TO KILL A SHADOW

JULIA CASTLETON

PENDULUM BOOKS

Cover design: Dare

For all the survivors

TO KILL A SHADOW

1

DARKNESS SHELTERED Michael Wilmore. He pressed himself deeper into the shadows of the empty doorway, shrinking back from the sickly yellow light cast by the streetlamp. He knew he needed to move; Ben wouldn't wait forever, and if he lost this chance, he wasn't sure how much longer he would last on his own. But fear made him wait; he had to be sure. Sure he hadn't been followed, sure Ben was alone.

The street was quiet. Somewhere a dog barked. A couple burst out of the student halls opposite, the girl laughing as she stumbled against her companion. Wilmore caught a sweet waft of marijuana as they passed his doorway, oblivious to his presence. The girl's high heels clicked into the distance. The street was empty again.

Now, he told himself. Now is the time. As if on cue, clocks across the city marked the quarter-hour. He checked the street again, pulled the collar on his wax jacket a little higher, and left the sanctuary of his doorway. His heart rate rose sharply as he crossed the pool of yellow light, exposed like an actor on a stage.

A shadow at the far end of the street caught his attention. A man with dirty ginger hair and a filthy, torn three-quarter length coat staggered into view, then leant against the wall of Exeter College. There came the wash of liquid against stone, and Wilmore released the breath that had caught in his chest. Just another Oxford drunk relieving himself.

He pressed on quickly now, slipping through a narrow door into familiar territory: his old college. This is where he'd first met Ben. They'd both been highfliers, enthusiastic drinkers, and creative pranksters, but their friendship had petered out in recent years as their careers had taken them in different directions. Howells was married now, a family man, and a writer for *The Times*. Wilmore had seen him on TV panel shows, talking about press freedom or the latest political crisis, and had noted with affection the changes in his old friend's waistline – expanding – and hairline – receding. Instinctively Wilmore ran a hand through his hair; he still had plenty, but it was greasy and unwashed. His reflection in the glass of the college lodge highlighted sunken eyes, dark stubble, lines etched deep across his brow. He was a stranger to himself. But not, it seemed, to the porter seated in the lodge. Derek Underhill didn't appear to have aged a day in the thirteen years since Wilmore's graduation, although he was perhaps a little stiffer as he leant forward to open the window.

'Evening, Mr Wilmore,' Underhill said with a smile. 'It's good to see you.'

'How do you do that, Derek?' Wilmore asked incredulously. 'You must have seen thousands of students since I left. Do you remember all of them?'

'Some make more of an impression than others.' Underhill looked pointedly towards Front Quad, a pristine square of green hemmed in by age-mellowed stone.

'Ah,' Wilmore replied, smiling despite himself as he remembered the night of the notorious medics' dinner when he'd risen to a dare and gouged a patch of the college's prize-winning turf, earning himself both a measure of infamy and a two-hundred-pound fine.

'You here for formal hall, sir?' Underhill asked.

'No. I'm meeting someone,' Wilmore countered.

'Mr Howells?' Underhill guessed.

'Yes.'

'He's in the bar,' Underhill advised. 'I doubt you'll have forgotten where that is, sir.'

The two men shared a wry smile, and Wilmore crossed the quad, his footsteps echoing off the fifteenth-century stone buildings. The pristine lawn in the centre showed no sign it had ever been vandalised. Movement drew his eye towards the hall. Through clear glass windows nestled in the spot-lit ivy, Wilmore saw a handful of men and women in long black gowns; members of the senior common room enjoying drinks ahead of formal hall. Wilmore had no desire to bump into any of his former tutors and hurried through a dark, narrow archway into another quad and down the stairs to the bar.

He paused, checking again that he wasn't being followed, before peering through a picture window in the heavy door. Ben Howells, in a pink shirt and blue suit, was alone at a table, head bent over his phone, a pint two-thirds down. Some of the other tables were taken by people Wilmore didn't recognise. The young staff were flirting and messing around during this lull. Later the place would be heaving, reverberating with the exuberance of youth, the ancient walls slick with condensation. Wilmore intended to be long gone by then.

He pushed open the door and crossed the room towards Howells, who looked up and smiled.

But Wilmore frowned. For days now he had lived in a state of hyperawareness and he sensed immediately that something was wrong. It was just a glimpse: two men, shadowed in the deepest recess of the bar, largely hidden from view by the stone columns that held up the vaulted roof. They didn't fit. One wore a thin woollen hat above narrow, dark eyes. A thick beard covered much of the man's face. He was wrapped in a short bomber jacket that could have concealed a catalogue of nightmares. The second man was clean-shaven and sported an aggressively short crew cut. He wore a thick navy-blue submariner's jumper. Almost certainly military. As Wilmore moved towards Ben, he saw Crew Cut glance at his bearded companion. Wilmore tasted bile in his mouth.

They had found him even here.

'Mike, everything alright?' Howells asked, standing now, his hand at Wilmore's elbow. 'You look like shit. Let's get you a drink.'

'Good idea,' Wilmore croaked, allowing Howells to manoeuvre him closer to the bar. In the mirror behind the bottles and optics he saw the men watching him impassively across the room. Wilmore leant into Howells, his voice a low snarl. 'Who did you tell?'

'What? No one. You know me, I love the cloak and dagger stuff.' Howells gestured to the barman for a couple of pints. 'You've got nothing to worry about.'

Wilmore didn't respond. Here, in the familiar bar, Howells with his belly straining against his pink shirt, the smell of stale beer, posters advertising student bops and rape crisis helplines, he felt a splinter of doubt. Maybe Howells was right; maybe he was being paranoid.

'Here, get one in you and relax. Doctor's orders.'

Wilmore stared morosely at the pint the barman carelessly slopped in front of him, foam trailing down the glass onto the well-worn counter. He had spent so many carefree nights in this bar. He would never have imagined he would stand here fearing for his life. He tried to steady his breathing and fight the effects of the adrenaline coursing through his veins. He told himself he was panicking about nothing but in the mirror above the bar, his eyes locked with the bearded man, and he caught a flash of recognition. Wilmore's hackles rose.

This wasn't paranoia.

2

'DON'T TELL me to relax,' Wilmore hissed at Howells. 'Who knows you're here?'

'What happened to you, Mike?' Howells' expression betrayed his concern.

'Who?' Wilmore pressed.

'Nobody,' Howells replied, genuinely perplexed. Wilmore saw realisation spread across Howells' face.

'What?' he challenged.

'David Gannon phoned me yesterday,' Howells began hesitantly. 'It's been ages since we last spoke. Your name might have come up.'

'Gannon?' Wilmore asked.

'Historian. Year below us. He works at the Foreign Office.'

'We need to leave,' Wilmore counselled. 'Now.'

Howells looked bemused and took another long draw on his pint.

'I mean it, Ben,' said Wilmore. 'Get up slowly, say something about the beer being better at the Turf.'

'Really?' Howells asked incredulously.

'Really,' Wilmore confirmed. 'They're here to kill me.'

Howells started to laugh but Wilmore saw him clock the men in the mirror and register their silent malevolence. Howells gave a nod of resolution, pushed away his pint and picked up his phone.

'Selfie time,' he said loudly, pulling Wilmore close and holding his phone in front of them. Wilmore was about to pull back when he realised the phone camera was focused not on him but on the mirror over the bar, capturing the two men in its reflection.

'Ben,' breathed Wilmore, part in admiration of his friend's Fleet Street cunning, part in fear. Now they were both marked.

Before he could say anything else, Howells was standing up, pushing back his bar stool. 'Let's go to the Turf. I need a proper pint.'

The two of them left, Wilmore nudging Howells on, the hairs on the back of his neck bristling. He didn't need to look behind to know the men would follow. He slammed the heavy door shut behind him and pushed Howells up the stone steps towards the quad. 'Run,' he said. 'We need to get out of here.'

Wilmore and Howells barged past a woman and sprinted through a narrow corridor into Front Quad. Wilmore didn't hesitate and charged across the lawn.

'Sir!' He heard Derek yell his disapproval, but the friends didn't stop. Wilmore could hear the echo of chasing footsteps.

'Which way?' Howells panted as they burst onto Turl Street.

'Bodleian. There'll be more of them,' Wilmore cautioned as they ran along the college boundary and turned into Brasenose Lane.

The ginger drunk was still there but he was standing alert now, his finger to his ear, murmuring into his filthy collar. Wilmore recognised the danger too late. He dived to pull Howells away, but the ginger-haired man lunged, pushing Wilmore's friend beyond his reach. The assault surprised Howells and he dropped his phone. Wilmore heard it clatter across the cobbles and saw a flash of steel as the man's hand jerked back and forth, driving a short knife into the journalist's gut. He kept stabbing like a jackhammer as he barrelled Howells against the wall of Brasenose Lane. Wilmore staggered back as his friend dropped to his knees, then fell flat, smashing his head against the slick cobblestones, blood pooling blackly. Ginger knelt quickly and patted down the prone journalist. Wilmore snapped out of his shock, pivoted, grabbed the fallen phone and wheeled away down Brasenose Lane, seeking out the shadows, his breath coming in short panicky gasps.

Heavy footsteps echoed behind him.

'Target heading east along Brasenose Lane!'

Wilmore heard the urgent words and a moment later saw a pair of large men running west along the northern edge of Radcliffe Square, blocking off his escape. Wilmore shoved Howells' phone into his pocket as he cast around, looking for an alternative way out. Lying at the heart of Radcliffe Square was his only hope of escape: the

Radcliffe Camera, a five-storey circular building that formed part of the Bodleian Library.

Wilmore's pursuers were closing on him. There was a thud to his left, and a cloud of fine dust burst from the eighteenth-century stone building. They were shooting. God, were they that desperate, that protected, that they would shoot him in the middle of a busy city? Heart pounding, Wilmore dashed across the lawn and bounded up the Radcliffe Camera steps, colliding with a couple of students on their way out.

There was another thud, more dust and then the crack of broken glass, just as Wilmore ducked inside. The librarian was open-mouthed in horror and students started grabbing their things, shouting, heading for the door. Wilmore barged past, aiming for the neck of a staircase that led down to the vaults.

He glanced back, and saw Crew Cut and Beard force their way through the door, looking around wildly, pistols raised malevolently. Wilmore half ran, half fell down the narrow staircase that wound towards the vaults. He stumbled into a dimly lit corridor. As he surged forward, Wilmore heard the thunder of heavy footsteps behind him. The nearest door was propped open by a maintenance cart, which he yanked clear. The door swung shut behind him, the latch catching with a satisfying snap.

He sprinted towards a door that capped the end of the corridor and didn't slow as he approached. He set his shoulder and barrelled into it at full speed. The pain of impact was lost to euphoria as the lock shattered the frame. Wilmore tumbled through the doorway, lost his footing and collapsed in a heap. He heard swearing behind him; his pursuers had reached the first door. There were two deep thuds as they shot out the lock and the door swung open. Wilmore didn't wait and was on his feet, running.

He sprinted into a huge storage facility that spread beneath Radcliffe Square and much of the Bodleian, a maze of floor-to-ceiling bookcases that housed the ancient library's extensive collection. It had been many years since he'd been down here for an illicit assignation with a librarian girlfriend, but he had a vague recollection of the layout and exits. Wilmore twisted his way between the bookcases, slowing to a creep so he could hear his attackers. His breathing was shallow and rapid, his heart hammering, fit to burst. His assailants said nothing, but he could hear their footsteps, which allowed him to stalk away from them. After a few moments, Wilmore could see the north wall between the bookcases. His pace quickened as he jogged towards a door that was cut into the old stone.

A bullet whipped past his head and tore into a nearby bookcase. Wilmore wheeled round and saw Crew Cut thirty feet away, sprinting along a parallel aisle. They were separated by rows of tall bookcases. The gunman's only opportunities to shoot came when they were both in the gaps. Wilmore paused behind a bookcase. He had to get to the door, but he couldn't outrun a bullet. There was every chance he wouldn't make it. He reached into his pocket and pulled out Ben's phone, his heart lurching at the picture on the screensaver: two carefree, gap-toothed kids in bright wellies and bobble hats. He choked when he thought of their father bleeding to death in a dark alleyway. Wilmore shoved the phone between two books. Now, he just had to survive long enough to tell someone about it. There was no sign of Crew Cut, so Wilmore retraced his steps, moving quietly, pausing to listen, then circling back, then forward again, his nerves fraying, his fears almost overwhelming him.

The shots came suddenly, as Wilmore was between bookcases. He leapt for cover and caught sight of Crew Cut before he made it to the safety of the next set of shelves.

'Keep exits covered. Target still on the loose. East side.'

Wilmore held his breath. He strained every sinew listening for them, then carefully edged forward to the top of his aisle. He could see the door, and the flat bar that marked it out as a fire exit. Wilmore took a deep breath and drove himself forward, gathering speed with every step until he was charging at the door.

'Over here. North side!'

A bullet whipped through the air. The shot went wide but it was near enough. More shots and voices behind him, heavy footsteps echoing around the vast room. Bullets thudded into the wall ahead, but Wilmore didn't slow and collided with the heavy door and burst into the cool, dim corridor beyond. He bounced off the walls until he came to another fire door. He tumbled through and was blasted by cold air, his breath misting like gun smoke. He hurried up a set of stone steps and got his bearings. The fire exit had brought him out by the Sheldonian Theatre, and Broad Street was just ahead. He could hear sirens behind him and saw blue lights flashing through the darkness. The road was clogged with cars and onlookers drawn to cries and commotion. An ambulance pushed through the crowds on Broad Street. Someone must have found Ben. *Please be alive*, Wilmore breathed into the darkness, but he'd treated enough knife wounds to know the ambulance was too late for his friend.

A crowd of rowers celebrating a win burst out of the King's Arms to his right, singing loudly, not yet aware of the drama unfolding in their city. Wilmore pulled up his collar and joined the drunken throng, heading towards the kebab vans of the High Street. He kept pace with them, and a girl linked arms with him, her face flushed with booze, her eyes glassy. As they passed the far edge of Radcliffe Square he saw more blue lights, police with guns, crowds huddling, talking nervously, phones held aloft to capture the drama. Among them, a dirty figure with ginger hair scanned the crowd, murmuring into his collar. Wilmore fought the urge to flee. He kept his head turned and forced himself to smile at the girl, who skipped by his side, singing.

As they reached the High Street, he peeled away and joined another crowd, jostling onto a bus heading south. He glanced around and saw Crew Cut further down the street. Wilmore ducked, fumbling for money, pushing onto the bus, ignoring the angry mutters behind him. Crew Cut was jogging purposefully towards the bus stop now. Wilmore dropped to the floor and pretended to tie his lace. He was buffeted in the face by a man's shopping bags. *Shut the doors, shut the doors,* Wilmore prayed silently.

More people pushed onto the bus, and he was forced to stand and shuffle further down, edging into a seat next to a woman holding a snivelling toddler. As the doors hissed shut and the bus lurched into the road, Wilmore risked another look outside. Crew Cut was level with him now, scanning the waiting crowds and the passengers already on the bus. Wilmore hid behind the toddler.

'What a sweet kid,' he said to its bemused mother. Her red-faced, whiny child might be many things, but right now sweet was not one of them.

Wilmore didn't care. The feigned attention had given him cover and as the bus started to move, he risked a glance outside. Crew Cut was still casting about, scanning for his prey. As the bus gathered speed, Wilmore urged it on towards the busy ring road and the thundering anonymity of the A40.

3

I WOKE up in the dim light of dawn, feeling the steady throb of my pulse beneath my fingertips. The clock read 4:53 AM, its soft glow a stark contrast to the darkness outside. Watching the luminous second hand sweep the clock face, I counted the beats for a minute: sixty-six, strong and steady. Satisfied my heart was working as it should, I released my grip, deactivated the alarm, and rolled out of bed, shivering. It wasn't just the cold of the early morning; I felt a deep chill of unease, as though something evil had touched me in the night, calling my name. Had I been dreaming again? There was something just out of sight, lost in the fog, a voice saying my name, a memory. My heart skipped, and I touched my fingers to my wrist again, feeling the pulse throb once, twice, but then forced myself to let it go. If panic took me in its grip, I could spend the whole day in bed, afraid to move in case it disturbed the rhythm of my heart. Pulling on my robe, I murmured to myself, 'This is real, this is real.'

I made my way down the hallway, moving especially quietly as I passed Alex's bedroom. My son had another two and a half hours of sleep ahead of him. I turned the thermostat, immediately feeling warmer when I heard the low thump of the boiler coming to life.

The kitchen was small and ancient, but with my landlord's permission, I'd painted the thirty-year-old units pale blue and replaced the cracked worktops with reclaimed marble. The walls were eggshell white and covered with photographs of Alex and me. The Bosch fridge freezer, sourced through Freecycle, was missing a handle and leaked occasionally, but it did the job. The rotten lino had been replaced with white tiles recovered from the old Seymour Swimming Pool before it had been demolished. A charity shop had yielded a cheap pine table and battered folding chairs, which I'd brightened with primary paints and a square of floral oilcloth. A table for two. We never entertained. Money was short, but I was proud of my efforts, turning this cramped inner-city rat hole into somewhere my son and I could call home.

While the kettle boiled, I checked my pill box to reassure myself I hadn't missed any meds. Whatever had unsettled me was just a dream, a normal dream. Touching my hand to the hot kettle, I pulled it back quickly: 'This is real, this is real.' A comforting mantra, the reassurance of ritual. 'Everything is OK.' I cradled a hot mug of camomile and lavender tea as I hunched over my laptop at the small table. The solid-state drive took moments to boot up, and I was soon staring at my own photograph next to the words 'Truth Above All,' the strapline of my website, The Castleton Files. The photo always made me wince. It was a projection of my brittle public face. I looked past the tidy light brown hair, the high cheekbones and grey eyes, and saw instead the strained smile and shadows that had haunted my eyes in the early days of my recovery.

I focused on the top story, an article I'd written about Sir John Phelps, a Conservative Member of Parliament I'd caught offering to table questions in exchange for cash payments. It had been a classic sting, involving a dummy corporation in Luxembourg I'd set up with my regular collaborator Joe Turner. The only surprise had been how quickly Phelps had fallen for it. His greed and hubris had made compulsive viewing, the grainy video spreading like wildfire on social media and catapulting The Castleton Files into mainstream news stories. The attention didn't come naturally to me, but the impact on my web traffic could not be denied. There were over six hundred comments beneath the article, most commending my work. A few longstanding readers congratulated me on finally getting the exposure I deserved.

It was a good feeling, but I knew success was almost as dangerous as failure, and soon stopped reading the comments. Instead, I logged into the administrator section of the site to see that traffic had indeed spiked two days ago, shortly after the first mainstream news outlets picked up my story. Instead of the usual fifteen to twenty thousand unique visitors per day, The Castleton Files had racked up over half a million visitors in the past forty-eight hours.

Another flutter of anxiety surged within me. Now I faced the challenge of coming up with enough high-quality reporting to merit the level of interest. There was a follow-up to the Phelps story, rebutting the official statement he'd made defending his actions, but I knew I needed something big, something fresh, to keep these new readers coming back. And I needed it quickly. The Castleton Files mattered more than I could ever make anyone understand. I wanted it to grow, to reach more people, to make a difference to the world Alex would inherit. And, deeper than that, deeper perhaps than I realised, the site was my baby, conceived amid the wreckage of my life, a purpose that had drawn me on, nursed me back to health. I brooded over it like an anxious parent, its momentum the litmus test of my own recovery. Without the site, without purpose, I feared I might return to the darkest of days.

My iPad vibrated, and I saw a FaceTime call coming in from Lyndsey Daniels.

'Mornin', beautiful,' Lyndsey beamed. 'How's superstardom treating you?'

I picked up my iPad and showcased my small kitchen. 'Well, as you can see, I've already moved into a mansion,' I replied. 'What time is it over there?'

'A little after nine,' Lyndsey answered.

I'd never met my webmaster in person, but I always pictured her having a glamorous Californian lifestyle. Late-twenties, blonde, blue-eyed, and elfin, Lyndsey was not a typical computer geek. She was a staunch social activist who had figured out early on that technology was the future. Majoring in computer science, she'd immersed herself in the world of alternative news and social media. She'd been in the first wave of visitors to my site and had offered to help when The Castleton Files had run into capacity difficulties.

'You've seen the numbers,' Lyndsey stated. It wasn't a question. Lyndsey was paranoid about security and monitored any administrator activity on the site.

'Thanks for keeping it up,' I replied gratefully.

'A couple of hundred thousand a day is interesting, but I'm waiting for when we've got two or three million.'

I laughed.

'I'm serious,' Lyndsey advised. 'Look what the Foundation story did for The London Record. One sensational scoop can put you on the map. The Record is averaging around four million hits a day. I'm telling you, it won't be long until you're in that league. What's next?'

I grinned. Despite the eighteen months we'd spent working together, Lyndsey was still as much a cheerleader as she was a colleague.

'I'm going to take Phelps' denial to pieces. After that, I've got a couple of leads, but nothing sensational. I might dig into the slush pile.'

'Good luck with that,' Lyndsey replied. 'Last time I checked, you had over seven hundred emails.'

'Wow,' I observed. 'I'd better get started. Let's talk in the morning.'

'Sure,' Lyndsey replied. 'Have a good day.'

'You have a good night,' I said as I ended the call.

Turning to my laptop, I signed into The Castleton Files webmail. Lyndsey was wrong; there were now over eight hundred emails waiting for me. Taking a sip of my tea, I began reading through them.

4

I WAS stiff and cold when the familiar insistent tones of Alex's alarm disturbed my reading. I was surprised it was already seven-thirty. I'd spent over two hours trawling the mailbox. Most of the emails were congratulatory messages advising me to keep up the good work. There were about half-a-dozen from people who claimed to know the truth about Russia's involvement in the US presidential election and twice as many from people who claimed to have proof that Islamic State operatives were infiltrating Europe as refugees.

A handful of emails unsettled me, with a couple of death threats, one promise of rape, and the usual collection of unsolicited photos. I decided to place these menacing emails in a separate folder for Lyndsey to analyze. I would pass any particularly ominous ones to the police, along with any identifying data I could find. Such communications were among the more depressing aspects of being in the public eye, and I muttered earthy curses as I shut the folder.

The alarm in the next room fell silent, and I knew Alex was awake. I pushed his bedroom door open and saw my five-year-old son was already out of bed and partially undressed. He'd somehow got it into his head that he needed to wear his school uniform to breakfast, and I didn't want to deter this show of independence.

'Morning,' I greeted him.

'Good morning,' Alex replied, pulling on his grey flannel trousers.

'You sleep OK?'

'Good,' came Alex's favoured response.

I smiled as Alex hoisted the elasticated waistband over his hips. He had become such a capable and independent little man. The first couple of years of his life had been hard for us both, and I had worried

I wouldn't be able to manage long-term. But he was maturing into such a wonderful, easy-going, peaceful person.

'Can I have a cuddle?' I asked.

'I'm just doing my buttons,' Alex replied, focusing on fastening his white shirt.

'Let me help,' I offered, kneeling next to him.

'I can do it, Mummy.'

I waited for him to finish methodically threading his buttons through the tight little eyelets. When he'd fastened the last one, he turned, smiled proudly, threw his arms around me, and squeezed me tight. I ran my fingers through his brown curly hair.

Like his caramel-coloured skin, Alex's curly hair was something he could only have inherited from his father. My own light brown hair was rail straight and my skin pale white. But for all the immediate differences, it was clear Alex was my son; we shared the same oval-shaped faces, almond, upturned eyes, refined button noses, and plump, full lips. Alex towered above most of his classmates, but his height could have come from either of his parents. I was a slim five-eight, and my family were all quite tall.

'You need a haircut, mister,' I observed, tussling Alex's hair. 'You ready for breakfast?'

Alex nodded, and I followed him out of his bedroom. He sat in his usual seat at the kitchen table, and I fixed him a bowl of Shreddies and milk, topped with a dollop of my homemade butterscotch sauce.

'Thanks,' Alex said, as I deposited the bowl in front of him. 'Spoon.'

I shot him a disapproving glance.

'Please may I have a spoon?' Alex corrected himself.

'Good boy.'

I handed him a spoon and watched with satisfaction as he set about his cereal with enthusiasm. I popped a slice of rye bread in the toaster for myself and noticed a new email had arrived, its bold text clearly visible from the other side of the room. The subject header caught my eye: **I know how Ben Howells really died**.

'Mummy, can I tell you something?' Alex asked between mouthfuls.

'Of course,' I said automatically as I curled over my laptop. I opened the email and started to read.

Dear Ms Castleton,

My name is Michael Wilmore. I am a captain in the Army Reserves. I was with Ben Howells when he died last night. He was murdered by men who want to stop me sharing what I know. My life will be in danger until the truth comes out. Email me if you are willing to meet.

Yours sincerely,

Michael Wilmore

You're not listening, Mummy,' Alex protested.

'I'm sorry, sweetie, you go ahead.'

'Yesterday we were playing funky chicken tag and William D knocked me over.'

'Were you OK?' I asked as I googled Ben Howells.

'I didn't cry,' Alex announced proudly.

'Did William do it deliberately?'

My laptop displayed a series of news headlines about the murder of *Times* journalist Ben Howells in Oxford, where there'd been an armed attack on one of the libraries. I vaguely recognized the name but couldn't recall the man's face. My time at the paper was now a blur of painful memories.

'I don't think so,' Alex replied.

'That's good,' I said absentmindedly as I scanned the first news report. The suspect wanted in connection with the murder was Michael Wilmore. My stomach churned with the familiar excitement of a story.

I typed a quick reply to Michael Wilmore.

Very interested in meeting. Let me know when and where.

'Should I get him back?' Alex asked. 'Should I knock him over today?'

'Maybe,' I answered vacantly as I hit send, before processing what my son had actually said. 'What? No! Of course you're not going to knock him over. What a thing to say. Go and brush your teeth, you cheeky monkey.'

Alex rolled his eyes, stood up, and left the kitchen. I shook my head at my son's desire for Old Testament retribution, then noticed that Michael Wilmore had replied. I opened the email.

The lobby of the Kensington Hilton. 11:00 AM.

My stomach rolled, and my pulse quickened.

This was real.

5

ST. DOMINIC'S WAS a sought-after primary school. We lived a few streets away, firmly in the catchment area. Those with pretensions referred to it as North Kensington. Older residents knew it as White City. The school's reputation attracted newcomers, driving up house prices, gentrifying the area in a grey wash of Farrow & Ball and trendy eateries with chalkboard menus. Alex and I walked to St. Dominic's, but we were in the minority. Every morning huge four-by-fours vied with neat hybrids for parking spaces near the school. I was on nodding terms with a few parents but kept a low profile, dodging the bake sales and quiz nights. Sometimes I worried that my isolation would mean Alex would miss out on playdates and party invites, but I reassured myself that he was only five. He had years to make his own friends.

I led Alex to the gate and gave him a hug.

'Have a good day, fella.'

'I will,' Alex assured me before running towards the playground. 'William,' he yelled, catching up with a friend.

I stayed until I saw the two of them walk into the school. It always felt like I was leaving a piece of my heart behind whenever I said goodbye. I sent a silent prayer down the corridor: stay safe, little one, I love you. Some mothers lingered long after the bell, dithering over PE kits and packed lunches, squeezing in extra hugs for tearful children, fussing like over-protective hens. It was at times like this I was glad of The Castleton Files. It gave me purpose and kept me from lingering. I checked my phone – 8:43 AM. Time to prepare for my meeting.

***

The Kensington Hilton was a large, modern four-star hotel clad in beige marble and gleaming gilt metalwork. I knew it well. The hotel was located on Shepherd's Bush Roundabout, less than a ten-minute walk from my sister's house. The lobby bar took up half the public space and overlooked the foyer. I arrived half an hour early, ordered a peppermint tea from the exceedingly polite waiter, and sat back to watch the to and fro of hotel life. Business travellers stooped over phones, parents weary with jet lag snapped at overwrought children, tour guides checked lists and distributed keys. I wondered when I would ever be able to afford a holiday with Alex. I couldn't imagine what it would feel like to be away from the flat with time on our hands.

A man in a grey suit caught my eye. He walked with the confident upright demeanour of a soldier but had a scruffy beard and nervous narrow eyes. It wasn't Wilmore. I'd already tracked his digital trail and found him tagged in Facebook photos and named in a local newspaper article praising the Surrey GP and Army Reservist as he prepared for deployment on a humanitarian mission to Syria. I watched the bearded man as he took a seat on the far side of the lobby bar and bent his head over his phone. I lingered for a moment, then returned my attention to the foyer, scanning for Wilmore. Eleven o'clock came and went, and I wondered whether my instincts were wrong. Maybe Wilmore was as much of a crazy hoaxer as the man who'd emailed me with badly photoshopped pictures that supposedly proved the Prime Minister had once been arrested for indecent exposure. Or the one who claimed the new home secretary was a Russian mole and was receiving coded messages through Russia Today broadcasts. I was never surprised by the elaborate delusions some people manufactured – I, better than most, knew the inventiveness of a sick mind – but I was often taken aback when I uncovered their identities and found them to be otherwise fully-functioning members of society. Postmen, accountants, even teachers, and once a magistrate.

At five past eleven, the waiter returned to hover at my shoulder.

'Julia Castleton?'

'Yes.' I nodded.

'There's a call for you. Lobby phone four.'

I left the bar and found phone number four in a row of carrels by the lifts.

'Hello?'

'Miss Castleton?' a deep voice responded.

'Yes.'

'This is Michael Wilmore. Do you know the Waterstones on Piccadilly?'

'Yes.'

'There's a bar on the fifth floor. I'll meet you there in thirty minutes.'

'What do you want to tell me?' I tried to get a sense of the man before I expended any more time on him.

'Not over the phone,' Wilmore said firmly.

'Do you know what the odds are of someone having tapped this line?' I retorted. 'You need to give me something.'

'I have evidence of a military conspiracy. One that cost Ben Howells his life,' Wilmore replied. 'I'll see you in half an hour.'

Wilmore hung up and the line went dead. I returned to my table and grabbed my coat. The waiter came over with the bill on a small salver.

'Was everything OK?' he asked.

'Yes,' I replied, dropping a five-pound note and hurrying from the bar. I suspected either Wilmore's knowledge of the London Underground was lacking, or he was hurrying me to flush out tails. Piccadilly in thirty minutes was going to be tight.

6

BY MY own reckoning, I was three minutes late when I hustled into 5th View Bar in Waterstones. Breathless from my dash across London, I scanned the room for the Army Reservist. The bar was busy, and I took a seat at the counter, using the vantage point to observe the other customers, most of whom admired the view from the fifth-floor windows.

An hour later, still nursing a lime and soda water, my head throbbing with the hustle and bustle of the busy London bar, I grew increasingly frustrated by Wilmore's failure to appear. I replayed our brief conversation, wondering whether I'd been the victim of a setup by one of my rivals. It wasn't unheard of. Time wasted following false leads was time not spent pursuing real stories. I looked at my phone. It was 12:38 PM. If I left now, I'd have just enough time to get home and write my criticism of Phelps' statement before picking Alex up from school. I paid for the drink, my mind already on my article as I took the broad, sweeping marble staircase down through the grand bookshop.

It was only when a man in a dark grey suit barged into me as he sprinted down the stairs that I noted the first signs of frenzied activity on the lower ground floor. I hurried down and pushed my way through the crowd that had gathered around the entrance to the men's toilets. The same man who had barged me on the stairs now blocked the doorway.

'What's going on?' I asked.

'A customer's been taken ill,' the man replied.

I craned to peer over his shoulder and saw two young men, a woman wearing a Waterstones badge, and a shocked old man gathered like shields round a prone body. One of the young men shifted to whisper something to the Waterstones lady, and through the gap, I glimpsed a face I recognized. It was Michael Wilmore.

'Let me help; I'm a doctor,' I lied to the man blocking my path.

He looked over his shoulder and called to the woman with the badge. 'She's a doctor.'

The woman nodded, and the man in the suit stood aside to let me enter the men's toilets. There was an acrid stench of urine, and a bed of fouler smells lay beneath.

'I'm Lucy Marks,' the woman said. 'There's an ambulance and police on their way.'

'Julia Danby,' I said, as I approached.

The two young men stepped aside and let me see Wilmore. His legs trailed inside one of two toilet cubicles and his body lay diagonally across the floor. Wilmore's face was contorted in a rictus of pain. I crouched down but it was already clear I'd find no pulse. I checked anyway and pressed my fingers firmly against his clammy skin. I noted his glassy eyes, the blood-flecked foam that ran from his mouth and the hypodermic needle buried to the hilt in his forearm. I looked up at Lucy Marks and shook my head slowly.

'Who found him?' I asked, and all eyes fell on the old man.

'I was at the urinal,' the old man said, trembling as he spoke. 'I heard a noise behind me. It sounded like someone choking. The cubicle door burst open, he fell through and cracked his head on the floor. He was twitching and choking. That's when I started shouting.'

'By the time we arrived, he was still,' Lucy added. 'We've had the occasional bit of trouble with local addicts, but never anything like this.'

I looked down at Wilmore's dead eyes and wondered what secrets they'd seen. Was he a crazed murderer turned suicidal? Or had he been right to be paranoid? I longed to go through his pockets but couldn't risk it, not with the police already on their way.

'There's nothing I can do for him,' I said as I stood. 'The police will take it from here.'

'Thanks,' Lucy replied. 'Thanks for trying.'

I nodded sombrely and patted the old man on the shoulder in a gesture of sympathy. He looked whiter than the corpse at his feet. I left the foul room and as I pushed my way through the gathered crowd,

I caught a glimpse of something that unsettled me. While everyone else was focused on the crowd outside the men's room, one man, a tall man with a crew cut, was looking the other way. From a vantage point at the top of the steps, he was watching me as I pushed against the crowd. A sudden surge of people blocked my view, and by the time I'd pressed past them, the man was gone. I hurried out of Waterstones and looked up and down Piccadilly, but the man was lost amid the thronging early afternoon crowds. I hugged my coat tight against the biting breeze and started to question myself. Amid all that chaos, the man could have been looking at anything or anyone. But an inner voice said the man had been watching me, making sure I failed to meet Wilmore.

Experience had taught me never to ignore the inner voice. I needed to find out whether Michael Wilmore was a murderous fantasist with a drug problem or whether that needle was a murder weapon designed to ensure his secrets died with him.

7

ALEX MOVED with the shoe-scuffing shuffle that signalled his displeasure. His Star Wars backpack hung low on his shoulders and lolled from side to side with each unenthusiastic step.

'I don't want you to go,' he said for the umpteenth time.

'I know, sweetie,' I replied, struggling with the holdall that held his clothes and the battalion of toys he'd insisted on bringing. 'But it's my job. I have to go away to earn money to pay for all the stuff we like.'

Alex gave me his most potent look of disapproval. 'I thought stuff wasn't important,' he challenged.

'It isn't,' I agreed, although, as I took in our surroundings, I wasn't so sure.

We were making our slow and, in Alex's case, reluctant way along Holland Villas Road, one of the most expensive streets in West London. Here, three-storey double-fronted houses, concealed behind high walls and mature trees, sold for upwards of twenty-five million. The horseshoe drives hosted Bentleys, Range Rovers and Ferraris. The people within these houses knew nothing of want or hunger. They had no idea what it was like to feel the toxic stress of an impending payday loan taken out to feed a hungry toddler. They had no experience of making a fifty-pound donation from a reader stretch for an entire week. They didn't spend long nights worrying about how to pay for new school shoes. Unless they'd come from real deprivation, wealthy people could never understand the corrosive effects of poverty.

I didn't crave the bigger house or faster car; all I wanted was the security to get through the month with bills paid and food on the table. There was no peace of mind to be found surviving hand-to-mouth, striving to claw a living from the only thing I felt able to do. For now, banner advertising and regular reader contributions enabled us to get by, and sometimes we could afford a few treats, but I was well aware how quickly the foundations of our lifestyle might crumble, exposing us to the cruel bite of poverty. Visiting my sister was always difficult, for many reasons, and the sharp contrast in our living standards added to my discomfort. It wasn't that I was jealous of her lifestyle; it was the guilt I felt for making choices that left Alex unable to enjoy similar luxury and security. I had always fought against the tide, and I now teetered on the edge of poverty. Emilia had swum with the tide and had washed ashore with everything.

'Why do you need to go?' Alex pressed.

'Things aren't important,' I replied. 'But food is. So are clothes. It takes money to buy them, and unless you've got a secret pot of pirate gold somewhere, I need to go out and earn some.'

'You can just take some money from Aunty Emilia,' Alex said. 'She's always offering.'

I frowned. My perceptive little boy was right, but I would never accept money that would only have come from Philippe, or even worse, my father.

'If I had a dad, you wouldn't have to work.'

I winced. The wound was so raw, and ran so deep, I almost couldn't bear it. And yet one day I would have to tell Alex. Tell my beloved boy, my living heart, about what happened. As always, I shied away from the subject.

'That's not true. Lots of children have mommies and daddies who work.' I stole a glance at him, my little man, wondering what thoughts churned behind that serious face. I crouched down and drew Alex towards me. 'I know you don't want me to go, but you'll have a great time with your cousins. And Aunty Emilia and Uncle Philippe always spoil you,' I said tenderly.

Alex pondered my words with the solemnity of an ancient sage. 'Can I ride in Uncle Philippe's car?' he asked finally.

'I'm sure he'll take you for a spin,' I confirmed. 'If you ask nicely.'

I embraced Alex and gave him a kiss on the forehead. When we separated, he smiled, restored to himself. I stood up wearily. I dreaded the day when a hug would no longer be enough to solve his problems. I picked up the holdall and the two of us continued walking.

The Garonne family home was located halfway along Holland Villas Road, on the more desirable east side of the street. The gates were open, so Alex and I walked straight up, past an impressive collection of cars: Emilia's Q7, Philippe's Aventador, and Clara the au pair's C-Max, although there was no sign of the family's seven-seat Range Rover. I led Alex up the stone steps and pressed the intercom. Alex and I waited patiently for a response that never came. I looked down at Alex, who was busy studying the Aventador's curves, and was beginning to wonder whether I had the wrong day when a black long-wheelbase Range Rover pulled into the driveway.

Emilia jumped out of the passenger seat. 'I'm so sorry,' she said, hurrying over. 'The sermon dragged on. Hi, Alex. How are you, little man?'

Emilia gave Alex a warm hug, then kissed me on the cheek. Emilia's soft tresses smelt of coconut. Her makeup was barely there, yet her skin was immaculate, dewy, and radiant, and her forehead was suspiciously unlined. I made a mental note to ask her whether she'd had Botox. As always, Emilia had that effortless chic that a certain budget can buy. Even in skinny jeans, a simple roll neck, and pumps, she looked groomed and polished, like she'd just walked off a fashion shoot. I, in my supermarket jeans and charity shop jumper, hair scraped into a messy, unwashed ponytail and with no makeup, felt haggard and dishevelled next to my vibrant, elegant sibling.

'Good morning, Julia. Bonjour, Alex,' called Philippe as he joined us.

I stifled my instinctive dislike of my sister's husband. I couldn't put my finger on it, but I never felt at ease with Philippe, never trusted him, always felt there was a hidden agenda. He was polite, excessively so, in a formal French way, and quiet, almost to the point of introversion. Perhaps he was just shy, but I found myself bristling whenever we spent time with one another.

'Ça va, Alex?' he asked. His French accent seemed stronger than ever though he had lived in London for more than ten years.

'What do you say?' I prompted my hesitant son.

'Ça va bien,' Alex replied to my relief.

'Good,' Philippe said. 'Soon you'll be speaking French as well as I can speak English.'

I looked at him sharply. Did he mean to sound so patronising? Surely he meant it kindly? Alex was only five, for Chrissakes, but something always seemed to get lost in translation, and even after all these years, I felt we still hadn't met the real Philippe.

'Apologies for not being here to greet you,' he said. 'Our service was a little long. But wonderful, truly, so wonderful. You must come sometime, Julia.'

I made non-committal noises. Philippe insisted on attending mass at the same Catholic Church as the French ambassador, and his social circle was a group of very rich, very successful, very French expats. He liked his family to speak French at home and had nothing but disdain for many aspects of British life, from the public transport he didn't use to the fish and chips he didn't eat. I thought he said these things to provoke, but I couldn't get upset; I wasn't that keen on buses and fish and chips myself. Every interaction with Philippe felt like we were locked in some unspoken battle, with his subtle needling – if that's what it was – only goading me into a kind of docile implacability.

'That would be lovely,' I murmured, my face impassive.

'Bien,' he said, clapping his hands together. He was tall, slim and had a long face that was capped by a mane of curly black hair. His delicately framed designer glasses made him seem even more serious than he was. Emilia always talked about Philippe's great sense of humour, but I struggled to recall a time I'd seen him truly laugh. Philippe was eight years older than Emilia, and perhaps it was this that informed the dynamic of their relationship. Emilia had lost something of herself in joining with this man. But every bargain has its price, and in return for being the obedient model wife, my sister lived a life of incomparable luxury. Philippe was a partner in a hedge fund that specialised in the financial services and technology sectors. Emilia once told me that during the first year of their marriage, Philippe had made fifty-six million pounds. I sometimes pondered this number. It seemed improbably vast, and the thought of it made me very uncomfortable.

We hadn't discussed money since.

8

CLARA, THE Garonnes' plump, friendly au pair, wandered over with the youngest child, little Jacques, asleep in her arms. The two older children, Veronique, a solemn seven-year-old, and bubbly Edgar, the same age as Alex, were doing an exaggerated tiptoe across the thick gravel so as not to wake the dozing toddler.

'Lexi!' Edgar hissed in a loud whisper, a huge grin on his face. 'I got the jumper board on Subway.'

'Cool,' I replied. I had a vague idea they were talking about a computer game.

'Let's go play,' Edgar suggested as he hurried up the steps. 'Come on, Mummy,' he said to Emilia impatiently.

I watched my sister unlock the front door and deactivate the alarm system. Edgar raced into the airy hallway and sprinted up the stairs, with Alex on his heels. The two were good buddies, a fact that both warmed my heart and also chilled it. Alex longed for a sibling, yet I knew I would never have another child. Not after what happened.

'Alex!' I called after him, but my son was long gone.

'Do you want to stay for lunch?' Emilia asked.

'I can't,' I replied. 'I've got a supersaver ticket.'

'What about a cup of tea?'

I hesitated.

'You can't go without saying goodbye,' Emilia pointed out.

I peered up the wide staircase and regretted not keeping hold of Alex. 'OK,' I said reluctantly. 'But I can't stay long. I've got a train to catch.'

'Jules is going to stay for a drink,' Emilia informed Philippe, who approached with the taciturn Veronique at his side.

'Good, good.' Philippe's thin lips smiled, but his eyes did not.

The Garonnes had spent more than the national average price of a house on their kitchen. The pristine room was bigger than my flat and its hospital-white cabinets and walls showed no evidence of children. There were no greasy finger marks on the walls, no colourful daubings or swimming certificates stuck to the vast American fridge, no random bits of Lego or treasured stones littering the empty black marble counters. I wondered how people lived like this. Where were the gas bills, the forms from school, the precious robot made from an old egg box, the lonely mitten waiting to be reunited with its lost mate, the paint sets, breadcrumbs and teabags? Why could my own kitchen never look anything like this?

I sighed, put down the heavy holdall and noted how the room had emptied. Philippe had disappeared with Veronique to help with her homework. Clara had taken a sleeping Jacques upstairs, and Alex and Edgar were lost to an iPad somewhere above us. I was alone with Emilia and the silence told me she had something to say.

I determined not to make it easy for her. I perched on a stool at the central island and watched my sister prepare our tea, scooping loose leaf Lady Grey from a high-end caddy into a fine china teapot, arranging the cups, spoons, seeking out sugar. I could tell that my younger sister was looking for a way to get started and raised an eyebrow as she began fiddling with teaspoons.

'Do you really have to go?' Emilia said finally, as she poured the tea.

I watched pale liquid swirl around the cups. We both liked our tea weak.

'I mean, I know a lot of people are talking about the Phelps story, but how safe is it? You know nothing about this man.'

I watched as Emilia spoilt her tea with skimmed milk. I took mine as it came; the aromatic flavours of Lady Grey were too subtle to withstand adulteration.

'I mean, *The Times* was one thing, but this is...You're on your own, Jules.' Emilia tried desperately to engage me. 'Alex needs his mother. Don't get me wrong; we love having him. But if anything were to happen to...Well, it just doesn't seem there's much point taking unnecessary risks.'

'I'm not going to have this conversation again,' I said finally. 'You know why I do this.'

Emilia fixed me with a familiar look of incomprehension. It didn't matter that we'd been raised in the same house; we came from different worlds.

'But things seem, well, more dangerous now,' Emilia said. 'There was that woman in Malta a few years ago—'

'Daphne Caruana Galizia.'

'Yes, that's her,' Emilia responded without missing a beat. 'She was killed by organised criminals. She left behind children.'

'And a husband,' I said sarcastically.

'And a husband,' Emilia agreed. I couldn't tell whether my sister had deliberately chosen to ignore the sarcasm. 'And then there was Veronica Guerin. She was killed and left behind a child.'

'Do you know the names of any male journalists who've been killed investigating stories?' I asked acerbically. 'Or do you just keep track of the women?'

Emilia hesitated, so I pressed home my advantage. 'Or do you think it's OK for men to put themselves in harm's way? But us women should just stay home drinking tea and gossiping?'

Emilia fell silent for a moment, and I knew I'd won that skirmish.

'He misses you, you know.'

'I don't want to talk about that either,' I responded firmly. I wasn't in the mood to discuss our father. 'I'm not like you, Em. I can't forgive him.'

Emilia looked away from me and studied the two cups of tea cooling on the counter. I could tell she was looking for another way to address her concerns. We used to have an easy, honest relationship. We talked, laughed, argued, and cried together, but Emilia had become detached and awkward ever since my illness. It was as though she feared saying or doing anything that might trip a fuse. Emilia's caution made me feel like a freak, but also gave me a certain licence to behave however I liked.

'I have to go,' I announced abruptly.

'Your tea,' Emilia reminded me as I started for the door.

'I've got a train to catch.' I stepped into the hallway and called up the stairs. 'Alex! I'm going.'

I could see that my sister wanted to say so much more, but Emilia went to the intercom panel located just inside the kitchen doorway and pressed the page button. 'Alex, Mummy's leaving. Come and say goodbye.'

Emilia's voice echoed from all the speakers in the house. The two of us stood in awkward silence as we waited for Alex to appear. Finally, we heard footsteps at the top of the stairs and Alex came into view, closely followed by Edgar. Alex hurried downstairs, threw his arms around me, and pulled me into a tight hug.

'Be good, Mister,' I instructed my son.

'I will,' he assured me.

'I'm going to miss you.'

'I'll miss you, too, Mummy.'

'I love you.'

'I love you, too,' Alex replied.

I pulled away from my son and backed towards the front door.

'His clothes and toys are in there,' I said, indicating the holdall I'd deposited in the hallway. 'Thanks for this,' I said to Emilia. 'Say bye to Philippe for me.'

Emilia smiled half-heartedly, clearly disappointed not to have convinced me of my folly.

'Be careful,' was all she said.

'I will,' I assured her before leaving.

9

I CAUGHT the bus back to my flat to pick up my satchel and overnight bag. Fondly, I straightened Alex's bedroom and held his discarded pyjamas to my face, breathing in the sleepy smell of him. The emptiness weighed heavily on me, as if somehow the flat knew he was gone for a few days. I was glad to shut the door on my home and shake off this disquiet with a feverish dash to Paddington. I always liked a train journey and, having boarded the train to South Wales with six minutes to spare, I happily settled in front of my laptop and notebook.

In the days since Wilmore's death, I had been busy filling my notebook with details of his life. Michael Wilmore was a thirty-five-year-old doctor, born in Oxwich, a small village in the Gower, Wales. He had studied medicine at Oxford, and I found him tagged in a Facebook throwback post, glassy-eyed and grinning at a medics' ball, medium height, floppy hair, brown eyes. There was evidence on his page of a few failed relationships: arms round a pretty girl on a beach in Goa, grinning with a vivacious redhead in a bar in London. But the next time he appeared on social media, he was in army fatigues, taking time out from his GP's practice in Cobham to serve with the Army Reserves. He was a member of the Military Stabilisation Support Group, an amalgamation of the old Engineering Corps. The few more recent photos I'd found showed the once fresh-faced medic carrying his life on his face, his eyes creased by squinting into a hot sun, his hair cut short and now flinty with grey, his face thinner and more guarded. And no wonder, I thought. My research showed he'd seen service in Afghanistan and most recently in Syria, where his unit was deployed to provide humanitarian relief and support reconstruction.

Looking back through my notes, I recalled interviewing Esther Thomas, the manager of Wilmore's practice. She had been surprised to learn he was even in the country. His tour hadn't been due to finish for another three weeks.

'Everyone is just devastated,' Esther had said. 'He was so popular with the patients. Nobody believes any of the things in the newspapers. I don't know why they're allowed to print lies like that, and he can't even defend himself.'

I wondered why Wilmore was home early from Syria. Was he absent without leave? The Ministry of Defence had resisted my requests for information, and I didn't yet feel I was in a position to push the matter.

The Waterstones staff had been far more approachable. I had spoken to Lucy Marks, claiming that, as the first doctor on the scene, I needed further information in order to file a full report with the police. Lucy had accepted the deception and allowed me to question staff who'd been on duty that day. Nobody had seen anything, and the store's CCTV footage had been removed by detectives leading the investigation. But Lucy had given me the details of the old man who'd witnessed Wilmore's death, and I'd met Solomon Grail in a small café near Piccadilly, where he described again the moments leading up to Wilmore's death, the awful crack as he hit the floor, and the convulsions that had wracked the doctor's body.

'Was anybody else there? In the other cubicles?'

If it had been murder, someone else must have been there, to insert the needle and press the plunger.

But no, Grail, still shaken, couldn't remember anyone else. 'You read about these junkies,' he said. 'You don't expect it to be a doctor. To see him like that, to hear those noises; it would put anyone off doing drugs. I'll never forget it. Utopia.' The old man shook his head sadly. 'Utopia.'

'What's that?' I asked, already putting the lid on my pen, getting ready to leave.

'That's what he said. Three or four times. Utopia.'

'He said that? Just one word. Utopia?' I frowned. What was it? A code word for a military operation? A password for an email account? Or just how it felt to have an overdose of opiates sweep through his body.

Am I just chasing a junkie, I pondered as the train rattled westwards, fields rolling by under a grey sky. A drug addict doctor, scarred by war zones, fantasising about conspiracies. Nothing to see here, just another crazy, move along, folks.

The murder of Ben Howells had been pinned on Wilmore. The local police surmised Howells had been targeted over some longstanding feud, and that Wilmore had killed him when Royal Military Police officers had tried to intervene, leading to a chase that had caused panic and damage at the Radcliffe Camera. Ravaged by guilt, Wilmore had overdosed on heroin in the Waterstones men's room. There had been speculation he was suffering from PTSD after his most recent tour in Syria.

It all seemed so plausible, but I had briefly spoken to Wilmore in the hour before his death. He hadn't sounded like a man at the end of the road. He'd sounded like someone on a mission, someone with a desire to expose the truth, someone who had tried to share his secrets with a trusted journalist. If the official account was fiction, whatever Wilmore knew had led to Howell's death and eventually his own. If I was right, then there was a level of official complicity that pointed towards the security services, and that suggested Emilia was right: I was getting myself into a very dangerous situation. But that was the very reason I had to continue. What kind of world would it be if you closed your eyes to murder and conspiracy? To powerful forces running amok in a university town? To slain journalists, hunted doctors, mysterious men watching in bookshops? I didn't want these forces running the world my son would live in, and evil would only profit from the complacency of good.

The inquest into Wilmore's death had been adjourned until June, but his body had been released for burial and the funeral was due to take place at St David's Church in Oxwich, the village where he'd been raised. I planned to be there, to learn more about the doctor from those who knew him best. His mourners.

10

THE TATTOOED Man had the devil in his eyes. Brimming with hatred, they stared out from his shaved skull and fixed upon Julia. Only, she wasn't herself. She touched a hand to her head and felt the barbs of closely shaved hair. She looked down and saw that she was wearing torn black leggings and a ripped black t-shirt. Black labourer's boots weighed heavily at the ends of her legs, which were spread wide under the table. She was aping the confident stance of the large, muscular man opposite her, and she knew that her eyes would be a hateful mirror of his. She knew the man, and he her. She knew that she'd lain with him, stripped him of his black vest and blue jeans, thrilled to run her hands over the skulls and lattices that covered his skin. But for all their intimacy, the beast opposite her was unfamiliar. To look upon his twisted, evil face was to see it for the first time.

The train sped through the countryside. Julia did not know where they had come from or where they were going. Her whole world had shrunk to this moment, to his dead black eyes, the stench of death on his breath, to the raw power pulsating from the two of them, filling the carriage, cowing the weak shadow dwellers who had moved seats and were clustered in a herd at the far end of the carriage.

'You're mine, you know,' the shaven-headed devil said in a gravelly, low voice.

Julia nodded. Of course she was. She saw how the tattoos permeated deeper than the skin, tainting his soul, drawing her in. She had seen signs that were beyond the sight of the shadow dwellers. She had been given a great gift, and this was her time.

'Pleasure me,' the shaven-headed devil instructed her.

Julia dropped beneath the table. She didn't care about the people watching them from the other end of the carriage. She served the Reaper without question. Julia felt a sudden change in pressure and the carriage went dark as the train swept into a tunnel. In the darkness, she knew she was close to the truth of this world.

I swallowed a scream. I woke to find myself in darkness, but my eyes quickly adjusted and picked out table lamps and overhead lights. My palms were damp and sweat pooled in the small of my back. The train shot out of the tunnel, and sunlight flooded the carriage. I looked around uncertainly. There was no one opposite me. No tattooed man. No intimate stranger with the devil inside. I was on the First Great Western train from London to Swansea. I checked my phone. It was 4:00 PM on Wednesday the 18th of March. My pulse was racing, the panic of the dream flooding my body with adrenaline.

I hadn't been troubled by my dreams for more than three years. The combination of routine and a regimen of meds had kept the nightmares at bay. I stood and paced a few steps up and down the carriage. There was no one there apart from a couple hunched over phones and a sleeping businessman, his head lolling.

I returned to my seat, trying to swallow the panic. Every sinew in my body wanted to flee, to climb out of my skin, then the train, and then the world. I checked my pulse again, forcing myself to count and breathe. *This is real, this throb of life under the fingertips. This is real.* I touched the table, my cold tea, my notebook. Real, all real. The Tattooed Man was just a dream, nothing more, a bad dream. Everybody had them from time to time. I tried to tell myself that it didn't matter, but deep down, I knew that it did. There had been a time when the dream world and the physical world had been as one, and I lived in fear of that time returning. I pinched my leg hard. Was it real? Was the pain real? How much did it have to hurt to be real? My eyes filled with tears as fear flooded my body. I couldn't bear for it to happen again. I wasn't strong enough. And I had Alex now. The thought of losing him terrified me more than anything. I trembled, and my breathing grew shallow and tight.

'Tickets, please,' a voice said.

The sudden interruption startled me.

'Sorry, love,' said the conductor, smiling down at me kindly. 'Didn't mean to scare you.'

I stared at him, taking in his salt-and-pepper beard, the laughter lines round his blue eyes, and the quizzical upturn of his eyebrows.

'Got your ticket, love?' he asked again, and I clung to this simple request as if it were a life preserver cast into a dark and tumultuous sea.

I rifled through my satchel, focusing on nothing but the ticket. Find the ticket. One thing at a time.

'I would have woken you earlier, but you looked so peaceful,' the conductor explained.

At least the screams of my night terrors hadn't returned.

'Here it is,' I said a little too enthusiastically. 'Have you worked here long?'

The conductor clipped my ticket. 'Twenty-three years,' he answered.

'Must be very interesting, meeting so many people. Or maybe not. Do you always work this route? You must know every twist and turn. Do you ever get off and visit the places you pass every day?'

I was babbling now, but couldn't stop, the words escaping like steam from a safety valve.

'Are you OK?' the old man asked.

A cold. Flu. Aids. Cancer. Ebola. All things one could discuss with a stranger. A broken leg. A broken wrist. A broken finger. Perfectly acceptable conversation topics. A broken mind? Not so much.

'I'm fine,' I responded. 'Just a little tired.' I knew I must seem ridiculous, prattling on, keeping him from his job. But I couldn't be alone with my thoughts. I had to hold on to this man until the danger passed. 'Actually, I'm going to a funeral,' I said. 'Not someone close, a colleague, but I—'

The conductor cut me off. 'I've finished with my round,' he said. 'I could sit with you if you want to talk. Death can do strange things, even when it's not a loved one. Reminds us all of what matters.'

I studied the conductor's warm, friendly face and realised that I didn't need to say anything to him. He'd lived long enough to know that I was not fine. He also knew better than to mention the fact.

I swallowed hard. I was never good at accepting help, but I needed this man's company. 'That would be very nice,' I said finally. 'But could you do the talking? I'm all over the place today.'

He smiled. 'Would be my pleasure,' he said. 'When you get to my age you have so many stories to tell but most folk you know have already heard them a hundred times. It's good to have a fresh audience.'

'I'd love to hear your stories,' I said. And I meant it.

As the train pushed on through the hilly Welsh countryside, I settled into my seat and listened to a complete stranger lay his life bare.

11

THE TRAIN pulled into Swansea a few minutes early, and I thanked the conductor, Tom, for his amusing tales about his long-suffering wife, Sandra, his three-legged dog, Beau, and his experiences of twenty-three years working on the trains. I didn't explicitly thank him for keeping me from spiraling into a full-blown panic attack or worse, but I felt he understood. Stepping off the train, I felt more like the person who'd boarded three hours earlier. The drizzle didn't bother me much. My heart felt lighter.

'Three Bays Bed and Breakfast,' I informed the taxi driver. 'Oxwich.'

'Near the beach, is it then?' he said in a thick Welsh accent.

'Up the hill, near the castle, apparently.'

'We'll find it,' the driver assured me as he set off.

The old Vauxhall rattled onto the High Street and headed west on the coastal road. Swansea Bay stretched away to our left, and sailboats skimmed over the foam-flecked waves. Before reaching the seaside village of The Mumbles, the driver turned right, leading us off the coastal road and up into the hills. There was something beautifully bleak about the tough Welsh terrain. Hardy sheep cropped endless fields of grass, and spring lambs frolicked around their mothers, oblivious to the rain and the deepening gloom. My bearings were lost as the taxi wound through small villages. I caught glimpses of the sea now and then, always in a direction that surprised me. The car twisted down a steep lane, and I instinctively clutched my seatbelt as the gradient intensified until we reached sea level. Beyond high dunes, I saw the long sandy beach of Oxwich Bay. It was too early in the year for holidaymakers, and the car park was deserted, and the beach shop shuttered. Out in the bay, two container ships and a tanker squatted on the churning grey sea.

Passing a hotel overlooking the beach, the taxi veered inward again, climbing a steep road that cut through a thick wood. Vegetation closed in on us, and branches scraped the sides of the cab.

'There it is,' the driver suddenly announced, pointing to a small sign on a stone gatepost: Three Bays Bed & Breakfast.

I peered beyond the gate and saw a sweet cottage painted in a pale-yellow hue. A trellis of hardy roses adorned the porch. A neatly landscaped garden was edged by mature trees, bent and wizened like old men bowed by the sea winds. Beyond lay a close-cropped field, thatched with gorse, and below, the thick woodland clung to the hill we had just climbed. I couldn't see the sea, but I could hear the distant rush of waves crashing against unyielding rocks.

The proprietor, Diane, greeted me with enthusiasm. She was a spry lady in her early sixties, sporting a tight blonde perm and a taste for vibrant colors. Flowers adorned every corner of the B&B - real flowers in vases, botanic prints on display, ceramic flowers in fine china pots, pressed flowers showcased in a display unit, and daisies blooming across the wallpaper that covered the hall and stairway.

Having paid in advance, I signed the guestbook, reverting to Julia Danby, and Diane showed me to my room.

'You're our one and only guest this week,' Diane chattered. 'Make yourself at home. I've put you in here,' and the hostess proudly opened the door to a large room, overlooking the sea.

I focused on the view, finding it calm and restful compared to the room's overwhelming chintziness that resembled a florist's paradise.

'This is our Country Rose suite,' said Diane. 'It's my favorite.'

'It's lovely,' I murmured politely.

Diane beamed. 'I knew you'd like it, the moment I saw you.'

Not sure how to respond, I simply smiled vacantly, allowing the conversation to fade into silence. Finally, Diane got the hint and left, and I flopped onto the bed, suddenly overwhelmed with tiredness. But the fear of the Tattooed Man's return surged as soon as I closed my eyes.

Hastily sitting up, I retrieved the B&B's Wi-Fi code and powered up my laptop. An hour passed in a blur as I checked emails and responded to journalist queries about the Phelps cash-for-questions story. After ploughing through my inbox, I engaged with followers on social media. It felt satisfying to see my new followers support me in shutting down my rival Chris Jones's attempts to latch onto my stories. So, this is what it would have been like to be the cool kid at school, I thought wryly. My tiredness forgotten, I posted a teaser on The Castleton Files, hinting at a new and explosive story. The speculation would surely rattle Jones.

I picked up my phone and dialled my sister's landline.

'De Garonne,' Philippe answered formally.

'Philippe, it's Julia. Is Alex around? I'd like to say goodnight.'

'Clara is bathing the boys,' Philippe replied. 'I will take you to them.'

As Philippe ascended the stairs, the distant sound of squealing laughter grew louder until he reached the bathroom.

'Boys!' he exclaimed, and the laughter faded. 'You're on speaker,' Philippe announced. 'Alex, it's your mother.'

'Hello, little man,' I said with a smile.

'Hey, Mum!' Alex yelled enthusiastically.

'How's life?'

'Good.'

'What've you been up to?'

'Stuff,' Alex replied.

'Good stuff? That's all anyone can ever hope for. I just called to tell you that I love you.'

'I love you too, Mummy,' Alex announced in the squeaky voice he reserved for moments of acute embarrassment.

'You be good,' I instructed him. 'And get a good night's sleep. I'll see you tomorrow night.'

'See ya,' Alex said.

I heard the acoustics change.

'Emilia is at her yoga class,' Philippe informed me, his voice deeper and closer now that the phone was off speaker. 'Do you want her to call you?'

'No, that's OK,' I responded.

'Well.' Philippe paused awkwardly. 'Good luck with whatever it is that you are doing.' His voice dripped with condescension.

'Goodbye, Philippe,' I said coldly before hanging up.

It was a little after seven when I took my coat out of my overnight bag, slung my satchel over my shoulder, and headed downstairs. Diane was watching Emmerdale. She paused the programme as I entered the room.

'Just catching up on the Dale,' Diane said. 'You off out for your tea?'

'Actually, I was hoping to find Grange Farm,' I replied.

Diane's expression changed, and she became quite somber. 'You knew Michael?'

'Yes,' I replied, trying not to feel guilty about stretching the truth.

'You should have said,' Diane responded with the awkwardness often accompanying the subject of death. 'I didn't know, my dear, otherwise I would have offered you my sympathies. What happened, it was a terrible thing. You'll not find Ashby at the farm. He's been down the Bay every night since it happened. I've got a mind he plans to drink himself into his son's grave.'

'The Bay?' I quizzed.

'The hotel. You'll find him in the lounge.'

'Thanks,' I replied.

'Give him my best,' Diane added as I left the room. 'Terrible thing to have to bury a young one.'

12

THE RAIN had stopped. The air was fresh and sweet and the sky streaked pale grey and rosy pink as the heavy sun sank beneath the sea. I walked down the steep hill towards the bay and pressed myself into the dripping hedgerow whenever a car passed. The vehicles blinded me with their glaring headlights in the deepening twilight.

The hotel sat at the bottom of the hill, overlooking the beach. Garden lights twinkled and shadows shifted under the high trees. Somewhere empty bottles clanked into a recycling bin and a woman laughed wildly. I drew my coat tighter. The briny air had taken on a decidedly chilly edge.

I stepped into the lobby and hurried past a receptionist who looked up from her desk and smiled vacantly. I found the lounge to be a cosy snug, decorated with black-and-white photographs and botanical prints. Leather armchairs nested round small bar tables, and a large log burner radiated heat. The room was empty save for two ruddy-faced old men, nursing a half-empty bottle of Scotch and two huge brandy glasses.

'Welcome, stranger,' the larger of the two men said loudly, raising his hand in salutation. 'Every stranger is a friend you haven't met yet. And once you meet them, they get stranger still.'

The large man had a tufted nest of grey hair, shaggy eyebrows and an untidy beard. He wore a green-and-beige checked shirt, brown trousers and a pair of brown boots. A green waxed jacket steamed on a peg near the log burner. His smaller companion was bald and sported a pair of large plastic-framed glasses that sat upon a red, bulbous nose. He was wrapped in a thick cream rollneck pullover that was covered in stains, some of which looked months old. A pair of muddy black trousers and wellington boots completed the outfit.

'I'm looking for Ashby Wilmore,' I said.

'Haven't seen him for years,' the shaggy man replied. 'Have you seen him anywhere, Arthur?'

The bald man shook his head, and his larger companion suddenly grew sombre. When he spoke, there was a morose edge to his voice. 'I don't know where he went, but he left a broken old fool in his place.'

'Mr Wilmore?' I asked uncertainly.

The shaggy man stared.

'His friends call him Lord Wilmore,' Arthur said suddenly. 'Thems that don't call him tosspot, that is.'

Ashby leant forward and glowered at his friend as his unsteady hand poured them both drinks. When he'd finished, he turned to me. 'Well, take a seat then,' he instructed. 'You obviously want something and you're not going to get it standing there like a useless cabbage.'

'Have a drink, my darling,' Arthur suggested. 'You can share my glass. I promise you won't catch anything a good dose of penicillin can't cure.'

'I'm OK, thanks,' I replied. I drew up a chair and slid my satchel under the table. 'I don't drink.'

'Don't trust a wench that doesn't drink, even if she is comely,' Arthur slurred.

'She doesn't want to hear your bawdy talk,' Ashby retorted. 'She came to bother me. Isn't that right, girl?'

'I came to ask you about your son,' I said honestly.

Ashby caressed his glass and fixed me with a hostile gaze. He took a slow, deep drink and then sat back in his chair and closed his eyes. He pinched the bridge of his nose with his fingers and rubbed his right eye, pressing hard enough to distort the shape of his eyeball. I got the sense he was trying to find a way to release an impossible pressure.

'You remember that bloody stump?' Ashby said, opening his eyes and looking at his friend.

Arthur grinned.

'Mavis, one of the old girls up the hill, she had this oak tree in her garden.' Ashby turned to face me. 'She asked me if I could get rid of it. So, me and Arth went and chopped it down for her. Got rid of all the timber, as a favour, mind. And then she says to me, 'Ashby, what about the stump?' What about the stump!'

'That bloody stump,' Arthur added.

'It was a blimmin' favour, mind. Anyway, we don't like to disappoint the ladies, do we, Arth?'

Arthur shook his head slowly, his grin never fading.

'So, I got my hands on some P4. Like C4, only it's powder,' Ashby explained.

'Boom!' Arthur interjected loudly.

'So, me and the smiling fool here, we're out in her garden, digging under the stump. "You alright, Ashby?" Mavis calls out her window. "You gonna dig it out?" she asks. Are we fuck? Bloody thing was as big as Moby Dick. Must have been a tonne at least. So, we dig under the stump and stuff the hole with powder. Arthur borrowed the detonator from a mate. We won't say where, like, not with all them ISIS fellas about.'

Arthur surveyed the room theatrically.

'Anyhow, we stuck the pins in the powder and ran the cables out to the detonator,' Ashby continued. 'We're crouching behind Mavis's shed, and I said to Arthur… what did I say to you, Arthur?'

'Put your fingers in your ears, Arthur, this thing's gonna pop,' Arthur replied.

'True. That's what I said,' Ashby confirmed. 'And I pressed the plunger.'

Ashby paused and looked sadly at me. I wondered if he'd forgotten he was in the middle of a story. I glanced at Arthur, who was still grinning, his eyes glassy and unfocused. How many bottles had they had, I wondered?

'Bang!' Ashby suddenly shouted, hitting the table for good measure.

The blow startled me, and I almost knocked the bottle over.

'It was like the bloody Blitz! That powder blew a crater in her garden the size of a flippin' lorry. We both looked up and there's the bloody stump trailing ten foot of roots and soil, weighing about a bloody tonne, flyin' through the air. And what does this idiot say?'

Arthur shook with the force of his sniggering. "Hey up, Ashby. Looks like the wind's caught it."

Arthur slapped the side of his chair and rolled about with laughter.

'Bloody wind's caught it. Thing weighs a tonne. He's making jokes, and I'm there peeking through me fingers, praying the damned thing doesn't come down on someone. That's hard time in the chokey if it does. Flaming stump flies for what seems like a day and a half and finally lands on the neighbour's roof, where it slides down, taking half the tiles with it, and falls onto their patio. Three thousand pounds that bloody favour cost me.'

'Three thousand pounds,' Arthur reiterated, suddenly becoming serious.

'And you know what I learnt?' Ashby stared at me. 'Once you start messing about with dangerous things, you never know how bad life is going to get.'

13

I ORDERED a lime and soda water and spent the evening sitting with Ashby Wilmore and his friend Arthur. I tried to probe for information on Michael, but the old farmers were canny. Every time I raised the subject, they would tell some irrelevant old story. As the night wore on and they drained the bottle, their drunkenness got worse. They were utterly obliterated. Neither man could string together a coherent sentence and they stumbled round blindly. Arthur went to the toilet and came back with his trousers covered in suspicious wet patches.

I directed all my mental effort at willing Arthur to leave, and eventually at ten to eleven, he did. He stood suddenly, mumbled incoherently, and then staggered from one chair to the next, holding their backs like a drunk man's monkey bars, before he disappeared into the night.

Ashby sat silently and finished the bottle of whisky. His unfocused eyes stared towards the red glow of the burning logs. He was lost in thought and his whisky glass was tilted at a perilous angle in his careless hand. I reached out to right the glass, but he batted me away and drained its dregs. I sat back, wondering whether to call it a night, when he suddenly stirred and cast his dull eyes towards me.

'You've had your time, missy,' Ashby slurred, hoisting himself to his feet. 'S'ome.'

I stood and tried to support him as he crossed the room.

'No!' Ashby said forcefully, brushing my hand away. 'No pity!'

The old man staggered out of the lounge and fell against the metal bar that ran across the fire exit on the other side of the corridor. The door swung open, triggering an alarm that rang throughout the hotel. I pitied any guests who had turned in early, carefully closed the door behind me and hurried after Ashby. The rain had started up again.

It seemed to come in sideways now, carried on a chilling sea breeze, cold and flinty. A night to be warm in my flowery room at the B&B, not chasing an unfriendly drunk across a dark car park.

'Mr Wilmore!' I called out, as he staggered towards a mud-spattered Defender that was parked at a haphazard angle. I caught up with him and cursed softly as I stepped in a puddle. 'Mr Wilmore, you can't drive.'

'Steering before you were born.' He leered suggestively. 'I've got a warm bed big enough for two.' He grinned, and threw the keys at me.

I fumbled the catch and the keys fell to the ground.

'Bloody girl,' Ashby snorted, before shuffling round to the passenger side.

I picked up the keys with a huff and let myself into the vehicle. I placed my satchel on the middle seat and unlocked the passenger door. After some failed attempts, Ashby finally climbed in. He groped for the handle and pulled the door closed. The small space stank of wet dog and whisky.

'Which way?' I asked.

'Up,' Ashby replied with more than a hint of irritation.

I started the engine and slipped the heavy Defender into gear. I over-revved the engine and the car lurched forward, buffeting Ashby in his seat.

'Bloody woman driver,' he complained.

I ignored him and turned left out of the car park. I finally found the lever for the windscreen wipers, but they didn't help much. The rain was relentless and sounded more like hail as it pelted the Land Rover. That, plus the angry throb of the engine as it climbed the steep hill up through the woods, made it difficult to speak. It was only when I'd shouted my request for directions twice that I realised Ashby was asleep.

'Hey, Mr Wilmore,' I said, shaking him. 'Where's your house?'

Ashby stirred and looked around in bewilderment.

'Where's your house?' I repeated.

'Up,' he replied. 'Past the green.'

Ashby slumped back in his chair, comatose again. I drove on, crawling up the steep hill, peering through the rain-washed windscreen, praying we didn't meet anything coming the other way on this narrow lane.

After a mile, we topped the hill and followed the road along a ridge, past a neat village green, its one streetlight a beacon in the darkness. A flash of lightning out at sea caught my eye and I almost missed the turning for Grange Farm. We bumped and skidded down a track for a quarter of a mile to a white farmhouse near the cliff edge. The Defender juddered to a halt, and I unclenched my hands from the steering wheel. For a moment, I wondered what to do and listened to the crashing sea and the drumming rain. Then Ashby snored, and I leant over and rifled through his pockets for his house keys. I found nothing but a mobile phone verging on vintage, a tatty wallet and some loose change.

'Where are your keys?' I asked. I shook Ashby, who did not stir.

I jumped out, shielded my face against the storm and ran round to his door. I hauled him out. The hard rain roused him, and he staggered to his feet and lurched towards the house. He shambled up the front path and barged his shoulder against the door. He stumbled through the unlocked door into a hallway and his shambolic momentum carried him inside a living room, where he collapsed face-first onto one of two old sofas. I stepped back and surveyed the fallen man. I thought about taking off his wellies but decided against it. It didn't look like concrete boots would bother him tonight.

The soft glow of dying embers lit the room. The sofas were positioned either side of an open fireplace. Behind Ashby's sofa was a dusty sideboard that was covered with photographs of Ashby, Michael and a woman I took to be Michael's mother. A large window rattled and shook. I shivered as I peered out to sea. I saw the lights of distant ships and the intermittent flashes of an offshore storm. The curtains smelt musty and felt damp to the touch. I left them open. I considered borrowing Ashby's Land Rover to get back to the B&B but decided against it. Ashby was in no state to be left alone and I couldn't bring myself to forego the opportunity to poke around Michael Wilmore's childhood home.

14

PITCH BLACK darkness. The sudden glare of a light, warping, changing shape. The air was thick with white powder, choking, blinding. Her head felt wet but when she tried to raise her hands, she found they were restrained by something unyielding. She realised now the light came from a growing queue of cars to her left. On her right was the Tattooed Man, blood oozing from raw gashes that crisscrossed his face. Everything was strangely silent. She could see his mouth moving, twisted in a maniacal grin as he fought with his seat belt and the intrusive airbags, but the only sound was the deep drum rhythm of her heartbeat.

And then a switch flicked. Sound returned.

'Fuck!' the Tattooed Man yelled. 'I'll always be one step ahead of you!'

Julia freed her hands, touched the wetness that smeared her face and cloyed her hair. She felt oddly calm even as she looked at the slick blood on her fingers. Orange flames started to lick the car's bonnet. Julia glanced at the Tattooed Man, his eyes crazed with the evil derangement that tormented him.

'He'll not take you!' he yelled at Julia, as he yanked one of his hands free and reached into his leather jacket. He pulled out a large hunting knife and sliced through their seatbelts, but as she moved to open the passenger door, the man with the devil in his eyes pressed the blade against her throat.

'You're forgetting something,' he purred.

She smiled as she leant forward. She gasped as the blade bit into her skin. Her bloody hand clasped the back of the Tattooed Man's head and she pulled him closer. She didn't care about the pain and pressed herself into him. The knife slid deeper, her blood like a river and the darkness pulled her under again.

'Are you coming or what?'

The words swept in like a gust of fresh air. Pulled from the sticky gagging darkness of my dream, I gasped. I sucked in light and reached for something, anything, to ground myself. Papers. Piles of papers.

Newspaper cuttings. A postcard of a golden beach. California, the sunshine state. A dead pot plant. My stomach lurched. I'd fallen asleep while poking around in Ashby Wilmore's office and had been caught in the act.

'You find anything?' he asked pointedly.

I shook my head. I didn't trust myself to speak, the residue of the dream still coursed through my mind like an infection. The Tattooed Man. That was twice now, and I fretted it was more than a dream. What if it was a memory, or worse, a symptom, an early warning sign that my brain was in crisis again? My GP had been tapering my dose of Tegretol over the last year, each carefully calibrated reduction a big boost in my confidence. Now I feared my confidence had been misplaced.

My confusion wasn't helped by Ashby's appearance. His thick grey hair had been brushed, his beard trimmed, and he'd ditched the muddy slacks for a black tailcoat, black trousers and black shoes, which had been polished to a high gleam. A white shirt and black cravat completed his transformation from drunken farmer to Victorian politician. Was any of this real? Was that why Wilmore hadn't shown up at our meetings? Was all of this just a figment of my imagination? Was I doing this? Was I really here or was it all happening again?

I felt a hot flush of panic and pushed back from the desk.

'Toilet,' I mumbled, unable to bring myself to look at Ashby in his mourning suit.

'Top of the stairs,' he said, bemused. 'But I bet you already know that.' He sounded very pleased to have caught me prying like this.

I fled for the sanctuary of the dated bathroom and, panting in the morning chill, I locked the door. There was cracked lino under my feet, an ancient bathroom suite in avocado green and a stained and crusty towel on a hook. I stood in front of the mirror and pressed my fingers to my face. No blood, no scratches, but my eyes were wild. I put my fingers to my wrist. My heart was beating fast, but I had just run up the stairs. I counted out a full minute, listening to the little changes in my body, the way my pulse steadied, the rise and fall of my breath. *This is real*, I said to myself, *this is real.* I didn't recognise the Tattooed Man from my patchy memories but that didn't mean he wasn't real. I couldn't bear to touch the towel, so I splashed cold water on my face and dried it on my sweatshirt. I returned to the mirror and checked my throat. No cuts, no scar on the white skin. *Just a dream*, I told myself. But I still wasn't sure. I'd been fooled before. And then there was Ashby, waiting outside. It felt so unreal to be in this tumbledown farmhouse as seagulls wheeled in the sky outside the window. The old man was like an apparition in his Dickensian getup. *Could this be a dream?*

I checked my pulse again. Counted my breaths. It had been a bad idea to come here. Emilia had been right; I wasn't strong enough for this. I swallowed. The thought of Emilia, of Alex, of what might happen if I couldn't control myself, filled me with terror. I had much more to lose this time. A son. A precious son. I opened the bathroom cabinet to discover a sticky bottle of cough medicine, some TCP, packets of aspirin, a large bottle of Pepto-Bismol, a comb and a multi-pack of razorblades. Like a nurse, I acted with quick and unthinking efficiency. Time to rip the plaster off, clean out the infection. I rolled up my left sleeve to the elbow, took a blade in my right hand and pressed it to the soft white flesh of my arm. The prick of pain was like a release and my brain was distracted by a sudden flood of endorphins. The blood welled to the surface, deeply red and vital. *This is real*, I said, cutting myself again. *Real.* I cut again. Heavy splats of crimson fell on the lino, on my jeans. *Shit, oh shit.* I ran the taps and washed my arm, the dark blood diluting to weak blackcurrant squash as it spiralled down the basin. I mopped up with toilet paper and welcomed the pain as I held my arm above my head to slow the bleeding. *This is real.* I sighed heavily. The release was like a warm blanket, soothing me with familiar reassurance. But it only lasted moments. Already I felt guilty. I had promised Emilia it would never happen again but today had been an emergency.

I hurriedly wiped the floor and doused my arm in TCP. The sting made me curse. I wrapped the blade in bloody toilet paper and flushed the lot down the limescale-crusted toilet. Nobody would know about this. It was just the once, and it had worked. The strong smell of TCP and my stinging arm were proof that this was real. I glanced in the mirror and wondered at the secrets my mind held. Did the truth of the

Tattooed Man lurk within? I thought I saw the flicker of a smile in my eyes but it must have been a trick of the light. I took a breath and unlocked the bathroom door.

Downstairs, Ashby was pulling on his stinking wax jacket over the tailcoat. He looked up as I descended the stairs.

'So, you're a reporter.' It was a statement more than a question.

I nodded slowly. My shame at getting caught at his desk was made all the worse by the fact that I hadn't found anything remotely interesting in his private papers or on his computer. Just a series of innocuous postcards and emails from Michael.

'I won't hold it against you,' the old man said quietly. 'Did you know him?'

'We spoke,' I replied. 'He said he had a story.'

'He had a story that would change the world,' Ashby countered. 'That's what he told me. Wouldn't say where he was or who he was with. And he wouldn't tell me what the bloody hell he knew. Said it was too dangerous.'

I watched as Ashby fretted with the lapel of his tailcoat.

'The Army says he deserted his unit. They say he lost his mind.' The words caught in Ashby's throat. 'The police say he did terrible things. But he was my boy, and he needs a good send-off.'

I waited, uncertain how to respond to the emotional old man. Ashby took a few deep breaths and pulled himself together.

'So, are you coming or what?' Ashby asked. 'Service starts at eleven.'

I looked down at my dishevelled clothes and then at the clock. It was already ten-thirty. 'Like this?' I asked.

'I'll take you as you are. That's all any of us can ever do,' said Ashby philosophically, 'whether we're coming into this world, or leaving it.'

15

GREY CLOUDS pressed the horizon and rain fell so hard that the tiny, worn wipers could barely keep the Land Rover's windscreen clear. Ashby's finery looked utterly out of place in the filthy Defender. His neck strained at the starched, tight collar as he peered out at the deluge. Torrents of water gushed either side of the narrow road and pooled at the bends. Ashby drove recklessly, pushing the car to the limits. Every time we came to a turn, I found myself bracing, my foot searching for a phantom brake pedal. He almost ran a small hatchback off the road as we climbed the hill at the other end of the bay. My knuckles were white, and my mouth went parchment dry with fear when we narrowly missed a head-on collision with a truck. *This* was real.

The small church was an island of brown stone in a sea of green fields. To the south, beyond the grazing sheep, lay the turbulent waters of Oxwich Bay. Thick sheets of rain hammered the high waves and large ships rolled on the horizon. The Land Rover bumped over the rutted field that acted as a car park. There were four other cars. The hearse stood on a patch of scruffy gravel in front of the church, where five men in black tailcoats waited in respectful silence. I looked at Ashby and saw that his gaze was fixed on something beyond the hearse. I followed his sightline and, in the small graveyard that flanked the church, I saw sheets of artificial grass laid over the edges of a freshly dug grave. Ashby, his eyes glassy with tears, looked away, cut the engine and stared morosely at the rain washing down the windscreen.

'Do you think it's true?' he asked at last. 'What they say about him?'

I shook my head.

'This story you're working on. Will it clear his name?'

'If something really did happen in Syria,' I forced myself to answer, 'then, yes, maybe.'

'My son didn't kill himself,' Ashby blurted out as he finally broke down. Tears flowed down his flushed cheeks. 'And he didn't kill that journalist. I don't care what they say.'

I nodded and placed a sympathetic hand on Ashby's arm. He looked down at the tender gesture with dismay, quickly pulled his arm away and stepped out. I watched him lift his face to the heavens and his tears were lost to the rain.

With a heavy heart, I climbed out of the Land Rover and followed Ashby towards the church. The men who stood beside the hearse nodded sympathetic, sombre greetings. As we neared the vehicle, my eyes were drawn to the other side of the church, where two outside broadcast vans and three cars were parked in the far field. A small crowd of reporters gathered under umbrellas, but the huddle broke the moment someone spotted Ashby.

'Mr Wilmore, have you had any further information from the police?' a female voice called out.

'Isn't that Julia Castleton?' a man asked.

I had trouble identifying the questioners. Ashby and I were surrounded by a swarm of reporters, as persistent as wasps, buzzing allegations and stinging questions at us as we approached the church.

'Have you anything to say to the victim's family?'

'Why was your son AWOL?'

'What do you have to do with Mr Wilmore, Julia?'

'Will you be making a statement, Mr Wilmore?'

'You weren't the first vulture drawn by his bones,' Ashby informed me loudly.

'I shouldn't come in,' I said, pausing in my tracks.

'You may be a vulture, Miss Castleton, but I know Michael would've liked you,' Ashby assured me.

He continued towards the stone porch and I followed him. The doors to the church seemed to offer some protection, and the reporters fell back as if unwilling to breach this sanctuary. Ashby pointedly shut the great wooden doors behind us, and I could no longer hear the reporters, or even the rain. In the calm stillness of the church, it was as though the world had stopped. My panic levels subsided as I breathed in the warm air, which was thick with the scent of wood polish and damp bodies.

My eyes followed the line of the church to the stained-glass windows that dominated the eastern end. Beneath them lay the wooden altar and next to it, Michael Wilmore's simple coffin. I glanced at Ashby, who took neat, almost robotic steps up the aisle, his back as straight as any parade ground officer. I wondered how he had the strength to do it, how he could face the horror of burying his child.

The vicar, a tall bespectacled man with thick brown hair, stepped forward to greet Ashby, and then led him to sit beside his drinking buddy Arthur in the front row. He wore a black suit and, like Ashby, looked almost unrecognisable now he was respectable and sober.

I slipped into a pew at the back to give myself a good view of the mourners. A man with blond hair and matching stubble turned and glanced at me, quickly appraising me with bright blue eyes. He wore a smart grey overcoat, the shoulders damp from the rain, and I glimpsed a regimental tie. One of Wilmore's comrades?

Everyone else was well over fifty and appeared to be friends of Michael's father. It seemed Wilmore's public disgrace had ensured a very private funeral. How must Ashby feel to see his son so poorly mourned?

A PA system crackled into life, and the vicar welcomed the meagre congregation. 'On behalf of the Wilmore family, I'd like to thank you all for coming to share our loving memories of Michael.'

'Get out of my way!' a loud voice bellowed from beyond the inner door.

Then came the sound of a scuffle and a muffled cry, and the inner door swung open with such force that it clattered against the back wall of the church. An irritated man entered, casting angry looks over his shoulder.

'Sorry,' he barked at the vicar, before taking a seat in the back pew opposite me.

I placed him in his early thirties. He wore dust-covered jeans, a dirty blue shirt and a black hoodie, and his thick black hair was matted and unwashed. He caught me watching him and stared back, his eyes hostile, burning from his sharp, angular face. Unfazed, I eyeballed him and then glanced pointedly at the open door. Already a cold draught was breezing through the church, and the mourners could hear the noise of the press pack. The vicar started down the aisle to deal with it, but I got to my feet and beat him to the door, happy to shut out the reporters again.

'Thank you,' said the vicar. 'And welcome all. Let us begin by bowing our heads in prayer.'

I watched as most members of the congregation lowered their heads. The blond soldier turned to look at the dark-haired newcomer, who stared back with ill-concealed contempt. The soldier gave nothing away, turned around and bowed his head. I watched, wondering at the dynamics, when suddenly the dark-haired man fixed his angry stare on me again. I met his eyes for a moment and felt nothing but the man's rage. I turned to face the vicar and bowed my head to listen to the Lord's Prayer.

16

THEY BURIED Michael Wilmore in the rain.

I stood beside the church and fiddled with the strap of my satchel as I watched the mourners gather beside the grave. The pallbearers, who had entered the church at the end of a short, emotional service, lowered Michael's casket. Ashby shook as he wept for his son.

'You're getting soaked.'

I turned to see the blond soldier approaching with a raised umbrella. He had wide, welcoming eyes and a friendly smile. His rounded cheeks had been scoured red by the chill wind. He drew next to me, standing a few inches taller than me, and held the umbrella above us.

'Thanks,' I said.

'James Newby,' the soldier said, offering me his free hand.

'Julia Castleton,' I said as I took it.

'I know,' Newby replied. 'Michael gave me something to give to you.'

I looked up at Newby.

'What?' I asked.

'Not here,' he replied, looking towards the journalists gathered at the edge of the graveyard.

'Did you serve with Michael?'

'Yes,' Newby confirmed. 'He discovered something.'

'What?' I quizzed.

'Something terrible.' Movement caught Newby's eye and I followed his gaze to see the dark-haired latecomer staring at us.

'Who's that?' I asked.

'Major Ivan Fox,' Newby replied. 'He's SIC – second in command – of Mikey's unit. Or was. I heard he's on civvy street.'

'He doesn't seem very fond of you.'

Newby shrugged. 'I don't think Foxy's fond of anyone. We can't talk here. It isn't safe.' He pushed the umbrella towards me. 'Keep it,' he advised.

I took hold of the tiny canopy and watched Newby stalk towards the grave. He stood opposite Ivan Fox and the two men eyed each other as a trembling Ashby Wilmore threw the first clod of earth on the casket.

***

I scanned the cramped sitting room for Newby, but couldn't see him anywhere. I'd returned to Oxwich with Ashby, the two of us sitting in silence as he'd navigated the wet roads. Ashby had parked the Land Rover by the village green and led me to one of the adjacent cottages, where an elderly lady called Mavis had offered to host the wake. I had been given a warm greeting but once they learnt I was a reporter people ebbed away, directing looks ranging from suspicion to open hostility. I didn't mind – after all, I hadn't come here to find friends – but it did make it difficult to pump for information about Michael. This trip was another void. No leads, no stories, more wasted money, and all the time The Castleton Files was pacing at my heels, a hungry beast waiting to be fed. I suddenly felt claustrophobic, sitting in this low beamed cottage, pressed in by hostile strangers, the pressures of my job getting to me. I picked up my bag and pushed past the mourners, desperate for air.

Cold rain revived me as I stepped outside. My fingers slipped to my pulse but my count was interrupted by the dark-haired Ivan Fox striding across the green towards me.

'Hey!' he yelled. 'I need to talk to you!'

Anger radiated off the man, and I felt a sudden tremor of fear, remembering Michael, his paranoia, the needle in his arm. I turned to re-enter the cottage and the safety of the wake, but Fox grabbed me and I cried out as his fingers bit into my lacerated arm.

'What are you and Newby playing at?' Fox snarled.

I didn't get the opportunity to answer. Newby emerged from an archway beside the cottage and tackled Ivan at full pelt. The two men fell to the ground, and Newby seized the advantage, pummelling the stunned major with his powerful fists. I was shocked by the ferocity of the beating, and rushed over.

'He's had enough!' I yelled, pulling at Newby.

He turned to face me, his eyes full of brutish rage. Fox lay senseless beneath him.

'We need to get out of here,' Newby said urgently. 'There will be more of them.'

I reached for my phone, but Newby shoved it back in my bag.

'You can't trust the police,' he said, and he grabbed my wrist and pulled me down a narrow, muddy path that ran between two cottages towards a dense copse of tangled trees and brambles.

I glanced over my shoulder and saw Ivan Fox stirring. I followed Newby into the thicket, where sharp spines tore at my coat and the thicker tendrils threatened to snatch my satchel from my shoulder. After twenty yards, the brambles thinned and I caught glimpses of the frothing sea between the trees. Newby ran alongside me.

'Move!'

The urgency in his voice spurred me faster and branches whipped at my face as I ran on. The trees gave way to an open field.

I heard a powerful male voice yelling behind us. I turned to look but Newby pulled me on.

'They killed Mikey,' he shouted. 'We have to get out of here.'

'Who's they?' I asked breathlessly.

'Come on,' Newby urged.

He vaulted a wooden gate and I followed awkwardly, slipping in the mud on the other side. I tumbled on, trying to catch up with Newby as he led me towards a farmhouse and some modern barns. A thick wood lay beyond.

'There's a path,' Newby said breathlessly, pointing to the trees that clung to a sharp hill, which fell steeply down to the bay below.

I saw a black SUV, a Toyota, speeding down a country lane that ran parallel to the field.

'Shit!' Newby exclaimed as the Toyota stopped and three men in black balaclavas jumped out.

They sprinted towards the buildings, on an intercept course with us. I looked back and saw Ivan Fox struggling to catch us. I turned to Newby, full of concern.

'We've got to beat them to those trees,' he said. He pulled at me, urging me on.

We sprinted through an open gate into a muddy farmyard. I slipped, skidded and fell hard. Newby yanked me to my feet, before my hip had time to register the pain, and bustled me on. I resisted his grasp, desperate to recover my satchel, which had fallen in the mud.

'No time!' Newby yelled.

'My life is in there!' I protested, snatching up the bag.

'Hey!' a middle-aged man yelled from the doorway of the farmhouse. He immediately withdrew as the first gunshots rang out.

Bullets thudded into old stone, throwing up clouds of dust, as Newby and I sprinted behind an old barn that shielded us from our pursuers. Breathing heavily, I was about to speak but Newby gestured for silence. The treeline was just fifty yards away. We had to reach it before our pursuers rounded the bend and had a clear line of fire. As we ran, I looked over my shoulder and saw Ivan Fox slow to a walk halfway across the field. He hesitated, and then sheepishly started to retrace his tracks.

But the rest of the men were coming, pistols in hand. I was running faster than I thought possible and we made it to the treeline. Hidden again among the trees, we watched splinters fly everywhere as bullets hit the trunks. Now we were descending steeply, slithering and stumbling down a steep rocky path that was slick with rain. I lost my footing and fell. I tumbled over roots, through mud and fallen leaves and finally came to a battered, dazed halt near the foot of the hill. I reared up in unfocused panic as someone approached. A hand grabbed my arm, and my eyes snapped back into focus. It was Newby.

'Are you OK?' he asked.

'I think so,' I answered groggily.

'We've got to keep moving,' he advised. 'We're nearly there.'

I followed Newby's gaze and, through the trees, I saw the Oxwich Bay Hotel, Ashby's watering hole.

People.

Safety.

I forced myself to my feet, swung my satchel over my shoulder and limped alongside Newby. We scanned our surroundings, looking for movement among the dank trees. I didn't see the man until it was too late. A dark figure stepped out from behind a tree and smacked Newby in the face with the butt of his pistol. Newby crumpled immediately. I screamed and turned to run, but was confronted by another masked man, who drove his gloved hand into my face. The stench of an acrid chemical filled my nostrils, and my head swam. My limbs suddenly went limp and useless, and my voice refused to come. A pair of strong arms grabbed me before I hit the deck, and I was dragged out of the woods, away from the prone Newby.

And then the world went black.

17

MY EYES rolled open. It was dark, so dark. Something had woken me. Something hard and violent. A second slap struck my cheek and my head snapped to the right. I cried out, but the sound of my pain was muffled by the black hood over my head.

'What have they told you?' A deep voice came out of the darkness.

'Who?' I asked weakly.

'Michael Wilmore. James Newby. We know you're investigating Wilmore's death. We know he tried to pass information to you. Before you die you're going to tell us what you know and who you've told.'

I felt the firm grip of a man's hand on my chin. The fingers pressed the rough hood into my flesh.

'I…' I began, but my words were cut short by the deafening sound of a nearby gunshot. The fingers fell away and there was the thud of a body hitting a hard floor. Then came the scuffle of rapid footsteps and a series of shots. More cries, and then silence.

I sat motionless, paralysed with fear. My breath came in rapid shallow gasps. I feared I might lose control of my bowels and focused on counting, in and out, four and five, six and seven. My ears were still ringing from the gunshot, but I strained to hear any sounds. Then, suddenly, there was movement. Footsteps, slow at first, then increasingly quick. I felt hands at my throat and recoiled.

'It's OK,' a familiar voice whispered. 'I need to untie the hood.'

'James?' I asked uncertainly.

Fingers worked the knot that secured the hood, and then it was off. Blinded by the light, I gasped the fresh air and squinted carefully until Newby came into focus. His blue eyes smiled down at me, bright as the ocean against his pale face, which was streaked with dirt and blood.

'I followed them,' he said, working quickly now on the ropes that bound my arms and legs to the chair.

I was in a large warehouse that was entirely empty apart from the body that lay at my feet and two others slumped by an inner door. I shivered, suddenly chilled to the bone. The sight of the corpses affected me as much as the stale chill of the empty warehouse.

The ropes fell away and Newby hoisted me to my feet. I felt shaky and one ankle screamed with pain when I put my weight on it. I hobbled closer to inspect the bodies. One ginger-haired, one with a harsh crew cut, and one bearded man. All had died with their pistols drawn.

'Who are they?' I asked, trying to get a closer look at the black guy.

'I don't know. Military Intelligence? MI6?' Newby pulled me away.

'I've seen him before,' I remembered, indicating the black man. 'He was in Waterstones the day Michael was killed, I'm sure of it.'

'We need to get out of here,' Newby urged. 'Can you walk? There could be more. We really need to go.'

I nodded and bit the inside of my lip to distract from the pain in my ankle. 'My bag,' I said urgently. 'My phone's in my bag, fuck, where is it?'

'Here.' Newby found it on the floor behind my chair. 'But no phones. You don't know who's listening. Come on, we need to move.'

Reluctantly I slung my bag over my shoulder. Every instinct told me to call for help but the dead men looked like military. The kind of people who could triangulate calls, tap phones and find me.

'Lean on me,' instructed Newby, and despite my instinctive dislike of accepting help, I took his advice.

We moved towards the large double doors at the front of the warehouse. Newby opened a gap and peered through.

'Clear,' he said.

It was pitch black outside. *How long have I been out?* I thought, suddenly panicked as I took in the heavy rain falling in flinty slivers from the night sky. I had promised I'd collect Alex. What would he be thinking?

'You're in shock,' Newby told me as he led me past the attackers' SUV towards a small hatchback parked in the muddy yard.

I realised I was shaking and that my breathing was shallow and erratic. I felt light-headed and dizzy as Newby helped me into the passenger seat. He ran round to the driver's side, jumped in and started the engine. He didn't put the headlights on until we had driven about a quarter of a mile down the lane that led away from the warehouse. We were on a narrow road that ran alongside a cliff edge. I looked down at the choppy waves and tried to bring the world into calm focus. The adrenaline that coursed through me was helping to dull the pain, but it was pushing me towards a full-blown panic attack.

'The British Government has been selling arms to Islamist fighters in Syria,' Newby announced suddenly. He reached for a folder that lay on the back seat, and deposited it on my lap. 'This is what Michael wanted me to give you.'

I examined the brown envelope folder, which was full of documents and emails from the Ministry of Defence and a variety of military contractors.

'They've been killing people to suppress the story,' Newby continued. 'We won't be safe until it's been made public.'

'Did you know about this?' I asked.

Newby shook his head. 'Not until the night before Michael died. He came to stay with me. Made me promise to hide him after what happened in Oxford. He told me he planned to contact you and gave me that,' Newby glanced at the folder, 'in case anything happened to him.'

'How did he get all this?' I asked, rifling through the papers. The panic subsided as I focused on the story and my brain started to whirr wildly.

'I don't know,' Newby replied. 'I need to drop you somewhere,' he added nervously. 'I've ridden my luck as far as it will go.'

I looked at Newby incredulously.

'I'm sorry. He was my friend, but I didn't ask for any of this,' Newby said earnestly. 'I just killed three men. These are bad people.

They killed Michael and that reporter in Oxford. I don't want to end up like them.'

Newby looked at me, then back out at the dark road.

'This isn't my fight,' he said emphatically.

18

NEWBY AND I parted shortly after ten o'clock. He dropped me off at a McDonald's on the outskirts of Swansea. The restaurant was busy with night-time trade.

'Thanks,' I said, as he pulled to a halt in the car park. 'I'll never forget what you've done for me. How can I reach you?'

'I'm sorry,' Newby replied. 'But it's safer if neither of us knows where the other is going.'

I stuffed the folder into my satchel and opened the car door.

'Be careful,' Newby counselled. 'We won't be safe until the world knows the truth.'

I nodded and hauled myself out of the car. Everything ached, my bad ankle throbbed ominously, and my cheekbone was tender to the touch. I limped over to the restaurant and watched Newby pull onto the main road. As he drove into the distance, I reached into my satchel for my phone, and saw that I had twelve missed calls, all from Emilia. I didn't bother listening to any of the messages and dialled Emilia's mobile. The phone was answered after a single ring.

'Where are you?' Emilia asked, her voice sharp with worry.

'I got held up,' I replied. 'Sorry.'

'We've been frantic,' Emilia countered. 'Philippe, it's Jules. She's OK.' Emilia directed her words away from the phone, and I heard a muttered guttural response in French.

'How's Alex?'

'Not good. He was worried about you, but we settled him down. He's asleep now.'

'Thanks,' I said awkwardly.

'Was it worth it? Was it worth making your son miserable?'

I shivered as I considered the question. I started as a group of teenagers exited the restaurant, jostling each other loudly. An old car with muted headlights pulled into the car park. The driver, a middle-aged man with boot polish black hair, eyed me as he steered the car into the drive-thru. My head went light with panic.

'Jules?' Emilia asked. 'Are you still there?'

'Yes,' I forced out the word. 'And yes, it was worth it. I'm on my way home. I'll pick him up before school.' My intonation was uneven, and the words were so rushed they almost ran into one another.

'Are you OK? Where are you?'

'I'm fine,' I replied. 'Just…a hard day. See you tomorrow.'

I hung up quickly, and switched off the phone, suddenly anxious about the exposure of the call. My paranoia ratcheted up another notch. I was almost overcome by a terrible fatigue that made me want to weep. I unzipped a pocket sewn discreetly into the lining of my satchel and pulled out an old Nokia I kept hidden for emergencies. I switched it on and dialled the only number in the memory. It would connect me to the one person who could make me feel safe.

19

I SIPPED the scalding tea, and my hands hugged the cup for warmth. I knew I should eat something – I'd had nothing except a cold sausage roll at Michael Wilmore's wake – but my stomach was rolling uncomfortably. I recognised the feeling, the churning excitement of a big story, mixed with the sharp twist of nerves that someone else would beat me to it, and an undertone of icy fear I might get it wrong. There was also the lingering unease that someone else would try to kill me.

It was clear that Wilmore's dossier was a big story, potentially my biggest yet. The kind of story that would make The Castleton Files front-page news, that could topple governments, ruin careers and send people to prison. The kind of story people are willing to commit murder to keep hidden. I took another sip of tea and nearly spilt it as my hands shook. I was scared but I knew I had to publish. This was exactly the kind of story that needed to be dragged into the spotlight. The perpetrators had to feel the heat of exposure; whatever power they had would wither in the light.

The truth was the only way to kill a shadow. I could not, in good conscience, read the dossier and turn my back on the story, no matter what the cost. At once I thought of Wilmore, of the price he'd paid. He had lost everything, his reputation, his friends, his life, to get this story into the light. His father was a broken man who would likely drink himself to death. Howells, a family man, would never return home. So many had lost so much because of this story. I thought of Alex. It caused an almost physical pain to contemplate leaving him, not being there to see him grow up, his grief…I added sugar to my tea, drank it down, refocused on the dossier in front of me and smothered my concerns with my growing anger at the corruption. I worked the angles and the first paragraphs started to form in my head.

How had Wilmore got all of this? There were documents here clearly marked for security clearance higher than any Army Reservist medic could attain. Procurement notices for some serious ordnance. An intercepted transcript of a telephone call between two men in Karachi discussing the British supply line. One of the men was relaying a request for a specific type of rocket launcher and the other man laughed, saying, 'Right now it's buy one get one free from our London friend.' There was a detailed Secret UK Eyes Only Options Paper compiled by the Overseas and Defence Directorate, which appeared to detail plans to supply arms to a number of Islamic militias operating in Iraq and Syria. One email, composed seven months after the briefing paper, showed the plan had been implemented but was proving hard to contain. The name of the author was redacted but I could see from the correspondence that it was a senior agent in MI6. A worried memo from a civil servant in the MoD advised a junior minister to consider exit strategies from Operation Entrust before the risks escalated.

'Initial objectives have proved harder to realise than expected and we have reached a crossroads. To go forward now will take us into dangerous territory from which there may be no return.'

There were many more pages. I flicked through, my eyes occasionally noting names I recognised: a senior MP on the Defence Committee, a minister in the Foreign and Commonwealth Office. I took out my phone and methodically photographed every page. When I finally finished, my phone battery was into the red, my eyes were gritty and sore and my body was wrung out with the tension.

It had been three and a half hours since I'd spoken to Joe. Just over two hours and twenty minutes since I'd posted in a Mumsnet thread.

Mumwherearemysocks

Kids in Port Talbot. Me in McDonald's. Keeping it real.

An hour later he'd replied.

DispicableMe93

Sweet as. Coming in fast. Big Mac meal.

There were a few bemused comments from other posters, but Mumwherearemysocks had laughed them off with a one-word comment – *Hic!* – followed by a series of emojis of wine glasses and grinning faces. I smiled ruefully. My infrequent postings as Mumwherearemysocks in those rare instances when I needed to contact Joe off-grid were always light-hearted and playful. They made me wistful for another life, one that might have been, if only…

I stopped the thoughts there. I knew from experience no good came from brooding over what might have been. I looked back at the dossier. Besides, if I was another type of person with another type of life, I wouldn't have The Castleton Files and the opportunity to make a difference to the world. And I wouldn't have Alex.

Movement outside caught my eye. A grimy white van with a dented bumper and a ladder on the roof turned into the car park. Signage on the side advertised the talents of Mr Tidy, a home maintenance service. But I knew anyone contacting Mr Tidy would soon find he was always booked. He was never to be found mending gutters or clearing gardens. He'd be staking out bent public officials, tracing girls spirited away for arranged marriages, or extracting befuddled widows from relationships with ruthless conmen. Mr Tidy's real name was Joe Turner, and he was a private detective who liked to keep his profile so low even I didn't know where he lived or where he came from. Yet I trusted him implicitly. I owed him my life.

I stuffed the dossier in my bag and stood awkwardly, gingerly testing my weight on my bad ankle, which was now swollen and stiff. My hip ached, a scratch from a bramble smarted over one eye, and I was bruised all over. But now that Joe was here, I felt better and even my appetite stirred. I ordered us both Big Macs, large fries, milkshakes, apple pies and a cup of ice to go, and limped out to the van.

I handed the food to Joe and then climbed carefully into the van, wincing with pain. I slammed the door shut and grinned into Joe's concerned face.

'You should see the other guy,' I said.

'I'd like to make his acquaintance,' said Joe with menace. 'Anything I need to know?'

This was his standard opener. It referred to any immediate threat in the vicinity.

'Clear, I think,' I said. I wrapped the ice into a wad of napkins and stuffed it down my sock in a bid to soothe my swollen ankle. 'But I wouldn't mind putting some distance between me and this place.'

The big diesel engine growled into life, and Joe eased us out of the car park, towards the M4. We didn't speak much at first. The combined roar of the engine and the van's heaters as Joe tried to demist the steamy windows made conversation difficult, and besides, we were both hungry and wolfed our burgers and fries and the gum-shrinkingly sweet pies.

It was late and the motorway was empty. With the business of eating done and the windows finally clear, I was able to tell Joe of my dealings with Wilmore, his death, the attack at the funeral and the intervention by Newby.

'This,' I said, patting my satchel, which contained the dossier, 'is pure dynamite.'

'Don't like dynamite,' said Joe bluntly. 'Dangerous, unpredictable stuff.'

'British Government selling arms to militants in Syria, Joe,' I said. 'The whole shitshow laid out. I'm amazed Wilmore lasted as long as he did.'

Joe chewed on his bottom lip. 'Okaaay,' he said. 'Let me check it out. Let's cross-reference what we can, and I've still got that mate in the MoD who owes me.'

'It's all here, Joe, honestly. And we can't wait on this one. They're going to come after me. I've got to think about Alex. We're only safe when it's out there. Sitting in my bag, it's like a hand grenade primed to go off. Set it free and the blowback isn't on me, it's on them.'

'Julia, your reputation is only as good as your last story. Phelps was a good story, a story we worked hard on, researched; armour-clad evidence that went viral. That was a game-changer for you. This, this is different. It's not you and me; it's someone else, someone you've never even met, someone who died a junkie. It just seems like a hell of a leap of faith to gamble all your hard work on him.'

'Joe, you're not listening,' I said. 'I make one call, one enquiry, try one meeting with any of the names in the dossier, and I may as well stick the needle in my arm myself. I have to publish. It's the only way out of this alive.'

I pulled out my laptop and got to work. By the time we reached the outskirts of London, I'd drafted the article and was mulling a headline. I read it out, listening to the cadence of each sentence, self-editing as I went. I knew it was strong. The story almost wrote itself. The dossier was like a dot-to-dot puzzle. All I had to do was draw the lines that pulled the picture into focus.

'Well?' I asked Joe, who brooded beside me.

'Like I said, dynamite,' he responded at last. 'Let me dig around this, Julia. Just me. It won't come back at you, and then—'

'Joe, they know I have this,' I said impatiently. 'They know. If I don't publish then I'm done. They've already killed two people that we know of. Newby could already be dead as well.'

'Let me at least check him out,' said Joe with exasperation. 'He could be anyone.'

'He saved my life.'

Joe muttered something and shook his head.

I looked down at the story. It was good. The evidence was compelling, and I would upload it for everyone to see. Only then would I be safe. Besides, there could be other copies of the dossier. I hated the thought of someone else getting this story out before me. I glanced sideways at Joe, saw the strain on his face, the tiredness of an all-night drive, and felt so glad to have him in my life. But I was the journalist, and it was my site. I paid him for his time – admittedly peanuts, though he never complained – but it meant I got to make the decisions.

Angling the screen away from Joe, I pressed *Post Now,* and it was done. I'd explain later.

20

WE HIT the early morning traffic as we drove through Chiswick. Commuters were already pushing into the city, one person per car, fingers tapping on steering wheels, faces a grey match for the gun-metal dawn. Perhaps later, sipping their expensive coffees in their shiny offices, they would surf the web and find my story. It always gave me a thrill to think of my work out there. Some of these people might already subscribe to my site, and the email alert advising them of a new story might be waiting in their inbox. I thought of my rival, Chris Jones. The news would sour his breakfast, a prospect I found immensely cheering. He was an angry man, who was clever enough to hide the more unpleasant aspects of his character beneath a veneer of righteous outrage at sneering elites and radical Islam. It was particularly sweet to think of him seething over his cornflakes when he went online this morning.

'Where am I dropping you?' asked Joe, frowning at the traffic now clogging the roads. 'I hope the answer's going to be home.'

'I need to pick up Alex from Emilia.'

Joe glanced at me. 'Home first. Seriously, Julia, you look like shit. And I mean that in the nicest possible way.'

I checked my appearance in the wing mirror. I did look rough. I was pale and drawn and had a bloody scratch down my right cheek. My hair was wild, and my face was grimy.

'See,' said Joe. 'You'll give the boy nightmares turning up like that. A shower wouldn't go amiss either.'

I knew he was speaking the truth and rolled a friendly punch at his shoulder. Emilia would only lecture me if I turned up looking like this. And I just had time. Home, quick shower, clean clothes and could still get Alex to school by 8:45. Like a good mother.

'OK, you're the boss,' I said. 'Home, please.'

'You got it,' he said, beeping his horn as a cyclist shot in front of him. 'And he's not got any lights on that bike. Death wish.' Joe used to be in the Paras and retained a rigid streak of adherence to health and safety.

I smiled and picked up my phone, which had been charging, and idly scrolled through my X feed. My post already had two hundred likes and seventy-nine retweets. A BBC journalist had picked it up and shared it with his thousands of followers with the message: *Expect some tough questions for the foreign secretary when she appears on BBCR4 Today programme #mustlisten.*

I felt my stomach lurch. What, already? I reached over and tuned in to Radio 4, where the guests were talking about an upcoming byelection. I quickly checked The Castleton Files. The story had been shared over four hundred times, there were 172 comments, and my email box was rapidly filling with queries from other journalists.

Joe turned up the sound to hear the foreign secretary stalling on a question about the revelations that the British Government had supplied arms to Islamic militias in Iraq and Syria. He looked across at me, his face grim.

'Something you want to tell me?'

I shrugged, listening to the radio.

'As I've already stated,' the foreign secretary was saying, 'I've only just heard about these allegations, and it wouldn't be sensible to comment at this stage. As you know, the situation in that part of the world is very complicated, very sensitive, and I really think media organisations, including these self-appointed bloggers, have a responsibility to check their sources and information very thoroughly because lives are at risk. In this instance, fake news could quite literally kill.'

'This isn't just any blogger though, is it, Foreign Secretary? This is the blog that just landed a blow to one of your own, Sir John Phelps, who sits on the Defence Committee.'

'As I said, Martha, I can't possibly comment until I know more.'

Joe turned off the radio. 'Well, you got what you wanted.'

'I had to, Joe.'

'It's going to be a firestorm today. You're gonna be in the eye of that storm. You ready for it?' He glanced at me meaningfully. I knew exactly what he meant.

'Yeah, I'm good,' I said. 'I can handle this. It's what I, what we, wanted, right? Expose the bad guys, bring them to justice.'

'Sometimes the bad guys bite back.'

'Yeah, I noticed,' I said, examining my bloated ankle in its soggy sock. 'I'll be fine, Joe.'

'You're not on *The Times* now though, Jules. It's just you.'

'I like it like that,' I said. 'On the paper this would be tied up with lawyers for weeks.'

Joe didn't say anything, but I knew he thought that was the sensible thing to do with a story this big.

'Fuck!'

He slammed on the brakes as a cab swung out in front of us. We were both flung forward until our seatbelts caught us. Joe honked the horn, and the cabbie flipped his finger our way.

'Nice,' I said. 'Classy. It's left here, Joe.'

'You're not alone though, Jules. You know I'll back you, whatever happens.'

We lapsed into silence as Joe circled the block in his van, looking for a place to pull over near my flat.

'You can drop me here. It's only round the corner.'

He pulled up and the diesel engine rattled as it idled. 'This good for you?'

'Perfect,' I said, grabbing my coat and slipping awkwardly down to the pavement. I leant into the van and pulled my satchel onto my shoulder. 'Thanks, Joe. For everything.'

He nodded. 'You know where to find me.'

I smiled. I didn't actually know where to find him, but I knew how to reach him and that was good enough. I limped hurriedly towards my block of flats, aware of my phone beeping and vibrating in my pocket as my story, like a stone lobbed in a lake, caused ripples that were felt across the world.

21

I TOOK a cab to Holland Park and tried to ignore the worrying hole it ate in my weekly budget. It was worth it, though, to take the strain off my throbbing ankle, and it gave me a chance to comb my still-damp hair and apply a little concealer to the dark circles under my eyes. I was wearing clean jeans, a pale blue linen shirt, a little frayed at the collar and cuffs, and my old trainers for comfort. I couldn't get my ankle back into my boots.

I arrived just in time. The au pair must have already taken the Garonne kids to their prep school in Chelsea, and Emilia was heading down the drive in her big Audi with Alex on a booster seat in the back. The two cars pulled up next to one another and Alex started yelling with excitement. I climbed in next to him for a big squealy hug. His school trousers were neatly pressed, his hair smelt of expensive shampoo and there was no trace of toothpaste on his jumper. I knew if I looked in his book bag all his reading would be done. I felt a rush of love for Emilia, who was now paying for the taxi. I sighed with relief, and was happy for the taxi driver. He'd get a much better tip from my sister.

Emilia returned to the driver's seat and eyed me in the rear-view mirror. 'Everything alright?'

'Yes, thanks, Sis,' I said. 'I got held up, and then the traffic across London was hell. But I made it.'

I high-fived Alex. He grinned and started to tell a long story about a game he and Edgar had been playing, involving dragons and dinosaurs fighting a Transformer, but it was unclear to me who the good guys were. I was just glad to see the smile on his face. Even in the two days I had been away he seemed taller, more confident and his vocabulary more mature.

'Veronique says one tiny poison dart frog can kill twenty thousand mice,' he said, his little face crinkling in a frown. 'Do you think that's true, Mummy? I hate those frogs!'

I caught Emilia's eye in the mirror.

'Sorry about that,' said Emilia. 'Veronique's obsessed with natural history at the moment. Especially the grisly bits.'

'That's all natural history is: grisly bits,' I said. 'Eat or be eaten. Did he behave himself?'

Emilia smiled warmly. 'Of course, he was a delight. As always. There's a letter in his bookbag for you. A school trip you need to sign for.'

My heart sank. There was a constant drip-feed of money to the school. Raffles and trips and dress-up-for-charity days that I always forgot until the last moment. Alex's World Book Day costume was the most recent in a long line of rushed disappointments.

I watched him stare out of the window. We were close to his school now and he kept spotting local landmarks – the park where we found the giant acorns, the café with the big hot chocolates, his friend Greta's house.

'I take it the trip was a success,' ventured Emilia. 'I heard the news on the radio.'

I nodded. 'Big story,' I said in an offhand way. I didn't want Emilia to pick up on the dangers that had rushed me into publication. 'Really big.'

Emilia pursed her lips. I could tell she wanted to say more but was reluctant to speak in front of Alex.

'How's Philippe?' I asked, changing the subject and scrolling quickly through my phone: eleven missed calls, and my post had been shared seven hundred times. 'And Jacques? Has his eczema settled down?'

'Yes, the new cream has made a big difference. He doesn't have to go back for six months now.'

I glanced at a text. From Lyndsey. *A hundred thousand hits before you've even had breakfast, sweetie. This is it!!!!!* Followed by a string of emojis. *Smiley face, smiley face, champagne bottle popping its cork.*

My stomach rolled. This was big. Definitely the right thing to get it out there. I realised Emilia had stopped talking, did a quick mental rewind and remembered our conversation: Jacques.

'Oh, that's wonderful, Emilia. I'm so pleased for the little fella.'

We chatted a bit more until we reached the school. It was strange to arrive in a big car like all the other four-by-four mums with their swishy ponytails and high-end gym kits. I couldn't help noticing the glances as they spotted Alex jumping down from the shiny Q7 with its tinted windows and personalised plates.

'What's wrong with your leg, Mummy?' asked Alex.

'I twisted my ankle,' I said. 'A real silly billy.'

'Did it bleed?'

I laughed. 'No, no blood, sorry to disappoint you.'

I gave him a big hug and kiss and breathed in the smell of his warm little body. Oh God, I loved him so much it hurt.

I watched him slip beyond the school gate and returned to the Audi where Emilia was waiting.

My sister appraised me like a doctor examining a patient. 'The limp?'

'Twisted my ankle. No, really, I did. Hurt like hell but nothing serious.'

'And the face?'

'Bramble. It was proper countryside, you know. It's dangerous.'

'Were you drinking?'

'No! I was stone-cold sober, and the countryside attacked.'

Emilia started the engine and pulled away, heading for my flat. 'I was worried. You didn't show up and then you sounded…well, you sounded distant, upset.'

I stared out of the window. Here, among the grime and stop-start traffic, the smart cafés with their chalkboards and gleaming coffee machines, the colourful tables of piled fruits outside the Turkish grocers, the to and fro of all the people, it felt as though my trip to Wales had been some strange dream. The endless rain, the cold farmhouse on the cliffs, the crashing of the sea, Ashby in his mourning suit, the miserable wake, the chase with Newby, the hood over my head, the dead bodies at my feet…Surreptitiously I let my fingers linger on my wrist and located my pulse and counted the steady drum under my skin. When I was satisfied, I let my fingers crawl up my arm and pressed them into the soft flesh I'd carved in Ashby's bathroom. *This is real.* It was all real. And it was mine: 102,000 hits and climbing. Before breakfast.

22

THE TATTOOED Man glittered. Lights shimmered off the tiny splinters of broken glass that crusted his head, shoulders, arms. He turned and the glass tinkled to the floor, before he crunched it underfoot. He held out his hand and pulled her close, his eyes black pools in which she could see the reflection of the smashed car, the approach of blue lights and her own white face streaked with blood.

'Move,' he commanded, and she followed.

She would follow him anywhere. They had crashed in a town square, and people were watching the smashed car as flames licked up the bonnet.

'Are you OK?'

A middle-aged man approached them, full of concern. The other shadow dwellers stayed back. They knew Julia and the Tattooed Man were dangerous. Why didn't this fool?

'I've called an—'

But the middle-aged fool never got to finish his sentence. The Tattooed Man swung an angry fist and silenced him. The other shadow dwellers melted away and the man on the floor moaned and clutched his bloodied face.

Nobody stopped them as they left the scene. Julia laughed hysterically. This is what it was to have magic. They were beyond all natural and human laws. They ran down a street. Julia didn't recognise the town and wondered why they were there. They burst through the door of a small shop and she blinked under the harsh strip lighting. She suddenly felt hemmed in by the overcrowded place, shelves piled high with stock, no space to run or breathe. A Sikh man in a yellow turban stood behind the counter, his face suddenly fearful. He knew. He could see what they were. Mortal devils, made of flesh, brimming with darkness. The shop spiralled blue and white as police cars raced towards the town square. The Tattooed Man growled, deep in this throat. His anger was so potent it had become physical. She sensed it filling the shadows of the shop. She glanced back at the shopkeeper and was startled to find he was no longer there. In his place was Michael Wilmore.

This is wrong, *Julia thought.* This isn't the world I know. I don't meet him yet.

'Is there another way out?' the Tattooed Man growled.

Wilmore watched them impassively. Julia felt a shot of fear. Why didn't he answer? Didn't he know the danger he was in? The Tattooed Man pulled out a knife.

'I asked you a question,' he growled.

Julia looked at Wilmore, willing him to speak. The magic worked. Wilmore opened his mouth.

'Utopia,' he said. 'Utopia.'

I woke up, panting. It was as if Wilmore had spoken out loud; I felt his breath on my ear, that one word spoken so distinctly. *Utopia.* I looked around. I was alone, on my bed in my flat, the dossier under my cheek, my computer humming hotly next to me. I couldn't believe I'd fallen asleep, on this day of all days. I'd taken my work to bed to rest my ankle. That was why Wilmore had been in my dream. That dream, that evil man. Why was I dreaming about him? Was it my illness again, or was it a memory coming back? The thought filled me with hot shame and cold dread, and the combination made me shudder. I took a deep breath and counted my pulse. Not today, I couldn't afford to be off my game today.

I'd already done two radio interviews and provided quotes for four print journalists and one blogger. I'd replied to a handful of comments on my social media accounts, updated the website and had been going back through the dossier, making notes on new angles and potential new leads when I must have dozed off.

I sat up groggily, feeling leaden and heavy, the dream like a fog, slowly clearing. *Utopia.* Michael Wilmore's last known word. It seemed to linger in the air. I shook my head, stretched and tried to pull myself together. There was still so much to do. An aeroplane tracked its way across my window, cranes worked the skyline, somewhere in the building I heard a TV blare the trumpet of canned laughter. I logged back into my email. Time for a new post, acknowledging my debt to Wilmore, calling on the police to re-open their investigation into Howells' death, given that Wilmore had clearly been trying to pass on the dossier to the murdered *Times* journalist. I made no mention of James Newby's role. He obviously wanted no part in this. I pressed Post Now, thinking of Ashby and what it would mean to have his son cleared of murder, his name no longer tainted with scandal and an ignominious death by his own hand.

Already I felt better. I had accomplished a lot today, and the sleep had done me good. I pulled on my trainers and coat, ready to fetch Alex. I felt like celebrating and decided to take him down to the adventure playground at Wormwood Scrubs. We could have fish and chips afterwards. I hummed as I tidied up the papers. I put them back inside the folder, which I slipped into what I called my safe. In reality, it was a vertical gap between two kitchen units, concealed by a narrow strip of wood. I pulled out the wood and put the dossier in, alongside USB sticks from previous investigations, Alex's birth certificate, the notes from the Mental Health Tribunal and my passport. I slid the strip of wood back. It looked just like part of the kitchen units, which some might describe as nineties MDF tat but which I, proud of my upcycling efforts, thought of as vintage and homely. I wrapped a thick scarf round my neck, pulled my cap low and picked up my phone, astonished at the heat the story had provoked.

I left the flat and on my way to Alex's school, I returned a call from a Channel 4 News researcher, talking him through the documents, the implications for the Government and the need for the police to re-examine the murder of Ben Howells.

It was only when I'd ended the call that I noticed the thin black man in the leather jacket. He was leaning against the bus stop, watching me. It wasn't the casual glance of the bored passenger waiting for a bus. It was direct, laden with intent, sending me a message. Instinctively I slowed and thought about crossing the road, but I had to pass this bus stop to get to the school gates. I told myself not to be silly. He was just another London nutter looking for attention. And besides, what could happen? It was home time, broad daylight, the four-by-four mums were congregating for loud chats, the nannies were pushing huge prams, waiting for their oldest charges, a few dads, vaguely uncomfortable, had their eyes on their phones. As I neared the bus stop, I picked up my pace so that I fell into step behind a couple of mums I recognised from Alex's year.

'Hi.' One of them smiled.

'Hi,' I said, keeping an eye on the man. I wanted to engage the woman in conversation but was suddenly shy. I had spent most of the past year studiously ignoring any interaction at the school gate.

The man unpeeled himself from the bus stop and stood in the pavement, hands on hips. Still, he stared at me, nodding his head slowly as if in agreement with some hidden voice.

'Do you know if they have any spellings to learn this week?' I gabbled at the friendly mum. 'I can't seem to keep on top of it.'

The woman smiled. 'I know what you mean,' she said, her soft Irish voice taking on a confiding tone. 'I lost the spelling book last week and Mrs Richards wrote me a stern note in his reading record. I felt this big—'

She was cut off mid-sentence by the man, who now blocked our way, still nodding manically. He was tall and wiry, his movements anxious and urgent, and his eyes darted everywhere, like some wild creature fearful of the wind. Yet I sensed this man was not afraid. He was dangerous. His leather jacket was scuffed, and one sleeve was torn. Underneath he wore a black hoodie and cheap tracksuit bottoms that hung over his trainers. His hands chopped the air, like a pound shop rapper. And suddenly he was in my face.

'Julia!' he barked. 'I knows it's you. Julia. Look at me, girl.'

I wondered how he knew my name.

'Don't you know me, girl? You can't say you forgotten me already. I know you ain't, not after what we did.'

He grinned, baring white teeth. One was missing. My insides ran cold. Did I know this man? I stared at him, desperately seeking some clue to our past.

'You OK?' asked the friendly mum quietly.

The man gave her a fierce look, before returning his attention to me. 'Don't you go pretending you don't know me in front of your friends. I know the real you, baby.'

'You OK?' the Irish woman asked again. She put her hand on my arm. 'Julia, we need to go in. It's the bell.'

I flushed with gratitude. The Irish woman didn't flinch from the man and stood at my shoulder.

'Bet your friends don't know 'bout your time on the street, eh, Julia? You told them 'bout that?' He grinned, his missing tooth a black hole that seemed to suck in all the air and light until I felt hot and dizzy.

I loosened the scarf round my neck, desperate to breathe, my mind working feverishly to understand what was happening. Was this real? How could he know that? Did I know him? *Was this real?*

'Julia,' said the Irish woman urgently, her face full of concern. We were alone in the street now. The other parents were safely inside the school gates. 'Come on now.'

'It's OK,' I said hoarsely, suddenly struck by the thought I didn't even know the woman's name. 'You go in. I'll be there in a minute.' I forced a smile and squeezed the woman's cold hand. 'Seriously, one minute. I'm fine.'

The man clapped his hands together, making me jump. 'I knew it, Julia, baby, I knew you'd remember me. Ole Wayne.'

'Wayne,' I echoed. 'Your name is Wayne.'

'Yes, ma'am,' he whooped. 'You knows it. I knew you didn't forget.'

He seemed delighted, and I stared at him as he jabbered on, his arms and head making jagged little movements, like he was attached to strings controlled by some crazed puppet master. Looking at Wayne's pupils, the sickly sheen on his skin, I guessed the puppet master came in powder form.

I took a step to the side, put a bright smile on my face. 'Good to see you again, Wayne. I have to go now. Take care.'

'Hey, hey, hey, not so fast,' said the man, looping and jerking into my path, blocking my way to the school gate. 'That ain't polite. You don't treat old friends like that. I wanna talk.'

'Talk about what?' I tried to keep my voice neutral, my face blank and forced myself to ignore the hard hammering of my heart and the sudden dryness in my mouth.

'About you. Me.'

I shook my head. 'Sorry, I really have to go—'

I moved to push past him, and he put his hand on my arm. I felt the fingers dig into the cuts I'd scored in Ashby's bathroom. The pain was as sharp as a shot of whiskey, hot, straight to the gut.

'Let go,' I said, wrenching my arm free. 'Don't touch me.'

He leered, and I caught the smell of onions and beer on his breath. 'You used to like me touching you. Remember that? I know I do.'

My stomach lurched. Did I know him? I couldn't remember him, but he knew my name, he knew about the streets...My head reeled. *Was this real?* Was this my past, at last, face to face? Was this the shape and colour and texture of the impenetrable blank of history?

'You and me. And the boy.'

'The boy?' I croaked. 'What boy?'

'Don't mess with me, girl. Our boy. Our baby.'

It was cartoonish, the way the world suddenly seemed to stop on its axis, the way my heart leapt, and the air rushed out of my body. Everything stopped, everything shrank to this moment. This stranger in a street, the words out of his mouth, his claim to my boy.

'I don't know what you mean,' I whispered, desperately searching his face for some clue that I had ever known this man, seeking out the tilt of the head, the curve of a cheek, a fleck of the iris, for any sign this wired, dirty man was anything to do with my precious, perfect boy. 'I don't know you. You need to leave me alone.'

'Don't play that game with me, Julia. I knows you had our baby, a boy. I have rights, girl. I have rights.' His voice was getting louder, his movements more urgent.

I felt he was enjoying this, like he'd been waiting for me to resist, that now I denied him he could be himself. He grabbed my arm again.

'I want to see my boy. Don't think you can leave me behind. I have rights.'

I pushed him off. 'Get off me!'

I was aware of people watching from the bus stop, but nobody intervened, nobody said anything. This was London and by-standing was a profession.

'Don't you turn your back on me. Don't you disrespect me. You ain't no better than me. I know where you been, girl. I know all your secrets,' he snarled.

Parents were emerging from the school gates now. Young children were gabbling about their day, clutching bright paintings that flapped like flags in the breeze as their mums and dads juggled PE kits and book bags. I needed to get to Alex. I needed to be with him, to make him as safe as all these other children, who were worried about nothing more than tea and bedtime cuddles.

I shoved forward. I had to get to Alex. I heard the shriek of another mum before I felt the hands on me. The man grabbed my shoulders and pulled me roughly round. I saw the anger on his face, the manic gap-toothed grin, his eyes wide and white. He raised his hand, and I ducked away. He missed me but lunged again, this time catching a glancing blow on my shoulder. I stumbled, my bad ankle faltered, and I fell into the road. A screech of brakes, a blinding white flash of pain, and air rushed from my body as the road raced up to meet me.

23

IT WAS the thirst that got me. My mouth was sticky and dry, my tongue furred and heavy. I opened my eyes and winced as bright lights seared them. Little shapes – orange triangles, brown circles, green squares – merged and danced before me. Nothing made sense. I shut my eyelids, but light scorched them red and orange. I wished I could slip under again. I was so tired, my body felt heavy, my limbs leaden as if gravity had strengthened its grip on me and was pinning me to the bed. But not my bed. I opened my eyes again, watched the shapes shift, flutter and finally settle. It was a curtain in a garish pattern. A curtain, fluttering as people moved beyond it. I heard them now, the muffled footsteps, the clatter of metal on metal, hushed whispers. A hospital. Nurses. They would get me a drink. I inched myself up and pain flared as my nervous system rebooted. Jolts of agony came from my ankle, hips, ribs and head. My parched mouth unstuck itself.

'Hello,' I croaked. My voice was thick and unrecognisable. 'Where am I?'

A head popped round the corner. A nurse, dreadlocks pulled back in a ponytail, his face tired but friendly.

'Hello, there, how we feeling?' He didn't wait for an answer but took my wrist and checked my pulse. 'You've had a good sleep. We'll get the doctor to come and see you but hopefully you'll be out of here soon. You know Fridays…'

A thermometer was in her ear now. He didn't seem to expect me to speak, for which I was grateful.

'Good, good,' he said. 'Doing nicely. Let's get you propped up. There, that looks better.'

'Alex?' I rasped.

'Your boy? He's with your sister. She's around here somewhere.'

'A drink,' I whispered. 'Can I have a drink?'

'I'll bring you one. Water alright?'

'Yes, please.'

The water was tepid. It came in a plastic cup, and I drank it down in one. The nurse came back with a jug and left it by my bedside. I suddenly wanted to cry at this kindness. It was so comforting to just be looked after. A drink. No questions. He put another pillow behind my head, and I closed my eyes, and felt the gentle embrace of sleep. Then it was ripped away.

'The nurse said you were—' It was a voice I knew.

Emilia looked down at me, my face full of concern. 'I'm sorry, were you asleep again? The nurse said…'

'I'm fine. Just so tired.'

'God, Jules, you gave us a fright. When I got that call from the school, saying you'd been knocked down…'

'I'm fine,' I repeated, suddenly recalling the thud of the car, the surprise as I hit the pavement – that would explain the scuffed palms, where I'd tried to cushion the fall – and the shock of the woman driving the shiny red Mini. Fortunately, the little car had only been nudging slowly forward, when I had stumbled into its path. Stumbled or was pushed? I had a sudden image of Wayne, his erratic movements, the gap-toothed leer, the sharp grip of his hand, twisting my arm, pulling me round…

'The school said you were run over—'

'I tripped,' I said, biting down my irritation. 'It was just a little tap. I probably did more damage to the car.'

Emilia wasn't buying it. 'But the car isn't in A&E, is it? The car doesn't have a son who was left crying at school while his mother was driven off in an ambulance.'

I bit my lip. 'Where is he?'

'I took him home. Our place, I mean. Philippe's with him.'

I pushed back my covers and swung my legs round, ignoring the protests from my bruised body. I had to be with Alex. I was suddenly fearful of his vulnerability in a world where his name, his school, were known to the likes of Wayne. The encounter had brought my nightmares to life. My past was a dark ocean that threatened the world

I'd created with Alex. He was a wonderful person, a creature of light, but he'd come from my very darkest experiences and that past would always threaten whatever we had. Wayne was a dangerous tide that could rip us apart and sweep away everything good. I gasped as my feet touched the floor and my legs trembled, weak as a rag doll.

'Er, what are you doing? Get back into bed right now.'

'I need to be with my son.'

I swore and fought back a wave of nausea as I reached for my shoes.

'The best thing you can do for Alex is stay in bed until the doctor says you're OK.'

I focused on forcing my swollen foot into my shoe, vaguely aware of Emilia flouncing out of the room. A moment later my sister returned with a stern-faced doctor.

'Mrs Castleton, I need to speak with you,' said the doctor. She looked as though she could do with a hospital bed herself. Her skin was grey with tiredness and her eyes were shadowed and bloodshot.

'I have to get home and see my son,' I said. 'I'm fine. Really I am.'

The doctor was small and wiry. She stood in front of me, a little too close for comfort, and I was forced to sit upright and leave my shoe.

'Unobserved, concussion can be very dangerous, Mrs Castleton. Think of your son.'

'I'm fine,' I said again, too weary to correct the doctor's assumption about my marital status. 'I've just been so tired. It's actually done me good to come here and have a nap but now I really need to go…'

The doctor looked at Emilia. 'Could we have a moment, please? I need to speak to Mrs Castleton.'

'Of course,' said Emilia, looking worried. 'I'll just get a cup of tea.'

I held my breath and steeled myself. In my experience, cosy chats with health professionals never boded well.

'Mrs Castleton, when you were admitted the paramedics advised there had been an altercation in the street.'

'Just one of those crazy London things,' I said. 'It was a misunderstanding. Mistaken identity.'

'You didn't know this man?'

I shook my head. That, at least, was true. I didn't know 'Ole Wayne'. Or, at least, I couldn't remember knowing him.

'And the bruises and cuts, Mrs Castleton?' The doctor lowered her voice, suddenly conspiratorial. 'If there's anything you'd like to tell me, it would be in complete confidence. I can put you in touch with people who will look after you and your son.'

I almost laughed with relief. *They think I'm a battered wife, not a nut.*

'No,' I said. 'Nothing like that. I don't have anyone in my life, not for years. Just my son.'

'Can you tell me how you got these injuries?'

The doctor was quietly insistent. I could smell the coffee on her breath, the sour tang of sweat. This was no doubt the dog end of a long shift and I was touched by the time she took to check on my purple bruises and scratched face.

'I went to a wake,' I said. 'In South Wales.'

'I'm sorry,' said the doctor. 'Someone important to you?'

I considered the word.

'Yes,' I said, thinking of Michael Wilmore, of the risks he had taken to give me The Castleton Files' biggest story. 'He was important to me.'

There was a silence, and I realised the doctor was waiting for more information. I shrugged. 'I had a few too many drinks and I fell down a hill.' I gestured at my sore ankle. 'Guess I'm not as young as I like to think.'

The doctor chewed her lip as she appraised me. 'Do you often drink so much you fall over, get injured?'

'No. I usually don't drink at all, actually.' I didn't mention it was contraindicated on my medication. 'Perhaps that's why it affected me so badly. Like I said, he was important to me.'

'Is that why you've been harming yourself?' The doctor looked meaningfully at my bandaged arm. Someone had carefully dressed the lacerated flesh while I'd been unconscious.

'It was an accident,' I blurted out, my face reddening. 'I didn't mean to.'

There was another long silence. I bit my lip. I didn't trust myself to say anything else.

'OK then, Mrs Castleton,' the doctor said finally. 'We can't keep you here against your wishes. But I strongly advise you don't go home alone. And no, a small boy doesn't count. Stay with your sister. She seems like a lovely lady. And if you start to feel unwell; vomiting, dizzy spells, you must come straight back. OK?'

I nodded. 'I promise,' I said.

There was a rustle at the curtain and Emilia reappeared, clutching two small plastic cups of steaming tea. I wondered if she'd been waiting outside, listening. I hoped my sister hadn't picked up on the comment about self-harming and studied Emilia's face for clues. But if Emilia had heard, she wasn't giving anything anyway. Besides, I couldn't be cross with her for eavesdropping. I would have done the same. I took the milky tea gratefully and grinned at Emilia.

'Looks like I'm bunking with you, Sis,' I said.

The doctor smiled. 'Good,' she said. 'Take care of yourself, Mrs Castleton. No more drinking and falling down hills.'

I nodded. That, at least, I could promise.

24

I WOKE in a cloud of pillows, cocooned in a warm duvet. The morning sun squeezed through a gap in the long drapes. Alex's tousled head was nestled against my shoulder, his arm flung across my belly as if he would never let me go. I watched him in wonder. That this little person belonged to me, that something so good and pure and clean should be born from the darkness of my past, was simply a gift that made all my pain worthwhile. His breath purred in and out, his eyelids fluttered, and one little foot twitched in time to some faraway dream.

Don't mess with me, girl. Our baby. Our boy.

The man's words rang round my aching skull. I closed my eyes but all I saw was the gap-toothed man, his manic eyes, the proprietorial way he held me, the sudden thud of the car, the rush of the road. *Oh fuck.* It would be the talk of the school gate. The Head would ask questions. It wasn't fair, not for Alex; he didn't deserve any of this. Could I really have slept with that man? I cringed with shame and self-loathing, and shrank back from myself, from what I had once been. I shook my head, as if I could stir the memory free. But there was nothing. I couldn't remember ever having seen Wayne before, but groaning with the frustration and shame of it, I knew how unreliable my mind could be.

'Are you alright, Mummy?'

'Morning, baby,' I said, smiling, tucking him closer to me. He was so warm and sleep-soft, and his eyes were still heavy. 'I missed you.'

'I missed you too.' A frown crossed his face. 'The school said you went to hospital. Uncle Philippe picked me up.'

'I tripped over, baby, right outside your school. Like a silly billy. They took me to hospital for a check-up. It was a bit of a fuss about nothing, really. Very boring.'

'Uncle Philippe said you got hit by a car.'

Philippe, you fucker, I thought.

'It was a misunderstanding. I tripped, and the car touched me. I think it hurt the car more than it hurt me.'

The quip worked better on Alex than on Emilia. 'Really, did you bang it?'

'Big dent.' I grinned. 'It's my strong bones.'

I flexed a bicep and frowned playfully. My strong bones were the stuff of family legend. This was why I was a bad swimmer but so good at opening jam jars, why the bad-tempered pony at the beach had tried to buck me off and why I always beat Aunty Emilia in an arm wrestle.

'You mustn't worry about me, baby,' I whispered. 'I am as strong as an ox.'

'Or a monster truck.'

'Yes,' I mused. 'I think I would make a good monster truck.'

There was a knock on the door and Emilia popped her head round.

'Oh good, you're awake,' she said. 'I've been checking on you all night.'

There was no sign of sleep deprivation on Emilia's unlined face. Her hair was shiny and bouncy, and her cheeks dewy. She tugged back the drapes and let the sunshine spill in through tall sash windows, and then caught sight of Alex peeping up at her from the bed.

'When did this little monkey creep in?'

Alex grinned cheekily at his aunt.

I shrugged. 'I woke up and here he was, fast asleep.'

'How's the head?'

'Fine,' I said. I glanced round the room and took in the pretty bed linen, the silk wallpaper and the tasteful botanical prints in wooden frames. 'Where's my phone? My bag?'

Emilia arched an eyebrow. 'Oh, I see we are feeling better. Normal service is resumed. You didn't even think about your phone in hospital. That's when I…' She looked at Alex and checked herself. 'Come on, monkey, downstairs. Clara's making pancakes.'

'Yippee!' yelled Alex, scrabbling out of the duvet. 'I love pancakes.'

Emilia waited for his footsteps to thunder down the stairs before she turned to me. 'Well? How are you really feeling?'

'Really, really fine. Seriously. Stop asking.'

'They said there'd been an incident…at the school gate…'

'Some loon. You know, London. You're never more than six feet from one.'

'I thought that was rats.' Emilia smiled. 'The police want to talk to you when you feel up to it.'

I couldn't face the prospect of dealing with the 'Wayne' issue. Procrastination and deflection were the answer. I snuggled deeper into the duvet, revelling in the luxury of the Garonne household. 'You certainly know how to make your guests comfortable, Em.'

'Never stint on tog rating or thread count,' Emilia said. 'Remember?'

I looked at my sister sharply. Of course I remembered. Our second stepmother's legacy had been a series of edicts on the finer things in life and a sharp dispatch to a distant boarding school. I couldn't even remember Collette's face now – the divorce had been brutal and our father had expunged this costly mistake from the family history – but I would never forget wasted summer afternoons trailing round Harrods' crystal department or the crack of a spoon across my knuckles for using the wrong fork.

'Seriously, my phone, where is it?'

Emilia reached into her back pocket and pulled out the phone. 'It drove us mad last night, vibrating and ringing. It was a blessing when the battery ran down. Philippe recharged it for you. He suffers from the same affliction as you. Can't bear to be unplugged from his tiny master.'

I was surprised by the thoughtful act. 'Thank him for me,' I said, holding out my hand.

'Breakfast,' said Emilia, keeping the phone. 'Before we lose you to work, come and have breakfast with us at least.'

I snatched the phone from my sister. 'Five minutes,' I said, my eyes already locked on the screen, my thumbs busy scrolling through a list of missed calls.

I thought I saw Emilia roll her eyes before she left the room, and within minutes all idea of breakfast was gone, my appetite lost as I realised my encounter with Wayne, far from being the talk of the school gate, was now public knowledge.

The first sign was five missed calls and a text from Lyndsey. *Er, what have you done to rattle Dumb Bones' cage? Other than being brilliant, of course. Don't let the bastards get you down.*

Dumb Bones was how Lyndsey always referred to Chris Jones, the sleazebag behind the eponymous Jones Report, a combination of nutball conspiracies and seething alt-right vitriol about the liberal elites, or Lib-Els, in Jones speak. Yet amid all the crazed bigotry, Jones had a knack of breaking enough big stories to give his site a shred of legitimacy, which swelled his legions of followers – the Jones Brigade – and meant the mainstream media could no longer dismiss him as a conspiracy nut. Sometimes he'd even pop up on Sky News as a pundit. He often claimed to turn down requests from the BBC to appear on Question Time although I thought this was fanciful.

Jones and I had crossed paths a number of times. He liked to refer to my much smaller site as 'The Crappington Piles', and I'd taken great pleasure in disproving one of his crazy theories involving lizard people and satanic rituals at a leading public school. But in general, we operated in different spheres. I suspected there was little overlap between our readers.

Yet after reading Lyndsey's message – and one from Joe saying 'You know how to reach me if this Jones situation needs sorting' – I visited The Jones Report with a sense of deep foreboding. The story was accompanied by a photo of me; not the headshot from my website but a grainy pic I couldn't remember seeing before. My head was half turned away from the camera, and my hair was scraped back. I wore no makeup and I was scowling at something in the distance. I looked just like the sort of bad-tempered harridan who might attack an ex in the street.

Revealed!! Establishment hack's walk on the wild side

You all know The Jones Report keeps it real. Now it seems Julia Castleton, the silver spoon hack behind The Crappington Piles, also likes to rough it. The

Jones Report can exclusively reveal that Castleton was in hospital last night after a spurned ex-lover attacked her in a Shepherd's Bush street. Eyewitnesses said Castleton was embroiled in a screaming match with ex Wayne Sloss, outside her son's primary school. Sloss turned violent and then pushed her in front of a moving car. Sloss, of no fixed abode, is known to local police and was apprehended by officers attending the domestic dispute. One eyewitness said Castleton seemed a little, ahem, 'tired and emotional', perhaps the result of ongoing celebrations after the Mainstream Media eagerly picked up her story bashing our armed forces. The Jones Report is no marriage counsellor but perhaps Ms Castleton should spend more time focusing on matters closer to home and less time undermining our heroes and brawling in the street...You heard it first on The Jones Report.

Blood roared in my ears. The anger was like an adrenaline shot. I read the article again and then paced the room, willing myself to calm down. I didn't trust myself to do anything until my anger abated.

The weasel Chris Jones. How dare he print those lies. *Tired and emotional, brawling in the street with an ex-lover, a silver spoon hack*...As always with Jones, there was just enough truth to give legs to the lies. My family cast a long shadow and it sometimes felt I would never be free of people making assumptions based on a name that I no longer even used.

Wayne Sloss. So, I now had the name of the man who claimed to be Alex's father. I dredged my memory, pacing the room, but drew a blank. I opened Safari on my phone and searched for Sloss. The top result was The Jones Report article. Beyond that there was a reference to a magistrate's court hearing for driving without insurance and some minor drug offences. No photographs, no social media profiles. Sloss cast no digital shadow.

I sank onto the bed, my anger momentarily spent but my mind churning. Should I respond, or let it go, rise above it like royalty? There was a thunder of footsteps up the stairs and Alex and Edgar burst into the room, laughing hysterically as they did a funny dance, wiggling their bottoms and singing some silly pop song, the lyrics all jumbled up. They scampered off to play before I could react. My stomach clenched and then I remembered it was Saturday. No school. No dreaded looks, sideways glances, or sympathetic questions hiding an avid hunger for gossip. How dare Chris Jones drag my life, my son's life, into the seedy spotlight of his sordid hate-spewing website? I wasn't going to let him get away with this.

25

THE CALLS started coming in just after nine. Lyndsey was already working hard to manage the increased traffic following the Wilmore scoop. Now the mainstream press was picking it up, their appetites piqued by the salacious side story of my personal life. I was hunched over my laptop in Emilia's clinical kitchen, a peppermint tea stewing on the counter, trying to compose a comeback to The Jones Report. I was repeatedly distracted by journalists who sought to clarify points, seek rebuttal to MoD statements and, more irritatingly, get my response to Chris Jones' story about my love life. Had I really been drunk on the school run? Was I injured? What was my relationship with Wayne Sloss?

After a while the two stories seemed to merge, so I'd be talking about Operation Entrust and then in the next sentence confirming I wasn't in hospital, that it was a minor incident, and no I hadn't been drunk on the school run. I felt my voice getting high and hysterical and my answers became increasingly abrupt. When Emilia got back from St Dominic's, I was ranting to a researcher for Channel 4 News about Chris Jones and I knew, from the look on Emilia's face, that I needed to shut up, quickly. I ended the call, apologising profusely, stressing it was all off the record even though I knew that nothing was ever really off the record. I had the sudden sensation I remembered from skiing, when a tricky descent unexpectedly crossed a line into a full-blown fall. I was gathering speed, veering towards losing control.

I put my face in my hands.

'What's going on?' asked Emilia. 'What's happened?'

I showed Emilia the Jones Report story.

'Wayne Sloss, who's he?'

I shrugged. 'I've never heard of him, never seen him before. And no, I wasn't drunk on the school run. I wasn't screaming and brawling. It's all lies.'

A notification popped up in my email. A high-profile *Daily Mail* columnist had just retweeted The Jones Report story to thousands of followers, adding: *Those in glass houses…*

'What the fuck!' I exclaimed. 'My story on the Wilmore dossier has nothing to do with this kind of muckraking!'

Another notification. Another retweet, this time using the unflattering photo from The Jones Report. Some wag had posted: *No wonder he pushed her in front of the car #helpforheroes #supportourforces*

'Gosh, that's so nasty,' said Emilia. 'Why do they do it?'

'If you spend all your time bringing other people down, you don't have to sort yourself out,' I replied.

My phone rang. We eyed it suspiciously.

'Here, let me,' said Emilia. She took the phone and stepped away so I couldn't snatch it back. 'No, I'm sorry, Ms Castleton is unavailable for comment. No, she's consulting with her lawyers. No, no further comment. Thank you for your interest.'

I listened in amazement. Of course, that was a better approach. Why hadn't I done that instead of engaging with these vultures? I looked at the rebuttal article I had drafted, full of anger and vitriol, and hit the delete button.

'Consulting with lawyers?' I said to Emilia. 'If only.'

Emilia put the phone down carefully on the counter, eyed the stewed tea with disdain and busied herself making a fresh pot of Lady Grey.

'It can happen,' she said, her back turned as she filled the kettle. 'You just have to say the word and you know you'll have the best lawyers in London fighting your corner.'

I grimaced. 'Thanks, but no thanks,' I said.

'But why? Why make life more difficult than it needs to be?' Emilia's voice was pleading.

'You know why. We've been over this a million times. It's bad enough, that bloody article…"silver spoon hack".' I almost spat the words.

'That's what gets you? Of all the horrible things in that article, *that's* what you're angry about!'

'I'm angry about all of it, believe me,' I responded. 'I just don't need *that* as well. It's another way of undermining me.'

Emilia removed my cold tea and put down a cup of pale Lady Grey. A buttery finger of shortbread was balanced on the saucer. 'I think you need to drink your tea, eat some biscuits and calm down,' she said.

'You sound like one of those cheesy chalkboard posters you get outside coffee shops,' I muttered, but I did what my sister suggested. The biscuit was sweet and woke my stomach. I gestured to Emilia for the biscuit tin, suddenly ravenous.

'I think you need to have a break from all of this,' said Emilia, gesturing vaguely at the laptop and phone. 'You're just feeding the fire by responding. Stay here for the weekend, switch off the phone. Just let it lie.'

'It's my name,' I said helplessly. 'This should be a big day for me, my biggest story, a really big important story. The numbers on the site are through the roof, and I'm dealing with this shit! Now my name isn't Julia Castleton, and I quote from *The Independent* here, 'a proven investigator and online crusader for truth'. Thanks to Chris Jones, I'll now be known as Julia Castleton, that woman who got drunk and was pushed in front of a car by her homeless bum ex and oh, did you know, her dad's a lord. Christ! I just can't believe it.'

I got up and paced the kitchen. 'And how did Jones get hold of this Wayne Sloss story? Who told him? Was it all just a setup to distract from the Wilmore dossier?'

Emilia shrugged. I could tell she was uncomfortable with this line of conversation, wary of feeding anything that she perceived to be paranoid thoughts.

'It's not paranoia if they really are out to get you, you know,' I assured her.

I knew from the guilty look on Emilia's face that I'd guessed right. My sister was worried I was losing my grip on reality.

'I have to ask these questions, Em. It doesn't mean I'm mad. It means I've just broken a big story that some people would really, really have liked to keep hidden. I've taken on the Establishment. This might be how it's fighting back.'

'I know, I know,' said Emilia. 'I believe you. The timing of this man's appearance is fishy. But why can't you write about Love Island or Farrow & Ball paint names or school gate fashions? It wouldn't save the world but at least people wouldn't be trying to ruin you.'

I grinned. 'Farrow & Ball paint names?'

Emilia shrugged. 'I'd read it.'

I smiled as I hugged my sister. I breathed in her expensive perfume and relished the warmth of her cashmere top.

'Thanks for reminding me there are far worse things I could be doing for a living.' I chuckled to myself. 'A thousand words on paint names. I wouldn't know where to begin.'

26

I WOKE late, groggy from a deep, dreamless sleep. I was back in my flat and could hear Alex next door, playing imaginary games with his Lego men. I strained my ears to listen, but it was mainly plane noises and little bang, bang popping sounds. Where did it come from, I wondered lazily, this urge to recreate battles between goodies and baddies with tiny plastic men? I'd never encouraged it, but my son seemed obsessed with building gaudy weapons from tiny bricks. Was this learnt, or was it innate? I stretched like a cat, before reaching over and pulling back the curtains to reveal a grey Sunday morning. I paused to register any aches and pains. Overall assessment: much improved. A lazy Saturday, eating cheese on toast and cuddling with Alex in front of mawkish Disney films, had done me the world of good.

I stretched for my phone. Just a quick check and then I'd switch off again to go do something nice with Alex. But within moments my heart was racing and my stomach churning. I was at the heart of a maelstrom. From the emails, texts and Twitter notifications, it was clear my story on Operation Entrust was big news – but for all the wrong reasons. I quickly found the source, a small story on the front page of *The Sunday Times*, that was reproduced on the newspaper's website. I logged in to my account and read with growing dismay.

Web of Lies: weapons to ISIS dossier faked by 'dark forces'

Police are set to investigate a blogger who claimed there was a high-level conspiracy to cover up British Government arms sales to ISIS rebels in Syria and Iraq. The Sunday Times *can prove the documents behind the sensational claims, which caused a diplomatic row with Britain's allies in the Middle East after they appeared on the website The Castleton Files on Thursday, were faked. The blogger, Julia Castleton, thirty-two, daughter of former junior minister for trade Lord Danby, also alleged that* Times *reporter Ben Howells and army medic Michael Wilmore were killed and she was abducted by the security services to cover up the illegal arms sales. Police commissioner Brendan Carter said it was unclear whether Castleton had faked the documents or had been duped by 'dark forces'. Castleton, who worked on* The Times *for six years until she left due to a long-term stress-related illness, was unavailable for comment.*

My skin prickled as cold dread crept through my veins. The article was a hatchet job. One paragraph quoted an unnamed senior intelligence officer who said the techniques used to fake the documents were 'schoolboy stuff that any respected journalist would have discovered during the most basic due diligence'. There were numerous references to my father, my scandalous exit from *The Times* and, of course, the Wayne Sloss story, which had been lifted from The Jones Report.

'This is the big problem with the alternative media and so-called fake news,' said a rent-a-quote security expert from Oxford University in a sidebar column, which must have been teed up from the moment the paper got whiff of the story. *'These sites don't have the same checks and balances as mainstream news outlets, so they can print their 'stories', regardless of the impact they may have on Britain's already delicate international relationships in the Middle East. Basically life for our soldiers on the frontline just got even harder, thanks to a dilettante blogger playing at being a journalist.'*

I cringed. I wanted to crawl under the duvet and never come out. But I forced myself to read my article again, and this time saw for myself the flaws in Wilmore's dossier, flaws I would have spotted had I not been so determined to publish as quickly as possible. And the speed was all down to Newby, his insistence that my life was in danger, that my only safety was to publish. Returning to *The Sunday Times*, I saw its reporters and the South Wales police had found no evidence of dead bodies in an empty Swansea warehouse. There were no eyewitness reports of black-clad armed men chasing me and Newby through the Welsh countryside. Had I imagined it all?

One woman, Janet Williams of Oxwich Bay, reported being at the funeral, where she said Julia Castleton appeared *'very overwrought for someone who didn't know the deceased – we all felt she was there to make more trouble for the Wilmores'.*

The journalist then helpfully added in all the detail about Michael Wilmore – absent without leave, suspected PTSD, his role in the murder of Ben Howells and finally his death by drug overdose in a public toilet in central London. So, no vindication for Wilmore and his grieving father. All I had done was put his death back on the front pages.

My phone rang. It was Emilia. My sister's fourth call that morning. I couldn't bear to speak to her. I burnt with shame and self-loathing and wanted to creep away from the world.

I watched the phone go to voicemail, then quickly fired off a text to keep my sister at bay. *Em, I'm fine. Just need some time to sort this out. Speak tomorrow. J x*

Almost at once the phone rang again. A number I didn't recognise. I let it go and then turned the phone onto vibrate only. I longed to disappear.

But that wasn't possible now. Alex bounded into the room. 'What's for breakfast, Mummy? Can we have pancakes like at Aunty Em's?'

He danced around the small flat, skipping through some imagined world, as I dragged myself from bed and shuffled into the kitchen. The words of the *Sunday Times* article ran through my mind. I felt like a robot, going through the motions of life while my brain spun in circles, trying to make sense of how my great scoop had turned to shit.

'Can I have the first pancake, Mum?' Alex twirled into the room, whooshing as he made a Lego man swoop through the air.

Pancakes. I remembered why I was in the kitchen, randomly opening and shutting cupboard doors. I realised we were out of eggs.

'It'll have to be toast,' I said, putting two slices of bread into the toaster. 'We've got no eggs. I'll get them later.'

Alex suddenly fell silent and went to sit at the little table. Perhaps he sensed the mood. I could barely bring myself to look at my son, so vibrant and full of life. I felt like a stone, a heavy stone that was weighing down this innocent child of light and joy.

I buttered the toast, then let Alex pick the jam. I made myself some tea while he ate, and when I picked up my mug, I realised my hands were trembling. This struck to the core of who I was, of the person I had carefully constructed from the wreckage of the past. Every time I glanced at my phone, it vibrated with messages and calls. I was under digital siege.

I saw Alex eying my phone dubiously.

'It's OK, Alex,' I said. 'I've got a lot of work on and…I'm not feeling well. Do you mind if we have another quiet day?'

'Do you need to go back to hospital?' he asked, wide-eyed with worry.

I forced a smile. 'No, it's just a tummy bug. I just need to get some rest. I'll be fine tomorrow.'

He pushed his chair back and gave me a big hug. 'I'll look after you, Mummy. Do you need the sick bowl?'

I fought back hot tears. 'No, baby. It's not that bad. I'm just going to lie down for a little while. You can watch some TV if you like.'

'Yes!'

He punched the air and raced from the room before I could rescind the promise of morning television. Moments later I heard the loud singing and bombastic dialogue of one of his favourite cartoons. I crept back to bed with my tea, my phone and my shame. *Worst mother ever*, I thought, as I drew the curtains to shut out the bright March sunshine. I hugged the duvet to me like a comfort blanket.

My phone was like a portal to a torture chamber. The reaction on X was feral. I was shocked by the number of strangers who suddenly felt impelled to publicly promise to rape, maim and murder me. I knew I shouldn't look, but it was like a car crash, and I found it hard to pull my eyes away, even when the blood in the road was my own.

I logged in to The Castleton Files and saw Lyndsey had been there first, closing down the comments section. I fired off a quick text of thanks to my IT guru for saving me from further public evisceration. My voicemails were mainly from journalists seeking comment. I deleted them as I went. With trepidation, I visited The

Jones Report. Another awful mug shot of me, this time grim-faced as I bustled out of a tube station. Where did he get them? Had one of his minions been following me? The story was the usual serving of half-truths and insults, slathered in a thick coat of glee. Jones clearly relished my public humiliation. Indeed, he seemed to think he'd played some role in my undoing, claiming to have called my Wilmore scoop a 'basket of lies' long before *The Sunday Times*. I shuddered as I read his piece.

Of course, Mizz Castleton has long had a flexible relationship with the truth. Her dazzling career at The Times *– nothing at all to do with her dad's job in the Department for Culture, Media and Sport, of course – ended in fiasco when Mizz Castleton's pharmaceutical habits (sniff, sniff) led to some dodgy expenses and questionable stories before she was quietly persuaded to recover from her 'stress-related illness' in a private clinic in Surrey…For those familiar with Mizz Castleton's erratic career, there was nothing surprising in the* Sunday Times *story…After all, you heard it first in The Jones Report.*

I flung down the phone like it was on fire. How could he write such things? And how did he get these snippets? Yes, I'd had a problem at *The Times*, but they had been so understanding because I had been so obviously unwell. And it wasn't pharmaceutical, it wasn't cocaine, and it wasn't a private clinic. It was an acute mental health ward in an NHS hospital. I shouldn't be ashamed that I'd needed help, but I was because idiots like Chris Jones still behaved as though there was some stigma attached to mental health issues. The horror of what had happened had eaten so many years of my life, led me into dark places I didn't think existed, and I now lived with the constant fear it could happen again. I hated people knowing – they couldn't help but treat me differently and even the most gentle kindnesses took on an edge. And now everyone knew something. The great horror of my life was now twisted into a parody of a spoilt rich kid with a pill problem, a sniff-sniff joke, a private drying out clinic…I pulled the duvet over my head and cried bitter tears.

At some point, I must have fallen asleep. There was a trace of a dream. A man, tattooed and angry, had been standing over me. He said my name, too close, his hot breath on my face. *Julia!* And suddenly I was awake, my heart racing, lost in the fog between sleep and nightmares.

Alex was crying by the bed.

'Baby, what's the matter? What's happened?' I folded my arms round him and pulled him into the bed.

'I was calling you. You didn't answer,' he snuffled. 'I thought you were…'

'Oh, baby,' I crooned, rocking him in my arms. 'I'm fine, see. I just fell asleep. I'm much better now. See?' I smiled brightly, then pulled a silly face. 'I always say sleep is the best medicine. I'm better now.'

'Really?' He rubbed away his tears, clearly wanting to believe me.

'Really. Come on, let's get more toast. It's just what I need.'

I left my phone in my muddle of a bed and busied myself in the kitchen. I made toast and peanut butter, and some hot chocolate, which we sipped in front of the TV. Outside, the world went by, planes tracked across the sky, toy cars and mini people went about their business. I imagined them all, reading their Sunday papers over cappuccinos and lazy brunches, dissecting my life and passing judgement. If I went out, would anyone recognise me from the photograph? Would anyone say anything? Would the Jones Brigade be waiting to get a photo of me, with my sore red eyes and unwashed hair? I sipped my hot chocolate and watched the cartoon animals solve their problems through friendship and honesty. I wished I could disappear into their simple, colourful world and that I'd never have to leave the cocoon of our little flat ever again.

27

I LONGED to wallow but instead had a shower and got dressed after lunch. It was important to show Alex I was well, to reassure him everything was OK even if we were spending another day in the flat. The phone called to me, like a scab I couldn't resist. There was more hate and bile on social media. The BBC had produced a long article looking at alternative media, using my downfall as a hook for a wider discussion about editorial controls, press freedom and libel laws. I was sickened to see my name had become synonymous with fake news, and the comments section made for painful reading.

The phone buzzed in my hand. It was Joe. I hesitated but then decided he was the only person I could bear to speak to.

'Plan?'

He always was to the point.

'Emigrate.' It wasn't even a joke.

'If you like. But before that? Plan?'

'Apologise to you. You were right. We, I, should have checked everything before publishing.'

'And? Plan?'

'Seriously, Joe. I don't know.' I scrolled through my X feed. It was brutal. 'This has buried me.'

'Then it's time to start digging.'

'What do you mean?'

'Well, the dossier was fake, right? So where did the faking start? Was Wilmore peddling a fake dossier? Or did Newby run interference?'

I chewed my lip. 'He seemed genuine,' I said. 'He seemed really frightened. And I saw him fight this other man, Fox.'

'Who's this Fox?'

'Hang on.' I reached for my notepad, flipped through it. 'Major Ivan Fox. Newby said he was second in command of Wilmore's unit. Said he didn't much like people. He seemed aggressive, angry, though…' I paused, remembering the moment outside the wake when Fox had approached me, asking what Newby and I were doing.

'Yes?' prompted Joe.

'Looking back, it was Newby that attacked Fox. Fox was trying to talk to me. He wasn't very friendly, like he was angry with me about something, but then Newby just flew at him, pummelled him, knocked him out.'

'You think Fox might have been angry about something else?'

'Maybe. It's another fuck up. I should have spoken to him.'

'Maybe Newby was making sure you didn't?'

I frowned, suddenly angry with myself. I'd put my life in Newby's hands and trusted him. I'd never questioned the possibility I was willingly running into a trap that would bring my whole career crashing down. Yet Newby had seemed so genuine. He'd been scared, he'd rescued me from those men, hadn't he? Had he? I clenched the phone between my shoulder and cheek, put my fingers to my wrist and counted out my pulse. *This is real.* The scars on my arm, scratched in Ashby's stained, cold bathroom, the sea pounding at the base of the cliffs, the bruising now green and yellow on my ankle. This was all real. And Newby, was he real? That I didn't know.

'You still there, Julia?'

'Yes. I'm here. Just thinking.'

'Good,' said Joe. 'Like I said, we need a plan. And my guess is it starts with Newby and Fox. You rest and I'll be round tomorrow.'

I hung up, my mind careening through fields and woods in the wet Welsh countryside. Newby had led the chase, but were we running for our lives, or running into a trap? I sprawled on the floor next to Alex, amid the felt tip pens and colouring books, and felt the first stirrings of hope. There might be a way out of this mess if I could only get to the truth.

28

IT HAPPENED at 2:03 AM. A massive crash that made me scrabble out of bed, convinced the building was falling in. Another series of blows thundered against the door. There was the terrifying crack and creak of wood splintering and the words 'home invasion' flashed through my mind. I switched on the light, grabbed my phone and dialled 999. Next door, Alex screamed, and I raced to his room. He leapt into my arms, trembling, pressing himself close as if to become part of me. I heard more wood splinter and looked into the hall to see the front door burst open. I withdrew and closed the door to Alex's room. I stopped breathing when I heard footsteps on the other side.

'Emergency, which service?'

'Police,' I jabbered as I piled a chair, a toy garage and a rucksack in front of the bedroom door. 'Someone's broken into my flat.'

I heard voices.

'Go away,' I called, trying to keep my voice calm and authoritative. 'The police are on the way.'

There was a sharp laugh and the door to Alex's room was roughly kicked open. My little barricade flew apart and a man walked into the room. He was tall, broad-shouldered, shaven-headed and wore jeans and a hoodie. A walkie talkie crackled from a holster, and he grinned as he caught my puzzled face.

'Yeah,' he said. 'We're the police, honey. No need for that.' He nodded at the phone still pressed to my ear. He pulled out his walkie talkie and spoke a jumble of codes and acronyms. I understood enough to realise that my emergency call was being stood down.

There were more people in the hall. Two men and a woman. All plain clothes, although two of them wore stab vests that made them look strangely bulky, their movements a little robotic as they plundered the tiny flat, carelessly rummaging through my things.

I felt my terror abate. It had to be a terrible mistake. I murmured into Alex's ear, trying to soothe him.

'It's the police, baby, nothing to worry about.' But he trembled like a wild creature, his head buried in my chest.

'What's going on?' I asked the shaven-headed man. 'You've got the wrong flat.'

Another man came in then. He was short, squat, with a thick bull neck and heavy stubble. His eyes flitted over me and Alex, and then swept the bedroom coldly.

'Julia Castleton?'

'Yes.'

'Then we've got the right flat.'

My mouth fell open. 'But why? What do you want?'

'My name's Conor Tull, DI Tull. We have a warrant to search your property and seize communications equipment. We have reason to believe you've committed an offence under Section 127 of the Communications Act. Is this your son?'

I nodded. 'The what act?'

'Communications Act. 2003. What's his name?'

'Alex, his name is Alex. Can you please stop this? He's terrified. He's only five.'

Tull was impassive. 'Anyone else here?'

'No.' I moved out into the hall with Alex clutching at my waist. A policewoman emerged from my bedroom holding my laptop, wrapping up my cable. 'What are you doing? That's private property.'

'We're taking these as evidence,' said the woman, her voice flat and business like. 'Do you have any other computer equipment here?'

I shook my head mutely. Boxes of files, my carefully collated cuttings and research, my notepads full of shorthand interviews, were being bagged up by the shaven-headed man, his walkie talkie still crackling under his arm.

Another man was going through my kitchen. I eyed my hidey-hole between the two wonky kitchen cabinets, but it went unnoticed. There was nothing of value there now anyway, I thought. The Wilmore file was a worthless fake. Tull was talking into a mobile phone in my living room. He paced absently, kicking at cushions and magazines that now littered the floor.

A neighbour hammered on the wall and a man's voice bellowed, 'Keep it down in there.'

Someone else in the building yelled back, 'It's the pigs,' and I burnt with shame. It was bad enough that my neighbours should see this, but that my son should be exposed was unforgivable.

Tull ended his call and walked over. 'We're going to need to take you in,' he said.

'Can't it wait for the morning?' I asked. My teeth were chattering. I recognised the signs of shock.

I gestured at Alex, trembling by my side.

'No, it happens now. We'll place Alex in temporary care for the night.'

'Wait, no,' I said, suddenly desperate as I realised this was just the start of the horror. 'Let me call my sister. She's in Holland Park. She'll come and pick him up.'

I pulled my phone from my pyjama pocket and began to scroll for Emilia's number, but Tull held out a stubby-fingered hand.

'I'm going to need that too, Ms Castleton,' he said. 'It's evidence.'

He took the phone without waiting for a response, then nodded to one of his officers, who produced a bag and put the device inside.

'Right,' he said briskly. 'I know this is upsetting but bear with us and hopefully it will all be sorted out soon.' If his words meant to reassure, the effect was undermined by the cold look in his eyes and lack of warmth in his voice.

'No, you have to let me call my sister. She'll be here in fifteen minutes. She'll take Alex. He has school tomorrow...' My voice broke.

Alex was crying openly. 'Mummy, don't go,' he sobbed. 'Don't leave me.'

I felt sick and the room swam as the horror of what was happening swept over me.

'Can we sort out his school things?' Tull asked. He spoke with the casual ease of someone ordering a pudding. 'Uniform, coats etcetera.'

I wasn't sure if he was talking to me or his minions. I hugged Alex close, not trusting myself to respond.

The female officer approached and gave Tull a meaningful look.

'Alex, is it?' she said, crouching down next to him. 'Don't worry, love. We just need to have a chat with your mum and then you'll be back together. Can you show me where you keep your uniform, anything you need for school?'

Alex couldn't speak; he just clung to me, whimpering.

'Let me call Emilia,' I pleaded. 'I'm begging you. She'll take him. Where's your humanity for Chrissakes?' My voice was high and screechy now. I saw an officer holding Alex's school uniform, bookbag, coat and shoes.

They were taking him. They were taking my boy. The one good thing in my life.

'You're not helping, Ms Castleton,' said Tull disapprovingly. 'And you're going to need to get some clothes on too.'

I felt my mind and body shift as though I was observing everything from afar, like it was happening to a stranger, an actor in a play.

The actor was pulling on tracksuit trousers and a hooded fleece over her pyjamas. Now the actor was weeping as her son, her little boy, was dressed in his coat. The son beseeched his mother for help even as he was led away by the policewoman. Now the actor was screaming, screaming and kicking, resisting the officer who held her, his mouth open, speaking words, words, words. And she couldn't hear them because her head was full of screaming. Hands grasped her roughly, her wrists handcuffed. She was screaming and kicking but the hands propelled her out of the flat, into the communal landing.

Then suddenly the distance was gone, and I realised with rushing horror that this was happening to me. I saw my neighbour then. A fat skinhead, his arms and neck purple with tattoos, his mobile pointing at me. I'd only ever nodded a greeting at him, and had always tried to shield my dark-skinned, corkscrew-haired little boy from the man with *that* cross tattooed on his forearm, *that* eagle insignia etched on the back of his shaven head. He watched me now, his gut spilling out over the top of his boxer shorts, his feet in a pair of incongruous pink Crocs.

'Don't worry, love,' he said. 'I'm filming them. You'll be OK. You hear that, pigs, no police brutality against this nice lady.'

I began to weep then. Big fat tears rolling down my cheeks and dripping off my chin. I was taken down in the lift, frogmarched outside and shoved roughly into the back of the unmarked car. My throat was sore and hoarse from screaming, and my body physically ached for Alex, who was somewhere out there, scared and alone, in the dark city.

This pain, this was real. But oh, how I wished it wasn't.

29

THE FOLLOWING hours were a blur. They had an unreal quality, as if I was watching events from afar. I was taken to Paddington Green Police Station, shell-shocked, tear-streaked, almost breathless with the physical pain of being ripped away from my son. In the station, various people in uniform told me things, asked me things, wrote things down and got me to sign things. I can remember none of the specifics. I was left to stew in a grubby interview room, sweating and light-headed with panic.

By the time the bull-necked detective returned, I felt punch-drunk with stress. He seemed to enjoy the situation and while normally such casual cruelty would rile my blood, Alex's removal had undone me. I was afraid. Afraid of this man who now wielded such power over me. I was consumed with thoughts of Alex, of how scared he must feel, how bewildered. Were people being kind to him? I could not bear to think of people being mean to him, and the pain of not knowing was a torture all of its own. I tried to answer the questions thrown at me, I wanted to help, anything to get out and back to Alex, but I had nothing to give him. And as the hours wore on, I was too numb, too exhausted, too broken to respond. Had he presented me with a statement for me to confess to the killing of JFK, I think I would have signed, anything to get out of there and win a promise to leave me and my boy alone forever. I suppose that's how these things happen. The miscarriage of justice isn't the false confession they want you to sign; it's what puts you in that room in the first place. That's what breaks you.

I was so lost in my own private hell I didn't notice the arrival of the lawyer, who entered in a cloud of plummy vowels and bespoke cologne. William Stone was my father's lawyer, though that didn't really sum up the range of services he performed for Lord Danby. I knew Stone had played some role in rescuing me from the darkest of times and that always made me awkward around him. It was possible he knew things about me no-one else did, things that not even I knew, and as a result I found it hard to be in his presence. He was always unfailingly polite, the product of a very expensive education and a long career at a prestigious law firm. When retirement loomed, he'd eschewed the golf course or the chance to bump up the kids' trust funds by taking on a few well-rewarded non-executive director roles in the City and chose instead to work for my father. Stone liked to joke my father had made him an offer he couldn't refuse. Whatever that offer had been, it was sufficient for Stone to be available around the clock with the kind of iron-clad discretion only the very rich and the very disreputable require. How he knew I was here, when I hadn't even been allowed to call Emilia, was a mystery but no-doubt was it a service that came as standard when you've been made an offer that can't be refused. Right now, however, I was too exhausted, too broken, to even acknowledge his arrival, never mind question how he'd found me.

'Ms Castleton is under no obligation to reveal her sources,' Stone said, taking charge as soon as he entered the room. 'I'd like to know the basis for her arrest and why you insisted on a night-time raid rather than asking her to attend an interview at a mutually convenient time. She's neither a threat nor a flight risk.'

I saw my interrogator bristle at the sudden intrusion of this urbane, expensively dressed lawyer, who projected a quiet and compelling authority and had instantly changed the dynamic in the room.

'We were concerned that the exposure of her mistakes would prompt Ms Castleton to destroy evidence,' the officer replied somewhat sullenly.

'And you are?' Stone quizzed.

'Detective Inspector Conor Tull.'

'William Stone. I'm Ms Castleton's solicitor. She won't be answering any more questions at this time. I trust you'll make arrangements for Ms Castleton's immediate release.'

Tull looked from me to Stone, studiously avoiding the puzzled look on the face of his colleague, a blonde uniformed policewoman.

'Let her go,' Tull said finally, and I slumped with relief in my chair.

It was only when we were signing the paperwork that I finally voiced my deepest fear. spoke, my words a raw rasp in my throat.

'Sorry, I didn't catch that, Julia?'

'Alex, my son. They took him into care.'

He looked at me, aghast. 'But Emilia only lives…that's so unnecessarily cruel.'

I nodded. 'Get him back, William. Please.'

He didn't need telling and swung into action. Calls were made and within minutes we were told we could collect Alex from temporary care immediately. I should have felt elated, but I was numb and full of shame. *I* had done this to my son, *my* career, *my* choices had led us to this.

I sat in Stone's luxurious Mercedes and rested my head against the window, my body limp, as the powerful car accelerated through the dark streets, thankful that Stone felt no need to fill the silence.

Dawn coloured the world a steely grey, and a light drizzle glinted beneath the streetlamps by the time we pulled up outside the emergency care home in a quiet street off Ladbroke Grove. I willed myself to stay calm, it was the least I could do for my boy. It helped that Stone was there: I knew any histrionics would be reported back to my father. But it took every ounce of strength not to break down when I saw my little boy, obviously shaken, dazed with tiredness. He flung himself into my arms, his body rattling with sobs.

I looked up at Stone and saw him battling for composure.

'Young Alex has grown up,' he said at last, as I cupped Alex's face in my hands and kissed his little nose.

I kept my voice light and chatty, wiping away his tears with my thumb, but inside I wanted to scream, to shout, to tear the world apart with my bare hands. But not here, not now.

Stone opened the door of his car to drive us home, but I shook my head.

'If I could just borrow the money for a taxi, please. I'll pay you back.'

'Julia, please, it's on my way home,' he began, but he knew me well and pulled out three twenty-pound notes.

It was too much but I figured my father was good for it.

'Will you be—' he began, but I was already hustling Alex towards Ladbroke Grove, my arm outstretched for a cab.

Every instinct in my body urged me to run from here and distance myself from Stone and by extension my father. I knew from Stone's unexpected intervention tonight that they were keeping tabs on me and the last thing I wanted was for him to take us home and see where we lived. Only as the taxi pulled away, Alex tucked against my body, did I look back at Stone and gave him a brief nod of thanks. His intervention had helped but it in no way meant I wanted my father back in my life.

30

I FELT the violation of my home like a physical blow. I had worked so hard to make our tiny rundown flat a sanctuary. And now it had been invaded, the lock smashed, our belongings kicked about, my son torn from my arms. I wasn't sure how we would ever recover from this. Some chipboard had been tacked into place across the smashed door. I touched it and quailed. I rested my head against the door jamb for a moment as I gathered the strength to go in and face the destruction. Alex still clung to me, his little face, streaked with tears, watched me quizzically. I forced a bright smile and squeezed his hand. A footstep made me jump.

It was the fat skinhead from across the hall, fully dressed now in his usual uniform of baggy jeans and an Arsenal top.

'Don't worry, love,' he said. 'My mate's a chippy; he put the board up for you. No one's been in.'

'Thank you,' I said.

He came over with a hammer, prised out the tacks holding the chipboard in place and tested the door.

'Not too much damage, love, but you're going to need a new lock on there today.'

He glanced down at Alex. 'Alright, little man? Don't you worry about nothin'.' He looked at me. 'I know when they raided my Ricky's place in Acton they weren't too careful about the kiddies' things. My missus, she's put something aside for your little lad if that's alright with you?'

I didn't know what to say. 'I, yes,' I stammered, but the man had already popped inside his flat and emerged a moment later with a large brightly coloured plastic garage and a bag of toy cars and trucks.

'Here, fella,' he said to Alex. 'See what you can do with these. Our grandkids got no interest in them now they've got the Xbox.'

Alex looked at me for reassurance before he accepted the toys. I was relieved to see a glint of excitement in his eyes as he peeked in the bag.

'Thank you,' he whispered. They were the first words he'd said since I'd collected him from the care centre and my heart swelled with gratitude for my neighbour's kindness. I'd misjudged the man.

'Thank you,' I said, forcing back tears.

'You want me to come in with you?'

I shook my head. 'No, we'll be fine, but thank you so much, Mr?'

'Stubsy,' he said. 'Everyone just calls me Stubsy.'

I nodded my thanks again and took Alex into the flat. It was a mess but not as bad as I feared. I bundled Alex into his room, quickly made his bed, got him into clean pyjamas and tucked him in with a mug of hot chocolate and a plate of buttered toast. He wouldn't let me go and insisted I stayed. I was itching to clean up the mess, to erase every trace of the horror that had smashed into our lives in the dead of night. But my little man needed me, so I drew close to him. He kept a hand knotted on my sleeve, humming tunelessly as he pushed a toy car over the bumps and dips of the bedding, his eyes heavy with tiredness. I listened to the drone of the traffic outside, people busy on the school run, the morning commute, the world rushing by as normal while we nested in this little bed, trying to heal each other just by being there, warm and close. My eyes grew heavy, and a great weariness descended as the adrenaline left my body. A moment later Alex's little hand loosened its grip and he slipped into sleep, and I soon followed.

***

I woke with a start. There was someone at the door, which creaked loudly as it swung on its buckled hinges.

'Julia? Hello, Jules, are you back?'

It was Emilia.

'In here,' I whispered loudly. 'He's just drifted off. I can't leave him.'

Emilia crouched by my side and hugged me, smoothing my hair. She inched back to study me and then looked down at Alex. 'How is he?'

I shook my head, my face grim. 'They wouldn't let me call you.'

'Oh, Jules. How could they? I want you to come back with me. Come and stay as long as it takes.'

I shook my head again. 'No, we need to be here. This is our home.'

There were more footsteps in the hall. Another figure appeared in the doorway of Alex's little bedroom. My father, hovering, unsure of his welcome. Or perhaps he was just stunned to see how real people live, I thought bitterly. I hadn't seen him for over a year and felt the familiar rage rising at the sight of him.

'Darling, how are you? What an ordeal. I'm so glad Stone could help you.'

I chewed my lip. Alex was still tucked into my side, twitching in his sleep. I didn't trust myself to speak. I had to stay calm now for my son.

'I need to change the locks,' I said to Emilia, ignoring my father. 'But they still have my phone.'

'I'm on it,' her sister said. She pulled out her sleek phone in its monogrammed leather case.

Soon she had booked not just a change of locks but a new door with steel frame too, paying extra for an emergency same-day call-out.

'Be here by five,' she said. 'On me. No arguments.' She slipped off her leather jacket and rolled up her cashmere sleeves. 'I'm going to get cracking on the mess through there. You stay with Alex. You both need some rest.'

My father, known to others as Lord Danby, had watched all this in silence. He was absently straightening the books that had been pulled off Alex's rickety little bookcase.

'I remember this one,' he chortled. 'Bear Hunt. You always used to cry because no one would play with the bear. You always were on the side of the underdog, even as a little girl.'

I eyed him coldly. 'You need to go.'

'Darling. I just want to help. Let me...'

'No!' Alex stirred in my arms. I lowered my voice. 'I need to do this myself. Just go. Both of you.'

Emilia looked at me, aghast.

'I'm fine,' I said. 'I need some sleep. I need to be here for Alex. Just go, please. But thank you for the new door.'

Emilia's chin wobbled. 'I hate to leave you like this.'

I held up my hand. 'Just go. When I get a new phone, I'll call you.'

'I'll come by tomorrow,' said Emilia. 'This isn't just about you, Julia.' She nodded at Alex.

'You know where I am,' said Danby stiffly. He was already pulling his scarf round his neck and started scrolling through his phone, car keys in hand. 'Don't make life harder than it needs to be, Julia, just to prove a point.'

I opened my mouth to protest but he'd already left the flat. Emilia scurried in his wake. It was only later, after I'd dozed fitfully with Alex in my arms, and got up to clean the place before the locksmith arrived, that I found the copy of *We're Going On A Bear Hunt* lying on top of the bookcase, with a thick wad of fifty and twenty-pound notes tucked inside.

31

IT WAS a bad night. Despite the new door, with its steel reinforcement, strong mortice locks and London Bar, I had struggled to sleep. I'd jumped at every little noise and kept checking my new phone to make sure it had a signal. Alex had woken up crying just after midnight. He'd wet the bed, and I had been distressed by how distraught he'd been at the loss of bladder control. After I'd soothed him, stripped his little mattress and dressed him in clean pyjamas, I'd brought him into my bed, where his kicking and twitching had kept me awake until I'd finally fallen into a restless sleep sometime around 6:00 AM.

It was only when my new phone buzzed with messages from my new network that I woke, gritty-eyed and pale, to find it was already after eight. I quickly decided to keep Alex off school again. He was too fragile and tearful, and I couldn't bear to be apart from him yet. Besides, his little primary school didn't feel safe now people like Wayne Sloss knew about it.

I got up and made cheese on toast for breakfast, which we ate in front of silly cartoons. Alex followed me from room to room, clutching one of the toys Stubsy had given him, a little red monster truck. I was relieved to see Alex was eating again, and by mid-morning he was giggling at the cartoons, and the tears seemed to have stopped. I picked up my phone and texted Emilia to let her know the new number and assure her that all was well. Then I emailed Lyndsey, letting her know her computer was gone, and the website would have to be suspended until further notice. Lyndsey buzzed back immediately. *Hey girl, what do you take me for? This ain't amateur hour. I've got everything mirrored my end. Don't let the bastards get you down. Keep writing. You need to put something up, and soon…or they've won.*

I chewed my lip, thinking. So, the site wasn't dead. Lyndsey would keep it alive. But I wasn't sure what to write. My last story had been a work of fantasy. Where could I go from there? Would I have any readers left?

I was disturbed by a sharp rap on the new door. Alex was immediately fretful and ran to my side. He twisted his hand into my waistband.

'It's alright, little man,' I said. 'It's probably just Aunty Emilia coming to check on us.'

But it wasn't my sister on the other side of my new spy hole. It was two women I didn't know, one of whom was checking some paperwork. I bristled. My brush with the police had left me raw and jumpy. There was another brusque, impatient knock.

'Who is it, Mummy?' piped Alex.

I grimaced. Now the women knew we were home.

'Julia Castleton? We're with Hammersmith and Fulham Social Services. Can we have a word?'

Social services. My heart plummeted. I wasn't dressed and noted with dismay my feet were still clad in the bright red ski socks I'd slept in. My grey joggers had a hole in the knee, my old boat club sweatshirt was stained with toothpaste and my hair was unbrushed. Alex was also in his PJs and had a smear of jam down one sleeve, which looked a little like a bloodstain. Reluctantly I opened the door. Identity cards were pushed at me, and one woman, the older one with a defiant stud in her nose and a streak of pink in her mousy hair, declared herself to be Elaine Blackwood. She introduced herself as 'the lead on Alexander's case'.

Alexander's case? Since when was he a case? But already Elaine had talked herself into the flat with a kind of false bonhomie while her pale blue eyes, cold and glassy in her pasty face, flitted across the space, taking everything in. Soon she was installed on my small sofa, pulling paperwork from a bright pink overstuffed backpack, commenting on the views, double-checking Alex's name and date of birth, asking if he was alright.

'Not up to school today then, Mum?' Elaine asked. Her tone was breezy, but I felt its icy edge.

'He's exhausted,' I replied defensively.

Elaine nodded sympathetically, but the smile didn't reach her eyes. She ran through a checklist, which I struggled to follow.

My mind was foggy and dull with this latest shock, and I was distracted by the other woman, who was trying to engage Alex, still mutely clamped to my leg. This woman – she said her name was Mandy something – was younger. Her black curls were heavily lacquered into a stiff, shiny bob, her trouser suit was neatly pressed and a silver cross lay at the opening of her white blouse. She was earnest, nervous and perhaps new to the job.

'What's this all about?' I asked, suddenly coming to my senses. It came out more belligerently than I intended, and there was a moment of silence. I saw the two women share a glance, and then Mandy tried to coax Alex to show her his bedroom.

'He doesn't want to,' I said. 'He's still very shaken.'

'Of course.' Elaine smiled. 'Alex, we just need to have a word with Mum. Don't worry, nobody's going anywhere. Perhaps you could show Mandy your room? She'd love to see some of your toys.'

Alex looked at me. He was a good boy, used to doing whatever grown-ups asked. I nodded at him.

'It's OK, baby, I'm right here. Why don't you show Mandy your new garage, and you come right back in here whenever you want.'

I saw Elaine watching me, silently judging. I had a horrible sickening feeling of déjà vu, of being back on the acute mental health ward at St Charles, of my every word and gesture taking on some grand psychological significance and of pens scratching on unseen forms, deciding my fate as I raged in impotence.

I swallowed deeply and offered the women a cup of tea. It was a poor bribe. A cup of tea to leave and never mention my son again. Elaine accepted the tea, but somehow engineered it so that Mandy made the brew. I gritted my teeth, kicking myself for giving the women such an easy excuse to poke around my kitchen, which was still in disarray. The breakfast things were piled in the sink and crumbs covered the countertops, but that was normal household mess. What made things worse was the lingering disorder of the police search; the upturned furniture, emptied drawers, dirty footprints and broken trinkets.

I tried to focus on what Elaine was saying but my mind was on the woman pulling open cupboards and drawers next door. Mandy was chatting to Alex, who was giving her a running commentary as he poured himself an orange squash.

Finally they came through. Mandy set down two cups of weak tea on the coffee table and then led Alex back to his bedroom. He seemed much reassured to see me sitting with Elaine, the mugs steaming beside them. Nothing bad can happen when you're chatting over tea, can it?

But this was bad, I thought. Elaine was explaining that I was subject to a Section Forty-Seven case, following a police referral. Elaine mentioned allegations of being drunk on the school run, an altercation with an ex-lover in the street, issues related to the posting of fake stories about abductions and murder. I tried to keep my voice calm and level and dug my fingers into my palms to try to control my mounting panic.

'And of course, we'll also be contacting your GP, and any other relevant mental health professionals to see their files,' said Elaine. She watched me closely, like a scientist studying a specimen.

'No!' I said. It came out too loud and Alex darted into the room, with Mandy on his tail. 'No,' I said again, trying to stifle my anger. 'No, that's just not acceptable. That's a complete breach of my rights. This is a fiasco. It's harassment. Surely you have real cases to investigate, real cases of neglect. Surely you can see he's well, and fed, and loved? Go down to the fifth floor and you can knock on any door and see—'

Elaine watched me coolly. 'Julia, believe me, we see neglect and abuse in all walks of life. Even lords and ladies.'

I seethed. 'Is that it? You want to take me down a peg or two? Look around, this isn't Mayfair. I'm just a single mum doing the best for my kid, and I'm also being subjected to police harassment because someone didn't want me to publish—'

'I thought that last story was all lies,' said Elaine, arching one eyebrow. 'I mean, isn't that why the police came round in the first place?'

I flared then. 'I was set up! But how dare you? What's that got to do with Alex? What's that got to do with me as a parent? Get out! Just get out both of you. Go and do some proper work, go and save a Victoria Climbié, instead of harassing me. Get out!'

By now my voice was high and screechy. I knew I sounded hysterical, but I couldn't help myself. It was like a valve had burst after the strain of the last forty-eight hours and now I couldn't reset. I just needed these people gone so I could shut my steel door and curl up with Alex. Mandy was already on her way out of the flat, looking shaken, but Elaine took her time, and rolled her head ruefully from side to side as she filled in forms and packed away her files. Her nose stud glinted, and a frown furrowed her doughy face. Her eyes were ice cold.

'This isn't harassment, Julia, it's procedure.' She spoke slowly, as if addressing an obstreperous toddler. 'It's how we keep children safe.'

Finally, the social worker was ready. She stood up, hoisted her backpack over one shoulder and cast a last judgemental look around the messy flat.

'Just go,' I said bitterly, shooing Elaine towards the door. 'You don't know me; you can't judge me like this. I love Alex. He's my life...' I caught myself just as my voice started to crack. 'This is just part of a wider plan to discredit me, to shut down The Castleton Files. I see what you're doing, and it sickens me.' I paused for breath, aware my voice was still high and hysterical.

There was a brief commotion at the door as Elaine had to edge round another figure, who had just arrived. I caught his eye but said nothing. I knew he wouldn't want to be identified.

'We will be back for another care assessment at the same time next week, Julia,' said Elaine. Her eyes coldly appraised the new arrival. She handed me a card with the date and time neatly written out. 'It's better if you co-operate with our visits. I can't stress how important that is right now.' She curled her pink streak behind one ear, then switched into best friend mode again. 'And make sure Alex is in school tomorrow, OK, Mum?'

I watched them leave, then wilted against the door frame, the fight leaving my body as their footsteps receded.

'Everything OK?' Joe Turner asked, watching me carefully.

I threw him a look and took a moment to catch my breath and count my pulse.

'I'll put the kettle on,' my friend said, taking charge. 'You look like you could do with a brew. And we need to talk.'

32

ALEX WAS soon happy in front of the TV, his eyes heavy, on the brink of sleep again. It seemed to reassure him to have Joe in the flat, and I felt a familiar twist of guilt, which stemmed from the fear that sometimes I just wasn't enough for my son.

Joe and I sat in the little kitchen and sipped tea. The small table and the countertops were strewn with papers. Joe had been busy and had read every page of the Wilmore dossier. I could hardly bear to look at the documents that had been the source of my public humiliation.

'Stop beating yourself up,' Joe said. 'This all looks plausible enough. A lot of journos would have fallen for it. See here, this email trail is entirely convincing until you cross-check names and travel diaries and actual receipts. Then you realise this David Manders couldn't have sent that email because he'd moved into the private sector two months before. And look here, this meeting in Geneva, well, it's only because the MoD has released the travel receipts that you see this fella was actually in the air en route to Qatar at that precise moment.'

He leant back in his chair and nodded with something like admiration. 'It's cleverly done. Enough nuggets of truth to make it look plausible. And it's funny how quickly *The Sunday Times* was able to pull it apart like that, almost as if someone had just handed them a mirror dossier with all the right receipts and job moves and details of the faked LinkedIn accounts so their story was ready to go almost as soon as you published.'

'It crossed my mind, but I was worried I was being paranoid,' I said. 'It was a quick takedown. But then the Establishment would be highly motivated to get its counter-story out there as soon as possible.' I put my mug down and ran my hands through my hair. 'I have to be hard on myself, Joe, because I've fucked up big time. I should have listened to you and done my job properly.'

'Julia, you couldn't have done this.' He gestured at the paperwork. 'It's impossible to get access to these travel remittances and phone logs without co-operation from the inside. And how were you going to get that? Show them the file? They'd have slapped a super-injunction on you and there'd be no story.'

'There is no story!' I cried. 'That's the fucking point, Joe.'

He cocked his head and gave me one of his looks. 'Oh, but there is a story,' he said softly, with the beginnings of a smile. 'It's just a different story to the one you published.'

'Newby?' I asked. His name had been running through my mind ever since I'd read the *Sunday Times* article. Had it all been a big setup? And if so, who had the resources needed to stage an abduction and murderous rescue?

Turner nodded. 'James Newby. It seems to be his real name.'

'I know, I checked him out,' I said, exasperated that all my careful research was now in Paddington Green Police Station. But the highlights were still fresh, the result of obsessive brooding over the events of the past week. 'Shrewsbury High, Sandhurst, Germany, stint in the Falklands, Afghanistan, Iraq. Then he left. Bit of a jock; rugby, rowing. While in the army, he clocked a sub-three-hour marathon.'

'Quite a looker too,' Joe needled me.

I ignored him. 'So, we go find him, right?'

'We also need to find the other one.'

'Fox?'

'Yeah. We need to find out what he knows. Why he was so angry.'

'There's not a lot on Fox,' I said. 'He's not a creature of the Internet Age.'

'Aye,' said Joe. 'Not so photogenic.' He handed me a scrap of paper with an address in Shropshire. 'Old army pal owed me a favour or two. You go for Fox. I'll track down Newby.'

I hesitated. 'Things are tricky here, Joe. I'm not sure I can leave Alex. Those women were social workers.'

He nodded. 'OK then. I'll do them both, Fox and Newby, and report back.'

'Thanks, Joe.' I hesitated. 'Can we talk money?'

'Julia.' There was a note of warning in his voice. We'd had this discussion before.

'Joe. I pay my way. I'm not running the site as a charity. It's a business.'

He gave me a sceptical look. I wondered if he'd checked the accounts at Companies House.

'That said,' I went on, 'I hate to ask but would mate's rates be OK again?'

'You know what I think,' he said. 'We can talk money when the site's washing its face.' So, he *had* seen the accounts. 'But,' he added, noting the stubborn tilt of my chin, 'if it makes you feel better, mate's rates are perfectly acceptable to me. Friends help the world go round.'

I grinned. 'Thanks, Joe. I appreciate it.'

'Now back to business. What about the guy who attacked you?' Joe asked. 'You know anything about him?'

I shook my head. 'Only that his name's Wayne Sloss.' I hesitated, before lowering my voice. 'And he claims to be Alex's father.'

'My guess is it was a stitch-up,' Joe remarked. 'The police released him yesterday. If he really was the boy's father, you'd have heard from him by now.'

I hoped he was right; I hated the thought that Alex might have anything in common with that dreadful man.

'Another blow to your reputation. If this was a stitch-up, it's a good one. They've not left any aspect of your life untouched. You starting to get the feeling you've poked a bear?'

He paused, then added a warning. 'You need to be careful round those social workers.' He leant back in his chair and stretched. I heard his shoulders crack, a legacy of too many stakeouts, crammed in that van. 'I mean it. You're in the system now. You need to record what they say. I'm not joking. Remember me telling you I had an, er, associate I was bringing on?'

I nodded. I vaguely remembered some talk about a new hire six months ago when Joe had been working a case that required a lot of travel. I'd been surprised. Joe didn't trust many people.

'If it's alright with you I might get him to do a little discreet digging into the social workers. You get their names?'

I nodded and wrote the names on a piece of paper and handed it over. 'Discreet,' I warned. 'I can't afford to make enemies of them.'

Joe tapped the side of his nose. 'Only you, me and the new boy will know. It never hurts to have some surprises in your back pocket.' He stood up. 'I'll leave these for you,' he said, gesturing at the Wilmore dossier, which had been annotated with his tiny spidery writing. He also left printouts of his Internet searches on Newby, Fox and other key figures mentioned in the documents. 'You take care, sweetheart.'

'You too,' I said as I saw him out.

Alex was asleep in the blue light of the television, so I picked him up, tucked him into bed and kissed his soft forehead before drawing the curtains. I thought about Elaine's warning and neatly folded his school uniform, checked his book bag and packed his PE kit. Tomorrow, I would be the model parent. Let Chris Jones or any of his spies make headlines out of that.

I returned to the kitchen and pulled together Joe's notes. I felt adrift without The Castleton Files. It had consumed my life for so long. Out of habit, I used my new phone to check the site. The top post was still a holding message about news and comments being suspended until further notice. I sighed heavily. A site without new content was a site on death row.

I checked my emails. There were more requests from journalists, another tech update from Lyndsey, and a notice that one of my key advertisers, an insurance company that targeted Millennials, was pulling the plug. I didn't blame them. It was one thing to back an alternative news service with a track record for breaking edgy stories that appealed to younger readers, it was quite another to have your company festooned across a website accused of running fake stories that put British troops in danger. *This is it*, I thought gloomily, *this is the end.*

I slumped over the table. I'd worked so hard. I'd got my life back on track, been a good parent, broken some decent stories, exposed corruption at the highest levels and now, now they were threatening to take it all away, even Alex. This was how it always worked, I thought angrily. The Establishment closed ranks and used its powerful tentacles to choke off any threats.

I looked around the kitchen and suddenly felt trapped by the long, lonely evening that lay ahead. I tried not to think about the expectations that weighed on me. I knew how I was supposed to behave. With my son at risk, I was meant to roll over and shut up for ever.

And there was no guarantee that even if I played ball I wouldn't be ruined anyway. The wheels had started turning and the system was messy and sticky, easier to get tangled in than to escape.

I felt a sense of purpose settle upon me. This dossier, whatever it was, wherever it had originated, held the clue to my ruin. I wouldn't be truly safe until I got to the truth of the matter. My only hope to save Alex, to rescue my career, was to do what I'd always done, shine a light in the darkness.

I read until my eyes ached and my back was stiff. I made another cup of tea, ate some stale biscuits and then paced the flat. Alex cried out. He'd wet the bed again. I cleaned him up, piled the wet sheets into the washing machine and then snuggled with him in my bed. He fell asleep quickly, and I re-read some of the documents, using my phone to cross-check histories and names and places.

I felt the quickening of my pulse, extricated myself from Alex and tiptoed into the kitchen, where I shivered in the cold. One photo on James Newby's LinkedIn feed showed him standing on a golf course, leaning on his clubs, squinting into the sunshine. A flag fluttered behind him. I peered closer and saw it was the logo of a company called The Harlen Group. The name tugged at a memory. I'd seen it before, recently. I shuffled through the papers and found it among Joe's spidery notes. One of the correspondents on the MoD email chain, Steven Burton, had, according to his LinkedIn profile, left Government to work at The Harlen Group. And one of the email addresses copied into another email trail had been a Harlen Group address. I tracked it down and searched for it: a Katrina O'Brian, assistant director, Middle East and North Africa.

The Harlen Group itself was harder to pin down. The website made it look as though it was some humanitarian outfit, with photos of smiling kids, a lab technician in a white coat bent over some vaccines, a helicopter flying low over an ocean, fields of yellow wheat under a blue sky. The language was opaque, the usual corporate guff about global citizenship, stewarding resources, protecting the assets that matter most. There were bios of smiling senior executives, black-and-white shots of men, the odd woman, talking animatedly around a boardroom table. The bios were brief, a mix of corporate and military experience, a smattering of MBAs, a sprinkle of Washington think tanks, at least one former minister, Sir Bryan Stevens. Google offered surprisingly little. For a company that boasted such a high calibre board, and claimed a presence in London, Washington, Houston, Dubai and Hong Kong, it was remarkably below the radar. I did find two note-worthy points: The Harlen Group was cited in a court case between a human rights group and an oil company in West Africa, where the company's security division had been accused of colluding with a military junta to deprive a local community of oil revenues. There was also a reference to Bryan Stevens in a *Guardian* article, which sniped at the five thousand pounds a month he was earning as a part-time non-exec for The Harlen Group so soon after leading public office. One comment under the article made reference to Harlen being 'a shady MI5 front with a clear neo-con agenda'. I took a screenshot of the comment and jotted down the username. My mind whirled. A shady MI5 front. Just the kind of outfit that could stage a black ops abduction, forge a fake dossier and drag its publisher through the mud. I messaged Joe. *I'm going after the fox. Let's keep the rest mum.*

I dropped my phone, sat back and stretched, suddenly exhausted. It was 3:37 AM. I needed sleep. It wasn't just the groggy bone-ache of tiredness or the deepening bags under my eyes I feared. I knew sleep deprivation was a key mental health trigger and I couldn't risk an episode, not when I had social services on my case. I pushed all the papers into a messy pile and switched off the light. My anger was gone and, standing in the cold, dark kitchen, I felt a clear sense of purpose. I was going to find out who framed me and why they'd ruined my life.

33

EMILIA SAID she will never understand me.

'Two days after a visit from social services and you're leaving Alex for another wild chase across the country?' She was incredulous. 'Think about what you're putting at risk. It's not just Alex. I'm thinking about you too. This, this' – she groped for a word that wouldn't offend – 'this obsession.'

'Obsession?'

I clenched my jaw. If I were a man, I'd be described as motivated, driven, ambitious, dogged, even pig-headed. But obsession came with connotations of mental imbalance, which, of course, belied Emilia's true concern.

She thinks I'm losing it. I'm on the cusp of another episode. This could all be a figment of my disintegrating mental health. But I steeled myself to stay calm. *Afterall, it's not like I'm not having mental wobbles right now. And, selfishly, I need her on side to look after Alex, again.*

So, I stayed quiet and instead crouched down to say my goodbyes to Alex, who was happily distracted by Edgar's latest iPad game and appeared, on the surface, relatively untroubled by my imminent departure. I knew Emilia and the welcoming home-from-home she provided was part of that. I owed my little sister a lot, even if we were like chalk and cheese.

I saw her watching me anxiously. She was worried she'd over-stepped the mark. That the obsession comment was about to blow up in her face.

'Don't worry.' I smiled. 'I'm going to the depths of the shires. Shropshire, the least inhabited county in England. The biggest risk will probably be boredom or frostbite.'

'You're right, it'll be cold up there. I'm going to gift you a new jumper and socks.'

'It's Shropshire. Not the Arctic,' I grumbled but it was for show.

Emilia looked much brighter, and I could see her doing a mental inventory of her extensive wardrobe, wondering what she could gift to finally part me from my 'interesting' charity shop cardigan that I knew she hated.

I cleared my throat. 'One more thing, Em. Alex has been a bit upset…crying at school yesterday. And, er, he's wet the bed a couple of times.'

'That's not a worry for us,' said Emilia, swiftly. 'The mattresses are all protected…Edgar's only been dry at night since Christmas. But Julia, if he's this upset, and with the care assessment coming up, are you sure…I mean, can't you just defer this trip for a week or two until things settle down?'

Her words were delicate as eggshells, carefully chosen to avoid another flare-up of an old sore. I sighed. I wished I could make her understand. 'I can't, Em,' I said sadly. 'I have to know the truth. It's the only way out of this mess. It doesn't mean I don't love Alex. I do, it hurts me every time I leave, but I'm doing this for him. If I don't salvage this, they will never stop until I'm destroyed.'

I saw Emilia wince. I know she hated this kind of extravagant talk, that she saw it as a gateway to another episode. 'But if they decide against you…'

I turned my face away. I couldn't bear to think about it. 'Don't. I would never let them take him.'

Emilia shivered. 'What do you mean?'

I could tell she had gone to a dark place, that she thought I'd be one of those cases you read about, desperate mothers who do unspeakable things…

'I mean I will do whatever it takes to clear my name,' I said slowly. 'I would never hurt Alex. I can read you like a book, Emilia. Never play poker.'

We both smiled then and spoke in unison. 'Poker is for men. Ladies play bridge or whist.'

It was another of stepmother Collette's golden rules. The tension passed and I left, certain my son was in the hands of one of the kindest and best people I knew.

34

JOE TURNER arranged the car. It was an old banger that belonged to his nephew, who was on a gap year. The stale odour of crisps and cigarette smoke was masked by an over-scented air freshener, a jaunty pineapple that dangled from the rear-view mirror.

'Easy on the clutch,' said Joe. 'And bring it back in one piece or Nate will kill me. It's his pride and joy.'

I grinned. 'Permission to ditch the pineapple?'

'Granted.'

I turned the key and the diesel engine throbbed into life. 'See you soon. Usual methods of comms, DispicableMe93?'

'Right-ho, Mumwherearemysocks.' He slapped the roof and I pulled away, heading towards the A40, feeling a little thrill in the pit of my belly.

I had always enjoyed driving. It was soothing, the closed metal bubble cocooning me from life beyond the road. And it was nice to have shed my old clothes for Emilia's cast-offs. A pair of grey skinny jeans, a cream silk top and a navy cashmere jumper that looked pristine but which Emilia had sworn was heading for the charity shop. It took three hours to reach Shropshire, and the skies darkened with every junction on the M6. By the time I found Ashley, a small village ranged along a steep hill, the first heavy drops were pelting the car. I pulled up by a large church to check the sat nav and listened to the rain. It was strangely relaxing. A stiff breeze whipped early blossom from a small apple tree and petals fluttered across the churchyard like confetti. It was nice to be out of London, and I decided to brave the weather and walk the last stretch to Fox's house.

It was a good decision. The rain eased and the sky lightened to duck egg blue. I found Fox's house down a muddy track. It was a detached Victorian redbrick that had seen better days. Paint flaked off the door and bowed windowsills, and moss lagged the roof and the broken doorstep. I knocked, but there was no answer. I peered through a window into a little sitting room, which was filled with boxes, an armchair and an old racing bike. The place looked as though it hadn't been lived in for some time. A wasted trip then.

There was a sudden whip crack nearby. A gunshot. Crows rose noisily into the sky. Another shot. Hair prickled on my arms and the back of my neck. A man shouted something indistinct. Then came the sound of glass breaking. I tiptoed over weed-strewn gravel round the side of the house. Overgrown shrubbery dripped water down my neck. I emerged into a large garden, long neglected, but clearly once a beautiful spot to sit, with its view of green fields and rolling hills. A man stumbled across the ragged lawn. Ivan Fox. He looked even more dishevelled than at the wake. His eyes were sunken and dark stubble covered his lower face, which still sported the bruises of his encounter with Newby. He had a shotgun in one hand, a dead squirrel in another. He jumped when he saw me and flung the dead squirrel into the undergrowth.

'They eat the eggs.'

'What?'

'Squirrels. Vermin. Eat the birds' eggs.'

He walked towards me and fumbled another cartridge into the shotgun. He smelt like a brewery and a can of strong lager protruded from the pocket of his wax jacket.

'I know you,' he slurred. He came a bit closer, peered at me, then in a movement that showed no signs of his inebriation, smoothly swung the shotgun round so that the two barrels were pointing at my belly. 'You're Newby's pal. From Mikey's funeral.'

'I'm not friends with Newby,' I said nervously. 'I only met him that day.'

The gun didn't waver from my stomach. I felt Fox's black eyes boring into me. I wondered how drunk he was and tried to calculate my chances if I ran.

'My name's Julia Castleton. I'm a journalist,' I told him. 'Michael Wilmore wanted to give me some information, but he died before we could meet. I think he was killed to stop him talking. And I think Newby might have had something to do with it.'

Fox laughed, a bitter cackle, then lowered the gun. I took a deep, shaky breath. He pulled out a small bottle of whisky from another cavernous pocket and took a long draw. He handed me the bottle. It was empty, save for a swig.

'No thanks,' I said.

'Not drink, throw it,' he slurred.

I looked at him quizzically.

He nodded. 'Toss it into the air.' He raised his gun to his shoulder. 'Target practice.'

I lobbed the empty bottle into the air, and Fox fired. I slapped my hands over my ears. They rang with the crack of the blast. The bottle fell to earth, untouched, landing with a dull thud in the long wet grass.

Fox swore, then stumbled back towards the house. I hesitated. Should I follow him?

Inside, the house showed the same neglect as the garden. A large kitchen took up at least half of the ground floor and I admired the potential, imagining it as it once must have been: the AGA polished, a kettle bubbling, the large farmhouse table scrubbed, sunlight gleaming on the glassware displayed on the Welsh dresser. Now every surface was piled with dirty dishes and empty bottles. A cat watched me from its perch on top of an old piano. The table was strewn with yellowed newspapers, a can of gun oil, old rags and a box of cartridges. The floor was sticky underfoot and everywhere smelt feline.

Fox put the gun on the table and busied himself unscrewing the top off another bottle of whisky. 'Top of the morning,' he slurred, before slumping into an armchair by the AGA. He took another long swig from the bottle, then spluttered as it hit the back of his throat. He raised watery eyes that looked like they hadn't slept for weeks. 'Just get it over with. I don't care anymore.'

'What, get what over with?' I asked but his head had already lolled forward. His chest rose and fell in time with his deep guttural snores. He was out cold.

I looked around the filthy kitchen, picked up all the cartridges I could find and hid them in my handbag and instantly felt slightly more at ease. Finally, I washed a mug, made myself a cup of tea loaded with sugar cubes from a dusty box and headed back out to the garden. Perched on a wooden table, my hood pulled up for warmth, I watched the March sun slowly sink. The garden filled with golden light and birdsong, and it suddenly struck me that Fox was expecting me to kill him.

What was it he'd said? 'Just get it over with. I don't care anymore.'

I listened to the birds and wondered what could make a man surrender his life so easily.

35

JOE TURNER made light work of tracking down his target. I trusted him implicitly, but he always gave me a full debrief afterwards though I guessed he often edited out the less salubrious elements out of a sense of proprietary. He started in Oxwich, reasoning that if Newby had faked my abduction, then he'd had help. That scale of operation couldn't go down in a place as small as this without people noticing.

It hadn't taken long for someone to recognise his printout of James Newby's LinkedIn profile picture. Newby had rented a caravan from a farmer under the name Neil Porter, telling people he was in the area to photograph sunsets. He'd driven a silver Honda Jazz, the kind of anonymous hatchback no one would notice, except the farmer, who was thinking of getting one for his wife and had chatted to Porter about fuel consumption and reliability. No, Porter hadn't had any visitors. He'd paid in advance in cash and had handed over the full week's rent even though he'd only stayed five days.

'Kept it nice too,' said the farmer. 'You should see the state some of them are left in. You don't know folk until you've run a caravan park.'

Next it was a trip to the McDonald's where Joe had collected me. This was the last place I'd seen Newby. Joe eyed the CCTV cameras, considered their angles, then pulled out his second wallet with its fake ID. Posing as DC Ryan Kozwincka, he'd talked himself into a cramped back office walled with corkboards pinned with cheerful corporate slogans, complicated staff rotas and reminders on food safety. He peered at grainy CCTV footage of the car park. Two hours, one Big Mac meal and three bitter coffees later, he found it: a silver Honda Jazz pulling into the car park, and me, ghostly white in the jerky monochrome images.

A cheerful assistant manager with acne and a nose stud brought in more coffee for DC Kozwincka. Joe winced at the pronunciation but was glad his borrowed identity was all consonants. It made the name harder to remember and trace should anyone later enquire about the policeman who'd turned up to check the restaurant's CCTV footage. He waited until the spotty manager had left the room, then paused the footage to jot down the number plate. He pressed play and watched the little car pull out and go east.

'Got you,' he muttered.

Then he'd headed out into the dismal dregs of the day, his mouth sour from all the coffee, his back stiff. Chasing the rest of the trail didn't take long. He called in favours, got a trace on the car through a source with access to the ANPR - the National Automatic Number Plate Recognition Data Centre. It was amazing what those little cameras on all the motorway bridges clocked. The Honda had filled up on the M4 just outside Cardiff with four men in the car. So somewhere east of Swansea, Newby, or Porter, whatever his name was, had picked up three more men – enough for a dummy abduction. Joe's mate with access to the ANPR was going to email over some photos.

'Then where?' asked Joe.

'It's a hire car. Outfit in South London. I'm texting you the address now.'

'I owe you,' Joe said, as his phone buzzed with the details.

'You always say that,' his contact replied. 'I'm still waiting.'

Joe grinned and climbed into his van for the drive back to London. He'd never told me why so many people seemed to feel obliged to help him out. He said it was his boyish charm. Charm that was now heading Newby's way.

36

IT WAS dawn when Fox finally stirred. I saw him wake with a start, his hand at once reaching for his gun. He rolled his eyes when he noticed me. I was sitting on the piano stool, flicking through a family album, and paused at a photo of Fox in combat gear in some desert, his eyes creased against the sun. The image opposite showed him in dress uniform at someone's wedding, cheering with his buddies. Beneath it was a formal photograph of Fox holding open a box that contained medals on their ribbons. I didn't know what the medals meant but I knew you didn't get them for just turning up.

'So,' I said, as he sat up in his chair and cradled his head in his hands. 'What went wrong?'

He groaned.

'Fuck off,' he muttered. He hauled himself upright and stumbled from the room.

I heard the sound of distant vomiting. The ancient plumbing creaked and thumped. When Fox finally appeared, he looked a little fresher. His hair was wet, his face was still unshaven and bruised, but his eyes were brighter. I noticed a tremor in his hands as he filled the kettle.

'You still here?' he asked gruffly.

'I want to know what happened in Syria. You were clearly Boy Wonder; medals, honours, and then this.' I gestured vaguely round the kitchen, at his dishevelled state.

'Nothing happened.' He kicked and poked at the AGA. 'Fucking thing,' he muttered. 'Out of oil.'

He slumped down again, dejected.

'How did you know Wilmore?' I asked. 'Was he the medic on your squad?'

He shook his head slowly. 'You know you're trespassing on private property? I've asked you to leave.'

I ignored him. 'What happened to Wilmore? Why did he go AWOL? Did something happen in Syria?'

Fox's black eyes flashed angrily but he said nothing. Again he touched his hand to his gun, like a child reaching for a comforter. I shivered. The kitchen was cold now the AGA had gone out, and the windows were misted with condensation. The cat had gone. I saw it flash across the dew-wet lawn.

'This is my parents' house,' said Fox, his gravelly voice making me jump. 'I'm supposed to be clearing it out. They died last year.'

'I'm sorry,' I said. 'That's hard.'

'Dad let it go after Mum passed. He couldn't cope. I was away.' He tailed off and his eyes glowered into the distance. 'How did you find me?'

I ignored him. My phone was buzzing in my pocket. I didn't recognise the number but was aware of Fox watching me so felt compelled to step outside and answer.

'Ah, Julia, so glad I caught you. I thought you might be on the school run.'

It was Mandy Walker, one of the social workers. I looked about guiltily, as if the social worker could see me, standing outside a rundown cottage in the middle of nowhere.

'What is it?' I said, my voice small and tight. I could feel my heart pounding high in my chest.

'I wanted to let you know we're bringing the care visit forward. We'll be with you this afternoon.'

'Wait, what? You can't do that.'

'I'm afraid we've had some new information, Julia. It really has to be today. How about one o'clock?'

I swallowed, desperately trying to calculate the drive back. 'No, a bit later than that,' I said. 'I'm, er, I've got a medical appointment. The dentists. Three o'clock would be better.'

'But won't you be picking Alex up then?'

'No, Alex is having a playdate with his cousins. His aunt picks him up today.'

At least that was true.

'How lucky for him,' said Mandy. But the way she said it made it clear she didn't think Alex was lucky at all.

I dug my nails into my palms and forced myself to stay calm. 'What new information?' I asked.

'I can't go into that on the phone. Elaine will tell you. Three o'clock then. Thanks, Mum.'

I felt suddenly dizzy. I put my hands on my knees, bent double and took deep breaths.

The door opened behind me. Fox stood watching but didn't say anything. I guessed in his world it was normal for phone calls to leave you reeling. He withdrew and when I finally went back into the house, he'd made me a cup of tea. I sipped it suspiciously, wondering where he'd got the milk from. I hadn't seen anything drinkable in the fridge last night. I'd poked around while he slept and had snacked on a packet of cheese crackers and had then found a tolerably clean bed in a cold box room. There'd been a large rucksack by the wall. I'd checked it and discovered changes of clothes, spare boots, a sleeping bag, a knife and Fox's passport. A get out of Dodge kit, all ready to go. But where, and why?

'I need you to tell me about Wilmore, Newby and Syria,' I said very calmly and slowly, as if to a child. 'I will never tell anyone that I've met you, but I need to know the truth. Wilmore's dead, another journalist, Ben Howells, is dead, I think Newby set me up and now they're threatening my job. I'm going to lose my child…' I paused, checking myself, trying to keep the panic from my voice. 'You have to tell me. Please, Mr Fox. Ivan. I stumbled into this because Michael reached out to me and now they want to destroy me.'

I couldn't say any more. I thought about loading the gun and threatening him but then remembered what he'd said last night before he passed out. Looking at his haggard face, his black eyes haunted behind those sharp cheekbones as he sat in the wreckage of his family home, I felt he would welcome death. I drank my tea and then stood wearily. I needed to be in London by three.

'Please,' I implored, 'whatever's happened to you, whatever you know, you're not going to make anything better by staying silent. The only way to kill a shadow is to shine the light of truth on it.'

I pushed open the door and the cat raced in, meowing loudly. It seemed to revive Fox from his silent reverie.

'Lockmere,' he said. 'You need to look into Lockmere. That's where they sent them.'

'What's that? What's Lockmere?'

He shook his head grimly. 'Lockmere,' he repeated, his voice heavy with regret. 'It's where they send the fallen. All of them.'

And that was the last I got out of him. I left him sitting in his chair, the cat rubbing round his legs, the gun by his side. As I steered the little diesel down the M6, the car shuddering in the backdraft of huge trucks, I was glad that the cartridges were still in my handbag.

37

AS I'VE said before, when it came to pulling in favours, no one worked it like Joe. It wasn't that people always owed him one, it was just that when you knew their dirtiest secrets, they liked to pretend it was a fair trade; one good deed for another rather than what it really was: blackmail. Not that Joe ever spelt it out. He didn't need to. People with big secrets are hyperalert to the possibility of exposure. They anticipate it at every turn and will do anything to keep their dirt buried. Besides, people tended to like Joe. Perhaps he was right, it was his boyish charm. He could play the cuddly teddy bear, there was a twinkle in his eye and he had that old-fashioned notion of honour. His word was still his bond, and that counted for a lot, even among the liars and cheats he dealt with.

It was certainly paying dividends now. He hadn't expected to get the close-ups on Newby's fellow passengers in the Honda Jazz so quickly, but his source in the NADC didn't know Joe had long ago burnt those pictures of him with other women. Joe's silence meant the man kept his wife, his job and his dignity, but in return he'd been attending Sex Addicts Anonymous UK and in gratitude was one of Joe's most willing and useful sources.

Joe studied the photos on his tablet. Newby, with his blond hair and strong jaw, looked a little harassed. Another man, his head shaved into a crew cut, had the build of someone who pumped a lot of iron and a neck like a bull. The third man was slighter, the wiry build Joe always associated with special forces, with short dark hair and a pinched face. The fourth was pale and rangy, with long ginger hair tied in a ponytail. Joe didn't like the look of them; they seemed handy, professional. He fretted. He used to know someone in facial recognition who was linked to the police database, but his contact was inside now after a small gambling habit grew into a large mortgage fraud addiction.

Joe looked up from his tablet. The woman he'd been watching for the last hour was finally locking up at the hire car company. It was time for DC Kozwincka to make another enquiry. It was amazing how a warrant card combined with the right blend of authority and bonhomie got civilians to bend rules to please you, particularly if you applied the pressure when they were already a little flustered with deadlines or keen to clock off. Indeed, it was only twenty minutes later that DC Kozwincka was back in his car, with Neil Porter's credit card details and billing address. Joe smiled as he pulled out into traffic and nosed the van south, heading for an address in Upper Norwood. Not too much of a diversion on his way home. That would do very nicely.

***

Less nice was the destination, a grubby doorway piled with black binbags from the adjacent takeaway. Behind the door lay a poky office and, from what Joe could see through the grimy window, the place had been deserted for some time. He ordered himself a spicy chicken meal from the takeaway, but the boys behind the counter didn't speak enough English to answer his questions about their neighbour. The other side was a nail bar, and the ladies there eyed him with suspicion.

'Been empty long time,' snapped one girl, flicking her long tresses back over her shoulder. 'We don't know them.'

She returned her attention to her client, who was having long pink talons gilded with shiny gems. Joe shuddered. They looked like horrible germ-catchers to him.

He loitered for a while, finishing his chicken, wondering why Newby had an address in a disused office. Or was it? He peered in again. There was no pile-up of post behind the door, just a couple of pizza menus, and now that it was dark he could see a faint blue glow further in the building. Perhaps an alarm, a Wi-Fi box or a screen left on.

Joe wiped his hands on his jeans and tried to shake off his fatigue. He circled the block, noting the signs of gentrification; the artisan baker, the little bistro, the Waitrose shoppers rubbing shoulders with the youths in hoodies, smoking weed at the bus stop. He trailed a side street past boarded-up shops with doorways that smelt of urine and garbage and came to the back of the building. Some of the guys from the takeaway were smoking by overflowing bins. They paid him no attention as he inspected the scuffed office fire door, which was tagged with graffiti. But to the left there was a fire escape, and Joe quickly ran up the metal stairway, which opened onto a flat roof. There was another door here, with a keypad on it. Joe guessed it led down to the dingy office. He would have liked to poke around but he suspected the door was alarmed and, besides, the fried chicken boys were watching him now. They probably thought he was police. He climbed down, nodded good night to them, and jogged back to his van. He circled for a while, holding out for the right parking spot, one that would give him eyes on the fire escape. His tablet was almost out of juice, so he plugged in his charger and settled in to wait.

He was dead beat from driving and fell asleep a little after midnight, wrapped in the sleeping bag he kept in the van for stakeouts. He woke with the rising sun and groaned as he moved. He was cold and stiff, and the van windows were misted with condensation. He struggled out of the sleeping bag and winced as he took a slug of cold coffee. Maybe he was getting too old for this lark.

Most places were shut at this hour. Only the corner shop, the tube station, the cab company and the supermarket were open. He checked with the dispatcher at the cab company. The postie usually did his round about eleven. Joe always kept a toothbrush, toothpaste and deodorant in the van, so he nipped into the supermarket and used its toilets to freshen up. Then he bought himself an egg bap, a paper and a cup of scalding tea and settled in for another wait.

The dispatcher's information was correct. The postie did make his round just before eleven. No mail was delivered to the office.

'There's a mail redirect on,' said the postman. He squinted up at Joe, his eyes hard like a policeman's. 'And no, I can't tell you where.'

Joe held up his hands in a gesture of surrender and backed off. He returned to the van and fired up his tablet to run checks on the address. He traced its ownership through a series of shell companies until he came to a name he recognised. One of the biggest shareholders in Norwood Enterprises, a tiny outfit with two directors that was late in its filings at Companies House, was The Harlen Group.

38

I FELT like Mary Poppins. Rooms were tidied, the bathroom scrubbed, and clean towels laid out. The kitchen sink was scoured until it gleamed, and the fridge was packed with fresh food. I even sprung for a bunch of one-pound daffs from Tesco, now prettily arranged in an old pickle jar on the table. I laid biscuits on a plate, set out three mugs and tried to picture myself chummily laughing and smiling with the people who wanted to remove my child. I chided myself. I mustn't think like that. They were allies, just wanting the best for Alex, as did I. I just needed to prove to them that his best was here with me. I was about to have a shower when there was a knock on the door. They were half an hour early, doubtless a ploy to try and catch me out. I caught my reflection in the mirror. I was pale without makeup, my hair was in a scraggy ponytail and I smelt ever so faintly of bleach. Well, there was nothing I could do about it now.

I opened the door, pulling on Emilia's cashmere to cover the ripped t-shirt I'd worn to clean and planted a smile on my face. The social workers were turning away from the door, and looked surprised when I flung it open. Elaine looked peeved. Were they planning to write me up as a no-show? I was happy to disappoint.

'Alex not here?' asked Elaine. 'You having some 'me' time, Mum?'

'His aunt's picking him up for a playdate after school,' I said, resenting the insinuation. 'I explained that on the phone.'

'How are your teeth?' asked Mandy.

'What? Oh yes, fine,' I said, flustered. 'Nothing to worry about.'

Mandy and Elaine shared a look.

I decided to ignore it and focused on winning them over. I busied myself making teas and handing out biscuits. When they'd settled on the sofa, I perched on an old wicker chair and tried to maintain my smile. 'So, what's the new information?'

Elaine began rifling through her bright pink rucksack. Today she was using a child's blue glittery hair slide to clip back her lock of pink hair. I found the look very contrived but supposed it might be designed to put the children she was assessing at their ease, although I recalled that Elaine had shown next to no interest in Alex at our last meeting.

'As you know, Julia, we had authority under a Section Forty-Seven to contact your doctor. I'm aware that at our last meeting you had some objections, but you must understand we're only doing this for Alex, making sure he's getting what he needs in terms of support and stability.' Elaine paused, tilting her head on one side, waiting for some outburst from me.

But I kept the polite smile on my face, though it hurt my cheeks to hold the position. I held my hands on my knees, my fingers rigid and tight.

Finally, Elaine started up again and flicked through my file. 'Well, your GP, what a lovely woman, you've got a good one there, Julia' – Mandy nodded as though they were discussing a husband, not a GP – 'filled us in on the psychotic episode five years ago. Now' – and here Elaine held up a hand, as if to silence an interruption, but she needn't have bothered; I didn't trust myself to speak and kept my face contorted into a tight-lipped smile – 'there's no stigma attached to mental health. I always say, don't I, Mandy, that you wouldn't be ashamed of a broken leg, so why do we feel ashamed when it's our brains?'

Mandy nodded vigorously. 'Everyone has their issues,' she said.

Elaine tilted her head on one side again. 'Anything you'd like to add here, Julia?'

'It was a long time ago.' My voice came out like a low croak.

'Of course.' Elaine smiled brightly. 'We know that. We just need to be sure everything's OK with you now. It was a severe mental health crisis.' Here Elaine paused to refer to her notes and shook her head slightly as she read.

I gripped the arms of the chair to stop myself ripping that silly slide from the woman's hair and kicking out this busybody. Who was this woman to judge me?

'You were fired from work in some controversy, then your family reported you missing until you were found six months later, living on the streets. I believe your father had you sectioned under the Mental Health Act.'

I nodded, my mouth too dry to talk. The horror of it all, so much horror, summed up in so few words. Joe Turner, hired by my father, had found me. Only he could have done it. I was quite lost by then, living my own private hell, so scared all the time, pursued by people I couldn't name, dwelling in shadows and darkness. With a tattooed man? I still didn't know. And Wayne Sloss, had he been there?

'Of course, later you challenged your detention. There was a Mental Health Tribunal. Two, in fact, after you appealed the finding of the first, and you were discharged the following year, and you were pregnant.' Elaine did the head tilt and looked expectantly at me. 'Alex must have been your silver lining from a difficult time.'

'Yes,' I whispered. 'He saved me.'

Elaine gave a tight little smile. 'And a lot of support from the specialist mental health midwives. I know they worked very closely with you.'

'There's no shame in that,' said Mandy. 'Especially for a single mum; it can be very difficult.'

I shrugged. 'My sister was very supportive.'

'Your GP said she hasn't seen you for a while?'

'We're tapering my meds. I'm fine now. That's a good thing, surely?' It came out a bit too defensively. I coughed. 'I mean I don't want to waste NHS resources.'

'No one would think that, Julia. It's very important you get the help you need as soon as you need it. You have Alex to consider.'

'Yes, of course. Sorry.'

'You're still taking medication?'

'Just Tegretol now.'

Elaine smiled brightly as though I was a toddler who'd presented a turd for inspection. 'That's great, Julia. And Alex's father?'

'What?'

'Does he have access to Alex?'

'No.'

'Would Alex like contact with his birth father?'

'No!' I pulled myself back under control. 'No, he's only five. He's happy and bright and settled just the two of us.' I felt like a heel. I knew Alex would love a dad.

'Do you have contact with the birth father?'

There was a horrible pause. I realised these women had read the filth on The Jones Report, repeated in lurid detail in papers that should know better. They wanted to know if Alex's birth father was a junkie who was known to the police.

'No.' It came out as a whisper. I took a deep breath. 'I have no way of reaching him.'

'Would you like contact, dear?' Elaine's voice was seductively soft now. 'Although I understand it could stir up a lot of memories. From the dates, I mean; Alex was conceived while you were in psychosis.'

I cleared my throat. 'I don't know who the father is if that's what you're getting at. I was sick. I have no idea who the father is. I didn't even know I was pregnant until they told me in St Charles.'

That moment was one of the few that I could remember. I had stabilised by then, but I could tell the consultant psychiatrist had been scrutinising my reaction. At first, I'd been numb. One moment it's just you knocking around in your body, a sentence later and there're two of you. It's quite a lot to take in. But very quickly my feeling was one of wonder and delight, that out of the horror I would have this gift. Of course, there were anxious and dark thoughts. Who knew what I'd been doing, what I'd smoked and drank and otherwise ingested on the streets? Who knew what diseases I'd been exposed to? What messed-up gene pool my baby would inherit? And then this medication that had broken through the psychosis, would it have harmed the child? I obsessed over all these questions. I had to stifle a laugh whenever other mums-to-be worried about eating blue cheese or a soft-boiled egg. If only they knew! I had researched obsessively while waiting for blood tests and scan results, which eventually came back all clear. I was fit and healthy, and so was baby. I really had won the golden ticket.

'You can't tell us who the father is, or you won't?' asked Elaine. 'It's been in the papers, Julia, that you had an altercation in the street with the father. I have to ask these questions, to find out if Alex is safe.'

'He's safe,' I muttered. 'That man was a bum. I suspect he was paid to attack me. It's part of a plan to discredit me.' I laughed bitterly. 'And by golly, it's working.'

Elaine had her patient nursery worker's smile on again. 'Do you see our problem, Julia? When you talk like this, when we know from your doctor you haven't been in for a while. When you print wild stories about MI5 or whatever trying to abduct you. And when you don't know who Alex's father is, even though you're fighting in the street with someone who claims he's the boy's dad. How can we trust you to keep Alex safe when you can't even trust your own mind?'

I stared at Elaine in horror. They were suggesting that everything that had happened – Michael Wilmore, the dossier, my abduction, the encounter with Wayne Sloss – were symptoms I was in psychosis again. And worse, when Elaine put it like that, it did sound mad. Was that why I was having the dreams? I started suddenly. I hadn't dreamt for a day or two but that was because I had barely slept. Was I entering another manic period? I flushed and realised I was very close to tears. I couldn't bear for it to happen again. I couldn't lose myself to darkness.

'I'm not sick,' I croaked, my knuckles white. My fingers dug into my thighs as I battled for self-control. 'I'll go to my GP tomorrow. You can speak to her. I'm not having another episode. I've had a lot of work stress but I'm not sick.' I was worried I was repeating myself, so I shut up suddenly, not trusting my treacherous mouth.

'Is Alex staying at his aunt's tonight? Emilia Garonne in Holland Villas Road?'

I nodded. I couldn't remember giving them the contact details, but perhaps it was because my sister was my named next of kin on some form. 'Yes, he's there. You can call and check.'

Elaine stood up and adjusted her hair slide. She pulled on a bright yellow rain mac. Mandy stood too, a little too close for my comfort, but I didn't dare move away. I felt my whole future balanced on a pinhead. The slightest misjudgement, a nervous tic, a sneeze, a curse, and I would tip into an abyss.

After they were gone, I lay on the floor for a long time, drained of all energy, counting my pulse, focusing all my thoughts on just breathing in, breathing out. I didn't trust my mind to think of anything else.

39

THEY CAME at night again. It was clearly an MO designed to cause maximum anxiety and distress. My only thought was at least Alex wasn't here. He was at Emilia's having a sleepover and I clung to his absence like a drowning person to a life raft. And this time, I didn't waste a second; I called Emilia, trying but failing to keep the edge of desperation from my voice. Because I was scared. The bull-necked copper Conor Tull was alleging his team had found indecent images of children on my laptop and I knew, with a sickening lurch, that they would try to use this darkest of smears to take Alex from me.

'Don't let him out of your sight, Em, promise me,' I pleaded down the phone. 'Don't let them take him.'

My phone was quickly seized and bagged as evidence. They cuffed me and walked me out like a perp, and I was relieved there was no sign of Stubsy this time: if he got wind of these allegations, there'd be no more sympathy for the nice lady. I wasn't sure I'd go back anyway. The flat didn't feel like a safe haven anymore.

The looks I got from the other officers when we arrived at the station told me they all thought the worst of me. I burned with shame and a sense of injustice. Back in the interview room, I felt like a wild thing caught in a trap, all tooth and claw and terror but ultimately powerless. My lead tormentor, Conor Tull, could barely disguise his relish at my predicament. He was baiting me, and I decided it was safer to keep quiet. I did not trust myself to speak wisely.

It seemed endless but it can't have been more than a couple of hours until William Stone made his polished arrival. And despite everything I felt about him, and my father, I was relieved to see him. This was too serious for me to fight on my own.

40

'I SEE the fancy lawyer's arrived,' sneered Tull as Stone took his seat next to me.

'May I have a quick word with my client?' Stone asked, and then without waiting for Tull's response, turned in his chair so we could whisper discreetly. 'Have you said anything I need to know about?'

I shook my head. 'It's all lies. They're trying to fit me up.'

'Have they told you what they found?'

'A hidden cache of pictures of children. Being abused.' My voice cracked. 'They'll take Alex from me.'

Stone shook his head, then turned his attention to Tull. The policeman's face was flushed. There was white spittle at the corner of his mouth and a vein pulsed in his forehead. I hoped he dropped dead.

'You're charging Ms Castleton with offences under Section 160 of the Criminal Justice Act?'

'Yes. She'd gone to great lengths to try and conceal the cache on her computer, but our people are experts. Won't be long until we've worked out who she's been sharing it with.'

'I haven't shared anything with anyone,' I protested.

'Just your personal enjoyment then.'

'This is a stitch-up, and you know it,' I muttered darkly.

'So you say,' said Tull, 'but there's more to you than meets the eye, isn't there? You're already on a Section 127 for the lies you peddle on that website. What else have you been sharing with your loyal fans?'

'For fuck's sake,' I muttered. 'I'm a reporter. I used to work on *The Times*.'

''Used to' being the operative words there,' sneered Tull. 'Left under something of a cloud. Even Daddy couldn't get you out of that one. Oh yes, you've had a very colourful past; a misspent youth, one might say.'

'If you call time being sectioned on a mental health ward a misspent youth,' I said flatly. 'It doesn't mean I'm a child abuser.'

The door opened behind us, and a WPC came in with a folder.

'Here you go, boss,' she said, handing it to Tull.

She shot me a dirty look before she left the room.

Tull perused the contents of the folder and his lips curled with distaste. Then he placed three grainy photographs in front of me and Stone. I glanced at them and quickly looked away.

'This is serious stuff,' said Tull. 'We're talking Category A under the Sexual Offence definitive guidance. We need to know where you got these from.'

'Those aren't mine and you know it. It's you who's broken the law here.'

'No one's going to believe you, Ms Castleton. Not after what you've done, so you may as well tell us now rather than dragging it out,' said Tull. 'You need to focus on how to co-operate with us if you want any hope of seeing your little boy again.'

Stone cleared his throat. I could tell the images had shaken him but surely he couldn't think I would be involved in something like this. But then he'd seen me at my worst, so perhaps he could believe even this. The lawyer kept his eyes on the policeman. 'My client denies ever seeing these images and she's never shared them.'

'We'll see,' said Tull. 'With these kinds of investigations, it's important we shut down the whole network of paedos, not just the odd nonce.'

'Fuck you,' I spat.

Stone leant into me again. 'Keep it together,' he whispered. 'Have you seen those photos before?'

'Fuck you too,' I hissed.

'Julia,' he cautioned. 'This is very serious.'

'I know,' I said. 'But they haven't come off my computer. I've already told him my system is mirrored; there's complete redundancy. Lyndsey Daniels can prove those files aren't mine, but this fucker won't listen to me.'

I sobbed, exhausted. I had explained this to Tull multiple times, but he'd just bellowed at me for hours until I'd stopped trying to defend myself. If I couldn't even get Stone to believe me, then I was done for. It seems, however, Stone had everything he needed.

'I'm going to need to speak to your superior,' he said quietly to Tull.

'Oh yeah? Time to pull in the old boy's network, eh?'

'Your superintendent is a woman, actually,' drawled Stone. 'And I think she's going to be very interested in the fact her CID team have planted false evidence. There appears to be a high-level attempt to smear my client, extensive collusion and corruption to incriminate a woman who is, by your own account, vulnerable' – and here he placed a hand on my arm, warning me to stay quiet – 'intimidation, collusion with social services…Ms Castleton's servers and hard drives are all mirrored, and it will be very easy for a computer forensics expert to not only prove these photos weren't ever on her computer but at what date and time they appeared on the machine that you have in your possession. Consider your next move very carefully, Detective Tull.'

I watched the words hit home. Tull's face was redder than ever. A nervous tic pulsed in his temple. Whoever planted those images hadn't known my system was duplicated somewhere across the Atlantic.

'That's your defence, is it?' Tull asked, his face still twisted in a sneer, but the bravado was punctured. 'That there's some malicious element at play. Then I guess we'll leave it here for now, pending further investigation. I hope you're right, Ms Castleton, for your sake.'

'Oh no,' said Stone. 'We are most certainly not leaving it here. This is a horrific smear on my client. You have threatened her, and her little boy. You, one of your colleagues, or some other individual has planted evidence of the most heinous nature in a bid to do maximum harm. That evidence has been planted while the machine was in your possession. I think you know my client is an investigative journalist. One has to wonder what interest you have in silencing her with this dangerous and criminal intimidation.'

He went on in this way for some time. It was, I have to admit, a tour de force. Eventually Tull just stopped the interview tape, stood up and left the room, and I was free to go. I found I was trembling and when Stone offered his arm to lead me down to his car, I didn't object. I whispered my thanks and he nodded, grim-faced, and I was grateful he had the good grace not to mention the brimming tears as we drove back to Holland Villas Road, back to my son.

41

I STAYED with Emilia all weekend. Alex was happy to have his mum back and seemed completely content for us to stay in the big house on Holland Villas Road forever. I wondered if he would ever feel safe at home again. He hadn't been there when Tull had come back and bundled me out of the flat on trumped-up indecent images charges, and I would never tell him our home had been invaded a second time. He was still so upset from the first police raid, I worried that the flat was now permanently tainted. Would we have to move for him to feel safe again? I couldn't even think about that now. I was exhausted from recent events and just allowed myself to float in a kind of half-sleep in the comfort of Emilia's guest room.

Philippe greeted me with his cold smile at breakfast. I tried to warm to him – after all, my son and I were frequent beneficiaries of his hospitality – but he didn't make it easy. Even my breakfast order – weak tea rather than the thick black coffee bubbling on the stove – led to raised eyebrows.

'The British and their obsession with tea,' he said.

I shrugged and spread raspberry jam on a piece of toast. Alex had already eaten and was playing in the garden with little Jacques, holding his hand and helping him water plants with a pink can. I knew he yearned for a sibling and hoped he would forgive me and find company enough from his cousins and friends.

I wondered if Philippe expected some breakfast small talk and was relieved when he pulled out the business section of *The Sunday Times*. He sipped his tiny cup of coffee and read some long piece on Bank of England policy.

Emilia burst in, dewy and rosy-cheeked. She smelt of perfume and soap and her hair was still a little damp from the shower after an early morning pilates class.

'Morning. You look better,' she said. 'Have you had breakfast? Did you try this rye bread?'

'It's very good, thanks.'

'Another slice? Some apricots?'

I smiled. Only Emilia would present dried fruit as if it were a treat. 'I'm good, thanks. I'll take another tea though if you're putting the kettle on.'

Philippe rolled his eyes behind his paper.

As we sipped our tea at the kitchen table, watched the children play in the garden and made easy chitchat about Jacques' refusal to give up the bottle and Emilia's concerns that Veronique might be dyslexic, I had a glimpse of the kind of life I could have led. One of comfort, easy company, long breakfasts, pilates classes and eye creams. The au pair loading the dishwasher, the husband making plans to pick up lunch from a deli in town. The security of a full bank account.

'We're going to see Daddy today,' Emilia said. Unusually for her, this wasn't a suggestion but an instruction. 'You owe him, Julia. William Stone isn't a guardian angel, you know. He was there because of Daddy.'

'That's what I hate. Everything in my life, good and bad, is always because of him.'

I saw Emilia shoot Philippe an imploring look, but her husband just ignored the silent call for support, shrugged and went back to his newspaper.

'Julia, this is so serious. And Daddy says he's got some information that could help.'

'I'm sure he thinks he does,' I muttered, but my interest was piqued. After all, he knew everybody. Besides, deep down I'd already decided to see him. The stakes were too high now not to take all the help I could.

42

OTHER THAN a clutch of early-morning tourists already thronging the steps of St Paul's, the City was quiet. Emilia glided her Audi through the streets until we reached a shuttered underground car park beneath a towering city office block. The spring sunlight flared off the building's huge glass walls, making it gleam like some inland lighthouse. I raised my eyebrows.

'Working weekends? All not well in the love nest already?'

Lord Danby, one year into his fourth marriage, had form for using work to retreat from strife at home.

'He thought it would be more private,' said Emilia diplomatically. She used a security pass to open the steel gates to the car park.

I did not approve of wife number four, an Argentinian who was only six years older than me.

We glided silently upwards in a mirrored lift. I frowned at my reflection. I looked pale and gaunt, and there was a smear of breakfast butter on the jumper I'd borrowed from Emilia. Next to Emilia's unblemished complexion, I looked even more drained and dishevelled than usual. Even in jeans and a sweatshirt, Emilia exuded grace. I ran my fingers through my hair and scratched at the butter smear with a bitten fingernail.

The lift doors slid open and I was for a moment taken aback by the view. London glittered below us like a jewel in the sunlight, the dome of St Paul's majestic in its solid rotundity amid the sharp edges and acute angles of twenty-first-century glass and steel. It was such a beautiful city, and Lord Danby's receptionist commanded one of the very best views of it. She smiled brightly as we approached and my hackles rose – as a girl I had always been suspicious of the brightly lip-sticked, immaculately dressed women who spent more time with my father than I ever did. This one was just as showy, even on a Sunday, in wide-legged slacks and a silk blouse that was slashed just a little too low for work.

'Samantha, I hope he's not working you too hard.' Emilia smiled.

'I was just catching up on some filing,' the pretty receptionist said. I glared. Did people even do filing in the digital age? 'Nice to see you again. Please go through, he's expecting you.'

Emilia led the way and I glowered by her side.

'Filing my arse,' I muttered.

'Play nice,' said Emilia. 'You know what it's like; people are always trying to impress him.'

'And he is so very impressionable.'

Emilia was about to say something but the door ahead of us was flung open and our father greeted us. *The Right Honourable Lord Danby*, I thought darkly. If only people knew the dishonour that blemished his seemingly charmed life.

His office was large and opulent. A fashionably sleek desk and Eames chair occupied one corner, while the huge modern painting that hung on the back wall looked vaguely familiar. Two sleek modernist leather sofas squared up across a glass coffee table. Floor-to-ceiling glass walls provided views that stopped a person in their tracks.

'It's quite something, eh?' Danby said, as I stared down at the city.

It looked so perfect and clean and peaceful from up here. Funny how a little distance was so purifying. I pushed away from the glass and turned my back on the view. I knew it was a beautiful lie. The city was far from perfect.

Samantha bustled in with a tray. A coffee pot, teapot, milk jug and tiny wafer biscuits. The cups and saucers rattled as she set them on the glass table.

'Wonderful,' beamed Danby, clapping his hands together. 'Please.' He gestured for us to join him on the sofas. He peered into the teapot and gave it a stir. 'Shall I play mother?'

The quip hung in the air like a bad smell. Even after all these years, it was an assault on the ears for him, of all people, to raise the spectre of our mother. Even twenty-four years later, the loss would sometimes catch me unawares, the grief roaring in like a spring tide. I still couldn't forgive our father. He'd already left the family home to live in a medieval house on the edge of Antibes marina with a French model, so our mother bore the cancer diagnosis alone and succumbed to the tumour's virulence within just eight months. I was convinced my mother's heartache and humiliation had hastened her untimely demise. And he never even married the French model. She had just been another diversion – the 'French fancy', our maternal grandmother had called her.

Our first stepmother hadn't appeared on the scene until the following year, by which time us girls were living with our father with the help of Nanny Girt, a big-bosomed German lady who'd been with us since infancy and remained until the reign of stepmother number two. Collette didn't like fat nannies cluttering up the place.

I watched my father pour tea and proffer biscuits. I wondered whether he had any idea of how angry I still was about his desertion of our mother. Perhaps he thought all was forgiven and forgotten. After all, it was so many, many years ago, and no one ever talked about it anymore. He looked up and smiled.

'Everything alright, dear?'

'How's the new wife?' I spat.

'Valentina, darling, her name's Valentina, and she's very well, thank you. We'd love for you and little Alexander to come and visit. Valentina loves children.'

'Of course she does. They're the key to a gold-plated divorce.'

'Julia, that kind of comment is beneath you.'

I fumed. This always happened. I thought I could cope with my father but as soon as I was in his presence, bile would percolate throughout my system.

Emilia cleared her throat. 'Daddy thought it would be a good idea if we talked tactics.'

'Tactics?' I echoed.

'William filled me in on the charges you're facing. The pornography—'

I interrupted my father. 'Not pornography. Children can't consent. It's sexual abuse, rape.'

Danby looked shocked and fiddled with his teacup. 'Yes, of course, what I meant is I understand you have proof that those, er, images weren't on your computer, so I'm hoping we can park that one with William to deal with. But I understand the Section 127 charge still stands.'

'I'm due in court next week,' I said. 'It's bullshit, of course. A tool to shut down freedom of the press.'

'Yes, darling. But it was false, wasn't it, that story about the arms sales?'

I stood up, exasperated, and paced the room. 'There's more to it than that. I just need a bit more time to piece it together. This charge is bullshit to stop me digging into what was really happening. Someone wanted to discredit me, and they bloody well succeeded.'

I saw Emilia and my father share a glance but swallowed my anger. I wanted to hear what he had to say.

'Regardless of the politics of it, Jules, the fact is you've been charged, and we have to deal with that,' said Emilia.

I saw Danby shoot her a grateful look. Emilia was always the balm on our fractured relationship.

'Now, William is a wonderful lawyer. I trust him implicitly. And he's a wily fox; never underestimate him. But I do think if there was a way for this not to reach court, to save you that stress at this terrible time when these awful people from social services are putting you under pressure, I do think that would be best.'

I stopped my pacing and sat down again. 'And how does that happen?'

Danby leant forward, conspiratorially. 'Well, I've taken soundings from some key people, very discreetly. The consensus is that this Section 127 charge, in fact all this nonsense with the pornogr— I mean, the abusive images, and the social services, could evaporate if we just make the right moves.'

I leant forward. 'What moves?'

Danby gave a nervous laugh. 'You're not going to like it but I implore you to think about it, for your sake, for Alexander's sake.'

'What moves?'

'Shut the website and retract that story about Phelps.'

I threw my hands up in the air. 'Man! I can't believe this!' I ran my hands through my hair. 'Shut the site. Retract the story on that shitbag! Are you kidding me?'

'I knew you wouldn't like it,' said Danby. He didn't seem at all perturbed by my reaction. 'But you need to think about this rationally.'

'But if I'm going to lose everything anyway, why not just go to court? At least there I'll have a chance to state my case. And give Stone a break, he might win!' I leapt up and started pacing again.

'I know it's a big ask,' pleaded Emilia. 'But, Julia, this isn't about you anymore. It's about Alex. It's one of those moments in life when you get asked to do something really big for your kid. And you just have to do it. Because some things are bigger than a career.'

'Career! This isn't a career!' I laughed hollowly. 'I barely scrape by.'

'Darling, if it's money…' broke in Danby.

'Money, it's always money with you. It can't solve everything. This isn't about a career, whatever that is, or money. It's about truth and justice. Things that really matter.'

'Of course they matter, darling. But this is your liberty we're talking about. Your son. Your name.'

'You mean your name,' I muttered darkly. 'God, this is why I didn't want to come here. You and Phelps stitching up backroom deals, it's the Establishment coming together. You always have to come out on top.' I was pacing feverishly now, my temper rising. 'What cosy little chats you've been having. This is exactly the kind of conspiracy I try to expose! Jesus! What the actual fuck!'

I stormed out, almost blind with rage. That was his solution! To shut The Castleton Files, which he'd always hated, and then retract my biggest story and give that greedy scumbag Phelps a free pass! How many grubby deals like this were done every single day? How many times were people cheated out of the truth? Or denied justice?

Samantha was scrolling on her phone when I strode into the lobby. She looked up curiously.

'And fuck you too!' I yelled as I got into the lift and descended to the streets of London, to real life.

The pavement was filthy, a McDonald's bag fluttered in the wind and there was some dried vomit by the wall. As ugly as it was, I preferred this grimy truth to the beautiful lie my father saw from his high tower.

I was desperate to get away from a world where back room deals and cosy handshakes still protected the rich and powerful, enabling them to twist the rules and rain down pain and inequity on those outside. I kicked the fast-food bag.

'Fuck!' I yelled, startling a lone cyclist, who whizzed through the empty streets in a blur of neon and Lycra. I didn't care. I yelled profanities into the wind until my voice was hoarse.

43

I MAY have declined my father's offer – and according to Emilia, he was still griping how I never thought how poorly my actions reflected on him, given he counted Phelps among his friends – but I was still glad to have William Stone in my corner for the hearing. Joe was escorting me, and I was always a little surprised when the two men greeted one another warmly. It always took me a beat to remember they had first met when Stone had tasked Turner to track me down and recover me from the streets.

They knew more about my past than I did. They had been there, at ground zero, the epicentre of my wrecked life, and had carried me to the safety of the secure unit at St Charles. Sometimes I wanted to ask Joe what it had been like, what I had been like, but I didn't dare. Even five years later, it was still too raw.

We met in a busy café near the courthouse and huddled round a small table. I took comfort from the noisy bustle, which would afford us a degree of privacy. Joe and Stone made an unusual pairing. Stone was urbane, smooth, effortlessly well-dressed in his bespoke suit and old boy cufflinks. Turner was in his usual uniform of jeans, polo shirt and bomber jacket. Yet the two clearly had a mutual respect and were at ease in each other's company. It was I who was awkward and out of place. I felt like I was playing dress-up, in a plain shift dress I'd got from a charity shop and Emilia's navy blazer. I wore my one pair of smart shoes, the heels of which clip-clopped like a show pony. I sipped my tea gloomily, wondering what I would have to wear if I got sent down. At least I wouldn't have to worry about putting food on the table, and Emilia would look after Alex while I was inside. I felt my heart lurch again. I hadn't been able to say goodbye to him this morning because

I couldn't trust myself not to break down in front of him. Emilia had taken him to school, again.

I am already slipping out of his life, I thought miserably. *Perhaps it's for the best; he won't miss me so much when I'm gone.*

'Julia, are you listening?' It was Stone, derailing my train of thought. 'If you plead guilty then we can work the case and I'm confident we'd be looking at no more than three months. You'd serve half of that.'

'Three months.' Joe whistled. 'People knocking off old ladies get less.'

'It's a serious charge,' Stone said, raising a hand to silence me. I'd opened my mouth to protest again about the inequities of the Communications Act, which apparently I'd breached with that damned Operation Entrust story. 'Julia, whatever you think of the legislation, the fact is you're here now. The time for campaigning is later, after we've dealt with this.'

I looked at Turner. 'What do you think? Do I plead guilty?'

He shrugged. 'If you plead innocent and it goes the other way, then the maximum's six months and a fine. You need to weigh the risks here, Jules.'

'It sticks in my craw,' I muttered, staring down at my tea.

'I know,' said Stone. 'But it's a question of damage limitation.'

Westminster Magistrates' Court was a short walk from the café. I felt as if everyone we passed knew who I was. I imagined them wondering about my crime, judging me. There were a couple of photographers loitering outside the building, bags of equipment at their feet, cameras slung round their necks. At first the dishevelled men didn't pay much attention.

'There's a big extradition case on today,' muttered Stone, and I remembered the case and felt a pang of regret that my own troubles had led me to neglect stories I'd been following for months.

But as we got closer to the courthouse, one of the reporters recognised me. At once, he sprang into action and others followed. Soon, the monstrous lenses on their cameras scoped out their prey. Turner took my elbow and quickly steered me through the glass doors of the courthouse, and his not insubstantial side profile prevented the reporters getting a clear shot.

'Nicely done,' said Stone. 'They'll be waiting on the way out again, but you just keep your cool. And say nothing. Absolutely no comment.'

I nodded. My anxiety levels were through the roof. My heart was pounding, my mouth dry. I saw a peripheral flicker. Someone I recognised just slipping round the corner out of sight. Or was it a figment of my imagination? I was exhausted by the nightmares that pressed in every night. The Tattooed Man embraced me and whispered my name in the darkness, as a ring of fire engulfed them. Sometimes he put his arm round my neck and crushed my windpipe until I woke up drenched in sweat, panting hard.

Instinctively I tugged my sleeve. I'd been cutting my arm again, neat little incisions every morning, like a prisoner keeping a tally of the days, an inventory of my sanity. And yet, deep down, I knew this wasn't the behaviour of someone who was well. But who could I tell?

Even my GP was out of the question now. Elaine and Mandy would pick over my medical notes like vultures plucking flesh from a corpse. I made a resolution. After the hearing, I was going to stop the cutting. It was too risky now I was under such scrutiny. I imagined the social workers searching my bathroom, finding the razors and the bloodied tissues, how damning it would look. There could be no cracks, no weak spots. I had to be rock solid for Alex.

We perched on metal chairs in the modernist building and waited. Stone and Turner shared observations while I brooded privately, rehearsing my plea.

Guilty.

It was the sensible thing to do. Yet I baulked at it.

Guilty.

The taint would be with me for ever.

'It's just a word, Jules.' It was Joe, reading my mind as always. 'It will keep you free so we can crack on and bury these guys.'

'Lockmere,' I said. 'The answer's there.'

He nodded grimly. 'We just have to get through this. This first, then Lockmere, then Newby, then Tull.'

'Tull? The policeman?'

Joe gave me a meaningful look. 'I'll tell you when we get out of here.'

I tried to get him to share, but it was time to go.

The courtroom was modern; sleek wooden benches, black chairs, muted greys and stone colours. Lawyers and courtroom officials mingled, sharing pleasantries, and there was the odd crack of laughter. Just another day in the office for them. A couple of reporters sat at the back, scrolling through their phones, looking bored. I vaguely recognised one of them as a former junior from *The Times*. I averted my eyes and kept my head down, awash with shame, battling to control my panic. What if I was sent down, confined in a small cell for twenty-three hours a day? Would the walls close in? How would I cope with no space to breathe, no chance to see Alex, to hold him? The panic was hot, like a burst of heat from an open oven. I couldn't breathe; it felt like my windpipe was closing. I looked at Stone to see if he'd noticed I was really ill, but he was on his feet, nodding and talking. The words were far away from me, lost behind the pounding of blood in my ears. I ran my trembling right hand up my left sleeve and pressed against the cuts, still weeping under the plasters on my forearm. The flash of pain surged through me, focused my mind, and brought me back to myself.

This is real.

Everything seemed to happen in a blur. Stone prompted me when to stand and sit. The charges were read, and I felt the frisson of anger. My story was incorrect, but it wasn't grossly offensive. Stone nudged me with his elbow, and I jumped.

'How do you plead?' repeated the magistrate, an avuncular-looking bald man with a twinkle in his eye. Time seemed to slow to a standstill. Then I caught a flash of Alex's smiling face, and I knew I had to be strong for him. The world came rushing back and suddenly I was speaking.

'Not guilty.'

44

THE WORDS surprised even me, and Stone twitched nervously beside me. The magistrate blinked at me a couple of times, then consulted his paperwork. A date was read out to go to trial: the 20th of April. And that was it. Moments later, Stone gathered his papers, gestured for me to stand and exit, and we walked out of the courtroom. The reporters glanced at me curiously. I caught the eye of the young gun from *The Times*. He was older now, his floppy hair cut short, his eyes tired.

'Be careful,' I said to him. 'This regressive law is an attack on a free press. Next time it could be you.'

The journalist nodded and scrawled in his notepad.

A court official stepped forward. 'Out,' he mouthed. 'This court is sitting.'

Stone jostled me forward impatiently.

'Well,' he said, when we were in the busy corridor, 'that was unexpected.'

Was he cross? He was so polite it was hard to tell.

'I couldn't do it,' I said. 'It just popped out.'

'And your comment to the reporters?'

'Popped out,' I said.

Stone grimaced. 'Well, we've a busy few weeks ahead. We'd better stay in touch. No disappearing acts.'

I shook hands with Stone, who stepped away to talk to Joe. When the men had finished, I approached and Joe told me he had arranged a meeting round the corner.

'We'll make our own way back, William,' he said.

'Don't get into any trouble,' said the lawyer, his eyes flitting anxiously to me.

'Safe as houses,' said Joe.

We went our separate ways. Joe led me out through a side entrance by the vending machines, and down a busy road that was choked with cars. We stopped at a nondescript office building, where Joe pressed a buzzer. The door opened and we crossed a shabby reception area and took a flight of stairs down.

'This is all very cloak and dagger,' I said. 'Who are we meeting?'

'An associate of mine,' Joe replied, pushing open a fire door to reveal an underground car park. 'Let me introduce Sam Harrison.'

A young man was kneeling down, fiddling with a motorbike. He stood up and wiped his hands on his leathers. He had blue eyes, like ink pools, dark skin and tousled black hair that flopped over one eye.

'Pleased to meet you, Julia,' he said, shaking my hand. His voice was pure London. Well-spoken, but with a slight Cockney edge. 'Joe's told me a lot about you.'

I flinched. I hated the thought of people talking about me, especially Joe, who knew more than most.

'Don't worry, nothin' bad,' Sam said. 'You're just about the only person he rates.'

'He must rate you,' I countered. 'I've never known him share before.'

'Sam's been working a few cases with me,' Joe said. 'He's a natural.' He grinned suddenly. 'And he's a drama school graduate, so plenty of time on his hands.'

This was clearly an old joke between the two of them. I wondered how a gruff PI came to work with a wannabe actor.

'So, what's this all about?' I asked.

'I've been following the social workers that are on your case, Elaine Blackwood and Mandy Walker,' said Sam. 'Both of them are all over Facebook. Mandy's deep in the church and doesn't do anything dodgier than sharing inspirational quotes, but Elaine is a bit more interesting. Got some hard left connections; she's dating some guy close to Momentum, likes to talk big on all the social justice shit. Massive chip on her shoulder. Fair to say she's relished investigating the daughter of a lord. She's none too careful about her privacy settings and passwords.'

'She's been posting about me?'

'She hasn't mentioned you by name, but knowing the back story I could piece it together. She's clearly got it in for you.'

'Why? Just because of my bloody dad?'

Sam smiled. 'It's more than that. I recorded her' – he pulled out a tablet and some headphones – 'and it's clear she's been primed to make life difficult for you.'

'Is any of this legal?' I asked, glancing at Joe.

'You planning to put it in court?' asked Sam, tapping at his tablet. 'This is just context, innit?' An audio file opened up on his tablet and he pressed play. He held the headphones out to me, and I put them on. The recording was crystal clear. My eyes widened as I realised it was Conor Tull in conversation with my social worker Elaine, who sounded as though she'd had a few drinks.

Elaine: Give me a mo, it's noisy in here [sound of her leaving busy room]. OK, say that again.

Tull: We have her. Let's just say there's some inappropriate images about to be found on her laptop. And when I say inappropriate, I'm talking Category A.

Elaine: Can't say I'm surprised. She's a fucking mess.

Tull: I told you.

Elaine: [unintelligible]…black and white. Can't have unsupervised contact.

Tull: Looks good for you. You were on her before we found it.

Elaine: Yeah, thanks for that. I owe you one.

Tull: Don't say anything for a bit. We haven't officially found it yet.

Elaine: I'm pretending I don't understand, Mr Policeman. [sound of cheers from noisy room] I gotta go.

Tull: OK. Just keep up the pressure, right? She's ready to crack.

Elaine: [laughs] Pleasure doing business.

The recording ended abruptly. I looked at Sam and Joe, infused with rage.

'What the fuck was that?' I asked, my voice quivering with anger. 'Why is he doing this to me?'

Joe shrugged. 'I don't know yet, but I want to find out. You OK if Sam keeps digging?'

I nodded. 'Get the goods on all three of them. I want to take them down.'

Sam grinned. 'I hate crooked cops. It will be my pleasure.'

45

A THICK mist was brewing outside Oxford, rising like a spell from the river. The miasma rolled into the lanes and billowed in the van's headlights. Witches' petticoats, I thought fancifully, and I shivered in my seat and pulled my coat a little tighter. Joe turned up the heater.

'It's OK,' I yelled over the roar of the vents. 'I'm not cold. It's just creepy.'

Joe was peering through the windscreen like an old lady. Visibility was down to a car length. 'I like it,' he said. 'Perfect for spooks.'

'Exactly,' I responded. 'Spooky.'

The van twisted and turned down the lanes, and the diesel engine chuntered through the whiteness. We pulled into muddy verges to let the odd car go by. Joe took a wrong turn but quickly realised his mistake and reversed at speed with the practised calm of a confident driver.

'Here we go,' he said as a distant lamp spread a gloomy yellow light.

Joe pulled the van off the road, crunched up a gravel track and parked behind a tumbledown cottage. A sign that had once hung from the eaves was propped against the wall and, judging by the grass and weeds grown up about it, had been earthbound for some time.

'The Loggerheads,' I read.

'Aye,' said Joe. 'We are officially at loggerheads.'

'What's with the puppets?' I asked, pointing at the three mannequins on the pub sign.

'They're not puppets,' a voice said.

It came from behind me. My heart jumped, and I grabbed Joe's arm in shock. A footstep crunched, and I turned to see a burly figure emerge from the gloom. 'They're men with wooden heads, block heads or, in old English, loggerheads.' The man spoke slowly, almost as if English wasn't his first language. I caught a hint of a west country burr.

'Good to see you, Al,' Joe said. 'Been too long.'

'Likewise, Turnip.'

The two men shook hands and then hugged, with much slapping of backs.

'Turnip?' I asked, still trying to recover my composure.

'Turner, Turnip.' Joe shrugged. 'Not a huge amount of imagination, I grant you.'

'It's on account of his great turnip head,' explained the stranger, rubbing his knuckles on Joe's skull. 'Obviously.'

'Alan, this is Julia Castleton. Julia, this is Alan Konsta, a buddy of mine from back in the day.'

I was never sure what day Joe was referring to – the Paras, whatever security service he'd been seconded to, or his early days as a PI. Now wasn't the time to ask. I felt Alan Konsta appraising me quietly, his dark eyes wary, his face careworn. He was a big man and his dark hair ran to grey. His chin was covered with a salt-and-pepper stubble, and a general air of dishevelment hung around him. Much like the pub, he seemed rundown, neglected. Finally, Alan stepped forward and shook my hand. His was large, the palm calloused.

'Come on, then,' he said. He led us through a small wooden door and advised us to duck under the low lintel.

It was perhaps the smallest pub I had ever been in, no bigger than the average sitting room. There was a little bar, done out in copper, and the polished metal glowed in the light cast by a fire that flickered in a black grate. There were two small coffee tables, each with mismatched armchairs arranged around them, and candles guttered in old wine bottles. A cat snoozed by the fire, a dog was asleep under one of the two bar stools, and an old man, dressed in a red hunt jacket and white jodhpurs, was asleep in a shabby armchair by the window.

'Wow,' I said.

'Ignore him,' Alan advised. 'He's been out hunting since dawn, but his horse ran off.'

'Is he alright?'

'The horse? She'll be back by dinner. She's no fool.'

'I meant him.' I nodded at the old man.

'Oh yes,' said Alan, puzzled. 'He's just having a nap 'til his daughter comes by.'

I felt like I'd stepped back in time. What a strange place this was. Alan fetched us a dusty bottle of red and three glasses from behind the bar. I accepted mine for the sake of politeness. I hated explaining that I didn't drink. We took the three armchairs by the fire, dislodging the cat who retreated with a look of high disdain.

'Is this your pub?' I asked.

'I'm just running it for a pal,' Alan replied. 'Keeps me in bed and board.'

'I've never seen anywhere like it,' I said, stroking the cat who had returned to favour me with its attentions.

Alan looked about him and shrugged. A log fell off the fire and sent sparks flying. The old huntsman snored loudly, then fell back into a quiet slumber. For some reason, I felt safe here. The little bar, with its vintage posters advertising Lucky Strike and its bowed low ceilings, stained yellow with tobacco, felt like a time capsule. Nothing from my present could harm me in this past.

Joe and Alan chatted, catching up on old acquaintances. I stroked the cat and listened with half an ear, noting how many were ill, dead or missing.

'So,' said Alan, 'I'm guessing this isn't just a social call. What do you want, Turnip?'

'Lockmere.'

Alan whistled. 'Go on.'

'We need to get inside.'

Alan chuckled and clapped his hands together. 'Turnip, if I didn't know you better, I would have a right laugh at a good joke.' He sat back in his chair and squinted at Joe over the top of his wine glass. 'But I do know you, so I guess…' He lapsed into a thoughtful silence. 'It's a big ask, Joe. The place doesn't even officially exist. You say Lockmere and I'm meant to say never heard of it.'

'And yet look at us,' countered Joe. 'It doesn't exist but here we are, three people talking about it.'

'I still don't get why it's so secret,' I said. 'I mean we all know military research facilities exist. A colleague of mine even had a tour of Porton Down a few years ago.'

'There's secret and then there's Lockmere,' Alan responded. 'Porton Down's got some good PR now, working on cures for Ebola, developing new types of battle armour, that kind of thing. But Lockmere…' There was another silence. '…Lockmere's the opposite of good PR. It's what comes out the other end.'

'The other end of what?' I asked.

Alan topped up the glasses with more red. The old huntsman stirred in his sleep and his feet kicked out as though he was dreaming of the chase.

'Doesn't matter how much you spend on defence research, or how many fancy new weapons or battle suits you have, if you send men to war, some are going to come back dead.'

'Humans,' I remarked.

'What?'

'It's not just men. Women go to war too now.'

Alan glowered at me over the wine. 'You know what I mean.'

'So what's in Lockmere?' I asked.

'The dead. That's what's in Lockmere. That's why we don't talk about it.'

'Dead soldiers? I thought they were repatriated, had honourable burials, crowds gathering to pay respects to the caskets.'

'Some cases are more…' Alan paused, searching for the right word.

'More?' I prompted.

Joe shot me a warning look.

'More complicated,' finished Alan. 'Sometimes they require further investigation.'

Alan drained his glass. He directed his next remark to Turner. 'So why the interest?'

'Julia's investigating the death of an army medic. We think he was offed because he knew something he shouldn't. And the something is in Lockmere.'

'Good place to bury secrets,' mused Alan, running his fingers over his stubble.

'How long since you were there?' asked Joe.

'Couple of years.' Alan stared into the fire. 'It was my last posting actually.' Another long pause. 'End of an era.'

'Could you help us get in?'

'Nah.' Alan shook his big head slowly. 'I mean you can't just walk in there. It's like Fort Knox for dead people.'

I twitched with impatience. This shambling man was out of the loop and coming here was a waste of our time. But from the corner of my eye I saw Joe make a little calming gesture. Alan was still talking.

'I can't get you in, no, no. But I know someone who could. Who might.'

I waited, holding my breath. Finally, I couldn't hold it any longer. 'Who?'

'Sheena,' replied Alan, directing his answer to Joe. 'She qualified about a year ago.' He smiled ruefully. 'It was her first posting. And my last. What are the chances?'

Sheena, it transpired, was his ex-wife. 'My fault,' he said. 'I changed. They say you always take it out on the ones you love most.'

'Will she help us?' asked Joe.

Alan shrugged and finished off the bottle. He gave Joe a meaningful look. 'You know she'd do anything for you, mate. Me too.'

He lumbered to his feet and shuffled off with the empty bottle. Watching him duck through a little doorway at the back of the bar, I saw that his skull was crumpled in on one side. I realised with a sudden hot flush of shame that his lugubrious ways were probably the result of brain trauma.

I caught Joe's eyes.

'IED in Helmand,' he revealed. 'Lucky to be alive. Lucky to be walking, talking, to be doing anything at all.'

'God, I'm an idiot,' I said.

The door to the pub opened and a ruddy-faced woman burst in, her wax jacket splattered with mud. She grunted with effort as she hoisted the old huntsman to his feet and staggered back through the door, dragging him to a waiting Land Rover.

Alan shambled in and noted the empty chair. 'Smithy's daughter turned up then. Good, good.' He sat down by the fire. 'Sheena's in. But it's gotta be tonight. They're short-staffed and there's an England match on. Says you'll never get a better time for a recce.'

Joe looked at me, eyebrows raised. I nodded.

'The sooner the better,' I confirmed. 'Thank you, Alan,' I added softly, trying to make amends for my impatience.

46

ALAN KONSTA drew us a map. I noted the tremor in his hands and tried not to stare at the depression in his skull.

I thanked him profusely, but he just held up his hands and said, 'Anything for Turnip.'

I wondered if I would ever inspire anyone to such acts of loyalty and friendship. Deep down I knew I was too prickly and difficult, pushing people away rather than drawing them in. We left the pub, got into Joe's van and headed east.

'Let me do the talking,' Joe said, peering at the road ahead. 'Sheena's an old pal.'

I looked at him, wondering exactly what kind of old pal. 'Alan said she'd do anything for you. What did you do?'

'When Al got injured, things were a bit of a mess at home. Their boy, Ryan, fell in with a bad lot. Got into a spot of bother with the cops. Drugs, you know. I managed to pull a few strings and then we sorted out the gang stuff, got him cleaned up. He's an electrician now, working in Melbourne, got himself a girl. Nice kid.'

I eyed Joe speculatively, mulling over what he meant by 'sorted out the gang stuff'. 'No wonder Al and Sheena owe you,' I said.

Joe shrugged. 'The lad just made a few wrong turns at a tough time in his life. It can happen to anyone. I like to think someone would do the same for my kid when I have one.'

I hugged myself in the darkness of the cab. I hoped Alex would never need that kind of intervention, but I knew better than most how easily life could unravel, and how important it was to have someone to help put you back together.

Lockmere was less than twenty miles away, but it was a long ride. The van followed a route that snaked through the foggy lanes and every so often we lost some time trying to make sense of Alan's map. His directions took us past the main gate. It didn't look particularly secure – just a sentry box and barrier blocking a single lane road that disappeared into fog – but Joe nudged me and pointed to a high razor wire-topped fence and directional cameras set further back. Alan's directions took us away from Lockmere but just as I began to wonder at the man's map, we made a sharp left and looped back along a single lane track through dark woods. Tendrils of mist wound through the trees, the fingers of some creature reaching out of the night. The lane twisted again and there was a wide muddy layby on our right, at the head of a footpath that ran into the woods. Two headlights flashed on and off, and Joe pulled over next to a large estate car.

Sheena's face was pale in the ghostly light from her dashboard. She had tired eyes, dark hair in a neat bob and wore no makeup. We got out of our vehicles, and she embraced Joe warmly, her head buried in his neck.

'You're looking good, girl,' he said, when they finally pulled apart.

She smiled ruefully. 'Not really. These night shifts grind me down.'

'Look good to me,' he said. 'It's been too long.'

'Funny enough I was thinking 'bout you the other day,' said Sheena. 'This place gives me the creeps anyway, but just lately...Well, I was thinking it was the kind of place you'd be interested in.'

'Anything specific?' asked Joe.

Sheena shook her head. 'Just a feeling. People higher up are twitchy, handling some of the paperwork themselves, urgent meetings...I don't know. You'll see. It's creepy.'

She turned to look at me. 'Who's this then, Joe?'

'Julia Castleton. She's the one who got me into this.'

Sheena glared at me. 'She's that blogger, isn't she?' She said 'blogger' like it was a curse word.

I bristled but said nothing.

'She's a journalist, Sheen, and she's solid,' Joe replied. 'Don't believe everything you read in the papers.'

Sheena chewed her lip, then gave me another fierce look. 'I will feed you to the dogs if you fuck this up for us.'

I held up my hands. 'I'm not going to fuck anything up. My life, my son's life, depend on me getting this right.'

'Let's do it then,' said Sheena. 'Get in my car. I'll take you in for the start of my night shift. Keep low and I'll park by the women's changing rooms. I'm the only woman on duty tonight so it's safe as anywhere.'

I could feel Sheena eying me as she got in her car. If this woman was representative of the public's perception of me, I absolutely had to restore my reputation. I couldn't go through life with people judging me like this.

The Volvo rolled along country lanes until the razor wire fence came into view. The road ran parallel to the fence for a mile until we came to a side gate. Joe and I ducked down while Sheena showed her security badge to a camera, and then we were in. We drove along a straight road that cut across empty grassland. In the distance, a cluster of one-storey buildings loomed out of the fog.

'The tip of the iceberg,' Sheena explained. 'Most of it's underground.'

She pulled up by one of the boxy buildings and used her key card to open the door, revealing a changing room, toilets, showers and lockers. The place smelt of disinfectant and soap.

'Here!' Sheena threw some combat fatigues at me. 'Put these on, you'll look less conspicuous.'

She rummaged through a locker and pulled out a set for Joe. 'Our SIC is, ahem, bigboned,' said Sheena.

'My kinda lady,' said Joe, taking the clothes and locking himself in a cubicle to change.

I found it strangely anonymising to be in uniform, and there was a certain comfort in that. The trousers were hanging off my hips, but I rolled the waist band over a couple of times.

'You need fattening up,' Sheena observed. 'You're too skinny to do any damage to anyone.'

I bit my lip. I hated the way it would be considered rude for me to comment on Sheena's sturdy figure, but people felt no such inhibition when it came to discussing those of slimmer build. And having been much heavier myself, when the pounds piled on relentlessly in the early days of my lithium and Zyprexa regime, I was still touchy about people making any comments about my weight, even if it was to say things had swung too far in the other direction.

'Julia can look after herself,' Joe remarked from behind the locked door. 'And there's more ways than one to hurt people.'

'I'm sure,' Sheena said dryly. She was in her work kit now; green medical fatigues, name badge and orderlies' shoes.

I was surprised. 'You're a nurse. But I thought this was a mortuary.'

Sheena gave me a look. 'Medical science doesn't end when the heart stops.'

I swallowed, suddenly feeling queasy. What went on here? A hot flush of apprehension swept over me. What were we going to see?

'You alright?' Sheena was peering at me. 'You look a little peaky.'

'I'm fine,' I replied. I did feel a little peaky but there was no way I was going to admit it.

Joe emerged from the cubicle looking every inch the army man. It wasn't a stretch for him given his background, but, catching my reflection in the mirror, I felt like a kid playing dress-up, albeit a particularly pale, gaunt-looking child.

'Right,' said Sheena, checking her watch. 'I'm due on shift in five. Stay close to me. It's a minimally staffed facility; after all, the dead don't need much, so we'd be unlucky to get stopped. But, just in case, you're auditors from DSTL.'

'DSTL?'

'Defence Science and Technology Laboratory,' Sheena explained, leading us into the dark night.

A security spotlight flicked on, illuminating us like actors on a stage. This was clearly normal practice as Sheena didn't bat an eyelid. She led us to another concrete box, swiped her card and opened the door. It was a largely empty room, just a few desks, all deserted now. At the back, there was a set of rough concrete steps that went underground. Our footsteps echoed off the bare walls as we descended.

'This is the back way,' Sheena told us. 'Bodies, equipment, supplies, all come in another entrance to the north. Big industrial lift.

But this is obviously quieter, and keeps me fit, especially at the end of a shift.'

I felt slightly dizzy and lost count of the number of stairs as we wound deeper and deeper. Every twelve steps or so there was a flat landing with doors leading off, with cryptic signs such as 'Radiology' or 'Biopharma', but still we wound down and down. At last, we stopped by a door marked 'Mortuary 1'.

'How many are there?' I asked.

'Four,' Sheena replied. 'Do you know what you're looking for?'

'Fox and Wilmore shipped out to Syria in September,' said Joe. 'So I'm guessing nothing before then.'

Sheena opened the door to Mortuary 1. I took a deep breath, and followed, keeping my eyes on the white tiled floor. The cool air smelt faintly of disinfectant, and there was a constant hum from unseen machinery. I looked around while Sheena crouched at a desk in a small side office and logged on to a computer. We were in a large underground bunker. There were metal doors set in one wall. I had seen enough TV to know these held the refrigerated caskets where bodies were stored. I counted twelve doors in this room and guessed each might conceal four caskets. That was a possible forty-eight bodies. Forty-eight bodies not released for burial. I shivered. I wasn't religious but it felt wrong to hold people in this cold limbo. Somewhere up above, families grieved. I glanced at Joe and saw that he too was unsettled.

There was a beep, and a printer started to spit out paper. 'We've had twenty-three back from Syria since September,' said Sheena. 'I'm printing off the details now. Have a look through. I've got to report to the duty officer. I'll be back in about twenty minutes.' She gave us a stern look as she handed over the papers. 'Don't wander off.'

But Joe and I were already pouring over the printouts. There were lists of names, shipping numbers, dates and various military codes.

'Doesn't twenty-three seem a big number?' I asked. 'If we'd lost twenty-three soldiers in Syria in that time, it would be front-page news. I'm sure I'd have covered it.'

'You're right. I thought we just had a humanitarian brief over there.'

'What do these codes mean?' I asked. 'These ones don't have any names, just numbers.'

Joe frowned. 'ID numbers maybe? Look, the ones without names are all from the same week in February.'

'That's not long before Wilmore went AWOL,' I said. 'None of these have been released for burial.'

'Eighteen of them. All in Mortuary 4. That's where we should start.'

I blanched and swore softly. I shivered just thinking about what lay behind those doors.

'Joe?' My voice was a little shaky. 'Whatever happened to those men upset Wilmore so much that he went AWOL.'

Joe nodded grimly. 'Yeah, I don't think it's going to be pretty. You up for this?'

I took a deep breath and nodded, despite myself. 'I have to know. But God, I don't want to.'

I tried to stop my mind picturing the horrors I'd see but it was impossible. My overactive imagination filled my head with gruesome images of the dead, which made me feel queasy. But it didn't matter what lay behind those doors, or how it made me feel. Finding the truth was the only way I'd get my life back. The only way Alex and I would be safe. And that was all that mattered.

47

WHEN SHEENA came back, she listened to what we wanted to do. Her face was stern.

'It would be Mortuary 4. You're going to need to suit up to go in there. That's where they store cases of suspected poisoning, chemical attack, radiation or bio-threats.' She sighed heavily. 'This is going to really complicate things. It's a controlled area, so I have to log every time there's access.'

'We really need it, sorry, love,' said Joe. 'I wouldn't ask if it wasn't important.'

Sheena rolled her eyes, but it was clear her gratitude to Joe ran deep and she took us down another level to Mortuary 4. She used her swipe card to access the outer room, where there were lockers containing hazmat suits.

'I'm going to log that I went to check on a faulty thermostat reading,' she explained, 'and hope no one notices that the hazmat suits were sent to decontamination.'

She supervised as we suited up clumsily. She put my phone in a medical bag so I could film proceedings. I could feel panic rising and tried to focus on my breathing rather than whatever lay beyond the metal door. Sheena helped fit the hood, and I fought the urge to back out. It was horrible. I felt trapped and my hot breath came in fast panicky gasps.

'Get in and out,' said Sheena. 'Don't touch, don't take anything and don't tell me what you find. I don't know what's in there and I don't want to know. I'll call your phone if we need to abort. Got it?'

Joe gave the thumbs up, and reluctantly I copied. Sheena tapped in the access codes and the door clicked open.

'You don't come out this door,' Sheena told us. 'You'll see the exit door. You go in there to decontaminate and take off the suits. I'll meet you on the other side.'

Once Sheena was clear, I started video recording on my phone. I took a long shaky breath and tried to compose myself. Inside the hazmat helmet, everything seemed more immediate and intense. I became very conscious of my breathing, which was rapid and shallow, and felt beads of sweat prick my brow. I watched Joe push the outer airlock door open, and we stepped inside a small windowless compartment. Joe shut the outer door, and an inner one opened with a hiss as the pressure seal deflated. We stepped inside Mortuary 4, which looked much like the one upstairs, except there were eighteen of the refrigerated compartments in here. Each was numbered and had a date. I held the printouts in my gloved hand and tried to concentrate on the numbers and codes in front of me. Joe saw I was having trouble and tried to take them from me, but we weren't used to the suits and the papers dropped to the floor.

'Shit,' I said, stooping clumsily to pick them up.

It was impossible. I couldn't get a grip on the papers through the thick gloves. Joe bent down and helped. The papers were all scrunched up and out of sequence, and I felt my heart rate accelerating with brewing panic. Joe tapped me on the arm and led me over to the metal doors.

'Let's just get started,' he said. 'I'll go left, you go right.'

I gave him the thumbs up and moved to the doors on the far right. I steeled myself, then quickly opened the top door and pulled out the long drawer that lay inside. It was empty. I let out a shaky breath, pushed the drawer back in, and closed the door with trembling hands. The compartment below was also empty. *Perhaps they're all empty*, I thought with a sudden lightness. Perhaps there was no horror to see. Perhaps Fox had thrown us a red herring. I glanced over at Joe. He was also making quick progress and hadn't found anything yet.

I moved to the next pair and pulled out the top drawer. It was empty. The bottom one, however, was heavier. I swallowed and looked down at the sealed body bag. My hands were trembling so much, and the gloves were so cumbersome, it took ages to pull down the zipper.

It was stiff but then suddenly gave and opened to reveal a woman. Middle-aged, weather-beaten skin, a mole on her left cheek. No obvious signs of trauma. I pulled the zip down further. The woman was in civilian clothes. A long, patterned dress, a black headscarf and shawl round her neck and shoulders. Her hands were rough, her nails cut short. Dusty buckled shoes capped her feet and the heels were worn down. Was this an intelligence or special forces operative in deep cover, travelling incognito? I'd heard whispers about black ops taking place in Syria. I couldn't see any evidence of injury, and then remembered what Sheena had said about possible poisoning or contamination. Yet the woman looked peaceful, like she was in a deep sleep rather than the victim of a chemical attack.

I opened the next drawer and found another body. I unzipped the bag and took a step back. It was an old man with dark brown leathery skin, his face deeply lined and creviced with age. He didn't have teeth and there was a spray of white hair on his head. He was dressed in a long dusty tunic, grey socks that had wrinkled round his ankles, and he wore leather sandals on his feet.

Again, there was no sign of what he'd died of. But one thing I did know: this old man wasn't a special forces operative. A spy maybe, but his age made field operations extremely unlikely.

'Joe, come and look at this,' I said, my voice muffled by the hood.

I touched the man's hand and turned it over to see prayer beads still clasped in his calloused palm. What had happened to bring him here? Was he an interpreter? An informant? Why had he not been buried in Syria?

'Joe,' I repeated. 'This is strange.'

'Julia.' Joe's tone immediately drew my attention. 'You need to see this.' His voice was shaky. I joined him by an open body bag, fearful of what might be inside. Joe didn't scare easily.

I looked down and saw what had shaken him. Lying cold and motionless was a child. I grabbed Joe's arm in shock. The dead boy was just a couple of years older than Alex. He wore a red t-shirt, jeans and a pair of scuffed trainers. My head spun and I took a step back. I thought of the boy's mother grieving at the horror of his loss but was suddenly struck by the thought she might be with him here in this place of death. I eyed the remaining metal doors fearfully. Why were these people here? What had happened? Why was a dead child in a military mortuary?

We opened another two drawers and found an elderly woman and a teenage girl; a sleeping beauty, her dark hair coiled in a long plait, her lips frozen in a curled smile. I stifled a sob. I didn't know what this was, but I knew I would never forget that little boy, this beautiful girl, so still, so far from home.

48

MY PHONE began to buzz and vibrate, and I shook Joe as he went to open another drawer.

'We have to go,' I said. 'Now.'

He nodded. I could see how pale he looked behind the face mask. This had shaken us both deeply. I had prepared myself for soldiers with horrific wounds, mutilations or chemical burns, not dead children. We moved as quickly as we could to the exit, pushed the button and heard the heavy door hiss open. Automated nozzles sprayed us with a clear liquid, and once the shower ended, we struggled out of the heavy suits and hoods. I immediately felt strangely weightless. I took my phone out of its bag and shoved it into my pocket. We left the suits in a large dump bin and exited into a long gloomy corridor.

'Where's Sheena?' I asked.

We lingered for a moment, but I felt dangerously exposed.

'We need to get out of here,' said Joe. 'We can't wait for her. This way.'

We set off down the tunnel at a brisk walk and soon reached the stairs and began to climb quickly. The sound of our footsteps and heavy breathing was loud in the otherwise silent place. I was unnerved by Sheena's absence. Had she been caught? We came to the door at the top but it was locked, and we had no way of opening it. We looked through the porthole but there was no one in the room beyond.

'Where the fuck is she?' I whispered.

'She'll have her reasons,' said Joe. 'I trust her.' But his face betrayed his concern. 'We can't wait here. Let's go back down and find that other entrance she mentioned.'

I felt an irrational fear of heading back underground. We could be walking into a trap. 'Wait,' I said, pulling out my phone. It showed the last dialled number, a mobile I didn't recognise. I rang it now but there was no answer. It went through to Sheena's voicemail.

I looked at the video file on my phone. It was a large file, four minutes, though it had felt much longer. I watched its progress as I uploaded it to my Dropbox account.

Thirty-two per cent, fifty per cent, sixty-seven per cent.

'Come on,' said Joe.

'Wait!'

I looked at Joe suddenly and saw that he shared my concern. There were footsteps coming up the stairwell.

'Julia, we have to go now,' he urged.

'Just a minute.'

Eighty per cent, ninety-two per cent. The footsteps were closer now. Two people walking up the stairs, talking. A male and a female. Maybe a couple of flights below.

Joe flexed his muscles.

Your file has been uploaded.

'Done,' I said.

He took my hand and quickly pulled me down a flight of stairs. He pushed me through a door marked 'Haematology'. The room was empty, but sensors noted our entrance and the lights flicked on, illuminating rows of lab benches, large fridges and filing cabinets. Joe pushed me behind a bench, and we crouched down. Moments later the door opened. We heard Sheena's voice.

'Lights on, what a waste.'

A male voice next to her mumbled something indistinguishable and she laughed. There was a click and the room plunged into darkness. The door closed. Joe and I slumped, breathing heavily.

'Come on,' he said, scrambling to his feet. 'We gotta go.'

'Where? How?'

'Just follow me.'

The moment we moved, the motion sensors triggered, and the lights came on. Joe turned them off and we exited into the now empty stairwell. Joe began to climb the stairs.

'Joe, that way's locked,' I advised. 'We've got to go down.'

He shook his head and ran up the steps. For a big man, he was surprisingly nimble. Exasperated, I followed. We were wasting valuable time. But as we reached the top, he broke into a big grin. The door was ajar. Something small and pink propped it open. A sanitary towel in its plastic wrapper, casually dropped, just stopping the door.

'Clever girl,' said Joe. 'Even if he'd seen her drop it he'd probably be too embarrassed to say anything.'

He picked up the pink envelope and tossed it to me. I gave him a puzzled glance.

'What?' He smiled. 'I don't need it.'

We entered the empty changing hut, moved cautiously to the door and went into the night. The base was deserted, and there was no sign of Sheena. As we crossed the ground, I shivered, and not just because of the cold. I couldn't shake the taint of death and kept visualising all those bodies in their cold storage bags, deep beneath our feet.

'You OK?' Joe asked.

I nodded. 'Let's get out of here.'

Joe scanned our position. We were huddled in deep shadow by the women's changing hut. The neighbouring buildings were also in darkness. Just one, three along to our right, glowed yellow behind standard-issue blinds.

'Sheena's car,' whispered Joe, pointing at the Volvo parked in a puddle of light, fifty metres ahead of us.

'Can you hotwire it?'

'Er, this is 2017,' said Joe. 'Go near it and we're talking immobiliser, alarm and a platoon of soldiers.'

'What's the plan then?'

'Well, we need to get the keys.'

I pulled out my phone and texted Sheena. A moment later a text pinged back. *Stuck in meeting. One hour.*

He jerked his head behind him. 'You nip in there and go through Sheena's stuff. If she's got them on her then we'll need plan B.'

'Which is?'

'Let's try plan A first,' he replied.

I took a deep breath and crawled round the side of the building. I paused to listen but could hear little above the hammering of my heart. This place gave me the creeps. I edged to the door, staying low. All was quiet. I pushed it open and moved in quickly. I soon found Sheena's locker and rifled through her stuff. I was relieved to discover the car key in Sheena's handbag. I was about to pull open the door and run across to Joe, when I heard the ring of boots on concrete and low voices talking. I shrank back and locked myself in one of the toilet cubicles. The door to the hut opened.

'That's what Connors told us, anyway,' a male voice said. 'I'm just sick of it.'

Another voice answered but was indistinguishable.

'Just checking it now.'

Footsteps scuffed across the changing room. I held my breath.

'Nah, no one in here. You'd think they'd keep it tidy. There's only three of 'em.'

The other voice spoke again and the man laughed.

'You filthy sod. I'm not touching anything.'

The footsteps clumped away, the lights went off and the door closed. I took a moment to calm myself. I counted to twenty, then slipped across the dark changing room and out into the night. I found Joe where I'd left him and held up the key in triumph.

'That was close,' he observed.

I noticed he was holding a brick. 'What were you going to do with that?'

He simply raised his eyebrows and scrabbled to his feet. 'Come on.'

We kept to the shadows all the way to the edge of the car park. Joe pressed the button on the key fob and the indicators winked. He started the engine, and we headed back the way we'd come, following the paved road that cut across the empty parkland. Joe kept the lights off. It was like driving into a wall of blackness. Every moment I expected to see Jeeps race up behind us, or helicopters loom out of the dark sky.

'You've watched too many films,' said Joe, when I shared my thoughts. 'No one's expecting anyone to bust out. They're guarding corpses. They're worried about people breaking in.'

'But why, Joe? Why were those people in there, those kids?'

He shook his head, as though trying to shake the image of those bodies from his mind. 'I don't know. Look.'

The fence was now in sight. Joe pulled up by the heavy gate. There was a small metal bollard by the side of the road, with a keypad, speaker and card reader.

'Fuck. What do we do?'

'I don't know,' Joe admitted, tapping the steering wheel in frustration.

'I have an idea,' I offered.

I texted Sheena. A reply pinged back within seconds. *Still stuck in meeting, so go ahead. Gate staff won't know. Tell Alan to drive the car back down and wait in the car park for me after the gate guards go off duty at 6:00 AM.*

I opened the driver's window, leant across Joe and pressed the button to activate the speaker. I heard the sound of a buzzer ringing somewhere distant.

'Julia, this is a fucking bad idea,' hissed Joe, trying to haul me back into the car.

The speaker crackled into life.

'Yeah?' drawled a voice.

'It's Sheena. My card won't swipe.' I focused, trying to recall the way Sheena spoke.

'What the fuck, Konsta.'

'Just buzz me out.'

'What? You're on duty.'

'I forgot something. Really need it. Personal. Women's stuff.'

There was some mumbling, then: 'Make it quick, Konsta.'

And with that the gate swung open. Joe gunned the accelerator and we sped into the darkness with the cold air whipping through the open window. We raced up the lane and wound into the dark woods, until we pulled up next to our van. Joe called Alan and told him he needed to drive Sheena's Volvo back onto the base after 6:00 AM and wait for her to finish her shift.

'What's going on?' he asked. 'Where's Sheena?'

'We got separated,' Joe explained as we climbed into the van. 'Had to borrow her car to get out.'

'Is she alright?' asked Konsta.

'She's fine. Her car's parked in that layby in the woods.'

'Joe, what the fuck? What did you find in there?'

Joe paused. 'Better you don't know. And I hope Sheena doesn't either. It ain't good, mate.'

He ended the call, started the engine and drove into the thickening fog, which swallowed the van in its clammy, white embrace.

49

JOE KEPT fiddling with the radio. I ground my teeth in irritation. Both of us were on edge.

'Just leave it,' I implored, as his hand reached to retune it again.

'I think we should take a break,' he said. 'I'm bushed.'

I was too wired to rest, but since it wasn't my van and I wasn't driving I didn't have much say. We pulled into a petrol station and Joe filled up. He bought us greasy microwave sausage rolls, chocolate bars and sugary teas. We ate in silence and watched cars emerge from the fog and then disappear.

'Where do we go with this?' asked Joe. 'There's no story until we know what happened and why those people are in a military mortuary.'

'We need to go back to Fox. He obviously knows more than he's saying.'

'If he's still alive,' said Joe gloomily. 'He's a loose end.'

I thought about Fox, drinking himself into oblivion every night with the gun by his side. I'd thought him a suicide risk but maybe the gun was protection against the people who kept their secrets hidden in Mortuary 4. I pulled out my phone and emailed Lyndsey. *I've got something in my Dropbox. Please make copies and keep them somewhere safe. Be in touch soon.*

'At the moment, no one knows we know,' I observed. 'They think I'm still at home, licking my wounds from the fake dossier and the police investigation. It gives us an edge. A small one, but I've worked with less. If he's still alive, we need to get to Fox before they do.'

'You've perked up,' Joe said. He started the engine and turned the demister up to maximum.

'It's the sausage roll,' I replied. 'I'm buzzing on chemicals and gristle.'

'I'll make a note to keep you fuelled with both.' Joe smiled and pulled onto the dual carriageway. 'So, where to?'

'North,' I said. 'To find a fox in his hole.'

It felt good to have a plan. We faced a long drive, but the roads were clear, and the van ate up the miles. I emailed Emilia to tell her that I would be away another day and night. I tried not to think about my sister's disapproval and my son's disappointment.

I'm doing it for you, Alex, was my silent prayer. *To keep you safe, to keep me sane, to keep us together. I'm doing it for you*. But I found myself wondering whether it was the truth. A better mother would have given up, backed down and surrendered her ideals for the safety of her child. But there were no guarantees they would ever let me walk away. Social services were out to get me, and the only way to prove them wrong was to break the case and demonstrate that I wasn't crazy. If he ever had cause to judge, I hoped Alex would understand my choices when he was older.

We swapped over somewhere around Birmingham, and I was happy to be behind the wheel while Joe nodded off next to me. I pulled off the M6 just before dawn. The skies over north Shropshire were clearing. A mist lay on the hills and a lone heron glided over a flooded field. I felt my heart lift at the sight and thought about leaving London. *Wouldn't this be a better place for Alex to grow up?*

When we reached Ashley, I parked by the church again and nudged Joe awake.

'We walk from here.'

We headed up the narrow hill to Fox's house. The air was wet and thick with the smell of farms, animals and muck.

'Fragrant,' Joe noted.

'I want to bottle it and take it home,' I replied.

'Eau de manure,' said Joe. 'I'll pass.'

We crunched across the weed-strewn gravel around Fox's house. The place looked as shut up and rundown as it had on my last visit. I led Joe behind the house, and we peered through the kitchen windows.

'Needs a woman's touch,' said Joe, noting the mess.

He was rewarded with a shower of raindrops as I shook a wet blossom branch over his head.

We knocked on the door but there was no answer. Joe walked round the side and climbed on a bin to peer in through a window.

'I can get in here,' he said, rattling the window, which showered me with flakes of paint and chips of rotting wood.

'Shh,' I cautioned. I could hear footsteps on the gravelled driveway.

It was an old woman, in brown trousers and a thick lilac jumper. She leant heavily on a stick.

'We've got company,' I advised.

Joe jumped down and the pair of us walked round to greet the new arrival.

'Can I help you?' the old woman called, peering at us.

'We're looking for Ivan Fox,' I said. 'But he doesn't appear to be in.'

'He's away at the moment. Asked me to watch his cat for him.'

'Do you know where he is? I saw him a week ago and he didn't mention he was going anywhere.'

'Friends are you, dear?'

'Yes, I wanted to check on him. I know he was still upset about his parents.'

'Oh yes, he's had a tough time. Lovely family, they were. Lot of happy memories here. He and my daughter were the best of pals, always in and out of one another's houses. But then he heads off and travels the world. My girl married the farmer up the lane. Real homebody that one.'

'You're very lucky.' I threw the woman a friendly smile.

'Sad to see the place looking so rundown. Lily used to be very proud of her garden. She and John really missed Ivan when he moved down south.' The old woman plucked some weeds that had overtaken a potted rosebush. 'It's very nice you're all coming to check on him. I suppose army people stick together, don't they?'

'Has someone else been here?' asked Joe.

'Couple of army pals looking for him.'

'Did you get their names?'

'No, sorry, dear. But I'll tell you what I told them. He headed off, said he had some things he had to put right. Truth be told, I think he was a bit of a mess. Felt very guilty not to be here when his dad passed.'

I pulled out one of my cards and gave it to the woman. 'If he comes back, would you call me?' I asked. 'I'm worried about him.'

'Haven't got my glasses on, dear,' she said, squinting at the card. 'I'll put it up safe for when he comes back. But I don't think it will be too soon. He left me two hundred pounds for the cat, and that's a lot of Whiskers, isn't it?'

She crunched back down the drive towards her own house.

'Looks like a dead end. I reckon he's gone to ground,' said Joe. 'If he's any good, we'll be lucky to find him now. And if we can, there's a good chance whoever's after him will get there first.'

I thought back to my encounter with Fox, recalling his haunted eyes, his guilt, his anger.

'He was drinking heavily. It makes people sloppy.'

Joe nodded and walked round the shut-up house. He clambered onto the bin and pulled a screwdriver out of his coat pocket to jemmy open the rotten window. He grunted and puffed as he hauled himself in and landed with a thud inside. I looked around guiltily but there was no sign of the old woman. Just a deafening chorus of birdsong. Then the backdoor opened and Joe beckoned me inside.

50

FOX HADN'T made any effort to clear up before he left. The place was a tip of papers and unwashed crockery, and a cloud of flies rose from a bowl of rotting cat food. Cornflakes and a smashed glass crunched underfoot. The AGA was out and the place smelt damp. I noted there was no sign of the gun.

'Here,' said Joe.

I followed his voice into the living room. It looked as though it had been hit by a hurricane. Cushions had been pulled off the sofas, books and magazines were strewn across the floor and picture frames smashed.

'Was it this bad before?'

I shook my head. 'No, someone's been here.'

Every room was the same. The disarray of a hurried search. I glanced round the bedroom I'd slept in. Amid the chaos – the bed stripped, the mattress upended, the chest of drawers violated – I noted the rucksack was gone. Fox had been ready to flee, but where?

Finding nothing, we left the house and trudged down the lane. I was suddenly bone tired. The trail was cold, and my adrenaline was ebbing away.

'I need food, and a kip,' said Joe.

'Yeah,' I agreed, climbing into the van.

A tractor and trailer thundered past us, spewing bits of hay across the lane. I thought idly how excited Alex would be to see the rumbling vehicle so close. I glanced up and glimpsed a head of golden curls and a pink fleece.

'Follow that tractor!'

'What? Why?' Joe asked. But already he was reversing the van into a gateway and turned to follow the tractor back up the hill.

'I want to speak to the driver. Quick, Joe.'

'It's a tractor, Julia, we don't need to be quick.'

We followed it past Fox's house, up the lane and along a narrow track to a modern farmhouse that was dwarfed by vast cowsheds. The tractor stopped by a barn, and the blonde woman in the pink fleece climbed down from the cab.

'Fox's childhood friend,' I noted triumphantly. 'The homebody.'

Joe shrugged. We got out of the van, attracting the attention of a sheepdog and a couple of Jack Russells, who yapped and darted round our feet. The woman called off the dogs and strode over. She was about the same age as Fox and her cheeks were rosy from a morning of fresh air and hard work. She had an easy, athletic stride and splashed across the muddy farmyard in her green wellies.

'Can I help you?'

'We're looking for Ivan Fox,' I replied. 'I was hoping you might know where he's gone.'

The woman's face darkened. 'Who are you?'

I thought about lying but sensed this woman would respond better to the truth. 'My name's Julia Castleton. I'm a journalist. I was talking to Ivan about a story I'm working on, to do with a friend of his, an army medic named Michael Wilmore.'

The woman shoved her hands in her pockets and planted her feet apart. Her green eyes levelled on me, and she waited for the story to continue. She looked like she could stand there all day and reminded me of an oak tree, enduring and unshakeable.

'Wilmore contacted me, said he had a big story. Something to do with the army, but he didn't live to share it. I think he was murdered.'

The woman's eyes didn't flicker.

'I met Ivan at Wilmore's funeral, and when I visited him, he started to open up to me, but now he's gone too. I'm worried about him.'

'You're the woman who stayed the night?'

I registered the funny look Joe gave me.

'He was off his face; I waited until he sobered up enough to talk.' I blushed, suddenly defensive. 'Nothing happened.'

'Yes, it did,' the woman countered. 'You stole his cartridges.'

'I was worried about his state of mind.'

The woman laughed. It was like the sun coming out. Her blonde curls danced, and her eyes shone. 'He's prone to being a miserable git when he gets drunk. Best to ignore him. Stealing his cartridges just gave him something else to complain about.' She laughed again.

'Do you know where he is now? Your mum said he'd gone away to put things right.'

The woman rolled her eyes. 'No secrets round here.' She chewed her lip thoughtfully. 'There's been people asking about him, watching the place. I know he was worried, scared even. I don't think I should say any more. You could be anyone.'

'Have you got the paper?' I asked. '*Sunday Times*? Open it up and you'll see my face in there. I've been dragged through the mud trying to find out what happened to Wilmore in Syria. They're trying to take my son away.' I felt the hysteria rising and shut up quickly. I couldn't talk about Alex's care assessment without being swept away by hot panic.

Joe reached over and squeezed my hand.

'Julia Castleton,' he repeated to the farmer. 'Look her up. She's not trying to hurt Ivan. She just needs his help.'

The farmer put her head on one side and eyed me as though she was judging a prize bull. 'He liked you,' she said at last. 'Maybe it was the drink, but he said he'd wished he'd been more helpful when he'd had the chance. Anyway, you made him think. He packed up the next day and headed off to help a charity he knew that's organising a convoy to Syria, you know, humanitarian stuff.'

'Do you know which charity?'

'Rebuild Syria. Got a depot in Warrington. He felt bad about what he'd seen out there and said he needed to keep busy. He's like me; I can't be doing nothing, it's not healthy. Speaking of which' – she checked her watch – 'I've got to get going. We got lambs dropping every five minutes and these cows don't feed themselves.'

We said our goodbyes and the woman strode across the farmyard with the dogs trotting at her heels.

'You stole his cartridges?' Joe asked as we climbed into the van.

I didn't say anything; I was already looking up the charity on my phone. It had been established about two years into the conflict by exiled Syrian doctors and engineers horrified at the destruction of their country. It seemed a bona fide outfit. An injured British colonel who had made a bit of a name for himself in the Paralympics was a trustee, as was an MP. I saw their latest campaign was to rebuild a village called *Al Hijjnah*, which had been reduced to rubble following desperate fighting between government forces and ISIS.

I glanced up as we drove past Fox's house. I wondered if he'd ever be back. It seemed a shame to let a family home in such a beautiful spot sit empty. Weeds would choke the garden and damp would rot the house. As before, I had the feeling of being watched, and scanned our surroundings. The windows were blank and unseeing, and the lane was empty apart from a few cars parked by the church.

Joe fiddled with the sat nav. 'About an hour to Warrington,' he said. 'But then we need to get some sleep.'

I nodded. I could already feel the flutter of paranoia, the hyper-alertness, the jittery energy of the hunt that was so seductive but so, so dangerous. And I was down to my last pill. I needed an appointment to pick up a repeat prescription. I pressed my fingers over my eyeballs. Thinking of home made me picture Alex, and I missed him so much.

'Let's go,' I said. 'Let's drill Fox for what he knows, sleep a couple of hours and then head home. I have to see Alex.'

51

IT WAS the diversion that saved us. Had he joined the M6 at Junction 15, Joe would never have noticed. But a lorry had overturned, blocking the slip road, forcing us on a long-winded diversion to Junction 16. And the grey BMW, which he later told me he'd first spotted parked by the church in Ashley, was there, always lurking one or two cars behind. Motorways made for easy tailing. Country roads required a team working in rotation and whoever was following us didn't have such resources to hand.

Joe glanced at me. I hadn't noticed the pursuing car and he later told me he didn't want to worry me. The strain of the past few days must have been written on my face and made him treat me with kid gloves.

He pulled into a garage, and I stretched while he filled up with petrol. I didn't realise at the time that he was watching the BMW slide by. He bought us supplies – croissants, sandwiches, muffins, cold cans and hot drinks – and we hit the road again. Two miles along, and the BMW emerged from a side road and coasted three cars behind us.

We were a couple of miles from the motorway when Joe took a sudden left onto a small industrial estate.

'Woah,' I said as my drink sploshed onto my hand.

'We've got company,' Joe revealed.

I glanced in the mirror.

'Been with us since Ashley,' he remarked. 'I'll see if we can lose them.'

He did a circuit of the industrial estate. It was empty apart from a couple of lorries, and the deserted streets exposed the BMW. There were two men in the car, and I had little doubt they'd realised they'd been made. The driver was black, the passenger small and pale, but I couldn't make out their features. It was difficult to be sure, but Joe was certain they were two of Newby's pals, the ones he'd seen on the NADC photos, the ones who'd pulled the stunt at Wilmore's funeral and abducted Julia. The ones who were supposed to be dead.

'Recognise them?' he asked as he stamped on the brakes so that the BMW was caught out and drew up behind us.

I peered in the wing mirror. 'Can't see well enough,' I replied. 'Not really.'

'They've obviously been staking out Fox's place, waiting for you,' Joe said. 'Or him.'

He stepped on the accelerator and the van lurched forwards. The BMW matched us. The driver was no longer making any attempt to conceal the tail. Within minutes, the van was back on the country road, taking the sharp bends at speeds way past the limit. But there'd be no outrunning them. The BMW was a monster.

'Plan?' I asked anxiously.

'I don't want to lead them to Fox,' he said. 'I'll try to lose them.'

He took the next right. We were no longer heading for the M6. My heart raced as he looped south and turned onto another road that snaked through a sleepy village. The road led us back into open countryside. The BMW glided implacably onwards, never letting us get too far in front. Joe glanced at the sat nav.

'Hold on,' he muttered.

At the next bend, he floored the accelerator and the van shot forward. I lost sight of the BMW in the wing mirror, and while the curve of the road concealed us, Joe killed the lights, spun the wheel sharply and took a hairpin left down a narrow lane into a thickly wooded area.

I glanced in the rear-view mirror and saw the BMW race past.

'That will buy us a couple of minutes at most,' Joe said.

He pressed the accelerator, and I was thrown around in my seat as he drove recklessly fast down the twisting track. We sped through a wood, and branches clawed at the sides of the van. The lane spat us out at a T-junction. Joe took a right, then another left.

'Every turn forces them to guess,' he said, 'and every wrong guess buys us time.'

Joe made another turn onto a narrow lane and a tractor pulled out ahead of us suddenly. Its high lights blazed like those of an alien craft and it rolled along slowly, filling the lane. There were no passing points. Joe hit the horn in frustration, but the farmer either didn't care or was oblivious. The sat nav showed another mile until the lane branched off.

'Shit,' he said.

I glanced at Joe nervously and he put the van into reverse and drove backwards down the lane recklessly fast. When we reached the junction, he swung the van round and sped back the way we'd come. We rounded a bend and as the road straightened, I saw the BMW coming towards us.

'Brace!' Joe yelled, and rather than brake, he stepped on the accelerator.

The two vehicles gobbled up the road and I gasped as they closed in on one another.

Joe held steady and didn't blink as the tarmac disappeared between us.

'Joe,' I exclaimed involuntarily.

The BMW driver chickened out and twisted the saloon into the hedgerow to avoid a head-on collision. There was a sickening crunch as the front of the van smashed into the rear flank of the car, grinding metal on metal.

I saw the airbags pop in the grey car, and Joe leapt from the cab and ran to the front of the BMW, where the driver, a bull of a man, with a crew cut and tattooed knuckles, was momentarily dazed. The air was thick with powder from the airbags.

Joe yanked open the door, just as the driver yelled to his passenger, a wiry, pinched man with a scar down one cheek, 'Get the girl!'

Joe leant in and landed a sharp jab on the driver's jaw. The driver, still wrestling with his locked seatbelt, attempted to fight back and landed a useful punch to the gut, momentarily winding Joe. This gave the driver time to release his seatbelt and swing round to kick Joe, his leg like a jackhammer, landing a savage blow just above the knee.

Scarface was out now, a gun in one hand, heading straight for me. I popped my seatbelt and jumped out of the van.

As Joe kicked the BMW driver in the face, dazing him and sending him reeling back into the car, I ran round the van and opened the back door. Scarface was almost on me, and I reached into the van instinctively. I grabbed a wrench from a pocket where Joe kept his tools and swung it round as the man raised his gun at me. The heavy metal wrench caught Scarface on his left cheek, and he went down hard.

I looked across to see Joe repeatedly slam the BMW's heavy door on the driver's leg until he was sure the guy was incapacitated. The man's howls became whimpers as he veered dangerously close to losing consciousness.

'Julia,' yelled Joe.

He ran over to me and registered Scarface lying at my feet, a handgun by his motionless hand.

'Nice work,' Joe said.

I dropped the wrench, and doubled over, hands on my knees, breathing deeply.

'Is he dead?' I whispered.

Joe crouched down and put his hand to the man's jugular. 'No. He'll live.'

Joe patted the man down and pulled out a wallet stuffed with cash. There were no cards and no ID. This guy was a pro. Joe put the man's phone in his pocket, then pulled down his sleeve to cover his hand and he picked up the gun.

'What are you going to do with that?' I asked suspiciously.

'Evidence,' said Joe. 'He's not wearing gloves.'

Joe dragged the unconscious man to the other side of the BMW and rolled him into the hedgerow. Joe was panting heavily now, and sweat ran down his back. I was shaking violently. It was shock. When we got into the van, Joe handed me a can of Coke.

'Drink,' he ordered.

He returned to the wrecked BMW. The driver was sweating with the pain of his crushed leg, but he still managed to fix Joe with a sneer.

'Don't bother asking,' he said. 'I'm not telling you anything.'

Joe shrugged and gave the door another vicious boot. The man cried out and, momentarily stunned by the wave of pain, his head lolled onto his chest.

'You don't need to tell me anything, pal,' Joe said. 'You just have to smile for the camera.'

He lifted the man's chin and took a photo of his sickly opponent, then walked round and took one of Scarface, lying in the hedge.

'Facial recognition technology is a wonderful thing,' he remarked to me. 'I'm sending these to my associate.'

I assumed he meant Sam.

He took a knife from his tool bag and slashed the tyres on the BMW. Then he reached in, took the keys from the ignition, and threw them over the hedge into the field beyond.

'Let's go,' he called to me. Then, speaking loudly, 'We'll catch Fox at Heathrow.'

He got into the van and reversed. Once we were clear of the scene, he floored it through the lanes. Neither of us spoke for a while.

I looked down at my hands and saw they were trembling.

'Pull over,' I said.

He stopped the van, and I jumped down and retched in a hedgerow. After a minute or so, I climbed back into my seat.

'Alright?' he asked.

I nodded, but I didn't feel alright.

When we reached the road that led to the M6, Joe put his foot down.

'Heathrow?' I asked at last.

'A little misdirection for the benefit of the guy in the car.'

'And the other one? You're sure?'

'I checked his pulse. Strong and regular. He'll be fine. Bit of a headache, but fine.'

'It was instinct. I lashed out and he just went down. I didn't think I'd hit him that hard.'

I groaned and hugged my arms tight round my body.

'He had a gun, Jules; you had no choice. Seriously, you did the right thing,' Joe said. 'Jules, listen to me. What are you going to tell Alex when he grows up? Don't fight back? Just stand there and let the bully hit you. Just stand there and let them shoot you, kidnap you, rape you. Just turn the other cheek? No, you're going to tell him to fight back, to protect himself, to keep himself safe because he matters. And it's the same for you. You matter. You're a mother. You couldn't have stood there and let that thug come at you. You did the right thing, the only thing you could do.'

I nodded slowly.

We hit the M6 and were soon sandwiched between two huge trucks heading north.

Joe reached into his pocket and produced the phone he'd taken from Scarface.

'This thing has buzzed a couple of times,' he said, handing it to me.

I checked the screen and saw messages from someone called DB. I wondered who DB was, and what he'd think when he couldn't reach Scarface. A call came in from DB and went to voicemail when I didn't answer. It rang again five minutes later, and then buzzed with another text from DB. *Any news? We need an update asap.*

I pondered the 'we'. How many people were in on this thing? And what was it they were in on?

I needed answers. We had to find Fox and persuade him to tell us the truth.

52

REBUILD SYRIA had a tatty warehouse on the edges of an industrial estate just outside Warrington. One side was like a vast jumble sale. Piles of shoes. A tower of folded blankets. A huge plastic skip marked 'Winter Coats'. In the middle, there were teams of people picking and sorting the items. A man in a high vis jacket and blue plastic gloves was sifting through a jumble of underwear. On the other side, the chaos had been ordered. Cardboard boxes lined with green plastic were being taped shut and stacked to make a neat wall. Each box had a list of its contents; everyday items from long johns to jumpers, socks to nappies, things that would help someone on the other side of the world survive another day.

A harassed-looking woman in trainers and a hijab approached Joe and me. A walkie talkie crackled in her hand.

'Greenbelt Pharma?' she asked hopefully.

We shook our heads, and she swore.

'We've been promised a shipment of meds before we fly,' she explained, checking her watch. 'They're cutting it fine.'

'We're looking for someone,' I said. 'Ivan Fox.'

'In the office,' the woman said. 'The paperwork is eyewatering.'

The office was a converted shipping container at the back of the warehouse. Inside there were two cheap plywood desks, a row of plastic chairs and corkboards covered with newspaper clippings that highlighted the charity's fundraising successes.

Fox was sitting at a paper-strewn desk, filling in forms. He looked up, took a moment to register me and stiffened, at once wary.

'What are you doing here?' He looked – and smelt – better than he had at our last encounter. His eyes were clear, his clothes washed, and the bruises faded.

'I went to Lockmere,' I said.

The dark eyes registered a flicker of surprise, possibly admiration. Fox looked at Joe. 'Who's the brawn?'

Joe stretched out his hand. 'Joe Turner. PI. I'm helping Julia on this case.'

The two men shook.

Joe nodded at the paperwork, Fox's passport and the rucksack by the side of the desk. 'You going somewhere?'

'I'm on the RS aid flight tomorrow. We're distributing care packages to *Al Hijjnah*.' He looked away, unsettled. 'You ever hear of it?'

We shook our heads.

'Doesn't surprise me. Just one more tragedy. It only matters if you were there. If you saw…' His voice caught, and he trailed off.

'Is that where you and Wilmore were deployed?' I prompted.

Fox didn't answer. He seemed lost in thought. When he spoke, it was as if he was talking to himself. 'I never set out to be a coward, but I let Michael carry the load. I should've said something, backed him up. But you can't change the past, only the future, right?'

He stood up abruptly and led us to a small circle of scuffed plastic chairs. In the centre stood a coffee table that was covered with tea-making paraphernalia. Used teabags stewed in a saucer and discarded spoons were crusted with sugar. Fox made us cups of weak tea and gestured for us to sit.

I pulled out a notebook. 'Can I?' I asked.

Fox shrugged. 'We were a new unit. Remember, Parliament voted against British involvement, but it'd become very clear that the situation in Syria was a whole new level of humanitarian crisis. There was clear evidence of chemical weapons attacks on civilians. There were mass graves. Women, girls, rounded up and sold in slave auctions. We were deployed with a purely humanitarian mandate. We were equipped to respond quickly and effectively. Nobody does it better than the British Army. We had shelters, water supply, latrines, medics when they could reach us. We started to clear *Al Hijjnah* of booby traps and rebuild what we could, which wasn't much. It's hard work, but satisfying, right? You can see the difference you're making.'

He lapsed into silence again, lost in memories, the pain etched on his face. A phone buzzed in Joe's pocket, and I frowned at the distraction. I didn't want to give Fox any reason to clam up. But if he registered the device, he didn't react to it.

'We worked well, especially if you consider we were a new team, a handful of guys I knew from previous deployments, but most were strangers. I hadn't met Wilmore before, but I liked him. He was a good laugh, and even though he was a doctor he wasn't afraid to get stuck in on some of the manual stuff as well. And he clearly cared, did a good job with some of the kids who were very traumatised. I didn't know Newby. He and his team were attached to our unit, but they were private contractors, all ex-military. He had four under his command. I was told they were working on a research project for DSTL.'

'The Defence Science and Technology Laboratory, right?' I confirmed.

Fox nodded. 'Something to do with checking for radioactive isotopes and chemical markers in the water supply. He gave me a scientific paper explaining what they were looking for and what they'd be doing but I didn't pay too much attention. I mean, everyone was worried about the use of chemical weapons and nerve agents. I was just glad they were collecting evidence and left them to it.'

He balled his hand into a fist.

'Big regret,' he said. 'I wish I'd been watching more closely. Newby and his men stayed away from the rest of us. They went off on missions. Sometimes they'd be gone two or three days. They were focused on a small area in the foothills, east of where we were, something to do with the water tables. I should have kept on top of it but, truth be told, I didn't like him. He was so' – he grasped for the right word – 'so slick, so glib. False somehow. A career man, not an army man, if that makes sense.'

I nodded.

'Anyway, I was glad he was out of my way.'

'What were the names of his team?'

'Karl Lazard, Peter Dunn, Dalton Brown, Brian Hinstock.'

I wrote the names in my notebook.

'What do you think he was really up to?'

Fox shrugged. 'It was Wilmore who raised it. He got first-hand exposure to casualties and noticed a spike in deaths of civilians centred around a little village east of *Al Hijjnah*.'

'Where Newby was working?'

Fox nodded. 'Their deaths weren't consistent with military operations. I mean, there were no signs of trauma. It wasn't explosion or shrapnel or sniper fire. Or any of the more medieval methods favoured by the militants.'

'Poison? Nerve agents?' asked Joe.

'Not that Wilmore could detect. He was worried. He said it was like these people had been perfectly healthy – well, not perfectly, they were malnourished, stressed, lacked access to medicines for chronic conditions – but well enough, you know, considering the circumstances, and one day they just dropped dead.'

'What did Wilmore think it was?'

'He didn't know, but he didn't like it. When Newby got the order to ship the civilians from *Al Hijjnah* back home, to Lockmere, I knew something was really wrong. Civilians don't get sent to Lockmere.' He hesitated. 'I raised it up the chain of command, but it was just ignored. I mean, they were dealing with a shit storm over there. And wherever Newby's orders came from, they trumped my CO. But I couldn't just leave it, so I ordered Wilmore to perform an autopsy on two of the bodies. Newby and his unit were off doing whatever they were doing, and he and his team were being shipped out the next day along with the bodies. The autopsies weren't authorised and were a violation of those people's religious views, I know that, but it was my watch.' He slammed his balled fist onto his knee to emphasise these last words. 'My watch. And civilians were falling down dead. We did it at night. Just me and Wilmore. No one else knew. It was horrible, I mean, horrible. I've never witnessed anything like it. One of them was a child.'

He trailed into silence and Joe and I shared a glance. I'd seen the bodies in Lockmere and could only imagine the horror of undertaking an autopsy in secret.

'There was nothing,' said Fox. 'According to Wilmore, everything looked normal, healthy.'

I felt deflated. *Nothing?*

'And then he cut into the brain.' Fox ran his hand over his face, as if he could wipe the memories clean.

I held my breath.

'He found what he called microscopic contaminants in the brain tissue. He couldn't explain in any more detail. He didn't have the kit out there.'

'Microscopic contaminants?' echoed Joe. 'What does that mean?'

Fox shook his head. 'I don't know. But whatever it was, I believe it killed those people. And Newby knew.'

'Did you tell him what you'd found?' I asked.

Fox laughed hollowly. 'No. Me and Wilmore were fucking terrified. Whatever it was, it killed those people instantly. Cleanly. Invisibly. The perfect weapon. We didn't say a word to anyone.'

'Then why did they kill Wilmore?'

'When they got the bodies back to Lockmere they must have realised Wilmore had done those autopsies. I mean there's no hiding it, it's fucking brutal. He used a saw, you know…' Fox downed his tea and lobbed the empty cup into the bin. 'And when he went AWOL, they knew he'd found something. Poor sod, it was only a matter of time.'

I chewed my pen top. 'So only you and Wilmore knew. And he's dead.'

Fox grimaced. 'And I'm going to Syria. Rather take my chances there than hang around waiting for them to find me here.'

'Let me record this,' I said. 'Names, dates, places. Everything. Make it public, put it out there. Then you'll be safe and we'll nail them.'

Fox laughed hollowly. 'Is that what Newby said when he gave you that folder about the arms sales?' I blushed, and he nodded grimly. 'These people are pros, and they're clearly protected at the highest levels. No disrespect but I'm afraid your little website isn't going to make any difference to them.'

I threw down my pad and pen. 'So that's it then? You go off to martyr yourself in Syria and they get away with it. There's nobody to hold them to account for all those deaths, nobody to stop them doing it again.' I pushed back my chair and paced the little office angrily. 'It makes me sick. I'm so sick of bad people fucking it up for the rest of us! Aren't you mad? How can you just walk away?'

Fox eyed me, his black eyes glittering. 'Though she be but little, she is fierce,' he said, looking at Joe. 'She always like this?'

Joe nodded. 'She's only just warming up. She won't let this go.'

'Then you'd better know something else.' He hesitated. 'Wilmore kept a sample of that brain tissue. I don't know what he did with it but he had it with him when he left Syria. He said it needed a specialist microscope. A transmission electron microscope. Find that sample and you'll find out what happened to those poor people.'

53

WE PARKED up in a quiet layby on a country lane outside Knutsford. Joe climbed into the back of the van and unfurled a pair of camping mats. I joined him and we wrapped ourselves in sleeping bags that smelt of engine oil and too many takeaways. A heavy vehicle rumbled past and the van rocked, like some crazed cradle. It had been many years since I had bunked with anyone other than my son. I lay with my back to Joe and my nerves jangled. Every single sense was hyperalert to the presence of another person.

'Julia, you're fidgeting,' mumbled Joe. 'Go to sleep.'

His tone was reassuringly matter of fact. He didn't regard this as a big deal and neither would I. Eventually, I relaxed and fell into a deep sleep.

She tumbled through dream worlds, dark halls, long corridors, a field. She was in an empty house, looking for somebody. There was a noise in a great wardrobe. She knew she shouldn't open the wardrobe but her hands were out of her control. She must look. The wardrobe opened. The physical world flipped. Now a great wooden drawer in the bottom of the wardrobe was sliding towards her.

A long bag. A body bag. She pulled at the zip. The Tattooed Man, his eyes shut, a peaceful smile drawn on his motionless face. Julia reached out a hand. If she touched him she would know this was real. Her fingers trembled like a butterfly's wings, and when they cast their shadow on his face, his eyes snapped open.

'Julia!'

The world shifted perspective. Suddenly he was behind her. It must be a dream, she told herself, but the voice in her ear echoed like a warning. She felt his hot breath, the pulsing ripple of his bunched muscles as his arm reached around her neck, the power and the hate of him suffocating her struggles to get free.

I woke to the sound of a scream. Was it real? Was it me?

'Julia, Julia, it's OK.' It was Joe.

He had his hand on my shoulder. I was in the van and the sleeping bag was twisted and knotted round my legs.

'You had a bad dream. You're safe. It's me.'

He murmured to me and stroked my hair, trying to soothe me. My breathing slowed and I returned to fitful slumber.

When I woke, the van door was open. I scrabbled upright, disorientated. It was two o'clock – we'd been asleep for almost four hours. Or was I still dreaming? My pulse was slow and steady. The plasters on my arm were loose. Underneath, the skin was white and clammy, the cuts red, a tally of fear and pain. I pressed the edges of the plasters down.

This is real, this is real.

'Sleeping Beauty awakes,' Joe interrupted me. 'There's a bush over there if you wish to avail yourself of the facilities before we hit the road.'

'Thanks.'

I was suddenly bashful. I knew I'd been dreaming, and he'd comforted me. I remembered the caress of his hand on my hair, those big hands surprisingly gentle. It felt wrong. We were battle-hardened investigators, friends, yes, but taciturn. Even after all these years I knew very little about his personal life. There was an ex-wife, and he'd had a partner, Trish, but I couldn't remember whether they were still together. I never asked Joe about his life. Ours wasn't that kind of relationship. And yet he knew pretty much all the grizzly details of my fucked-up existence.

I climbed into the cab, tied my greasy hair into a ponytail and swigged some water. I was sick of the van, with its detritus of food wrappers and coffee dregs, sick of my dirty clothes, my mossy unbrushed teeth, sick of the noisy rumble of the engine and the ache in my back from too many hours sitting down.

I pulled out my phone and texted Emilia. *Heading home. Can't wait to see my little man. Lots of love and hugs from Mummy xxx*

'Sam's been busy,' Joe said. 'The black guy is Karl Lazard. The one you knocked out is Peter Dunn.'

'Part of Newby's unit,' I remarked. I checked my notebook and confirmed those were two of the names Fox had given me.

The phone Joe had taken off Lazard buzzed. 'That's eight missed calls and a couple of texts,' said Joe. 'Someone's getting anxious.'

'DB.' I checked my notes. 'Could be Dalton Brown, another one of Newby's men.'

'They're going to be looking for us,' said Joe. 'I'd like to get the van off the road. It's too recognisable.'

'I have to be back in London tonight, Joe. I need to see Alex. And I've got a doctor's appointment.'

I didn't want to make a big deal of it. But it was a big deal. I no longer trusted my GP, but I had to go and play nice to keep the social workers sweet. I needed a check-up and a repeat prescription, the next stage in the seemingly never-ending tapering of my meds. I had thought the end was in sight. I'd dropped lithium and Zyprexa, which had made me fat and sluggish, and was reducing the Tegretol every six months. But the dreams, that voice in my ear, the obsessive counting and cutting...was it just stress, or did I need to up the Tegretol again? Yet how could I talk about this with my doctor now, knowing that social services might use it against me?

'What time?' Joe asked.

'Six-thirty.' I prayed he wouldn't probe any more.

'I'll get you there.'

'Thank you, Joe.'

We drove back to the motorway in silence, and I brooded about my illness. Was it coming back? It was hard to tell what was a symptom and what was a trigger. I was doing everything wrong. Not sleeping properly, getting stressed, angry, and isolating myself. I had to get a grip. If I relapsed, I'd lose Alex for sure.

'So,' said Joe, breaking into my thoughts. 'You're an Army Reservist, a GP by day, and you think you're in Syria helping people when you dig some, what did he call them, microscopic contaminants, out of some kid's brain. You're terrified. Where do you go? What do you do with that sample?'

I sat up and mentally shook myself. 'He didn't go home. He'd know it was being watched. And no one at the GP's practice even knew he was back from Syria, so he didn't go there. His dad hadn't seen him.'

'He must have known that sample was a death sentence,' said Joe. 'So where did he go? It wasn't on him when he died, so where did he hide it?'

I thought back to my brief conversation with Wilmore. He'd been in control, setting the terms of our meeting, taking sensible precautions to make sure we weren't followed. He knew his life was in danger but he wasn't gibbering with panic. He was a doctor. A man of science. And a humanitarian, who'd been deployed to help rebuild a ravaged country. At great personal risk, he contacted me and Ben Howells, to expose wrongdoing. Which meant he knew what that sample was. Not just a hunch, he *knew*.

'He got it tested,' I suggested. 'He knew what he had when he got in touch with me.'

'So where do you test a sample of illegally obtained brain tissue that you've smuggled into the country? Fox said it needed specialist equipment, so where does he go? It's not like you can just walk in off the street and start using state-of-the-art electron microscopes.'

'Someone he was at medical school with?' I suggested. 'Or a tutor? We know he was in Oxford. That's where he and Howells met.'

'Those colleges always track alumni,' Joe said. 'They're relentless at tapping them for donations. Should be quite easy to get a list of his former pals who have access to the right kind of equipment.'

Soon we were south of Warwick. Oxford was ahead. I felt a surge of excitement, the rollercoaster queasiness of a big story. The sample could be sitting in a lab less than forty miles away.

'Forget it,' said Joe, reading my mind. He kept his foot on the accelerator, and the van shot past the Oxford junction, heading relentlessly for London. 'You've got a hot date with your doc.'

I said nothing and rested my cheek against the window. My brain fizzed. Car lights flickered in the corner of my eye, shadows of clouds raced across green fields and a train sped by. The constant travel was destabilising, I told myself. I needed to be still, to feel the ground under my feet. We overtook a minibus, and the driver caught my eye, and winked. The gesture unnerved me. Was it a message? Did he know me? Had we met when I'd been on the street? The six missing months were more than a blank; they were a burden that tainted every subsequent moment of my life. I didn't know where I'd been, who I'd known or what I'd done. I counted my breath and felt my pulse.

'Joe,' I said.

'Mm.'

'Am I like I was? When you first knew me.'

'No.' He kept his eyes on the road. 'Why? You worried?'

'No.' I hesitated. I could only have this conversation with him, and only here in the van, while his eyes were on the road. 'Yes. Maybe. I have bad dreams. I worry about it happening again. Would you tell me if you saw the signs?'

'I haven't seen any signs, Julia. You're under a lot of stress. But I promise I haven't seen anything.'

'You would tell me?' I had to know. He was my security. 'I can't trust myself. I need to know you wouldn't let me go again.'

'I promise. I would tell you.'

I nodded, blinking back tears. I couldn't contain my relief. He would watch me. Protect me.

'Joe?'

'Yes?'

'When you found me, you know, was I with anyone?'

'Anyone? Like who?' His voice was carefully neutral as though we were discussing the weather.

'A man. A big man. Covered in tattoos. Inked all over. Black eyes.' I spoke quietly, as if my words would tempt some dark magic, that even to describe this dread creature would summon him and put flesh and bone on my half-remembered dreams.

Joe reached out and squeezed my hand. 'No,' he said firmly. 'No one like that. That was the worst thing, really; you were mostly alone then. But you're not alone now, Julia.'

I nodded, squeezed his hand and then let it go. The gesture was too intimate. Already I regretted opening up. I closed back in on myself and pressed my cheek against the window, realising his protection was worthless. He couldn't see inside my mind. He could only see what I let him see. It meant only I could protect myself. I couldn't rely on anyone else. I was truly alone.

54

IT WAS so good to wake in my own bed. Alex was already up, lying on the floor next to me, his pens all over the carpet.

'Don't look,' he said, cupping a hand over his artwork. I caught the words 'Luv Mummy' and smiled.

'I won't,' I said, and rolled back onto my pillow. I felt as though I could sleep for ever but instead, I stretched for my phone to check the time. Already the horror of the last two days was receding. Sleep, a hot shower and Alex had helped ground me. The meds had helped too. The evening GP had been a locum, so I'd escaped any potentially dangerous admissions. It would be unreasonable to launch into my worries with someone who didn't know my history. So I'd answered the GP's questions with bland platitudes, remembered to smile, made a joke as he took my bloods, and had then skipped out with another three months on my current dose. That in itself had lightened my mood. *See, nothing to worry about.* And it would look good for the care assessment. I was a responsible parent who kept my appointments and took my meds.

I tiptoed round Alex and went into the kitchen, where I shivered while I waited for the kettle to boil. I checked my emails on my phone. Emilia wanted to compare diaries for a weekend at Arlet. I ignored it and scrolled down. I needed to reply to Lyndsey, who was worried about a potential hack of our subscriber list and suggested we talk that night. And William Stone had been in touch. The police were dropping the offensive images charges, but another serious matter had come to light. Could he please see me today?

I suggested meeting after I'd dropped Alex at school and Stone replied immediately, saying he would pick me up at the school gates. I raised my eyebrows. Was he already in the area? I wouldn't put it past my father to get him to spy on me.

Alex burst in with felt tip on his school shirt. He thrust his homemade card at me. Two figures, one big, one small, floating against a backdrop of spiky green grass, and a little pink cat with spiky legs. Emilia had warned me that Alex had fallen in love with the Garonne household's latest addition, a bundle of grey fur called Grundle.

Deer Mummy, I mis you. I luv you. From Alex

I kissed him. 'I love you too, baby. It's so good to be back home. Now come on, let's get ready.'

I made scrambled eggs for breakfast, and we bundled out of the house for school. Alex was full of talk about Grundle.

'If we have a girl kitten, then she could marry Grundle and they could have babies,' he said. 'We could, couldn't we, Mummy?'

'But we don't have a garden.'

'Aunty Emilia says you can get house cats.'

'Does she,' I said dryly. 'I'm not sure it's fair to have a cat that can never go out to play.'

I saw his crestfallen face. This was where my commitment to truth was eroded. My love for my son, my urge not to crush his hopes, led me into twists and compromises, away from truth, into a vague greyness where his hopes could live on. 'Let me think about it. OK?'

He was mollified by this and trotted towards school quite happily. I glanced around anxiously as we neared the gate but there was no sign of Wayne Sloss or any of Chris Jones' sleazeball informants. Still, I kept my head down. Was that a disapproving look from the teacher? Were those mums whispering about me? When Alex was safely inside, I scanned the street, studiously avoiding eye contact with any other parents. It was a relief to see William Stone's Mercedes glide into a parking space across the road. I jogged over and got in beside him. The car smelt of leather, polish and cologne.

'Slumming it?' I asked.

He smiled faintly. 'You were on my way into town.'

I was going to ask about his wife, stuck down in the country, but the woman's name was lost to me. 'What's so urgent?'

'Good news about the images. They're claiming an administrative mix-up with someone else's laptop. There'll be a fulsome apology, of course, but you may decide to launch an official complaint. However, I would park that for now, keen as you may be for revenge on dear Mr Tull. Something else has cropped up.'

'What?' I asked anxiously.

'Your name has come up as a suspect in a hit and run.'

'What!' I burst out laughing. 'I don't even have a car.'

'It was in Cheshire,' said Stone. He was studying me closely and I suspected he was watching my reaction. 'A collision with a BMW.'

I felt myself flush. 'It wasn't a hit and run,' I muttered. 'They attacked me and Joe.'

'They?'

'Two men. Peter Dunn and Karl Lazard. Dunn came at me with a gun.'

Stone pulled into a supermarket car park. He stopped the car and shuffled in his seat to face me.

'Julia, the car is registered to a lady called Simone Bentley. A 52-year-old housewife. She says you shouted a lot of abuse at her and drove off after smashing into her car and running it into a ditch.'

My mouth fell open. 'There was no woman. It was two men, Dunn and Lazard. They were in Syria with Wilmore and Newby.'

I could tell by Stone's face that he thought I sounded utterly crazy. He rubbed the bridge of his nose with his thumb and forefinger.

'I know it sounds mad, but it's true. There was no woman. Ask Joe. He was with me. He was driving.'

I swallowed, wondering how much I dare tell Stone.

'What?' he asked.

'I hit one of the men, knocked him out. Joe hurt the other one. It was awful. Horrible. But we had to. They had a gun.' I risked a look at Stone and the lawyer's face lived up to his name. 'Joe had photographs of them. That's how we got their identities.'

'I'll speak to Joe about this. Tull doesn't know yet. He's on leave until tomorrow. I'll see if I can shut it down before then. But, Julia, really, it's like handing ammunition to a firing squad. They've got you in their sights and they're determined to get you for something.'

I looked down. My hands were trembling. I couldn't afford any more legal problems, not with Alex's care assessment pending. 'Is there any news on the men, their injuries?'

'Julia, as far as I or the authorities know, there was no one in the incident but you and Simone Bentley. There were no men. No injuries.'

'They'll be off-grid,' I muttered. I saw the worry and disbelief on his face. 'I know it sounds mad. Please talk to Joe. I'm not making this up.'

Stone nodded, restarted the car and drove me back to my flat.

'William, please don't tell Emilia or my father,' I said, as I released my seatbelt. 'They already think I'm nuts.'

Stone hesitated, clearly torn. Danby was his client, after all.

'Please. At least wait until you've spoken to Joe.'

He nodded slowly and I climbed out of the car, shaken by his revelations. Stone drove off without another word and I wondered if I could trust him not to betray me to my father.

When I got upstairs, I took a seat in the kitchen and checked I'd taken my medication. Had it been one big delusion? Had I really run into a woman in a country lane in Cheshire? Had my sick mind somehow twisted it into some gun-toting black ops hit? Was it happening again? I would lose Alex. I would lose The Castleton Files. I would lose myself to delusions and mania, running mad, locked up, sedated, heavily medicated, fat and useless.

I picked up Alex's homemade card and studied the colourful image of the two of us. My son loved me, but was that because he was too young to know better? If there was any doubt about my state of mind, should I be left alone in charge of him? When I'd suffered a psychotic break, I'd been alone with no one relying on me. But now I had Alex, and if things went wrong...I shook the ugly thought from my mind, but the panic bore down on me like a tidal wave. I started to pace, trying to catch my breath. It had all seemed so real. The bodies in the morgue, the car chase, hitting that man. Had it been like this last time?

When I'd been at *The Times*, ranting about Russian spies, running up all those expenses, had it seemed just as real then? I couldn't bear it, not again. I rifled through the bathroom cabinet and knocked a bottle of Calpol to the floor. It smashed into slivers of brown glass, and the sickly-sweet smell of the medicine made me dizzy. I pulled out my washbag and emptied the contents, desperate now to find a razor and release the panic poisoning my system. Sobbing with frustration as I remembered how I'd purged the flat of razors, so confident I'd never need to do this again, I lurched into the kitchen and quickly picked up the bread knife and ran it once, twice, three times across my arm. The pain made me gasp, and I felt a flush of release.

This is real, I chanted, *this is real.* The blood oozed thickly to the surface, and I breathed into it, suddenly calm.

This is real. I dropped the knife into the sink, watched the cuts fill, and then spill. Red rivulets ran down my arm and dripped onto the floor. And, just like that, the calm I scored into my body turned to growing dismay. There was so much blood, more than before. I grabbed some kitchen roll, but the blood quickly soaked the sheets. It was on my jeans, my fleece. The metallic smell made me feel sick. I got a clean towel and wrapped it round my arm, cursing myself. Another fuck up.

My behaviour wasn't normal; I knew I needed help. But I couldn't seek it, not if it meant losing Alex. I was trapped with myself. Doctor and patient. Flawed and broken. I sat at the kitchen table and raised my arm above my head, trying to stem the flow, feeling vaguely woozy. And I still didn't know if Simone Bentley was real. I laughed, on the verge of hysteria.

And then I blacked out.

55

'JULIA, WHAT the fuck!'

How long had I been out? Suddenly Joe was there. He pushed my head down between my knees.

'Take a deep breath. Breathe. Good, you're OK, you're OK. Good girl.'

He sounded as though he was talking to a startled horse. He was even stroking my mane. I laughed, too loud, too wild.

Not a mane, my hair!

He stroked my hair, talking to me. He unpeeled the towel and checked my wounds. I heard him exhale, sadly.

'How bad is it?'

The words sounded far away, and slurred, like I was drunk. Had I taken another pill by mistake? I couldn't remember.

Joe was talking to me, but the words were lost somewhere else. I could hear his feet coming and going. I stared at my kitchen floor. There was a corner of toast, smeared in butter, a piece of Lego, and little red puddles of shiny blood.

Rubies on my kitchen floor, I thought.

He was doing something to my arm now. Throttling it. No. Bandaging it tightly. It hurt, but I reminded myself that pain was good. I should welcome the pain.

I don't feel real pain in dreams. This is real, I breathed, *this is real.*

He made me a drink, a mug of weak tea with lots of milk and tonnes of sugar and watched me drain it to its sickly dregs.

I was on the sofa now. Had he carried me? I wasn't sure. My arm was swaddled in white bandages. I recognised them from that time I'd twisted my ankle in Wales. There was a faint trace of pink, but the blood had only got so far and been held back. The platelets must be clotting by now, surely, my body mending itself. If only I could put a bandage on my sick mind. I took a long, shuddery breath. Had I been crying? No, I didn't feel upset. Just tired, so tired. Footsteps, another mug of tea. Joe perched on the chair next to me, his fingers stroking his chin, his eyes thoughtful.

'You made me promise to tell you if there were any signs,' he said. 'This, Julia, this is a sign. You need to see someone.'

I took a swig of tea. 'I wasn't trying to kill myself. I just wanted to check it wasn't a dream.'

He shook his head slowly. 'This is not a dream. It's very real. Your kitchen looks like an abattoir.'

I laughed then, and he did too. I could see the relief on his face.

'I'm not mad, Joe. I just worry I might be going mad, and it makes me do stuff like this.'

I took another gulp of the horrible sugary tea. 'William told me I've been accused of a hit and run. By a woman called Simone Bentley, driving a BMW in Cheshire.'

Joe nodded. 'Yeah, he called me. That's why I came round, reckoned you'd be freaked out but Christ…Anyway, don't worry about Stone; I put him straight. If you're mad, so am I. But we're not mad, are we? Wilmore was killed because of what he found out. And now they're coming for you, and they're using the police, social services and Chris Jones to do it.'

'They're trying to hack the website,' I said. 'They're going to go after my subscribers too.'

Joe rubbed his hands through his hair. He looked tired. 'I'm worried about you being here,' he confessed. 'I'm not sure it's safe for you and Alex. They know where you live.'

'You've seen my new door?' I was trying to make light of it but I couldn't help feeling uneasy. They'd found us before.

'Come and stay at my gaff,' he suggested. 'Both of you. I'll keep you safe.'

I shook my head. 'I can't, Joe. I've got to be seen to be providing a stable home life for Alex. If they get a hint of danger, instability…Besides, what about Trish?'

'She'll be OK.'

I caught a flicker of pain flash across his face.

'Joe?' I asked.

'I'm still in the doghouse about not phoning in. I promised it would be different this time.' He shrugged. 'It's the job, innit?' He got up and paced the room. 'Go to Emilia's,' he said. 'Her husband's got that place tight as Fort Knox.'

I wondered how he knew this. The full extent of Joe's dealings with my family was still a mystery to me.

'You think it's necessary?'

'Yeah, I do. You can play it with social services that Alex is still unsettled after Tull's night-time visit. Blame the police for scaring him out of his own home.'

'OK.' I nodded. I would feel safer there. And, with The Castleton Files in abeyance, my bank account was bumping along the limits of my overdraft. My fridge was bare and the electricity meter was nearly empty. At least we'd be fed and warm at Holland Villas.

'I'll run you down,' he said. 'Don't pack much though – the van's in for an overhaul, so it's the bike.'

'Thought Trish had made you get rid of that thing.'

'Rumours of its demise have been greatly exaggerated.'

I could sense the sadness behind his smile, and guessed he and Trish were headed for another break.

We talked as I told him what to put in my rucksack. Spare clothes for Alex, his favourite teddy and his trucks from Stubsy.

'And you?' he asked.

'I'll do me in a minute,' I said.

I didn't want him going through my things but wasn't quite ready to stand up and do it myself. He rolled his eyes at my bashfulness, but didn't push it, and instead handed me a sheaf of computer printouts. Somehow, he'd already got the matriculation lists of students who'd been at Oxford five years either side of Wilmore's stint at med-school. That made up sixteen years' worth of names. He also had the med student alumni records from most of the colleges, which provided patchy insight into the destinations of the bright young things. I didn't ask how he'd come by the information, but I noticed his young associate's name cropped up a few times during the conversation. I suspected Sam's talents were a little more sophisticated than a typical drama school drop-out.

'You've been busy,' I observed.

Joe shrugged. 'The hard work starts now. We need to figure out who on these lists would have access to powerful electron microscopes.'

'There's no guarantee he contacted any of them,' I said, frowning as I flicked through page after page of names. 'He could have been in touch with other army medics, an old buddy from school, anyone.'

Joe hid his irritation well. 'You have a better idea, smarty pants?'

'Why don't we start with the equipment first? Fox said it was very specialised, right? So let's track down which labs have it, and then see if any of these people are connected.' I pulled out my notebook and flicked through pages of shorthand. 'Fox said that Wilmore's field kit couldn't cope. Wilmore needed a transmission electron microscope.'

'OK, let's find one of them. My guess is still on Oxford. That's where he got Howells to meet him, and it won't just have been for old times' sake.'

'I agree,' I said. I straightened up and made to stand but suddenly felt woozy.

'You OK?' asked Joe anxiously. 'Sit down.'

I did as I was told and waited for the room to stop spinning. I heard him in the kitchen. 'No more tea, Joe,' I said. 'I beg you.'

He came out and watched me.

'Put your feet up,' he ordered.

He fetched a blanket and made me lie down, then tenderly took my arm, checked his handiwork with the bandages, and nodded, satisfied.

'You've stopped bleeding,' he said. 'You just need to rest now. You can't get on the back of a bike. Not yet anyway. And you certainly can't show up at Emilia's like this.'

I smiled thinly. 'Does that mean we're keeping this our little secret?' I asked.

He muttered something I didn't quite hear. My eyelids were so heavy and, no matter how hard I tried, I couldn't keep them open. Soon, sleep settled on me like a heavy blanket.

56

WHEN I felt strong enough, Joe biked us over to Emilia's house. I'm not a fan of motorbikes but there was something energising about zipping through the traffic with 152 hp throbbing beneath me, my good arm wrapped tightly around Joe's solid waist. I'd called Emilia to warn her of our arrival, but she still seemed a little flustered and uptight. I wondered if she and Philippe had had a row. Was it to do with me and my frequent impositions on their hospitality? I knew he disapproved of my lifestyle. I told myself not to be so egocentric; not everything in the world revolved around me.

Whatever was going on with Emilia, she was still a gracious host. Joe was invited to stay for lunch, which he accepted. This seemed to wrong-foot Emilia, who seemed unusually skittish as she darted about her vast kitchen, and I wondered if maybe she had a bit of a crush on Joe? He couldn't be more different from Philippe, but perhaps that was the attraction. I observed her for a few more moments, until she shooed me and Joe into the den with a tray of tea things and the biscuit barrel. Occasionally though, I would glance up from the files I was going through with Joe, and catch her watching us through the French doors, her face unreadable.

When Philippe emerged from his study, he looked a little non-plussed to see Joe and me there, but he chatted warmly enough with Joe over a lunch of quiche, salad and cold roast chicken. Indeed, Philippe was the most animated I'd seen him, talking about biopharma and some new intellectual property regulations that I'd never heard of.

The French man laughed heartily at something Joe said.

'Can I use that one?' he asked.

'I'm not going to patent it.' Joe grinned, and they both chuckled at some in-joke.

I caught Emilia's eye and shrugged. It seemed Joe was better at talking to Philippe than either of us.

Later, when the two of us went upstairs to wake little Jacques from his nap, Emilia asked me how well I really knew Joe.

'Can you really trust him?' she said. 'I'm worried he's egging you on when you should be focused on Alex right now.'

I knew this was a coded way of addressing my questionable mental state, and tried to reassure her that Joe wasn't enabling my paranoia.

'No-one knows better than Joe what happened before, and no-one knows better what to look out for,' I assured her. 'I trust him implicitly.'

She nodded and said no more, but I could see the strain on her face. I felt bad to be the cause of so much worry, but I also knew I could not, would not, walk away from this case. Not when we were getting so close.

'Come to Arlet with me and the children in the holidays,' she suddenly blurted out. 'Remember how much fun it can be. Alex would love it.'

I did remember. We used to run wild as kids, climbing trees, bareback rides across the estate, attempting to skate on a barely frozen pond. And even wilder as teenagers, smoking weed on the roof, pinching rare wines from our father's cellar and driving the old Range Rover without a licence to visit the boys in the local boarding school. I'm not sure it's the kind of absentee parenting either Emilia or I would endorse, but she looked so hopeful, so desperate almost, that I found myself agreeing to think about it. Emilia looked so relieved and gave me a goofy hug. And then I put Arlet firmly from my mind. Joe and I had business to attend to.

57

WE MET in a gentrified pub in Bethnal Green. The interior was all wooden floors, mismatched armchairs, ironic food served on wooden platters and blackboards chalked with motivational quotes. Even the staff seemed to have a carefully curated kookiness. The barmaid had an elaborate dragon tattoo curled round her arm, bubble-gum pink hair and steel toe-capped boots. At little more than five feet, she looked like an Anime character, but she had the smoky laugh of a mature woman and a book of mid-twentieth-century poets stashed under the bar, which she read between pulling pints of craft ale and dishing out bar snacks drizzled with tahina and harissa. Sam and I nursed mugs of peppermint tea while Joe rolled his eyes and tackled a pint of ale. He was still reeling at the cost of our sharing platter of pitta bread with dips and olives.

'Get over yourself, big boy,' said Sam, loading up a slice of bread with some baba ganoush.

Yet again, I wondered how Joe had hooked up with someone like Sam. They did strange work that required the kind of skills you couldn't publicly advertise. But even GCHQ ran recruitment adverts now. It was no longer a nod and a wink on the back staircase of an Oxford college.

Sam reached into his messenger bag and pulled out an iPad. He tapped the screen, opened a file and pulled up relevant photos as he scrolled down.

'Elaine Blackwood. As I said before, she's connected to Momentum. Went to Leeds Becket University to study social care. Involved in animal rights stuff, was an active hunt saboteur. There's a caution on file for aggravated trespass at a kennels. But she's got on with life, had a couple of jobs before moving to London, been with

Hammersmith and Fulham for three years now. She might be a committed socialist, bless her, but she's still got her foot on the property ladder. A little one-bed in Crouch End. But she spends half her time with her boyfriend, nice chap called Rod Kennett. Very active on social media is our Rod, very vocal. Depending on your views of Karl Marx, he's either highly progressive or very regressive. Works at Middlesex University, teaching, but has a double life as an agent provocateur. A real fire starter, loves any opportunity to smash a window or daub a bridge with a catchy slogan, disrupt meetings of Tory politicians he doesn't like, agitate crowds at demos. Bit of a rent-a-thug really. It's unclear to me how much Elaine approves of, or even knows of this, or indeed of his other lady friend, a nice yoga teacher who lives in Stoke Newington.'

I glanced at Sam, my mouth open. 'How do you know all this?' I asked.

He smiled. 'Do you really want an answer?'

I looked at him, then shook my head decisively. 'No. I suppose not.'

I studied a photograph of Elaine's agitator boyfriend, a short man with a receding hairline and a stud in his nose. He had his arm draped casually round a thin blonde woman and they were walking along a busy high street. The blonde's trendy yoga gear showcased her toned limbs and protruding pregnancy bump.

'Looks like an August baby,' Sam remarked.

'I almost feel sorry for her,' I said.

'Don't,' Sam responded. 'Elaine is not a good person.' He swiped to another picture. It was grainy and indistinct, shot at some distance through the window of a café. 'That's her having a little tête-à-tête with your friend Conor Tull.'

He tapped on the iPad and opened another file. 'Now Tull is an interesting character. Did his four years' basic in the army, then joined a roofing company that went bust in the housing crash. Applied for the Met and scraped in. Let's say he's not the sharpest tool in the box. Divorced, one kid with the ex-wife, who he doesn't see much, and another kid he doesn't see at all – it was a work fling, and it didn't end well. There was a complaint of harassment from the woman, though it didn't stick, and she was transferred.'

'He sounds like a real charmer,' mused Joe.

'Now all this procreating has left our Casanova with some money worries,' said Sam. 'The ex-wife has kept the house, a little association two-bed in Uxbridge, and he's supposed to pay another five hundred pounds a month. He contributes the bare minimum towards the second kid. He rents a two-bed flat in Pinner. Got a couple of maxed-out credit cards. Every month should be a real squeeze on his salary.'

'What's he on?' asked Joe.

'Just over forty-eight.'

I sipped my tea, and my eyes flitted from Joe to Sam. How had he got all this detail on Tull's finances? And if he had these kinds of skills, what did he know about me?

'Why's he after me?' I asked. 'Is he another social justice warrior trying to strike a blow to the aristocracy?' It didn't seem likely to me. I didn't think the man had a principled bone in his body.

'He's no revolutionary,' Sam replied wryly. 'On the contrary, I think Mr Tull's interest in you may be motivated by more material concerns.'

'What do you mean?' I asked sharply.

'For a man who claims not to be able to pay more towards his kids, he enjoys a relatively affluent lifestyle.' He swiped open more photos. 'That's a twenty-thousand-pound car he's driving, yet there's no car finance in his name. Every year he takes a two-week trip to Vegas. He's always nicely togged up. Season tickets at Arsenal. Took a girlfriend to Paris, first class, stayed at the Ritz.'

'Flash,' said Joe. 'Very flash for a copper.'

'So, what? You think he's bent?' I asked.

Sam smiled again. He clearly enjoyed keeping us in suspense. He opened a photo of a dark saloon car parked in the street. Another image showed a man walking past with a baseball cap pulled low, his shoulders hunched as if against the cold, hands in coat pockets.

'Tull has a lot of little meetings; car parks, McDonald's, those kind of places. At first, I thought it was informants but that felt wrong.

Never seemed like he was the boss man, more like he was getting orders,' Sam said.

'Orders, what kind of orders?' I asked.

Joe pored over the photos. He tapped one with his finger. 'I recognise this place,' he remarked. 'Norwood, in South London, right? Scruffy little office.'

'Yeah,' said Sam, who quickly pulled up the Google Maps location where the photo was taken. 'He went in there with this chap.'

Another photo, this time of Tull and a tall man. Both wore baseball caps, had their backs to the camera and their hands in their pockets as they stood in front of an estate agent's window.

'Got any more of this chap?'

'Not many,' sniffed Sam. 'He was careful. Cagey. This is someone used to keeping a low profile. This is probably the best.' He flicked through more photos until he came to a profile shot of the man. His head was down and he was half obscured by Tull as they went through a doorway.

'Can you enlarge this?' I asked, swiping back to the one of the two men staring into the estate agent. Sam used his fingertips to zoom in on the photo, quickly recognising what I wanted to see.

I caught my breath. There, reflected in the window of the estate agent, were the chiselled features of James Newby.

'Newby and Tull know one another,' said Joe. He ran his hands through his hair. 'And that' – he swiped back to the picture of Tull and the tall man entering the office – 'shitty little office is registered to a subsidiary of The Harlen Group.'

I sat back in my chair. 'They're paying Tull to do this to me.'

I took a deep, shuddering breath. Was this good news? It meant I wasn't paranoid; there really was a conspiracy to silence me. But it also meant my opponents were well-funded, very organised and extremely well connected, with the right kind of pull to kill journalists, bury evidence and use any means possible to quash all opposition. It meant I was right to be paranoid, right to be afraid.

'How is Harlen involved in this? How can they do this?'

'This is dark stuff,' noted Joe. 'These guys are serious.'

'At least you've got Tull,' said Sam, stirring his tea.

'None of this is admissible in court,' I observed gloomily. 'And it's the care hearing on Tuesday.'

'Don't worry,' said Joe. 'There's enough here to bury Tull in internal inquiries for the next two years.'

'You want more?' asked Sam. 'Joe had me research those names you got from Fox. I've got a match on another one.'

He pulled up a picture on his iPad. It was poor quality, and at first glance a nondescript misfire of a photo, just a shot of a dimly lit bar. There was no one in the photo until you looked closely: two men, their faces reflected in the mirror behind the rows of spirit bottles.

'That's Lazard, from the BMW,' I said. I squinted at the other man. He had a beard and sharp eyes and I recognised him from the staged killing in Oxwich.

'And that is Brian Hinstock,' said Sam. 'But the really interesting thing is who took this photo.'

Joe and I looked at him expectantly. Sam smiled; this was his greatest trick yet. 'This photo was found on Ben Howells' phone. The police discovered it last week. It was hidden in the vaults under the Bodleian. From the date and time stamp, it was taken in Oxford moments before Howells was stabbed.'

'This is proof Newby's men killed Howells,' I remarked. I felt a great release. Wilmore's name would be cleared.

58

THE NEXT thirty-six hours were purgatory. I had barely slept since Sunday. Whenever I got the chance, I worked on an article that detailed the links between Tull and The Harlen Group. I didn't have enough to publish yet, but the connections Sam had discovered were sufficient to start fleshing out a piece. Work kept my mind busy, but during my quiet moments, my mood swung between anger and a horrible lurching fear about the upcoming care hearing.

Now nerves made me clumsy. I had already laddered one pair of tights and a second pair had a run down the leg. I didn't have the patience or budget for this kind of dressing. How did other women do it day after day? I tugged impatiently at my skirt, pulling it down an inch so it covered the worst bit. Already I felt hot and uncomfortable, dressed in another woman's clothes. Emilia's silk blouse was a fussy style I would never choose for myself, and the skirt was too tight at the waist. I may have lost most of the weight gained in the lithium haze of my early recovery, but my body shape had changed, a visible reminder of my past.

Still, I had to admire Emilia's efforts with her makeup kit. There was an unfamiliar sheen to my skin, my lashes were thick with mascara, my lips tinted with a hint of gloss and there was a permanent artificial glow to my cheeks. A sweet chemical smell hit me when I turned my head, the hairspray ensuring not one hair fell out of place. It was like looking into a crystal ball and glimpsing another life, another me. The woman who'd stayed at *The Times*, a corporate woman, an editor, a success. It was unnerving and I pinched myself hard on the arm. *This is real*, I thought, *this is still me*.

I ran the tap and washed my hands again, resisting the urge to splash the cold water on my face and scrub away the mask. *I'm doing this for Alex*, I told myself, *I have to play their game for him*. But inside I was brimming with anger. I felt the injustice of the care hearing burn like poison through my veins. I touched the folder I'd put in my satchel as though it was a talisman. It was my last line of defence. Joe said dynamite was a poor weapon, but I'd use it if I had to. I wasn't going to lose Alex without a fight.

I left the ladies' toilet and met William Stone in the entrance hall. He was anxiously checking his watch but smiled warmly when he saw me.

'Julia, you look wonderful,' he said. His lips brushed my hair as we hugged. 'Can I get you anything before we go in? We just have time.'

I shook my head. I just wanted to get it over with.

A middle-aged woman bustled over and introduced herself as a representative from Cafcass. 'I've been trying to call you,' she said.

I glared at her. Was this another Harlen Group stooge?

'Who are you?' I asked. 'What do you want?'

'Children's and Families Court Advisory and Support Service. You should have had a letter from us.'

'I've been away. Staying with my sister.'

'You really need to make sure you let us know where you're staying,' said the woman, frowning down at her notes.

Stone intervened and smoothed the waters. I felt unsettled. What had I missed? Was this Cafcass something important? My stomach churned anxiously. I never seemed to get things right. But Stone was smiling now, and the woman was looking fondly at me.

'Don't worry, dear,' she was saying. 'I'll update our records and be in touch soon. We're here to help if needed.'

I tugged at my skirt and fussed with my blouse. I felt out of place. This whole process was a fog of acronyms and procedures and timelines, the kind of thing I used to navigate easily as a reporter on the court beat but now I was adrift, wholly dependent on Stone to keep me afloat. I wondered, not for the first time, if it was the medication; was it dulling my brain? Or was it just the lack of sleep? What was I even doing here in a court? I'd committed no crime and yet here I was surrounded by criminals, being hauled up in front of people who could punish me with something far worse than a prison sentence. They could take my son.

I fought the nausea and let Stone guide me down the corridor to a small waiting area. Elaine Blackwood was there, with another woman, in a black suit. Elaine's companion had long swishy hair and a large handbag that even I recognised as a designer label. This woman now joined Stone and me. She was the lawyer advising the local authority, and she and Stone chatted about points of procedure. I scowled and felt like a naughty child. I didn't know how Stone could talk to these people. To me they were all the enemy.

When we were alone again, I told him this and he laughed.

'They're not the enemy. This is just a process. You're inside the system. No one here wants to do you or Alex any harm.'

'This *is* harming us,' I said. 'He's been wetting the bed since they arrested me. I'm struggling to work or sleep. How is this good for us?'

'They just want to make sure Alex is getting the care he needs. You and I know he is, beyond a doubt. It's just a question of proving it to them.' He smiled at my cross face. 'Which we will do. This is just the first hearing and their case is so weak…You've had a wonderful letter of support from Alex's head teacher – it will count for a lot.'

I nodded, trying to take heart, but deep down I worried that The Harlen Group had everyone on their payroll. A company like that could afford to buy whoever they wanted. Even my father's lawyer, I thought bleakly as I cast Stone a suspicious look. *Don't go there*, I cautioned myself.

The usher came over and led us through into a small courtroom. The royal coat of arms hung above the raised judge's bench. Stone and I sat on the left side of a long wooden table facing the bench. Elaine and her department's lawyer sat on the right. The judge came in and we all stood up. I forced a nervous smile on my face. There was no wig, no gown, just an old man with thick-rimmed glasses and a green bow tie. Rather a jaunty look, I felt, for such a serious occasion.

Soon proceedings got underway. I tried to take notes but my hands were shaking too much. My shorthand looked like a drunk spider had roamed the page with inky feet. A door opened behind me and I turned to see Conor Tull slip in to sit behind Elaine. I glowered and my fists bunched in my lap. My skin prickled with a visceral reaction to his presence and my blood roared in my ears. I focused on my breathing, turned to face the royal arms, and tried to recall the history of the heraldry: the rearing lion, the shackled unicorn, the symbolic flowers under their feet, the Tudor rose, the thistle, the shamrock.

The judge was speaking again now, and I tried to concentrate. They were talking about Elaine's initial report. I bit my lip, my head bowed, hands balled in my lap. This person they were talking about – erratic and paranoid, recently hospitalised following an altercation with a former partner, my son in emergency care following my arrest under Section 127 of the Communications Act – certainly didn't sound like a fit mother. And it was all true, yet it wasn't true, but how would a judge who didn't know me understand that? I flushed with panic. The hearing wasn't going my way and things were going to turn against me.

The council's lawyer called Conor Tull and my hackles rose as he passed me to sit at the witness table. I didn't trust myself to look at him and kept my eyes fixed on the floor as Tull spoke.

'We had a report in of a road accident in Cheshire. Miss Castleton is alleged to have fled the scene. We are still making enquiries. It isn't clear that Miss Castleton, if she was driving, even had insurance for the vehicle involved. The other car was badly damaged, although the driver, a Mrs Simone Bentley, was thankfully unhurt. We are still pursuing this as an active case in addition to the Section 127. Miss Castleton has been hard to pin down, even though I believe she had given assurances to the case workers that she would be providing some stability for her son, rather than continuing to travel the country in pursuit of her so-called stories.'

Fury gripped me. I'd listened to Tull's lies, and every word had chilled my blood with a terrible icy anger. I clenched my fists, suddenly filled with a dangerous cold resolve.

'Thank you, DI Tull,' the judge said dryly. 'Let's limit your commentary to your area of expertise, shall we?'

But I was already on my feet.

'Julia,' Stone hissed angrily.

But I ignored him and hurried towards the bench. I wasn't going down without a fight. To the horror of Stone, the usher and the court officials, I handed the dynamite manila file to the judge.

'Julia,' Stone tried again, more weakly this time.

'It wasn't a hit and run, sir. They tried to kill me.'

I turned to face Tull, who smiled like a snake. 'He knows who I'm talking about. They're all in cahoots.'

'I bet they killed Kennedy too,' someone shouted, and it was then that I knew I had gone too far. I saw grins and smirks around the courtroom and Stone shook his head sadly as he approached.

'Julia.' The way he said my name made it sound as though I'd lost everything in the whole world.

59

I WASN'T about to give up. 'Two men attacked me and my colleague.'

I shook off Stone's hand, as he tried to tug on my sleeve. 'And I am insured to drive. I'm a good driver; I would never run someone off the road. This is all lies, a complete stitch-up designed to bring me down and silence The Castleton Files, and he,' I jabbed my finger at Tull, who sat smirking, 'he's up to his neck in it. He's tried to plant evidence on my computer to separate me from my son.'

I saw Elaine and Swishy Hair shake their heads sadly. I knew what they were thinking. I was mad, raving, and this case hearing would quickly proceed to Alex being subject to a care order. The prospect filled me with a righteous anger, and my voice only grew louder, the words rattling out like a machine gun. Stone rubbed his forefingers on his temples, no doubt wondering how he was going to explain this to my father. But I wouldn't sit here and let them lie about me like this.

'That man,' I said, my finger stabbing at Tull, 'that man is out to ruin me. He already knows her.' Now I pointed at Elaine. 'They speak on the phone, talking about evidence that's about to be found on my computer. I have the tapes, sir, I can prove it.' I saw Elaine and Swishy Hair urgently whispering, and the senior social worker's face suddenly turned the colour of chalk.

'And as for him, he's in the pay of The Harlen Group, the very company I am investigating.' I had no evidence that Tull had taken money from Newby, but he didn't know that and visibly blanched. 'He should be on trial here, not me!'

I sat down suddenly, as if winded. The judge peered at me over his glasses. 'Nobody's on trial here. This is an initial case hearing to see what next steps might be taken regarding Alexander's care. Now any documents I see are also shared with all parties, and we don't do last-minute evidence. This isn't an episode of The Good Wife, you know.'

There was a polite titter of laughter from the lawyers and court officials, but the reference was lost on me.

'But I will look at what you have given me, and share it with my learned friends, so that we all understand your point of view. Our only intention here is the very best care for Alex.'

He smiled kindly at me, and then talked with the court official about the next hearing date. Swishy Hair and Elaine were still whispering, when suddenly Tull broke out.

'This is a farce,' he said, suddenly looming over me, his aftershave making me feel woozy. 'I'm arresting you for fleeing the scene of an accident, and that's for starters.'

Stone stepped in. 'Seriously, Tull, you need to walk away now. I think you should take a look at that file. If what my client says is true, your arresting days will be over soon. If I were you I'd apologise to this lady for all the distress you've caused her and her son, and then I'd get yourself a good lawyer. You're going to need one.'

Tull opened his mouth as if to speak, but quickly thought better of it and stormed out of the courtroom.

I looked at Stone with new eyes. 'That was truly wonderful,' I said. 'Thank you.'

Stone smiled thinly. 'Another close call,' he said. 'And yet again you didn't trust me enough to tell me about your secret dossier, or your evidence against Tull and the social workers. Was this material obtained legally? It puts me in a very awkward position, Julia.'

'I'm sorry,' I said. 'Everyone thinks I'm mad when I say these things, so I try to keep them secret. And that dossier's only the tip of the iceberg…'

'Not here,' said Stone, his eyes locked on the contents of the file, his face visibly paling as he read. 'Christ, Julia, where did you get this stuff? Have you hacked his accounts?'

I shook my head. 'What's the phrase? Don't ask, don't tell.'

Stone shook his head wearily. 'Julia, I am never going to get to retire while you're around.'

I nudged his arm playfully. 'That's why you like me, William. You're far too young to go out to pasture. You need me.'

He smiled, strangely affected by my comment. I grinned back, suddenly high with relief. Surely the judge would read my file and understand I was the victim of a conspiracy, that I was a good mother, that Alex was safe with me. For the first time in days, I suddenly felt hungry.

'Treat me to lunch, William,' I said. 'I need carbohydrates and cream and cheese, and I know my father's account is good for it.'

He nodded. 'One condition: you tell me everything. Full disclosure and I'll treat you to the finest antipasti in London.'

I laughed and stepped outside to call Emilia, while Stone checked some paperwork with a court official. It was a bright day that offered the first hints of summer. The skies were blue, and I felt warm April sunshine on my face. I pulled out my phone and turned it on, hoping Emilia had remembered Alex's wellies. He was going on a nature walk today. I was almost shivering with anticipation. For the first time in weeks, I felt like a proper mother. I had no reason to be worried or ashamed or full of self-doubt. The investigation had taken me away from my son, but I had also felt myself retreat from Alex, as if my very presence could taint him with my unhappiness. Now we could go back to being a family.

The road was clogged with traffic, the thunder of buses, the over-revved scream of a motorbike. I ambled around the corner, away from the high street, and scrolled through my contacts for Emilia's number, noting I had two missed calls from Joe. I wondered if he'd narrowed down where Wilmore might have taken that sample. With the care hearing over, I could concentrate on chasing down the truth of what happened to Wilmore, to those poor people buried in a secure mortuary in Lockmere.

'Your phone, now.' The voice was right behind me, and it made me jump.

I whirled round and saw Scarface – Peter Dunn – standing there. So, I hadn't killed him in that country lane in Cheshire. Now I almost wished I had.

He reached out and snatched the device and slipped it in his pocket.

'Hey!' I exclaimed. 'What do you think you're doing? I know who you are.'

He scoffed. 'Like I give a fuck. This is what we're doing. You're going to walk down here with me, nice and casual, arm in arm, two lovebirds strolling on a lovely sunny day.'

'I'm not going anywhere with you.' I tried to sound brave but there was a quiver in my voice.

'You're going to do as you're told,' he said, and he pulled back his coat to reveal a gun in a holster. 'You're going to do as you're told or I'm going to kill you right here, right now.'

60

DUNN REGISTERED the fear on my face, then pulled something from his jeans pocket. I caught a gleam of metal in the sunlight and saw the serrated blade of a vicious knife. He put his arm round me, and I felt the prick of the blade in the soft flesh of my lower abdomen.

'Don't do anything sudden,' he hissed. 'If I stumble, this will slice you wide open. You won't even feel it until it's too late and you'll bleed out before I get to the end of the road.'

He held me close, and I recoiled from the smell of him, an acrid stench of sweat and cheap aftershave.

A woman passed us, clipping by on high heels, talking into her phone. The woman didn't see beyond the illusion; Dunn and I were a couple walking down a street in the spring sunshine.

Dunn smiled and glanced at me. He was short – we were almost eyeball to eyeball – but I felt the strength of him. His arms were like steel. We were moving away from the courthouse now, away from the bustle and roar of the main road. A couple came towards us, both with their heads bowed over their phones. I felt the knife press a little deeper, and I said nothing as the couple passed. They didn't even glance up from their screens.

A black van pulled into a parking space ahead of us.

'That's our ride,' said Dunn, nodding with a grim satisfaction.

I felt panic rise. I knew I must not get into the van. I had no choice; I would have to scream for help. Fear robbed me of my voice, but I told myself the outlook was bleak, regardless of anything I did. I would either die here, stabbed in the street, or wherever they planned to take me in that van. Better to go down fighting.

I focused on my steps. The van was getting closer. It wasn't the black guy driving, but another man, with ginger hair. He watched us approach, his eyes hidden behind aviator sunglasses, his fingers tapping anxiously on the steering wheel. I spotted a couple of men in high vis jackets crossing the road towards us. They carried hot drinks and packed lunches. I would wait until they were on my side of the street and then I'd scream for help. Perhaps Dunn would scare and run. Perhaps I'd get away with it. I braced myself and took a deep breath. I kept my eyes on the workmen, hoping to catch their attention with a fearful glance. I was so focused on my situation it took me a moment to realise why the workmen were suddenly scattering, dashing for the pavement, why the van driver's mouth suddenly fell open in surprise. A noise had filled the street, an angry, rumbling roar that pounded my ears. Dunn pulled me sharply round, and as his grip loosened, I jerked myself free. I gasped as a large motorbike skidded to a stop on the pavement between me and Dunn, its engine pulsing with menace. Its black-clad rider levelled a sawn-off shotgun at Dunn and shouted at me.

'Get on,' the motorcyclist yelled from behind a tinted visor.

I didn't hesitate. Dunn's hand was moving inside his coat as I pulled up my skirt and straddled the bike. The hot exhaust scalded my leg, but I didn't have time to register the pain. The huge engine growled, and we accelerated down the street. I instinctively wrapped my arms round my leather-clad saviour, gasping for air as the bike leapt forward, my eyes blinded by tears. My saviour stowed the gun in a leather holster that hung off the fuel tank and we wove through traffic at speed. Cars beeped and pedestrians whooped as we dipped down into Farringdon, racing through the narrow streets, my skirt up round my thighs, my hair streaming behind me.

We came to a stop in an underground car park and pulled up behind a yellow Transit. A door opened and Joe emerged and helped me dismount, chivalrously turning away as I pulled my skirt down. My tights were ruined, and I'd lost a shoe, but I was alive. I stood awkwardly in one stockinged foot, shivering with cold and shock.

I turned to look at my saviour. He pulled off his helmet and shook his hair. It was Sam.

'Nice work,' said Joe. 'Thanks, mate.'

'Best day ever!' Sam grinned.

'How did you know?' I asked.

'They were going to come for you at some point. They knew you'd be at the hearing. So, I had Sam tail you. They must be pretty desperate to try and snatch you outside a courthouse. There's CCTV everywhere.'

Joe opened the Transit and pulled out some planks for Sam to roll the bike into the back.

'We'll change the plates back at the garage,' he said to Sam, as they secured the bike with cargo straps.

Sam pulled the shotgun out of its holster and handed it to me. I was surprised how light it felt.

'Theatre prop,' Sam revealed with one of his sly smiles.

Joe threw a blanket to me. 'Don't worry,' he told me. 'We got you.'

'Thanks, Joe,' I said, hugging the blanket tightly round my shoulders. I couldn't stop shivering. 'Joe? They took my phone. We can track it.'

'Already on it,' Sam remarked as he studied his iPad. 'Got 'em. They're heading over Blackfriars.'

'Joe? Do you think they'd go after Alex? Or Emilia?' I asked.

Joe and Sam shared a look. Clearly it was on their minds too. Joe shuffled uncomfortably.

'What?' I demanded. 'What is it?'

'I already had a word with your brother-in-law.'

'You spoke to Philippe?'

'Yes. He's paid for some discreet security. Couple of fellas watching the house, driving Emilia and Alex. I know the firm, they're good.'

I bit my lip. 'Why didn't you tell me?'

'You've got enough to worry about.'

'You think I can't cope?' I knew I was being silly, but I hated the thought of Joe and Philippe organising this, protecting the little women and keeping them in the dark like we were children who couldn't be trusted with the truth.

'I know you can cope,' said Joe. 'But I also know you don't like taking help. Particularly from your family. So I sorted it. I need your focus here.'

I took a deep breath, then nodded for him to continue.

'OK,' he said. 'I've got a shortlist of places Wilmore might have taken that sample. We need to work on this quickly because I can't help thinking Newby is going to be making the same deductions.'

'What've you got?' I asked.

'I'll show you as we drive,' he said. 'We need to get moving.'

We climbed into the van, and I found myself sandwiched between Joe and Sam. The burn on my leg was throbbing and I looked at it gingerly.

'That needs seeing too,' said Sam, eyeing the oozing wound on my inner thigh. The shredded tights stuck to the damaged skin.

'Later,' I replied, pulling my skirt down.

But he was already rummaging through Joe's first aid kit. He pulled out scissors and a medical dressing.

'Permission to operate?'

I swallowed and nodded reluctantly. As Joe drove the van, Sam cut away my tights and then ripped open the pack holding the sterilised dressing.

'It's treated with silver,' Sam said, as he placed the dressing over the wound. 'It helps burns heal.'

'You're a man of many talents,' I noted. 'You're wasted on the stage.'

Joe chuckled next to me. 'Luckily, he's never on it. Have you finished, Doogie Howser?'

'Who?' Sam said, handing me a couple of painkillers. 'I don't get your old man references.'

I swallowed the paracetamol and my body slowly relaxed.

'Let's see this shortlist then,' I said.

Sam tapped on his iPad.

'Don't you ever write anything down?' I asked.

'Why would I do that?' He seemed genuinely puzzled.

I looked at the list he produced. It was a spreadsheet, with four entries highlighted in yellow. The remainder were shaded in grey.

'We worked out it couldn't be the ones in grey,' explained Sam. 'Either they had access to the wrong type of equipment, or there was no connection with Wilmore. But this one here, this is our top pick.

The senior fellow at Oxford Science Department. She was at college with him, so they'll know one another well. They're even friends on Facebook. The others, here, this one at Imperial, he was at Oxford at the same time. This one at Rutherford is another Army Reservist but we don't know if they met. This one at—'

'It's none of them,' I said decisively. 'It's her.' And I stabbed my finger at one of the names shaded in grey.

'No,' said Sam. 'She's got no known connection to him. And that lab doesn't have the right microscope, we checked.'

'It's her,' I said. 'I know it is. Look, it's only UCL. We're almost driving right by. If it's not her, then we'll go straight up to Oxford.'

I stared down at the name, certain this was their target: Utopia Robins, her name had been the very last word Wilmore ever spoke.

61

IT WAS easy to spot Utopia Robins. We'd been directed to the canteen, and I'd surveyed the bustle of students for a moment before spotting the one who looked like they were living on over-stretched nerves in the wake of a high profile and traumatic bereavement. Nursing a mug of coffee at a corner table, she looked young and pinched, her slight frame drowned by her lab coat, like she'd recently lost a lot of weight. She startled at a crash of plates, clearly jittery. I glanced at Joe, and he nodded. He'd spotted her too. We navigated the room to her table and asked if we could join her.

She jumped, looking up from her phone where she'd been doomscrolling the news.

'What? Sorry?'

'Can we join you, Utopia?' I repeated to the woman. 'We want to talk to you about Michael Wilmore.'

She froze at the name. 'Who are you?'

'My name's Julia Castleton. I'm a journalist. Michael reached out to me before he died. And this is my colleague, Joe Turner.'

She stared at us and colour rushed to her pale cheeks as panic flushed her body. I felt a rush of excitement. I could tell we were close to something. I nodded to Joe and we sat down without waiting for her to answer.

'What do you want?' she asked.

'How did you know Michael?' I asked.

'We were friends.' She could tell we didn't believe her, and blushed. There was a horrible silence, and she felt compelled to fill it, suddenly gabbling. 'He's my godmother's GP. I did a work placement at his surgery after university.'

I smiled and shot a meaningful look at Joe.

'See?' I said. 'Not all connections can be traced online. You stayed in touch with Michael? You must have been close?'

Utopia glanced down at her hands, painfully aware of her bright red cheeks. She thought they'd been close, but in the end, it seemed she barely knew him at all.

'We went out together for a few months after I moved to London, but he ended it. The age gap, you know.' She shrugged. It was clear it still hurt.

'But he trusted you?' I persisted. 'He came to see you when he returned from Syria?'

Utopia nodded. 'He said he needed my help. But he didn't realise I'd moved to another department.'

'What did he want you to do?'

'He had something with him, a sample, and he needed access to one of our electron microscopes in the pathology lab. I couldn't help him. I'm working in radiography now.' She sighed. Her failure to make headway on this new project weighed heavily on her.

'Did he tell you what the sample was?'

'Brain tissue. He said it was a difficult case. He needed a more powerful instrument. He was hoping it could be some breakthrough. But who knows what it really was. I saw the news, read about his issues. I never realised he was so ill.' She hesitated, suddenly suspicious. 'Why are you asking all these questions?'

'Michael contacted me before he died, saying he had a major story. But I think he was killed to stop him talking to me.'

'Killed?' Utopia said in disbelief. 'The papers said it was suicide. They said he murdered that reporter.'

'Well, I don't believe Michael killed Howells, and I believe that sample holds the key to what happened to him in Syria.'

'What?' Utopia looked at the pair in horror. 'I feel awful. I didn't help him. Maybe I could have stopped it.'

'You couldn't have stopped it,' said Joe kindly. 'The people after him are professionals. It was only a matter of time.'

'But if I'd been able to look at the sample…'

'Do you know what he did with the sample?' I asked. 'Where did he go next?'

Utopia looked at me and I could tell she was wondering how far to trust me.

'Michael wanted Julia to know,' said Joe quietly. 'He risked his life to get this information to her.'

Utopia glanced down at her long fingers, which were twisting in knots. I held my breath.

'He didn't take the sample,' she said at last. 'I still have it.'

I sat back as if stung.

'You have the sample. Where?'

'In the freezer. Here. At work. It's stored at minus eighty.' She blushed. 'I didn't know what it was, so I labelled it as mouse brain.'

'Mouse brain.' I felt almost faint. The key to everything could be an unguarded wrongly labelled sample in a university lab.

'Michael asked me to keep it safe until he came back, but then he didn't come back.' She trailed off. 'When I read he'd died, I thought about throwing it out but I never got round to it. Or maybe part of me wanted to believe him when he said it was important, so I kept hold of it. So it's still here.'

'Well done,' said Joe. 'You have to help us now, Utopia, help us look at this tissue. It's the key to everything. If we're right, it's the reason Michael was killed.'

She nodded. 'How did you find me?' she asked. 'Nobody knew about our affair.'

I looked at her with a sad smile.

'He died with your name on his lips,' I said. 'His last word was Utopia.'

62

UTOPIA HAD asked us to meet her after hours.

'There'll be fewer people around then,' she'd said.

So, Joe and I had spent the afternoon in the van in a state of nervous anticipation. The wait, when we were so close, was frustrating.

'Do you think we can trust her?' I asked. 'She could be in there flushing it down the plug hole right now or calling Newby.'

'She seemed genuine,' mused Joe, and he was usually a good judge of these things.

'Will the sample even be valid now?' I asked. 'I mean how long do these things last?'

Joe shrugged. 'We'll know soon enough. No use worrying about what we can't control.'

'God, you're so bloody zen,' I said. 'Doesn't anything ever get to you?'

He looked at me sharply, and I quickly averted my gaze. Things that could rattle Joe were probably best left alone.

'Do you think Newby's lot will trace her?' I asked, keen to fill the silence.

'Unlikely. I mean, unless they're somehow going to track down each of his ex-girlfriends in case one of them happens to have access to a super electron microscope…Utopia. What a name. Imagine the playground.'

I shrugged. 'Her parents must have been Thomas More fans. Or hippies. Like you.'

Joe's phone buzzed and he read a text.

'It's William again. He's glad you're OK and said he checked in with Emilia earlier. Alex is fine. The security's in place.'

I nodded. 'And my phone?'

'Sam says it disappeared somewhere near Elephant and Castle. They must have neutralised Find My Phone or ditched it.'

I brooded. I'd so been looking forward to picking up Alex tonight. Instead, I was cold and hungry, wearing horrible clothes and plastic trainers Sam had grabbed from the market near Barbican, cooped up in a van to check on some month-old brain tissue. I pulled up my hood and tried to nap but was too wired to relax. Finally, the day dragged into dusk. I watched the students and staff head out, and the lights wink off.

At half past six, Joe got a text from Utopia. *Meet me at Queen Square, five minutes.*

'Come on,' said Joe, stretching. 'Time to go.'

Utopia met us on the square in the shadow of the huge hospital and led us to a side entrance. She was very slight, almost childlike, with big eyes and blonde hair that tumbled messily out of a ponytail. She led us down to a basement and our footsteps echoed along the empty corridors.

'Neuropathology,' I remarked, looking at the sign above the door. 'Does that mean dead people?'

'Don't worry,' Utopia reassured us. 'We won't go near the morgue.'

'I don't want to see any more bodies,' I said without thinking.

'More?' queried Utopia, her eyes opening wide.

I shook my head. 'Figure of speech.'

Joe shot me a look. We didn't need Utopia getting cold feet.

We followed Utopia through to the electron microscopy department.

'I'm not based down here anymore,' she said, looking around wistfully. 'But I told a friend, well, colleague, I wanted to recheck some slides from a paper I worked on.'

'Thanks.' Joe smiled. 'We really appreciate it.'

'You've got the sample?' I asked.

'Yes.' She hesitated. 'I don't know what you want to see but it's likely to be highly degraded. When Michael brought it to me, it was packed in ice but nowhere near the optimum temperature. And he'd already travelled with it, God knows how, out of Syria. Time and temperature are key when it comes to post-mortem preservation, so I just want to prepare you that we may not get much from it.'

She pulled on her white coat and gloves as she spoke. 'I can do tests, mono- and bidimensional gel electrophoresis, Western blotting, and mass spectrometry to gauge the extent of degradation but it's all going to take some time.'

I glanced at Joe. I was itching with impatience. 'Is this all necessary? Can't we just stick it under one of these microscopes?'

Utopia looked at us. 'You sound like Michael. He just wanted access to the Philips TEM.'

'The TEM?'

'The transmission electron microscope. It's super powerful. The image quality is excellent.'

'Let's do what Michael wanted,' I said. 'Stick it under the TEM.'

Utopia showed us the machine. It was unlike any microscope I remembered from school. It stood on a desk, a thick barrel, about four feet tall, that reminded me of a rocket launcher. There was a console of switches and dials, and a computer monitor.

I didn't know what I'd been expecting. Maybe a small lump of grey meat in a petri dish, but instead Utopia retrieved a series of slides from a huge freezer.

'Michael had already sectioned the sample,' explained Utopia. 'He'd had access to a lab in Surrey, but it didn't have the right cryo or microscopy services to do any more.' She hesitated. 'And he said it'd been too easy to find him there. He told me people had followed him; he'd only just managed to get out in time. I didn't know whether he was joking or crazy but I didn't take him seriously. I should have listened to him, trusted him.'

I felt a wave of sympathy for Wilmore. I knew what it was like to have the world lose faith in you, to have the people closest to you think you're mad. I was familiar with the frustration of speaking the truth but seeing nothing but disbelief, and worse, pity.

Utopia got to work. She seemed more at ease down here in this basement with the hum of the microscope, the blinking switches and dials, scribbling calculations on a piece of paper.

My burn throbbed under the dressing. I hoped Alex was tucked up in bed, and longed to hold him, to go home. I glanced at Joe. Was Trish waiting for him, another dinner in the bin? He was humming tunelessly, reading posters, flicking through a folder of protocols, looking at incomprehensible equations on a whiteboard. He nudged me and pointed to a quote written across the bottom: *I've got the brain of a four-year-old. I'll bet he was glad to be rid of it.*

'Groucho Marx,' said Joe happily.

'Brain science humour,' I replied.

It took us a while to notice that Utopia was very still and very quiet. Her whole body was frozen and rigid, as if all her energy was concentrated on one spot: whatever was under the microscope.

'Everything alright, Utopia?' asked Joe.

She jumped. 'Yes. No. I've never seen anything like this.'

She sat up. Her face was pale, her eyes wide. She fiddled with the monitor, and it blinked to life. We could see on the big screen what she'd seen through the viewfinder. There was a grainy image of organic circles and blobs of biological life. And then, clustered in the bottom right of the screen, tiny grey shapes, straight edges, sharp angles. Inorganic. Manmade. And before our eyes, these tiny contaminants began to move, microscopic hinges opening and shutting, almost like pincers, blindly moving left, then right, as if lost, unsure what to do.

'What the fuck are they?' asked Joe.

'Nanomachines,' said Utopia. 'They're tiny. Smaller than a skin cell. I mean, I've read about them, but I've never seen them. Hardly anyone has. This is cutting-edge stuff.'

She turned to look at us, her eyes shining. 'Whose brain is this?'

I shook my head. 'We don't know. But we think those things killed whoever's it was. Is that possible?'

Utopia was transfixed by the tiny devices. Finally, she spoke. 'I don't know. Yes, maybe. It depends. People are working on lots of therapeutic treatments using nanotech, creating particles that kill specific viruses, deliver medicines, kill tumours. There are only a handful of labs with this kind of technology.'

'So, it could be an experimental medical treatment gone wrong?' I asked.

Utopia nodded. 'I can't think what else it could be. I mean, Elon Musk is working on Neuralink, but I didn't think anyone had got this far. This is state-of-the-art stuff.'

Medical researchers don't kill doctors and journalists, I thought grimly.

Utopia wanted to call her old boss and show him. 'I've never seen anything like it,' she said. 'We're not really set up to analyse this. I should call the Centre for Nanotechnology on Gordon Street. They've got the proper facilities—'

She reached for the phone, but I put my hand over it.

'You can't tell anyone about this, Utopia.'

The scientist opened her mouth to protest, but I shook her head firmly. 'Nobody. Michael's dead. People he tried to tell are either dead or in hiding. Whatever this is, it's a death sentence. You must keep it to yourself.'

'But what do I do with this?' Utopia gestured at the monitor. The nanomachines were making tiny movements. 'I can't just flush this down the sink, you know. It's a biohazard.'

'You're not flushing anything,' I said. 'Put the mouse brain back in the freezer and keep it hidden until we get back to you.'

'That's what Michael said,' Utopia noted sadly. 'Only he never came back. I'm so ashamed. I should have taken him seriously but he was so…it was so outlandish, I…'

'It's OK,' I said. 'It's hard to accept the abnormal.'

'We'll come back,' Joe assured Utopia. 'And when we do, it will be with the force of the law and then you can get the nanotech experts on it. Just give us a bit more time. It doesn't look like these things have been harmed by storage.'

'No,' breathed Utopia in admiration. 'They've survived far better than the brain tissue, and they appear to be waking up. I mean, this is amazing. I'd love to run a full analysis on this sample. Perhaps we could see if the person was suffering from a neuro-degenerative disease; I've read about nanomachines being used to repair faulty—'

'No, Utopia,' I said sharply. 'You can't do anything else with this. We don't know if those things started sending a signal when they woke up.'

Utopia looked at the screen fearfully.

'It's too dangerous,' I pressed. 'Forget what you've seen. Promise me.'

Utopia nodded. 'I won't tell anyone. But I can't forget this. I've spent years studying diseased brains. This is the kind of technology that could potentially revolutionise treatment.'

I couldn't help but admire Utopia's excitement. The scientist saw hope, but the journalist in me only saw death and corruption. *People being treated for degenerative brain disease don't end up in a military-grade biohazard mortuary complex*, I thought. Whoever developed these machines had only murder in mind, and they needed to be stopped. I could tell by Joe's solemn face he was thinking along the same lines. Could we trust Utopia to keep quiet? Her tiny frame seemed to vibrate with excitement at what she had just seen. It was a risk, but we didn't have any choice.

***

We headed west in the yellow van, which had yet to gather the detritus of crumbs and chocolate bar wrappers that characterised the old one.

'This is luxury, Joe,' I said.

'Don't get too comfortable,' he growled. 'Mr Tidy will be back on the road next week.'

We stopped for food at the McDonald's on Baker Street.

'What next?' I asked between mouthfuls of fries.

'I'm still trying to get my head round what we just saw,' said Joe. 'Those were tiny machines inside a human brain. I mean, what the fuck?'

'I want to know who put them there. I mean it has to be Newby, right? That's what's really going on here. They're testing this stuff on civilians in Syria.'

Joe shrugged, his mouth full of burger. He swallowed. 'The military has a long history of using combat operations as a cover for testing new weapons,' he observed.

'Yeah, but we're not fighting in Syria. Wilmore was out there on a humanitarian mission.'

'But Newby wasn't. He was attached to Fox's unit, but he was operating outside the chain of command. Fox didn't know what was going on.' Joe wiped his mouth with a paper serviette, thinking. 'Harlen Group,' he said, at last. 'It's got their fingerprints all over it. They have the budget, the technology, and the access. They're a private contractor to the military.'

'But someone in Government knows about this,' I said. 'Newby's team was given access to Fox's unit, and then there was approval for the bodies to be removed to Lockmere. Remember Sheena said the top brass were twitchy about something.'

I sighed, suddenly tired from the long day, bloated from the rush of sugar and junk. 'I can't publish any of this. My reputation is shot. If I hint at nanoweapons being inserted in people's brains, my sister will have me sectioned.'

'We need an in to The Harlen Group. But they're going to be a tough nut to crack,' Joe said.

A warped idea formed in my mind, and I smiled. 'Actually, thinking about it, we may already know just the hammer for the job. Someone who can help us bust them wide open.'

63

I KNEW Joe didn't like the plan, but he was a pragmatic man. The Harlen Group was inaccessible, they stonewalled interview requests and refused to engage via phone or email. Most organisations leak – unhappy workers, disgruntled ex-employees and squeezed suppliers – but The Harlen Group was watertight. Perhaps it was gold-plated remuneration packages, or its reputation for being an aggressive litigant. However they did it, there was an impenetrable wall of silence around the organisation.

So, we were going to need a bigger hammer. And I'd found one. But Joe still didn't like it. It had given him great personal pleasure to expose Sir John Phelps. The man represented everything that was wrong with politics. He was venal, corrupt and steeped in the lazy prejudices of his class, which he'd never bothered to shed by spending time with the people he claimed to represent. And so arrogant. That had been his undoing. It had been so easy to bring him down because he believed himself untouchable.

But now he was to be our hammer. It felt like some kind of karma to me. I'd trashed Phelps's reputation and he'd threatened to ruin me with a libel claim, and yet now I was phoning to ask for his help bringing down a bigger enemy.

'You've got balls,' said Joe, and I grinned. Big compliment from him.

We were in his bolt hole in the East End, where he'd finally persuaded me to stay. The fact they'd tried to snatch me outside a courthouse showed how desperate Newby's crew was getting. And desperate people were dangerous. They'd almost certainly be watching Emilia and Alex.

'You keep them safe by staying away,' Joe had said, and I'd seen the sense in that.

His bolt hole was a one-bed second-floor flat off Roman Road. It was basic. A battered sofa, table and chairs, and a kitchen stocked with enough tins, teabags and powdered milk to hole up for a few weeks. It had superfast broadband, a clear view of the street and Joe's lockup where he kept the vans, and, most importantly, a good exit.

'This door is reinforced steel, but if we need to get out in a hurry you go to the bedroom, lock the door, climb on the chest of drawers and go into the loft. There's a walkway above the next two houses – you have to crawl on your belly past one cos they've stuffed it with bloody insulation, but you'll drop out into another little gaff of mine three doors along. Out the fire escape, down the alleyway and head for the Bow Road tube or hop on a bus.'

'I never knew you were such a property mogul, Joe.'

'Gotta subsidise the sleuthing somehow,' he replied.

'Sorry, Joe. This is taking up so much of your time. And I can't even afford mate's rates now. But I'll pay you back one day. I promise.'

'Julia, please. It's not about the money. I want to be here. This matters. If we're right, this will make a difference.'

'I know, Joe, but I will pay my way. It matters to me.'

A shadow passed over his face and I could see something wasn't sitting right with him. I told him to just spit it out. He took a deep breath.

'Look, Jules, I want you to stop worrying about the money. I know you'll pay when you can. And I'm not short. The PI business pays well. I can afford to turn work down if it doesn't interest me. And, as you see, I've got a few properties. More than a few actually. And I've got you to thank for that.'

'How so?'

'I was doing some low-key surveillance stuff, just covering costs really, when Stone called me about finding a missing person. It seemed an impossible job, but he knew I've got contacts and can keep my mouth shut. When I found that person, well, Stone's client was very grateful. There was a bonus, a sizeable one. I put it into property, round here and further east. It's proved a nice earner.'

'I was the missing person.'

He nodded. 'Your dad really loves you, you know, Julia. He was desperate to get you back, whatever the cost.'

I scoffed. 'That's his solution to everything. Throw money at it.'

'You didn't see him, Julia. He was broken.'

I digested his words, pacing the flat, running my hands through my hair. Joe watched me anxiously, like I was a bomb about to explode.

'It never sat right with me that you're fretting about paying me while I'm sitting pretty based on the bonus your dad paid me. Anyway, I wanted you to know.'

I stopped pacing and faced him, controlling the feelings that always surged when I thought about my father. Joe looked so worried, like a man on trial for his life.

'Jules,' he said gently.

I held up my hand and gestured for quiet. 'So, my dad threw a load of money at you and this is what you got?' I gestured round the poky one-bed, with its tired wallpaper, the stained carpet and the sagging sofa. 'You know, Emilia would faint if she saw that kitchen.' And I broke into a big grin. 'Don't look so worried, Joe. I'm glad for you. But seriously, man, you should have asked for more. I'm worth at least a Dulwich three-bed.'

He smiled, relieved. Was I really so scary?

'Come on, man, let's get back to work. Now I know the price that was paid for me, I'm going to be getting my money's worth.'

He grinned. 'Alright then. Anything from Phelps?'

I shook my head.

'Still nothing.'

'It's not like he's going to be in a hurry to call,' said Joe. 'We're not exactly his favourite people.'

He ran his hand over his face. He looked dog tired. He'd taken a call from Trish earlier and while I'd tried not to listen, it was hard in this small flat not to get the gist that he'd had an earful about his latest disappearance.

'Look, he's probably not going to get back to us tonight. Why don't you get some shut eye? There's clean sheets and stuff in the bedroom. I'm gonna watch a bit of telly, then have a kip out here.'

But even as he spoke, the phone in my hand began to vibrate.

'It's him.'

'Put it on loudspeaker,' Joe suggested.

I pressed the button and moments later Phelps' plummy tones filled the little flat. His voice instantly grated on me. I'd grown up around posh people, but Phelps was so over the top.

'You've some nerve,' Phelps began. 'I hope this is an apology.'

'Not exactly. I need your help with a story.'

He laughed luxuriantly. 'Oh, I rather think you do, my dear. Not had much luck lately, have you? What is it this time? Extra-terrestrials ate my baby? Or is it the lizard people? All you conspiracy nuts seem to love that one.'

'Nothing like that,' I said, willing myself to stay calm. 'It's to do with your seat on the Defence Committee.'

'What about it?' barked Phelps.

'You do a good job on there,' I told him. Joe raised his eyebrows. He loathed Phelps.

'It pains me to admit it, but you do,' I continued. 'We have a story about a company that may have crossed your path, The Harlen Group. You need to probe them, and their activities in Syria. There are some troubling unexplained civilian deaths in an area where their contractors were operating. You might be greedy but you're no murderer. And if Harlen had you in their back pocket, then you wouldn't have been looking for cash from us. Ask some questions. If this gets out, then it's the kind of thing that could really blow back on the Government. The committee could get out in front of the story and set the agenda. You could look like a hero.'

There was a pause that seemed to last an age.

'Send me a briefing paper,' he said. 'And I'll look into it. But it had better not be any more of your cock-and-bull.'

'It's not,' I replied. 'This is big. And it needs the weight and gravitas of the Defence Committee behind it.'

I knew Phelps would already be imagining himself grilling some hapless Harlen Group executive, preening for the Today Programme and BBC News. Maybe get himself back on Question Time. Win some brownie points from the PM.

'If it's good, I'll drop the libel suit,' Phelps offered.

Joe and I shared a look of surprise. This was an unexpected bonus.

'I don't need to waste money on lawyers,' Phelps advised. 'You've wrecked your credibility so thoroughly on your own, most people think your story on me was also bullshit. Job done.'

I fought for composure. 'Well, that's very magnanimous of you,' I managed.

'He conquers twice, who shows mercy to the conquered,' remarked Phelps, clearly pleased with himself. 'Julius Caesar.'

'I'll get that brief to you,' I said and ended the call with a shudder. I felt unclean even talking to the man. 'Urgh, he has no shame.'

'But he's no fool,' remarked Joe. 'Don't underestimate him. He knows this is an opportunity for him to make headlines for a different reason.'

'I'm going to have a shower and I'll dress this bloody burn,' I said, picking up a bag of my things Sam had dropped off. 'Is that OK?'

'Go for it,' said Joe. 'Make yourself at home. *Mi casa es su casa.*'

I grinned and headed for the bathroom. It was reasonably clean – old military habits die hard – but it was still basic. I'd noticed earlier that under the pretence of doing a wipe around, Joe had surreptitiously removed the nail scissors and razors. But he didn't need to worry. The case was keeping me focused and I didn't feel the need to cut. I turned on the shower head and let clouds of steam eclipse my reflection in the mirror. Stay focused, I told myself, this could be the fight of my life.

Feeling cleansed by the shower, my burn dressed and healing nicely, I left the bathroom just wearing my t-shirt and pants, and a towel wrapped round my hair. For a moment, I felt embarrassed by my near nakedness but when I glanced at Joe he was in front of the TV, feet up, engrossed in football digest.

'Night, Joe,' I said. 'Try to get some rest.'

'You too,' he replied, keeping his eyes firmly on the football.

64

IT FELT good to be back in business. I phoned Lyndsey to talk through the status of the site following the attempted hack. We discussed how to rebuild my profile on social media, and Lyndsey mooted a redesign for the site now that most of the advertisers, except my loyal wine club, had fled. Then I FaceTimed Alex. He looked well, tousled with sleep, another tooth gone, pure delight flashing across his face when he saw his mother. But too soon he was distracted, seduced by the lure of his cousins, and breakfast, and kittens under the bunkbeds. I knew he loved me, but youth is like a butterfly, flitting from one interesting flower to the next. I was pleased, of course. This was how it should be. I did not want him to sit and pine for me, but it was like a little stab of ice in the heart, how quickly the call ended, his relief to be off the phone, racing to join his playmates.

Emilia's smile now filled the screen. Even the unforgiving medium of FaceTime, with its unflattering angles and brutal lighting, couldn't dent her fresh-faced beauty.

'Don't worry, Jules,' she said. 'He is missing you. He asks about you every day. They all get on so well. And he got a gold star of the week in Friday assembly. For being a helpful friend at lunchtime.'

My heart swelled. 'Oh, that's wonderful. And another tooth gone.'

'Yes, Philippe thinks the tooth fairy's out to bankrupt us.'

'Don't set the going rate too high, Em. I've got to finance the rest of the mouth.'

'So,' said Emilia, a false brightness in her voice. 'What's going on? When are you coming back?'

'William told you what happened outside the court? I'm keeping away until we have this cracked. But we're close now, very close.'

There was a pause, long enough that I wondered if we'd lost connection. Eventually Emilia spoke again. 'Did you get the message from William about Arlet? The last Friday in April, maybe make a long weekend of it.'

Now it was my turn to hesitate. 'Is this his idea?'

'It just came up in general conversation, organically,' tinkled Emilia. 'Daddy really wants to reach out to you. And it would be wonderful, all of us together. The kids would love it. Alex and Edgar are inseparable and Arlet's like a giant adventure playground. Do you remember?'

I sighed. That was the problem; I did remember. The lonely nights in cold bedrooms; the stepmothers, successively erasing all traces of my mother; the shooting weekends, with a changing gallery of strangers, braying drunks, red-faced and half cut by teatime; children to be seen and not heard.

'Let me think about it,' I said.

'Jules, come on, one weekend,' pleaded Emilia. 'It would do us all good. The bluebells will be out. Come on, Alex would love it. He could help with the lambs on Lower Farm. Come on, for me.'

Every instinct told me not to go, but Emilia never asked for anything.

'OK, for you. And Alex.'

Emilia's face burst into a radiant smile.

'But Em, if he starts on me, I won't be held responsible for my actions. My life is what it is. I'm not going to change. Not for him.'

Emilia released a little high nervous laugh. 'Don't be silly, Jules. We'll have a lovely time.'

Privately I thought it would be anything but lovely; however, I would bear it for my sister, and Emilia was right, Alex would love it. If the weather was good, they could even take a boat on the lake and go fishing. And maybe a riding lesson at the farm.

I said goodbye to my sister and hung up as Joe came in, bearing bacon butties and mugs of tea.

'Plan?' he asked.

'I'm going to draft the brief for our new friend on the Defence Committee, and then I'm going to publish a teaser story.'

'Really?'

'Yeah, I think we need to make sure Phelps doesn't duck out on us. And it wouldn't hurt to give The Harlen Group a poke.'

'A poke?' Joe seemed uncertain.

'Yeah. We know Newby's on the Harlen books because you've got him tagged to an office registered to one of their affiliates. And then there's the credit cards. We have the statements from Fox, that Newby was up to no good in Syria. We've seen dead bodies in Lockmere. We've got Lazard and Hinstock at the scene of Howell's murder. I can run a story that The Harlen Group needs to expect some tough questions about its activities in Syria, unexplained civilian deaths with, how many was it?' – I flicked through my notebook – 'eighteen dead bodies brought back to the UK for post-mortems.'

I chewed my pen lid. 'Hm, we have the footage from Lockmere but I'm reluctant to run it yet. They'll slap an injunction on us and Sheena will be in deep shit.'

'I'm also not keen on showing the dead kids on the Internet,' pointed out Joe quietly. 'This isn't just a story. It's a crime. A tragedy.'

'Yeah, I know,' I said, booting up Joe's laptop. 'But I want to get this out there. I think we need to get people asking questions, put some pressure on Newby and his friends. If they've been using the cover of war to perform sick experiments, the world needs to know about it.'

'Yeah, I've been trying not to think about what they were doing,' said Joe. 'It's creepy, right? I mean these things, these nanomachines, you inject them. Utopia said they could be used to mend brains, but what if they do the opposite; what if they destroy them? It's the perfect weapon, undetectable but completely deadly, no environmental fallout, completely targeted, no collateral damage.'

'That's why we have to stop them, Joe,' I said.

I started typing, my fingers flying over the keyboard, lost in the flow of words.

65

I CALLED William Stone later to let him know that Phelps was in play. I wanted, I suppose, to reassure Emilia, and by extension my father, that I wasn't mad. That my teaser piece on The Harlen Group wasn't a sign of a paranoid mind unravelling.

'I saw your latest piece,' he said. 'Anything I need to know?'

'I wouldn't have published if I didn't have the evidence, William. Harlen Group won't admit to anything, but I have evidence I haven't published and may never publish. But believe me, I can link their people to Syria, to bodies in a secret military morgue, to what can only be described as a highly experimental weapon.'

There was a pause while he digested this. I suppose it did sound a little mad just blurted out like that.

'I'm not mad,' I added for good measure, though I suppose that's what a mad person might very well say.

'I've had a lovely letter from their lawyers,' Stone said.

'Why you? You don't represent me.'

'And yet they have made the connection. They clearly know a lot about you.'

'That doesn't surprise me. I'm not paranoid, by the way. It's just a fact of life, working on these kinds of stories. You ever hear of Tyrone Hayes?'

'No.'

'He was a researcher whose life was almost ruined by a biotech firm. When there's money at stake, big business plays dirty.'

'I didn't say a word,' said Stone. 'Emilia's worried about you.'

'I know. I'm sure she's planning some kind of intervention. She wants us to play happy families at Arlet next month.'

'She's a fixer,' Stone said. 'She has been her whole life. It's her strength and her curse.'

'Gosh, William, you do sound wise. A wise owl.'

'My wife says I'm a silly old coot. How nice to be an owl instead. Something else you should know. Emilia told me Philippe isn't happy about your latest activities. Apparently, his firm has some investments in this Harlen Group, and he thinks Joe pumped him for information about some new IP at lunch the other day and that you're somehow using The Castleton Files to manipulate the value of the company.'

I laughed. 'Now who's being paranoid? Come on, William, you and Emilia really don't think that, do you? I mean Joe's got as much interest in money as I have in Farrow & Ball paint colours, which is apparently something some people are interested in.'

Now William laughed. 'Actually, they do have some lovely greens this season. But I'm just giving you the heads up. Tread gently with Emilia. She's a rock, but she feels a lot, you know.'

'I understand.'

'And while I know I'm not your lawyer, I'd still like to help you,' he went on. 'If you're to go ahead, then you need to have a strategy for dealing with The Harlen Group, and somehow you need to disentangle from this fake news agenda. One of their spokeswomen was on earlier, calling you a fake news blogger and a danger to democracy.'

'Don't worry, I've got that sorted,' I said. 'Defence Committee today. Watch it. You'll see. It's going to be a physics lesson.'

'A physics lesson?'

'At The Castleton Files, we don't have the mass to open The Harlen Group. So we're going to use a lever. Look, William, don't worry. Watch the Defence Committee. You'll see what I mean.'

We ended the call amicably enough, but I couldn't help wondering what report would be sent back to my father. Everything rode on Phelps now.

66

I WOKE at 6:00 AM. The thin cotton curtains were little defence against dawn. I immediately reached for my phone and squinted at the bright screen as I tried to shake off the fog of another broken night. Had I been dreaming? The covers were twisted round my legs. I remembered footsteps echoing down endless corridors, a darkness behind me, or was it darkness ahead? It was unclear in these dreams why I was running. Was I searching for someone? Or fleeing from them? No wonder I was always so tired.

I checked my emails and notifications, my brain fizzing with excitement as I realised my plan had worked, it had really worked. I had to hand it to Phelps, he was a consummate performer. I had almost believed him myself, his impassioned plea that the honour of British armed forces, working on a humanitarian mission for some of the most vulnerable people on the planet, not be tarnished by the activities of unregulated contractors. That the activities of The Harlen Group in Syria be investigated:

'I see no reason why this humanitarian mission needs the assistance of a private contractor, for surely, here, at this time, in this place, in the face of so much suffering, there can be no profit margin. So, I think, even before we investigate some of the more alarming allegations about the unexplained deaths in the local population and the transportation of bodies to the UK, we have serious questions to ask about the involvement of The Harlen Group, about the scope of its contract and its remuneration.'

And that, it seemed, was sufficient to turn the tide. The civil servant put up by the MoD had blustered and obfuscated, clearly blindsided by Phelp's sudden interest. And that obfuscation, tinged with panic, was enough to give credence to Phelp's claim that something untoward had happened in Syria.

There were small pieces in *The Times* and *The Guardian* – although only the latter namechecked The Castleton Files as having broken the story ahead of Phelp's intervention – and a couple of human rights bloggers had started tweeting about the issue. *The Harlen Group must be sweating,* I thought. That no comment strategy wouldn't work for much longer.

There was a knock on the door. 'Are you decent?'

I sat up hurriedly and pulled the hoodie over my pyjamas. I ran a hand through my tangled hair. I knew I smelt of sweat, of morning breath, and clothes too long lived in. But it was only Joe. He'd seen me far worse.

He poked his head round, bearing a steaming cup of tea. I was getting used to his tea-making now. Weak, too much milk and in heavy chipped mugs, but the thought was kind.

'I wanted to make sure you were up,' he said. 'Phelps is going to be on Today in ten minutes.'

I high-fived Joe. 'There's no burying this now.'

He grinned. 'The irony of it all is, this is your biggest story, and the person fronting it is bloody Phelps!'

'You can't script life, Joe. And you know what, it's better this way. He has a better face for radio than me.'

We laughed. I was suddenly giddy with the release. If the story was moving into the daylight, then we would be safe. Officialdom would grind into action, questions would be asked, investigations opened, and Newby and his hoodlums would be imprisoned or disappeared.

We went into the kitchen and gathered round Joe's paint-spattered radio to listen to Today. I sipped my tea cautiously – it was so insipid yet also strangely nourishing – while Joe fiddled with his phone to record the feature. There were some serious questions, which Phelps handled competently, giving the air of a serious politician with a lifelong commitment to victims of civil war. The presenter reiterated that The Harlen Group had declined to be interviewed, and then the tone lightened as he joked about Phelps' recent discomfort at the hands of what he called 'the largely debunked alternative news blog', The Castleton Files.

'I mean, come on, what's really going on here?' the presenter asked.

'Far be it from me to tell you how to do your job, but I think I, and many licence fee payers, will be wondering why it's an independent website and not the BBC that has raised these important questions about The Harlen Group. Yes, I've had my run-ins with The Castleton Files, yes lawyers have been involved about possible libels, so I'm not going to comment further on those' – at this I shook my head, *the sly old fox* – 'but I have my own research on what The Harlen Group has been doing in Syria and I have come to the same conclusion as Miss Castleton: questions need to be asked. And if it's not by the mainstream media like the BBC, then I think we need to be thankful we have a thriving independent news sector out there ready to tackle these big stories.'

My mouth dropped open. Phelps had namechecked me on Radio 4's flagship news programme. He'd done more to repair my reputation than I could ever have imagined. He had defended The Castleton Files on mainstream news.

'I could kiss his big bald head,' I said to Joe when the segment ended.

Joe smiled, draining his tea. 'You've got a big story to write,' he said. 'Everyone's going to be chasing this now, so you have to get out in front.'

'On it,' I said. 'I've already written the skeleton.'

'We still need to deal with Utopia's brain sample.'

'Yeah. With everything that's happening, I'd like that to be in official hands sooner rather than later.'

My phone buzzed. It was a text from Phelps. *Just been on* Today. *Had them eating out of my hand. Planning to call Harlen before committee for thorough roasting. Rather enjoying myself and I've not even had breakfast yet!*

Two minutes later there was another text. A selfie of Phelps at Broadcasting House. Ten minutes later, a photo of his breakfast.

'No wonder he's so porky,' mused Joe, peering over my shoulder. 'That's a lot of carbs.'

Another text. *Just got a thumbs up from PM's press secretary.*

'You two best mates now?' queried Joe.

'He's going to want something in return,' I cautioned. 'Right now he's on a high to be back in the limelight for something other than his hideous corruption, but it won't be long until his baser instincts kick in again.'

I stood up, stretched and paced the room. I would write the story today, as much as I could, publish it, let the proper authorities know about the brain sample at UCL and the bodies at Lockmere. Once it was all in the open and the evidence in the right hands, my job would be done. I'd be safe and I could collect Alex and go home. Home. I hugged myself at the thought. Fresh clothes, hot shower, my own food, my boy in his own bed.

I sat down at the rickety table, opened the laptop and began to write.

67

IT WAS early evening when I finished. A light drizzle was falling, and the traffic hissed through the wet streets. I called Alex, told him I'd be back tomorrow, and we would go home. His response, a mix of delight and something else – relief? – left me ashamed at how long it had been. I had disrupted his life enough. It was time to get back to being a mother. *A mother and a publisher*, I thought with quiet satisfaction, casting my eye over my day's work. It was a good story, a huge story, and my evidence, from the video footage of our investigation at Lockmere to the recording of the outputs of the microscope, was incontrovertible. I still didn't have a comment from The Harlen Group but that was OK. I had made repeated requests for an interview and their silence was louder than any PR-crafted corporate word salad.

I stood up, stretched and paced the little flat. I was anxious to be done with it all now, to publish the piece and send all the evidence to William Stone. He would know who to give it to. I didn't trust the police, not after Tull. I stood by the window, fiddled with the flimsy slats of the cheap grey blinds and peered out. The rain was heavier, caught in the lights like shards of glass. The doorway to the lockup glowed yellow. Joe was doing some work on the van. It had been a strange few days, cooped up together in this flat, eating down his tins, drinking his milky tea, growing used to each other. It had been easier than I'd thought. We hadn't spoken much. Joe was taciturn by nature, and I was given to long broody silences at the best of times. I wondered if Trish was a talker, and then questioned whether it was natural to spend so much time speculating about his other half. *It's only because he never talks about her*, I told myself. *It makes her a mystery, a blank. It's normal to be curious.*

I sat down to copy-edit my work. I was ready to publish but I wanted Joe to have a final read to make sure I wasn't missing anything obvious. My phone buzzed. It was Phelps. Again. *Got something new on Harlen Group. You only have part of the story. Meet me tonight. Urgent. My place.* The phone buzzed again. This time it was his address, a block of flats in Pimlico.

I frowned, disliking his proprietary air. I only had part of the story? I couldn't really publish without checking what Phelps had. My experiences with the Wilmore dossier had made me very cautious.

I texted him. *What is it? Call me.*

A response pinged back. *No. Don't trust phones with something this big. Come now. Urgent!*

I was ready to bet my laptop it wasn't big or urgent, but could I take that risk? I phoned Joe but it went straight to voicemail. He'd be elbow deep in the guts of the van. I pulled on my trainers and coat, borrowed one of Joe's baseball caps and ran down to the lockup.

I smiled then. The radio was on and he was singing along to some pop song. Clearly, he was no stranger to the collected works of Little Mix.

'I didn't know you were a fan,' I said.

He looked up, at once alert, wondering why I was down here. 'Everything alright?'

'Another text from Phelps. He says he's got something for us on Harlen and wants to meet now, his place.'

Joe raised his eyebrows. 'You said he'd be wanting something in return. He's not wasting any time.'

'But what if he really has got something? I need to check it out. I can't have any hole in this story. Not after what happened before.'

Joe wiped his oily hands on a rag. 'Come on then, I'll take you. I'll be chaperone; that will kill his ardour.'

I laughed. 'I can handle him. No, what worries me more is if he has some kind of business proposition.'

'Business?'

'I don't know. But I don't trust him an inch. And I'd like a recording of anything he has to say to me. To protect myself in the future.'

Joe rubbed his hands together in glee. 'Lovely jubbly,' he said. 'Let me get Sam on the blower. He's got some new kit we've been dying to try out.'

68

HALF AN hour later I was sitting in the back of the van with Sam bent low over my cleavage. His tongue was between his teeth, his breath soft on my neck. Joe was holding a flashlight so the young man could get a better look. I focused on sitting very still. Sam was holding a needle very close to my chest, finishing his alterations.

He rocked back on his heels, his head on one side, and admired his handiwork. 'Not bad, eh? You're a one-woman covert camera crew.'

I looked down. The button camera was installed on a red polo shirt borrowed from Joe. They'd had to change the other buttons to make them match, hence the impromptu sewing session. I straightened the top self-consciously, hoping Sam hadn't noticed the stained vest top and greying bra that lurked underneath.

'Nice work,' I said. 'But I never wear polo shirts. I feel like I'm about to start a shift at McDonald's.'

'That's Ralph Lauren,' said Joe, mock offended.

'You've been done, mate,' scoffed Sam. 'That's not one of Ralph's.'

Joe looked genuinely surprised. 'It looks real. Got the labels.'

'Nah, you can tell by the seams.'

'Er, sorry to break up the fashion show but does this thing work?' I asked.

Joe was fiddling with a box that fitted in his palm. It was a small monitor, with headphones.

'Yeah, coming through loud and clear,' he said. 'It's wireless, so you won't need to worry about him finding anything.'

'I hardly think he's going to search me,' I said. 'This is Sir John Phelps of the Defence Committee, not the Mafia.'

'Same difference, innit,' Sam responded. 'We can record and livestream. I love this stuff.'

I pulled on my jacket but made sure the buttons of the polo shirt were uncovered. 'Does it matter if it gets wet?' I asked. 'It's pouring out there.'

'Better zip up for now,' said Joe. 'You can take your coat off when you get inside. Just be casual though. Don't be looking at the buttons, fiddling with them. He's a fool but he's not an idiot.'

We climbed into the cab of the van and set off for Pimlico. The rain had driven most people inside and the streets were empty. The puddles gleamed thick and oily under the streetlights, and the van's window wipers thumped rhythmically. An ambulance raced by, the blue lights reflected in the wet road, and I suddenly thought of the bodies in the Lockmere mortuary. It wasn't cold but I shivered inside my thin coat. Really, I hoped this was just a clumsy pass from Phelps. I'd have a drink, give him the brush off and laugh about it with Joe on the drive home. I wanted rid of this Harlen story. I'd be glad to publish and let it be someone else's problem, let someone else rip the company apart, drag the directors through the courts. Let the mainstream media dig into the Government, harry ministers, shake sources, broadcast questions and conjecture until the truth – who sanctioned what, who knew about Mortuary 4's grisly remains – at last tumbled free. I thought of Philippe and wondered how much money he stood to lose. Did he know about the nanomachines? Was that the IP he was so keen to monetise? He couldn't know. Despite my distaste for him, I couldn't believe he was that kind of man. He was an investor, but the massively complex world of corporate finance meant that it was easy for people like Philippe to own stakes without having to ask difficult questions.

My phone buzzed again. Another text from Phelps. *On phone. Important call. Just text when you get here and I'll buzz you in. Come straight up.*

I rolled my eyes. It was my natural instinct, when told what to do, to resist. It was one reason school had been such a torment for so many years. I didn't like Phelp's assumption that because I'd asked for his help, I was now his to command.

'What is it?' asked Joe.

'Phelps. Wants me to go straight up. He's on an important call.'

'He thinks everything he does is important,' said Joe. 'Pompous prick.'

He double-parked outside a nondescript block of flats, brown brick, white security shutters over the ground floor windows. A pair of sad-looking potted bay trees guarded the double glass doors that opened onto a dimly lit lobby. Most of the building was in darkness.

'Investment flats,' Joe noted. 'Absentee owners banking on London property. Better than gold.'

I shrugged. It was a world away from my grotty flat in White City. I watched a well-dressed woman, all flicky hair, oversized bag and carefully styled scarf, exit the building, a little pug trotting at her heels. *That could be me*, I thought, *if I'd chosen easy street.* So many decisions – some I couldn't even remember making – had brought me here, to this van, in my cheap jeans and borrowed polo shirt, my bank account empty, my kid the subject of a care hearing. Which one, I wondered, which was the pivotal decision? The choice that had divorced me forever from a life like Emilia's, or the unknown flicky-haired woman's? Would I be happier, I wondered, if I lived here, if I lived that life? Would Alex?

A horn tooted behind us.

'Fuck,' said Joe. 'I can't park here. We're going to have to circle the block.'

'I'll get out,' I offered, opening the door. 'You get a spot and I'll find you when I'm done.'

I jumped down, slammed the door and gave Joe a thumbs up. Phelps was on the tenth floor. I rang his flat, and the glass door buzzed and clicked open straight away. I crossed the lobby and my shoes squeaked on the highly polished floor. I called for a lift and got in. It smelt of polish, and a hint of expensive perfume, no doubt the lingering aftermath of Flicky Hair's ride down. I checked my appearance in the mirror and inwardly groaned. Flicky Hair had looked better groomed just to walk her dog. *Still, at least Phelps won't think I'm trying to lead him on*, I thought, as the lift doors pinged open. I stepped into a corridor of magnolia walls and beige carpet. An arrangement of silk flowers stood on a small table. Everywhere was so quiet. It was a Mary Celeste of a building, so different from my block, where you could hear people's lives being played out at full volume. There were always kids crying, the distant thud, thud, thud of a sound system and the rattle of applause on a neighbour's telly.

I reached Phelps' flat and found the door ajar. It was quiet, but I could see the yellow glow of lamps further inside. I hesitated for a moment, assailed by a fleeting mental image of him in a bathrobe, champagne in a cooler, lounging on the bed, a picture of seduction, but I shook myself, and pushed the door wide.

'Hello,' I called softly, wondering if he was still on the phone. I headed towards the light and passed a small cloakroom with its smell of bleach and aftershave, and another doorway, all in darkness.

And then I saw Phelps lying on the floor, his face turned away from me. I quickly went to his side, but as soon as I dropped to my knees beside his body, I saw this was no accident or tumble and that it was already far too late for any first aid. Phelps was lying on his side, one arm pinned under his body, his bald head twisted at an awkward angle, a pool of blood, thickly black, shiny as a jewel, spread across the beige carpet. There was a wound, and I instinctively looked away. I caught just a fleeting impression, bits of pink flesh, yellow fat, white bone, some horror where once an eye had been, a cheekbone.

My mouth filled with saliva, my face suddenly hot, and I forced myself to breathe and count, breathe and count, fighting back the impulse to retch.

Sir John Phelps had been murdered. Shot in the eye.

69

A DOOR shut behind me, and I wheeled round. There was someone else in the flat. The killer, of course, hiding in the darkness. Suddenly my nausea was gone. Now every sinew was tensed. I could feel the little hairs on the back of my neck standing to attention, my hearing catching every sound, near and far, from the tick of a little travel clock on the mantelpiece to the throb of adrenaline-laced blood pulsing through my body.

This, I thought with a sudden blinding flash, *this is the moment that will determine everything else*. A sudden calm descended, driving out the panic, like the muffled silence that comes with heavy snowfall.

This, I told myself, *this is what it is to be truly in the moment, to be real.*

My breath was caught somewhere high in my throat. I heard the rustle of material, then the living room door pushed a touch wider. James Newby. His blond hair was damp, as if he'd been in the rain, but then I saw the towel in his hand and realised, with a horrible sickening feeling, that he'd probably just been in the bathroom, washing off blood.

'Julia, Julia,' he said, in that public school drawl. 'So good to see you again.'

'What the fuck have you done?' I asked.

'What? Phelps?' He walked over, still drying his hands on the towel, to where I remained crouched by the politician's body. Newby's polished leather boot gently nudged Phelps' skull. 'This upsets you? You surprise me, Julia. He was ready to ruin you.'

There was another noise, deeper in the flat. A voice. 'Search her, she'll be filming.'

Newby smiled, thinly. 'My esteemed colleague makes a very good point. Stand up, please.'

I swallowed and panic flooded my body again. I stood and tried to still my trembling limbs. I could hear someone lumbering through the flat. It was the black guy from the BMW. Karl Lazard. I noticed with some satisfaction that he was limping heavily, leaning on a stick.

'I think you two have met before,' said Newby with a thin smile.

Lazard glowered at me. 'Get her phone,' he growled, gingerly lowering his bulk onto the arm of a cream sofa.

Newby flashed an apologetic smile at me. 'Sorry about this, Julia, but I'm afraid you're terribly out of your depth.'

'Fuck you,' I muttered.

Newby raised his eyebrows, like a teacher giving an unruly pupil an early warning. He threw the towel down, then quickly grabbed my right wrist and twisted it roughly behind my back. I gasped with the pain. It felt as though he might snap my arm. He patted down my pockets with one hand, never once releasing the pressure on my right arm. He retrieved my purse and my phone, then let me go, pushing me roughly down onto a chair.

I rubbed my arm. His fingers had been like steel pincers gripping to the bone, and I suspected this was just a taste of the violence that was to come. He may have the blond good looks and suave vowels of a public schoolboy, but this man knew how to hurt, how to kill. But he hadn't spotted the button camera. I swallowed nervously, praying he wouldn't come back for a closer examination. I watched him warily as he examined my phone and flicked through my purse casually.

'No wires?' he asked, looking at me. 'Bit amateur hour?'

'Don't take any chances,' said Lazard from across the room. 'Toss it out the window.'

Newby smiled. 'Oh, we can do better than that,' and he crossed to the small open-plan kitchen, separated from the living room by a shiny marble-topped counter and three bar stools. He dropped the phone into the sink and there was a horrible crunching and grinding noise. Newby grinned manically, shouting above the noise.

'I love a good garbage disposal. Best. American. Import. Ever.'

He seemed to be enjoying himself. There was a terrible familiarity about him. I recognised the raw and powerful energy. It reminded me of the Tattooed Man who plagued my dreams. Lazard, on the other hand, seemed resentful and tired. Perhaps it was the pain in his knee.

'Someone's waiting for me,' I said. 'Downstairs. If I don't go down, they'll call the police.'

Newby scoffed at this. 'You mean Joe Turner, your White Van Man. How very democratic of you, Julia. Don't worry, Dunn's dealing with him.' He checked his watch. 'He'll be here in a minute. No police. No, I'm sorry, Julia, I really am. I like you. You've got balls. We threw some heavy stuff your way, the kind of stuff that would make most people fall apart, but you kept going. A dog with a bone. I respect that. There aren't enough people in the world with principles anymore, prepared to do what it takes. So seriously, I salute you.'

And he turned to face me, and threw a solemn salute, and a little formal bow.

I glared at him, and he laughed casually.

'That's my girl. What a shame it has to end this way. But I suppose it was inevitable. I wanted to kill you before now, but orders are orders and my superiors didn't believe you posed a threat. I mean, who takes conspiracy nuts like you seriously? So I was tasked with discrediting you.'

I nodded down at Phelps. 'Why?' I asked. 'You didn't have to kill him. He's the kind of man you could pay off.'

Newby shrugged. 'He was causing too much trouble, got carried away with himself. And besides, it's a wonderful smokescreen, just what we need to help tidy up the loose ends. It's so useful, you see, that you have been so wonderfully, delightfully, publicly crazy.' He reached inside his blazer, and I watched with a kind of fascinated horror as he pulled out a gun with a long barrel, and began to screw what I realised was a suppressor into the muzzle. 'It's the perfect back story and we didn't even have to make it up. Just perfect, isn't it, Karl?'

Lazard just grunted as he watched me resentfully from across the room.

'You see, crazy journalist lady fixates on corrupt politician. Kills him, then kills herself. It's so neat and so believable. A murder-suicide. The final tragic end of a broken mind. There will be a lot of hair-pulling and chest-beating about the decline in mental health funding, the state of our NHS, perhaps the role of social media. Because you're very active on social media, aren't you, Julia?'

He chuckled then. 'But you've been so busy running around after us you haven't even noticed we hacked your social accounts. Some of your posts, well, seen with hindsight, in the wake of a murderous spree, will point to an obvious decline. Such a shame, everyone will say.'

I realised I was shaking. Was it fear? Was it anger? I watched the gun and desperately tried to figure a way out. I thought of Alex and was almost overcome at the prospect of never seeing him again. I had to buy time.

'Fuck you,' I muttered again.

Newby snorted. 'For someone who works with words you're surprisingly unimaginative. Is that all you have to say? These are your last moments, Julia, these words your last testament. Give us something to remember you by.'

'If you kill me, you'll never know what hit you,' I threatened. 'I've made contingency plans.'

Newby hesitated and cast Lazard an uncertain look.

The intercom buzzed and Newby went over and peered at the screen.

'It's Dunn,' he said, pressing the button that unlocked the front doors.

I thought how stupid I had been, just blindly following those texts when they had clearly been sent by Newby. I wondered how long Phelps had been dead.

The door opened and Dunn walked in. He smiled nastily at me.

'Your pal went down quickly for a big fella. Flabby, soft. Disgrace for a former Para.'

I reeled with the horror of it all. Joe, wonderful, protective Joe, the man who'd saved me so many times, was dead, and he'd been killed because of me.

I had to fight the urge to be sick.

70

'YOU AND him have been bumbling around like a pair of bloody Miss Marples,' mocked Dunn. 'Well, this is the big league, you fucking numpties.'

I tried to control my breathing. Panic bubbled up but I forced it down.

'Miss Marple always wins the day,' I said, sounding calmer than I felt. 'You'd know that if you could read, you moron.'

Dunn slapped me across the face. The shock of it was like a tonic. I lunged at him and landed a sharp kick on his thigh bone. I'd been aiming higher but was still pleased to see it hurt.

'Bitch,' he shouted, raising his hand, but Newby caught him and pulled him back.

'Stop it,' he said. 'We can't have her looking like she's been scrapping. PC Plod isn't entirely clueless.'

Dunn shook off Newby's hand and stalked away. I eyed him carefully, wishing I had hit him harder with the wrench when I'd had the chance. I glanced around the room. Newby had pulled the curtains – gold silk that hung in big frothy folds – and lamps threw pools of warm yellow light. Two cream sofas faced each other across a glass coffee table piled with tasteful books about architecture, a small bust of Churchill and an ashtray purloined from the House of Commons. I imagined Phelps hosting jolly soirees, pouring drinks from a little gilt drinks trolley, sharing gossip from the House, holding court. I saw no hint of Lady Phelps here. Perhaps the dutiful wife was stuck in the constituency, some draughty old hall with dry rot and greyhounds steaming by an open fire. I glanced at Phelps' prone figure, felt anew the shock of discovery. He never would have imagined that his questions at the Defence Committee would have led to this.

I did this to him, I thought. *I killed him, and soon I'm going to join him.*

I felt nauseous and unsteady.

'What do you think about her contingency?' Newby asked Lazard.

'It's a bluff,' the big man replied. 'Because she knows if she pulled something like that, we'd go after her son. An eye for an eye, so to speak.'

'See, Julia, you're only making things worse,' Newby said. 'You might think you're being clever, but if you do have a contingency, Laz is going to slit your boy's throat.'

I felt sick. That was the deal they were offering me. My life for Alex's. I took it without hesitation. 'He's right,' I confessed. 'There's nothing. No contingency.'

Newby smiled and produced a tape measure. He took a measurement from Phelps' cold hand. He saw me watching him, and smiled smugly. He was enjoying the theatre of this.

'It's all in the angles, Julia,' he said. 'We're dropping little crumbs for the police. Your X feed, that's the juiciest one, but making sure they walk in here and immediately get the story we're trying to tell, that's an art. Aha, over here, please.'

He gestured for me to stand, and I found myself compelled to obey when he waved the gun airily in my direction. I thought of Alex as I sat down in a corner of the cream sofa, of the life he'd have because of the sacrifice I'd make here tonight. Tears sprang unbidden.

'Now, now, don't get upset. It will be over so quickly,' said Newby as he pulled on a pair of leather gloves. 'Comfortable? I think if I was going to blow my brains out I'd pick a nice chair too. Cream though, going to be a terrible mess. Still, I suppose upholstery isn't high on your list when you're putting a bullet in your skull.'

I looked at him distastefully. And then felt a wave of nausea. The button camera. If this was going out onto the Internet, if it recorded my death, then it would be there forever, for Alex to stumble across. I felt sick. No child should ever have to see something like that.

'I can't do it,' I cried. 'I can't pull the trigger.'

'Not even for your boy?' Newby smiled darkly. 'Don't worry, Julia. We have our own contingencies for people who lack courage.'

He gestured to a metal briefcase that Dunn carefully placed on the glass coffee table. 'It will all go according to plan, with or without your co-operation.' He nodded at his sidekicks. 'Set it up, lads.'

Dunn winked at me, and then clicked open the briefcase. I caught a glimpse of medical equipment: syringes, phials, swabs, test tubes, all packed in custom-cut foam. I realised with a sickening lurch how they planned to make me co-operate. I fought for composure. There was no reason I had to give them the satisfaction of an easy death.

'I've seen them, you know,' I said. 'The nanomachines. I saw them moving in one of the brain samples.'

Newby looked up from his tape measure and beamed. 'They're a thing of beauty, aren't they? I'm impressed they were moving – what's that, over a month since the host terminated?'

He glanced at Dunn and Lazard. 'I told you. They're more resilient than Kniver said.' He looked back at me. 'Where's the sample then? We couldn't work out where Wilmore took it. I'd rather hoped he'd flushed it.'

'He was smarter than you give him credit for,' I replied. 'He kept the evidence safe.'

'Where?' snapped Newby, and for a moment the upper-class chumminess disappeared, and I saw the flash of a ruthless operative. 'Where did he put it?'

'Somewhere you can't get it,' I said. 'Even as we speak the researchers at the London Centre for Nanotechnology are all over it. Christmas come early for them.'

Newby roared with anger, kicked over a small side-table and sent a delicate orchid crashing to the floor. Its pot smashed, and moss and soil mixed with Phelps' blood.

'For fuck's sake, Newby,' said Lazard, looking up from a test tube.

'We'll blame that on her too,' Newby countered, his voice suddenly calm, though he was breathing hard. 'Trust Wilmore. The last boy scout.'

'Don't know why he even signed up,' Dunn observed. 'Fucking Reservists. Don't have the stomach for the real thing.'

I looked at him icily. 'What's the real thing? Injecting kids with nanomachines?' I saw the look of puzzlement on Newby's face. 'That's right. I filmed the bodies in Lockmere.'

'You have been busy,' said Newby. 'I'm intrigued how you got in there. It's a classified site.'

'You're not as clever as you think,' I said. 'You left plenty of crumbs of your own.'

I could tell this got to him. He clearly thought he was some kind of military genius. Well, I'd had plenty of practice dealing with arrogant narcissists in my time; after all, I'd grown up with one.

'You're not exactly subtle, James. Running all over the Welsh countryside, faking abductions and rescues, the dodgy dossier you got me to publish.'

'Darling, who needs subtle? You published it, didn't you? You took the bait, hook, line and sinker.'

'Done up like a kipper,' sneered Dunn.

I ignored him and focused my attention on Newby.

'Women and children,' I said. 'What heroes you are.'

'Don't look at me like that, like I'm the bad guy,' snapped Newby, and I saw a flash of something else in his eyes. It was important to him to be perceived as the good guy. He was on a mission. And that, I realised, made him all the more dangerous, fanaticism always did.

'You ever been to war, Julia? Have you?'

I shook my head, watching him carefully. I had poked a snake and now I was waiting to see what it would do.

'Then you don't know what it's like. The death. The fear, the stink of it, your buddies cut down next to you. The injuries, the torture... My God, the injuries, you would not think humans could do such things to one another. And the beauty of modern warfare is now we survive. I have seen men, horribly mutilated, just a collection of organs and a pulse and somehow the medics put them back together. But it's no way to live. And that's not even accounting for the mental scars. And these are hard men and women, as hard as it gets, and they're broken.'

He faltered, his blue eyes distant, fixed on some horror in his past. He shook himself and appealed to Lazard and Dunn. 'Am I right?'

'Right,' said Lazard wearily. He looked at me with angry, scornful eyes. 'You don't know shit.'

I watched the three men warily. Emotions in the room were high.

'This technology gives us a chance to end all of it,' said Newby. 'You ever seen a bunker-buster in action? No, of course not.'

'Boom,' said Lazard, across the room, and his big hands splayed to mime an explosion.

Newby started pacing again, and his speech got faster, like the words had long been rehearsed inside his head and were now tumbling out, a crazed recital of death. 'Or white phosphorous, old Willie Pete? It burns to the bone. Cluster bombs. Thermobaric bombs. They're a nice invention; they suck up all the oxygen in the air like a vacuum cleaner. Can you imagine what that does to a kid's lungs?'

I shook my head, mute.

'Turns them inside out,' he revealed. 'We will look back on these days and wonder how we could ever call ourselves civilised. The future, Julia, the future will be much cleaner, neater, pain-free. Nanoweapons, Julia, they're going to change everything.'

He stopped in front of me, sweat patches on his shirt. I caught a tang of BO and aftershave and the horse-sweet smell of real leather as his gloved hand touched my forearm and traced a route upwards, across my shoulder, round the back of my neck, to the small hollow at the base of my skull.

'Once in the bloodstream, the nanomachines make their way to the brain, where they wait for the signal. Each batch has a unique identifier, allowing operators to make precise decisions about which ones to activate, and when. They can be triggered by satellite, smartphone, Wi-Fi, then they shut down the brainstem, killing instantly. Think about it, a single serial number tapped into a phone and the bad guy drops dead. No collateral damage, no comeback.'

While he was talking, I watched Dunn and Lazard. Dunn was checking a barcode on a test tube, tapping something into his phone, while the big guy was pulling on a pair of medical gloves. I couldn't bear the thought of those tiny machines in my body, burrowing into my brain, the horror of knowing I'd die the instant Dunn triggered his smartphone.

An app. A fucking app would kill me.

Newby sensed my dismay. He took two steps back, inserting himself in my eyeline, holding his arms slightly away from his body, palms upwards, as if he were an entertainer inviting applause for his latest trick. His blue eyes were fixed on my face. I cleared my throat. A hard ball of dread seemed to have cut off my air supply, but before I could speak he clapped his hands, making me jump.

'Or a million at once,' he said, a maniacal gleam in his eyes. 'One code activated by your phone and an entire enemy army drops dead, all of them, millions of them, in a single moment. No damage to the infrastructure, the cities, the oilfields, the buildings. No casualties, no orphans, no pain.'

'Mass euthanasia,' ventured Dunn. 'Putting them out of their misery.'

'I like that,' said Newby, pointing at Dunn. 'Mass euthanasia. God knows, it's not like the human race is endangered. Plenty of us to go around.'

He wheeled to face me. 'And here's the thing; we lead the world in this. It's going to give Britain a military advantage we haven't had since, when?' – he appealed round the room for answers, like a game show host – 'I'm saying Nelson. I mean most of the last century it was the Germans and the Americans. I think you've got to go back to Nelson.'

'Bloodstream,' I said, finding my voice. 'How do you get it into the bloodstream of a million people?'

Newby looked delighted, like a teacher thrilled a pet pupil has asked the right question. 'You're right, Julia. In time we'll figure out how to deliver the nanomachines through the food and water supply, but right now delivery is very tricky. In Syria we had a fortunate set of circumstances. A prison full of people nobody wanted, guards willing to look the other way when we came in with some experimental shots against TB and, let's face it, given Assad's enthusiastic interrogation techniques, a bunch of captives probably happy for a quick way out. But there's so much corruption, Julia, you would not believe it. That's what you really should be covering. Write about that, the never-ending graft, people with their hand out all the time, looking for what they can get; *that's* your story.'

He looked at me as if he expected me to agree with him, for me to start taking notes there and then. He shook his head and recovered his train of thought. 'Anyway, some bright spark decided that it was better not to waste good medical supplies on prisoners who are only going to die anyway. Why not sell the batch of TB inoculations at an extortionate mark-up to some makeshift NGO trying to rebuild a village? He broke into our storage facility and stole the so-called vaccine.'

'Oh God,' I said. 'You told them they were being protected against TB.'

Newby narrowed his eyes. 'No, it was the NGO who gave the shots to the villagers. When we found out, we were mad. The beauty of the prison was that it was contained. We knew who had what, when, what worked, what didn't. Those prisoners were on death row. They were dead anyway. We're not monsters; we never set out to kill women and children. But this stuff got out there, in the fucking desert. These peasants and goatherders walking around with millions and millions of dollars of R&D in them! Can you imagine!'

'How could you activate them knowing it would kill innocent people?' I asked. 'Why didn't you abort?'

'A couple of them died before we activated. We didn't know if it was a bad batch, or if it was just coincidence. Some people said it was a reaction to the jabs. One of the NGO workers was lynched for being a spy for the regime. The whole situation was getting out of hand. We couldn't risk an investigation. Imagine if someone had found out what was really in their bloodstreams.' He shrugged. 'So we activated. It was a tough call but it contained the situation and allowed us to take the evidence out in body bags. It sounds bad, but the world needs this, Julia. We can't keep killing each other like barbarians. This technology civilises the business of war. The world should be thanking us. It *will* thank us one day. We're making combat clinical.'

I looked at him in disgust. 'Don't pretend you're a hero,' I said. 'You're just another corporate shill, turning a profit from death. The

Harlen Group aren't in this to save the world from bombs and pain. They're in this to make money.'

'Nothing wrong with making money,' piped up Dunn. 'Only rich girls like you sneer at money. For the rest of us it matters.'

'I'm tired of this,' said Newby suddenly. He checked his watch. 'She doesn't get it and I'm tired of explaining myself to civilians who lack the balls to do any of the messy business themselves.'

'Fox and Wilmore weren't civilians, and they didn't agree with you either,' I said.

'Pussies,' spat Lazard, lumbering to his feet. He steadied himself against the table with one hand. In the other he held a syringe. 'It's time to give her the good news,' he told Newby.

I felt weak with panic. They were going to inject those microscopic machines into me, activate the code and then, after I was dead, they'd force a gun into my lifeless hand, blow out my useless brains, ruin my reputation, and leave my son an orphan.

'Don't come near me with that stuff,' I yelled, unable to control myself.

I scrabbled out of my seat and put the sofa between me and the three men. I was taking a huge risk, but I longed to spend a life with Alex, to see him grow into the man he had the promise to be. A better man than any of them. 'Did you really think I'd come in here unprotected? You made it so easy for me, you didn't even search me properly, you fucking amateurs.' I knew that would hurt. 'Smile for the camera, boys; this has been filmed and livestreamed to YouTube. I think I can guarantee it will be going viral.'

71

'WHAT THE fuck,' bellowed Lazard.

There was a flicker of doubt on Newby's face, then his eyes narrowed to thin slits, and I was reminded again of a snake, getting ready to strike.

He lunged at me, spotting too late the slight variation in the buttons on my polo shirt, the bottom one with its opaque camera eye squinting up at him. I tried to jump free of his grasp, but my back was pressed against the kitchen counter. He held me roughly and tore wildly at the fabric, pulling the buttons free and ripping off the top. Stripped to my vest, I felt even more vulnerable.

Dunn and Lazard were arguing heatedly – clearly, they hadn't anticipated their exploits being livestreamed across the Internet. Newby ran into the kitchen and pushed the top into the waste disposal, which rumbled to life as it shredded the red material.

This was it. This moment of uproar and noise was my chance, and I took it. I ran from the room, toppling a bar stool in my wake. I raced out of the little flat and sprinted down the dimly lit corridor towards the lifts. I flung open the stairwell door and careened down, banging off walls, taking the steps two at a time. The stairwell was a functional service area with plain white walls and motion-activated lights for each flight, which meant that I was bathed in a harsh glare, but above and below was darkness. I sensed, rather than heard, the presence of someone beneath me. Then the lights flashed on briefly below, before being extinguished with a tinkle of broken glass. One of them must have taken the lift to the ground floor and was now waiting in the shadows for me. I stood still, straining to detect their presence, but I could hear nothing above the hammering of my own heart. Then the lights went out on my flight of stairs and in the sudden darkness, my senses went into overdrive. I heard footsteps, quietly, stealthily moving up towards me.

I steeled myself. To wait here was certain death. I ran quickly, suddenly exposed as the lights activated, and at once a shot rang out, nicking the concrete by my shoulder as I pulled open the door and drove myself forward, back into the padded softness of the corridor and the closed doors of the luxury apartments. If I knocked, if I screamed for help, would anyone answer? Would anyone come to my rescue? I didn't have time to find out. There was a voice on the staircase. It was Dunn.

'She's on the third. Close her down.'

I felt a flash of hot panic and my legs went weak with fear. These men were trained killers. What chance did I have? But I refused to go quietly. I would run and fight to the end. I thought of Alex and knew I'd do whatever it took to see him again. I sprinted hard and my breath came in hot, sharp gasps. The building was in an L shape. I had run down the long vertical and was now in the short foot, which ended in a fire door.

'Oh, thank God,' I whispered.

There was a small window in the back wall, a vase of dried flowers that shed dusty lavender beads on the windowsill, and through this I could glimpse the black metal stairs of the fire escape.

But my relief was short-lived. I flattened myself against the wall by the windowsill as legs descended the metal staircase and Newby passed by. The fire door thudded and rattled as the former soldier threw his weight against it. This was it. I was trapped and would die here in this horrible beige corridor.

Oh, Alex, I love you beyond words. You will never know how much you mean to me or that I spent my last moments thinking of you.

I closed my eyes. There was a noise, the pop of a gun, the thud of something heavy falling. Newby was still throwing himself against the fire door. He swore, then there came a barrage of shots into the wood. I cowered on the floor under the windowsill, palms pressed over my ears, when suddenly hands grabbed me and yanked me to my feet. This was it. My last moment. I wouldn't go down without a fight and balled my hands into fists. I'd meet death the way I lived my life, on my own terms.

72

I TURNED, ready to attack, but saw a face that almost made me weep with joy.

'Joe!'

He smiled weakly. There was blood on his forehead, and one eye was puffy and purple. His left arm and his abdomen were completely drenched in blood. I gasped. He was a mess.

'You should see the other guy,' he said with a wink of his good eye, but his words were breathy, and the joke had no conviction. He was so pale and sweat beaded his forehead.

'Come on,' I said, as the fire door took another pounding from Newby. 'Can you walk? Let's go.'

We rounded the corner of the corridor. Joe moved carefully, like a punch-drunk boxer trying to stay upright. Dunn was sprawled in the corridor, a single gunshot through the chest, blood spreading like a poppy in bloom. Joe shrugged at me.

'Now we're even,' he told me.

'They said you were dead,' I whispered.

He grunted. 'It didn't take.'

We reached the lifts. One was at the tenth floor, the other on the ground. Joe pressed the button while I glanced anxiously behind. I wondered how long the fire door would hold Newby, and where was Lazard? The lifts hummed into life and the one from the tenth floor moved down. Joe readied his gun in his good hand. The red arm hung lifeless and heavy. He levelled the weapon at the lift doors, which opened with a jaunty ping. The car was empty. We saw nothing but our own pale faces, streaked with blood, staring back at us from the mirrors.

I exhaled, a long shaky breath. But the ground floor lift was moving now.

'Let's go,' I urged Joe, but before we could get in the empty lift, the stairwell door opened, and Lazard stepped through and pointed a gun at me.

'Drop the gun, big boy,' he said to Joe.

'Shoot him,' I urged. 'Joe, just do it.'

'He's not going to do that, are you, Joe?' said Lazard confidently. 'Think you can get me before I shoot her? I've seen the way he looks at you, lady. Drop it, mate. Or I'll end her.'

And to make his point, he took another step forward, his gun now levelled just inches from my heart.

'OK, OK,' said Joe, raising his hands. 'I'm going to put the gun down.'

'Slowly,' said Lazard.

Joe nodded, then paused. There were footsteps behind, and Newby appeared, a little dishevelled, splinters of glass on his shoulders, sucking a cut on his hand. He'd climbed through the little window.

'All reunited, I see, very nice.' He looked at Lazard, then spoke softly. 'Pete's taken one for the team, I'm afraid.'

Lazard swore and his face contorted with anger and grief – but his gun never wavered from my chest.

'Drop the gun,' he said to Joe. There was a nasty new edge to his voice.

Perhaps Joe registered it because he complied. He bent down to put the gun on the floor and his movements were slow and awkward.

'Nice and slow, that's it,' said Lazard.

The soldier relaxed and shifted the weight off his bad leg. It was all Joe needed. He toppled forwards and his great bulk crashed into Lazard's injured leg so that both men fell awkwardly. A gunshot splintered the ceiling. It rained plaster, and I instinctively ducked, snatched up the gun Joe had dropped and spun round to face Newby. But he was quicker than me. His pistol was already pointing at my head.

I held my own gun with both hands. It was shaking with the violent tremors that afflicted me. Could I do it? Could I shoot?

Newby's eyes glittered, the corners of his mouth turned up. He clearly thought I wouldn't.

There was another bright ping. The ground floor lift had arrived. And with it came a scream that assaulted the senses. It was Flicky Hair, back from walking her little pug. Perhaps it was just a reaction to the scream, but I twitched, and the gun fired, kicking back and throwing me off balance. Newby dropped to the floor, clutching his side, disbelief on his face. Flicky Hair screamed again, and her little dog yapped and growled. The lift doors shut, and the scream descended.

I scrabbled to my feet. Joe and Lazard were slugging it out, Joe on top now, his fist pounding the side of the other man's head. I pressed my foot onto Lazard's busted knee, and he roared with pain. Joe delivered a dose of temporary pain relief in the form of a heavy uppercut to the jaw, which hammered Lazard's head into the floor and knocked him out. Joe slumped back against the wall, panting heavily, his hands slick with blood, his and Lazard's.

'God, Julia,' he said, his face a clammy grey. 'Got to be worth a Pulitzer at least.'

I tried to speak but my teeth were chattering too hard, my brain too full of screams and gunshots to find the words. Instead, I just crouched by his side, stroked his damp forehead and listened to the sound of distant sirens approaching.

EPILOGUE

PANSIES SHIVERED in the sea breeze. Blue and purple, with ink-stained hearts, they turned their faces to greet the sunlight that streamed in through the open patio doors. It was one of those bright days when anything seemed possible. The sun bounced off the glittering water, bright as a flashlight. Boats unfurled their sails and skittered towards distant horizons. Gulls cartwheeled through the salty air. Everything was in bud or bloom, and lovers walked near the water's edge, hatching plans.

I watched from behind my sunglasses. I felt the heat on my skin like a lover's caress. I stroked a pansy in its little pot, its petals as soft as a baby's cheek. I thought of Alex and smiled. As a baby, he'd had the most pinchable peachy cheeks.

'You seem happy.'

'I am.' I surprised myself.

I was usually too unsure of my feelings to commit to such bold proclamations but here, in this moment, it was true. I was happy.

'Good.' Emilia smiled at me across the tablecloth and the debris of a cream tea. 'You should be. You've had quite the year.'

I smiled wryly. That was an understatement. My story had been front-page news for weeks, eventually forcing the Government to announce a ban on the weaponisation of nanotechnology. Ethics committees had been set up. There were calls for a public inquiry into how a rogue unit within the biotech division of The Harlen Group had embedded itself within the British Army, and how much the Government and The Harlen Group had known about its activities.

Among other things, the story had shone a light on Army requisitioning. Battlefield commanders had the ability to requisition experimental weapons for live testing, which made them susceptible to inducement by companies like The Harlen Group. Until the official inquiry published its findings, no one could be sure how Newby and his crew got permission to go to Syria, but someone in the chain of command had signed off on their mission, and I was almost certain that person would now be sweating bullets.

I had been invited to speak at conferences and address the UN. I smiled when I thought about the invitations. Did this mean I too was now part of the Establishment? High-level negotiations were underway with Syria and local NGOs to ensure the repatriation of the Lockmere bodies and the payment of generous compensation to the victims' families. The Harlen Group faced a barrage of civil lawsuits, and criminal prosecutions were being discussed, though I suspected these would be buried in a relentless mire of claim and counterclaim, official secrets and old boy deals. The Harlen Group was one of those fortunate institutions judged too big to fail. Besides, who was left? Directors were pleading ignorance. A lone scientist, the company's head of biopharma and nanotech research, a Dr Christian Kniver, had been thrown to the dogs but I doubted he'd ever live to see the inside of a courtroom.

Dunn was already dead, of course. Lazard had died of a suspected stroke while on bail and Newby, recovering in a secure hospital from his gunshot wound, had gone into a coma following a pharmaceutical mix-up. His life support had been turned off in June. I had my own suspicions about the true cause of Lazard's and Newby's deaths, but I wouldn't be investigating them.

The mysterious Simone Bentley, the woman I was supposed to have crashed into, had never been traced, nor had the other member of Newby's team, Dalton Brown. Brian Hinstock, the man photographed with Lazard by Ben Howells moments before his death, was rumoured to be fighting with the Kurds against ISIS, location unknown. But I knew these names were just the tip of an iceberg. Newby and Kniver had not masterminded this operation. It had been a systemic conspiracy to weaponise and monetise nanotech. The Harlen Group's weapons division was being investigated on both sides of the Atlantic and its nanotech labs had been shuttered. For now.

Closer to home, Philippe was still sulking about his firm's losses, opining about the importance of nanotech to future health breakthroughs, stressing they shouldn't allow this one mistake to halt all research. I changed the subject whenever it came up. I would be forever haunted by the image of the little killing machines trapped in the dead brain tissue, awaiting orders, pinching and snipping.

'I like it here,' I said to Emilia. 'You made a good choice.'

Emilia beamed. The vintage tearooms at Broadstairs had been her choice for a sisterly catch-up, while the children watched a Punch and Judy show with the Garonne's nanny, Clara.

'Collette would approve,' I remarked.

'Indeed, she would.' Emilia paused. 'And I'm glad we came here to Broadstairs. I think it's done us all good to be by the sea, just having fun.'

I nodded in agreement. We had decided against Arlet after all. Too many memories, too much Valentina, too much my father's domain. A long weekend in a cottage by the sea was proving a hit with them all. The children, fuelled by fish and chips and sand-crusted ice-creams, spent their days excavating vast trenches on the beach and bodysurfing the waves until they tumbled into exhausted windswept dreams. Emilia and I watched idly, scrunching our toes in the gritty sand, admiring pretty shells, and, when all fell quiet in the bunkbeds above, sipped wine and watched the lights twinkle around the bay, reminiscing about childhoods past.

'Salt water heals all,' I said, reminding my sister of another of Collette's sayings.

And it was true. I *did* feel healed. My GP was pleased with my bloodwork and recommended maintaining the current meds regime. Alex was happy. He had a part in the school's summer show, and I was delighted to see how steady he was, how kind, a peace-maker to squabbling cousins and a devoted protector of little Jacques. My Section 127 prosecution had been dropped and social services had melted away like ice in the desert. There had even been an official letter of apology from the Met about Conor Tull, now suspended pending a formal investigation.

'So, what next?' asked Emilia.

'More cake?' I responded flippantly. I knew what Emilia meant.

'No,' said Emilia in horror. 'I'm already close to bursting out of these shorts.'

Nothing could be further from the truth. Emilia was fit and lithe, her crisp white shorts showing off lean legs that were the colour of golden sand, and a pretty sun top revealing tennis-honed arms. I cast a rueful look at my own outfit. Rolled-up jeans, battered flip flops and a white linen top with long sleeves. I was still self-conscious about the scars on my arms.

'No, I mean what are you going to do next; you, and Joe?'

'He's still officially recuperating, but you know him. He's always looking for his next adrenaline rush. He has a sidekick now, an IT whizz kid, Sam. The two of them seem to spend their days plotting and scheming.'

'No more big cases, I beg you,' groaned Emilia. 'My nerves can't take it.'

The waitress brought our bill and we both reached for it, but I got there first. 'Seriously, Em, you've paid for the cottage. You can at least let me buy tea and cake.'

It felt good to pay. And for once, I wasn't worrying about the hole it would leave in the weekly food budget. Subscriptions had surged in the wake of the Lockmere story, and advertisers were back. The Castleton Files was a success. My longstanding backer at the wine club had even sent me a celebratory case of English sparkling wine, though I'd noticed that the writing in the accompanying congratulations card was very similar to the penmanship of William Stone. I wouldn't press the matter. Not now, at least.

I paid the bill, put my purse away, and then froze. At the back of the café, a man was talking animatedly to a young woman, his hands gesturing, his teeth glinting white, like the snarl of a startled wild animal, raw and dangerous. I swallowed, unable to take my eyes off him. I knew him, that face, those black pitiless eyes, the inkings that traced every contour of his muscled arms, his thick neck, his shaven head. The Tattooed Man. I gripped the edge of the table until my knuckles turned white. I held tight, as if to anchor myself in this reality.

'What is it, Jules?' Emilia touched my hand lightly and followed my stricken gaze. 'Do you know him?'

'He's in my dreams,' I replied. 'But I don't know if they're dreams or memories, you know, from before.'

'You're sure?' Emilia glanced round again, caught the man's eye and turned to me. 'If you're going to cover your face in tattoos you should expect people to stare.'

'You sound like Collette,' I said, standing up. 'I'd know him anywhere. I have to speak to him.'

I could sense Emilia's disappointment. Everything had been going so well, so normally, and now her crazy sister was stirring things up again.

'Supposing he knows something about Alex.'

I didn't wait for a reply and started across the little tearoom. Teacups clinked above a hum of conversation and a coffee machine frothed against the far wall. Everything was so normal, yet I felt I had slipped into an alternate reality and walked as if in a trance towards the tattooed man, who sat back now and watched me approach. The tattoos made his face seem like a mask. It was hard to read what he was thinking.

'Yes? What do you want?'

His voice was brusque, an edge of Estuary English and something softer, maybe Welsh. His huge hands were pitted, scarred and threaded with tattoos. They lay on the tablecloth, out of place amid the chintz and dainty crockery.

His companion, a young woman with multiple piercings and cropped jet-black hair, eyed me contemptuously.

'Do you know me?' I asked.

There was a pause as his black eyes fixed on my face. It felt like my whole life hung in this moment.

At last, he shook his head. 'No. Never seen you before.'

'Are you sure?' I pressed, beginning to doubt myself. Was this the man from my dreams?

'Yeah, Dave, are you sure?' the pierced woman asked, her voice tinged with hostility.

'I've never seen her before,' Dave assured his companion. 'Listen, you've got me mixed up with someone else,' he told me. 'It's an easy mistake. People don't see beyond the ink.'

I ignored the glares coming from the pierced woman and studied the tattooed man. His features were different, his tattoos softer, and there was no sense of the anarchic energy that emanated from the man who haunted me. Up close, I caught no hint of the brooding evil of the man in my dreams. This wasn't my spectre.

'I'm sorry,' I said, flushing with embarrassment. 'You reminded me of someone. I'm very sorry to have disturbed you.'

I backed away, leaving Dave with the task of mollifying his suspicious companion.

'Well?' demanded Emilia as we stepped outside.

The two of us walked into the sunshine and the sea air was like a balm on my flushed face.

'I thought I recognised him,' I replied. 'But I got him confused with someone else.'

'I don't see how,' my sister responded. 'There can't be too many people with tattooed faces. Who did you think he was exactly?'

I ignored the question. I was thinking about my sister's observation. *There can't be too many people with tattooed faces*. If my tattooed spectre was real, there was a good chance I'd be able to find him. And if I did, he might be able to reveal something about Alex's heritage. Wayne Sloss had never been seen again, and I was in no doubt he'd been a Harlen Group stooge planted to sow scandal and discredit me. The Tattooed Man might be a key that could unlock the truth about Alex's real father. I felt the familiar shiver of excitement at the prospect of a new chase.

'Come on, Em, let's go and see Mr Punch get his comeuppance,' I suggested.

I took Emilia's arm, and we walked towards the pier. Two more holidaymakers enjoying the sunshine, shadows at our heels.

JULIA CASTLETON RETURNS IN

TO CATCH AN ANGEL

ABOUT THE AUTHOR

Julia Castleton is the creation of an internationally bestselling and critically acclaimed writing duo. Blurring the lines between fact and fiction, she takes us into a world that could have been torn from the headlines.

ACKNOWLEDGEMENTS

The authors would like to thank their families and friends for their ongoing support, Victoria Goldman for her editing work, and you, the reader, for spending time with Julia. We hope you enjoyed the ride. Please consider leaving a review on one of the many bookish platforms if you would recommend *To Kill A Shadow* to other thriller fans.

DON'T MISS

"A MESMERIZING AND BEAUTIFULLY HAUNTING THRILLER STEERED BY A POWERFUL PROTAGONIST, BRILLIANT PACING, BLOODY ACTION, AND EMOTIONAL PITH THAT INJECTS EVERY VEIN OF THIS NARRATIVE WITH EXCELLENCE. IT'S ONE OF THE BEST BOOKS OF 2023 AND I'M GLAD TO BE ENDING THE YEAR ON SUCH A HIGH NOTE."

KASHIF HUSSAIN, BEST THRILLER BOOKS

ENJOY THIS PREVIEW OF THE

FIRST THREE CHAPTERS OF

THE GIRL BEYOND FOREVER

ADAM LOXWOOD

PENDULUM BOOKS

1

I wasn't in the car.

I was somewhere else.

The last place I'd ever been happy.

The sun shines through the trees. Leaves cast dappled shadows on the dry grass as branches sway in the gentle breeze. I am barefoot, and my feet crunch the brittle summer earth into dust as I move stealthily towards the big oak at the bottom of our garden.

She's hiding there.

She always hides there.

A flutter of purple flowers on pink cotton. A small, perfectly formed cheek. She can't resist peeking, but I know the rules and pretend I haven't seen her. I know her stomach will be churning with the excitement of the chase, anticipating that sudden moment of discovery.

The roar.

The run.

The hug. The rush of adrenaline giving way to the relief that it's all pretend. That she's safe, wrapped in my arms. That I'm never going to let her go.

I forced myself to relive the memory every single day, so that my recollection was always perfect and my pain raw. So I never forgot her. My little girl, running through the sunlit garden. Sweet. Innocent. Beautiful. Forever just out of reach.

The plastic bites into my left foot, and I look down to see a blue shard, a relic of some old garden toy chewed up by the mower. I move, swiftly now; I can hear her tittering with excitement. She takes another peek, this time from the right side of the tree. I pretend I haven't seen and swing to the left. As I round the gnarly old tree, I see her.

Amber.

Ten years old.

Ten years of innocent perfection.

I growl.

Amber jumps and squeals, 'Monster!'

She runs across the lawn, and I pursue, growling and roaring with every step. Halfway to the house she turns to make a stand, trying to intimidate me with her sapphire blue eyes. I scoop her up, burying my face in her platinum blonde hair and roaring with renewed fury.

'Stop it, Daddy,' Amber squeals. 'It tickles!'

'Of course it tickles,' I say. 'I'm the tickle monster.'

'You cheated,' she tells me. 'You didn't count properly. You're supposed to count like this.'

She holds up her right hand and taps her thumb over her four fingers.

'One,' she says, as her thumb returns to her index finger and repeats its bounce over the other digits. 'Two.'

I'd taught her a way to count out seconds properly, something I'd learnt in the field, and she never let me forget it.

'I'll count properly next time, I promise,' I say.

'Hey, you two, lunch is ready!' Sarah yells from the patio.

Sarah.

Beautiful Sarah.

Our love died that night.

Withered in the face of horror.

Amber wriggles free and runs towards her rotund mother. Sarah can't pick her up because of the baby in her belly: the boy is seven months along and puts enough of a strain on her back.

I watch her stroke Amber's head.

I don't know how much this mundane moment will come to mean to me.

It's just another day.

Just another game of hide and seek.

I cannot guess at the number of nights my eyes will run dry at this memory.

Blissfully ignorant of the future, I join my family for lunch.

2

'You with us, Schaefer?' Jean asked, bringing my wandering mind back to the car. 'Schaefer?'

Detective Sergeant Peterson Jean. Family originally from Haiti, tall, thin, late-thirties, wide eyes. He'd helped me on some cases and we'd struck up an uneasy alliance. I looked past him, through the windscreen at a hooded figure walking our way.

'That's him,' I said.

'You sure?' Noel asked.

Detective Sergeant David Noel. Yorkshireman. Army veteran, like me. Short, wiry like a terrier, face pockmarked and scarred from a roadside bomb near Kabul. More to my taste than Jean, but still police and not to be completely trusted.

I couldn't see the hooded figure's face, but the clothes matched my informant's description. Noel scanned my face for doubt and found none.

'Let's call it,' Noel told his partner.

Jean grabbed the radio. 'Visual on the suspect. Everyone stand by.'

I sank a little further into the back seat. The hooded figure wasn't cagey, even though he must have known he was being hunted. He wasn't using any counter-surveillance techniques. He wasn't even checking the street. But I'd learnt to be cautious. I peered over Jean's shoulder and watched the hooded figure go into a front garden and walk up the short path towards one of the red brick terrace houses. He didn't even look round when he put the key in the lock. This was a confident man, afraid of nothing. The hooded figure stepped inside and shut the door behind him.

Noel and Jean both looked at me. Were they expecting me to say something? It wasn't my place to order the raid.

'You sure that's him?' Noel asked.

'It's him,' I replied.

'Okay. Let's go.'

Jean radioed the news. 'We're moving.'

I was the first to get out of the car. Up ahead I saw a squad of six SCO19 officers exit a battered, old, unmarked van. Their matt black Heckler & Koch submachine guns were deadly shadows clasped close to their chests. I felt a gentle tug at my arm. It was Noel.

'You know the deal: stay back,' he instructed.

I was certain I'd seen more action than Noel or Jean, but I wasn't police, so they wanted me well clear of any danger.

We quickly crossed Chapel Street, which was otherwise deserted. It was the middle of September, and the first chill of autumn was in the air. I pictured all the families living on this quiet South London street, sat in front of their televisions, or sleeping in their beds, unaware of the darkness just outside their own front doors.

As we reached the other side of the street, Noel signalled the armed officers, and the squad split in two. Three of the SCO19 officers followed Noel towards the front of the house. The other three joined Jean and followed him down a dark alleyway that cut between two of the houses. I went with them, plunging into a narrow strip of darkness as the houses either side blocked the sulphur glow of the streetlamps. A few steps further and I was back in the yellow haze of London at night. I could see Jean ahead of me, moving well: deliberate and silent. He led the SCO19 squad right, along a service road that ran behind the terrace. I followed, and was ten yards behind Jean when the landmine exploded.

3

The battlefield had taught me how time plays tricks. It slows and you can pick out the most exquisite details, but you still find yourself longing for more time to avoid the knife, bullet or blast.

Light travels faster than sound, and I saw the flash of the fireball first, and then felt the shockwave pick me up and toss me against a garden wall. I felt the intense heat of the inferno that broiled two of the police officers ahead of me. They were still alive and screamed like children as they burnt. Jean and another officer were knocked to the ground not far from me.

The world went muffled and distant and for a moment I thought I might lose consciousness. A loud hum pushed my eardrums into my head, creating an uncomfortable pressure, but I stayed with the world. My arms and legs weren't responsive and moved wildly when I tried to stand, like a marionette tangled in its own strings. My body trembled and my aching muscles were unable to coordinate their way upright.

Jean and the other officer groaned and floundered, and as my hearing returned, I realised their radios were alive with chatter.

'Bravo, what's your status?' It was Noel, speaking from the front of the house. 'Jean, are you okay? What just happened?'

Neither man could reply, so I crawled towards them.

'Open it,' I heard Noel say.

His officers would be going in through the front door, and I wanted to warn them this was no normal raid.

The radio broadcast some thuds and crashes and the sound of glass shattering. Then shouts and gunshots.

'Officers down, officers down,' Noel yelled over the radio. 'Get them out of there. We need immediate medical assistance.'

There was a pause. Then, 'Jean, I don't know if you can hear me, mate, but the suspect is coming your way. He's armed and very dangerous.'

Peering through the flames, over the bodies of the fallen police officers, I saw the back door open. I lay motionless the moment I saw Leon Yates step out, gun in hand. A gun that told me he wouldn't hesitate to put a bullet in my head. I could see his pasty skin, dark hair and angry, shadowed eyes beneath his hood.

He stumbled down the back steps and ran through the flaming ruins of the garden, past the dead policemen and Jean and the other cop, who were both out of it. He turned left and ran past me. As he neared the end of the alley, I took a deep breath. If I lost Yates now, there was a real chance of losing him for good. I had no idea what had happened to Noel's team, but there was no sign of them. I would have to go after the man myself.

I took another deep breath and forced myself to my feet. I was unsteady and dazed, maybe even concussed, but I could move. I took a couple of unsteady steps, and built up speed, gradually remembering how everything worked. It all hurt, but it functioned, and I was running now. I chased Yates to the end of the alleyway. Ahead of me, he turned left onto Galton Street, and I went after him.

Printed in Great Britain
by Amazon

48890735R00189